MY DARLING KATE

Elizabeth Graham

D1565333

Zebra Books
Kensington Publishing Corp.

http://www.zebrabooks.com

ZEBRA BOOKS are published by

Kensington Publishing Corp.
850 Third Avenue
New York, NY 10022

Copyright © 1997 by Elizabeth Graham

Zebra and the Z logo Reg. U.S. Pat. & TM Off.

First Printing: July, 1997
10 9 8 7 6 5 4 3 2 1

Printed in the United States of America

Chapter 1

Maryland Colony—1759

"Ah! Sweet, sweet Alyssa! At last you're here!" The two workers standing beside Nicholas Talbot on the wharf gave him curious glances, but his anticipation and excitement were so great he didn't even notice.

His heart pounded in his chest as he watched the *Rosalynde* come ever closer. A vision of Alyssa's blonde curls and sky-blue eyes filled his mind's eye. Then a frown drew his dark brows together. Blue eyes and yellow curls, yes, but what did she really look like?

He firmly pushed down the doubts trying to surface. Doubts that had plagued him on and off for months, ever since he'd sent the letter and passage money to his fiancée. After all, he told himself as he had a dozen times before, it had been five years. No wonder he couldn't remember the shape of her face, the way her features were arranged.

It didn't matter. In a few minutes now she'd be here in person, no longer the dream woman he'd worked so hard and so long to bring over from England to be his bride.

Nicholas pulled his dark-blue cloak closer against the chilly wind sweeping across the wharf from the creek. It was an unusually cold day on the Tidewater, and dark, lowering clouds filled the sky.

He hoped it didn't storm. Alyssa had probably had a rough passage. Late November was a bad time to sail the cold Atlantic, but when Henry Aldon had told him his ship would make a late crossing this year, Nicholas hadn't been able to wait until spring.

He needed Alyssa now. Both for himself and ... he pushed these thoughts aside, too. He wouldn't dwell on his recent problems. Time enough for that later when he had to explain to her.

But maybe he should have sent another letter after all, telling her that considering his changed circumstances they must wait for yet another year. His tumbling thoughts reversed themselves again. No, they'd waited far too long already. His darling wouldn't care. Of course she wouldn't.

She loved him. As he loved her. And that was all that mattered.

The square-rigged ship came alongside the wharf. The deckhands, aided by the two men on the pier, made the vessel fast, then put the plank walkway in place.

Nicholas erased the frown and summoned a smile as he eagerly studied the people on the deck, searching for a head of golden curls, a sweet smile, and blue eyes.

Recognizing a familiar face, he lifted his hand in greeting to Morgan Lockwood, the *Rosalynde's* personable young captain. Lockwood, pushing a lock of black hair off his forehead, smiled and waved back.

Two women dressed in coarse garb, obviously bond servants, made their way across the planks. One of them gave him a smile full of invitation as she passed.

A new frown drew his brows together. Where was Alyssa? Was he to be disappointed after all the years he'd waited? Had she fallen ill? Or had something happened to prevent her sailing?

He peered at the only woman left, his heart sinking. That couldn't be the girl he'd fallen instantly in love with the first moment he'd seen her in her father's greengrocer shop.

No, this woman was too tall. As she made her way across the planks, she clutched her hood around her face with a slender, long-fingered hand, obscuring her features. But the errant curls tossed about by the wind were most definitely not blonde. They were red. An uneasy feeling stirred inside him. No, she couldn't possibly be Alyssa. His sweetheart was small and cuddly. Born to warm a man's bed during the long winter nights.

"Careful, now," Nicholas warned.

Automatically, he took the woman's hand, surprised by the firmness of her grip. She was even taller than he'd thought.

And something about her seemed familiar. Had they perhaps met at one of the Tidewater gatherings? Could she be a daughter of a local landowner, returned from a visit to England? Again, that uneasy ripple went through him.

Wind gusted across the wharf, flipping back the woman's hood, revealing her face. Nicholas drew his breath in sharply, dropping her hand as if seared.

"Kate! What in God's name are you doing here? Where is Alyssa? Has something happened to her?"

Katherine Shaw felt her throat tighten at Nicholas's question, his anxious and dismayed expression.

She clutched her gray cloak tighter against the biting wind, hearing a protest from the kitten in its left pocket.

"My sister was in perfect health when last I saw her," she assured him. Postponing her answer to Nicholas's other questions, she slipped her hand into the pocket, smoothing the unseen tiger-striped head, and was rewarded with a vibrating purr.

She glanced quickly around. Formal gardens, frost-blighted now, made their way almost to the creek's edge to left and right of the oystershell lane.

Far up the lane she glimpsed an imposing manor house. She'd seen several others as the ship stopped at various points to pick up cargo and unload people and supplies, but this one looked far grander than the rest.

As Nicholas had written, his plantation truly was prosperous and beautiful.

And despite the gulls and the sea smells, this Maryland Colony was very unlike her home in England! Overriding her nervous exhaustion, excitement filled her. She'd made the long, uncomfortable voyage in search of a new life completely different from the one she'd left behind in Devon.

Finally, she let her gaze fully meet Nicholas's and felt a pulse leap in her throat.

She would have recognized him anywhere, too.

His richly colored chestnut hair was as unruly as ever, his thick-lashed eyes dark brown. His wide-legged stance still held a touch of arrogance.

But his face looked different—older, hardbitten, as if he'd gone through some bad times. A scar now slashed across his forehead. A few lines had etched themselves around his eyes and mouth. His voice had sounded harder and deeper, too.

But none of this detracted from the potent male attractiveness that had stunned her from their first meeting.

Kate pulled her hood back around her face and pushed straying wisps of hair under it, delaying a moment longer.

But there was no way to break the news to him gently.

She lifted her head and met his frowning gaze again.

"Alyssa can't marry you. She's betrothed to John Latton."

The anxiety left Nicholas's eyes, his expression changing to incredulity. "What are you talking about?" he demanded. "Alyssa's been *my* betrothed for five years!"

Kate nodded, her throat tightening again. He wasn't

going to take this well. Dread for what she still had to tell him swept over her.

"I know. But Alyssa was so young when you left—hardly more than a child. You couldn't expect—"

"I couldn't expect her to wait for me as she promised?" Nicholas interrupted. "Why not? Her letters never hinted that she tired of the waiting. That she had found another man."

Kate hadn't read her sister's letters to Nicholas, but she didn't doubt he spoke the truth. "You know Alyssa can't bear to hurt anyone. She just couldn't bring herself to tell you."

Even as she said the words, Kate knew she didn't fully believe them. True, Alyssa hadn't wanted to inflict pain on Nicholas, but her overriding concern had been to keep unpleasantness away from herself. Kate realized some of this was her fault. She'd spoiled her younger sister since their mother's death seven years ago.

Nicholas's brown eyes narrowed. "So she sent *you* to tell me? Wasn't that a rather extravagant gesture? Didn't she perhaps think it more sensible to write me a letter and return the coin I sent her instead of spending it on *your* passage? Or have you suddenly come into a windfall?"

Kate swallowed with difficulty. Her throat felt very dry. Why had she let her sister talk her into this plan?

Then her innate honesty resurfaced. Alyssa hadn't had that hard a time convincing her. She'd gently reminded Kate of her meager options. One was marriage to Cecil Oglethorpe. Seventy if he were a day, he'd already buried three wives and was panting to make her the fourth. Two or three other would-be swains were little better, even if younger.

And well she knew her person wasn't the big attraction. Once she married, the greengrocer shop she and Alyssa had jointly inherited would no longer be half hers, but her husband's.

The other choice was remaining single and running the

shop until she dropped dead behind the counter as her father had done a year ago.

Both were bleak alternatives.

Was it any wonder the plan Alyssa suggested had sounded so attractive? Had seemed to settle all their difficulties? Kate coming here for an exciting future in the New World, leaving the shop for Alyssa and John to run.

She shook her head. "No, no windfall. I used your money for my passage. You see Alyssa and I thought . . ."

Embarrassed dismay hit her as at last she fully realized the sheer audacity of the plan they'd concocted.

But she *wouldn't* stand here stammering like a ninny! She'd done this of her own free will and now she'd face up to Nicholas Talbot and tell him the whole of it.

She lifted her head and looked him straight in the eye. "I've come to take my sister's place. I've come to be your wife."

Kate held his gaze, watching as his expression changed to dumbfounded amazement—then true and intense anger.

"Woman, you have lost your wits," he said, biting the words out. "Why would you think I'd want to take *you* to wife?"

Kate felt her fair skin warm, her embarrassment deepen at his scornful words and tone. Her left hand curled around the kitten in her pocket as much for her own comfort as the animal's.

"Because you want a wife and it's common knowledge that women are scarce in the Colonies," she told him, forcing her voice to remain cool.

She noticed that more people had come to the dock and were boarding the ship, giving an occasional curious glance toward her and Nicholas. They were simply dressed and some of them were dark skinned, African slaves she assumed, disapprovingly. She hated the idea of one person owning another.

Confusion swept over her. Then why had she come here,

prepared to live under such a system? She brushed the thoughts aside. It was too late now for regrets.

"I'm strong and in excellent health. I'm skilled at running a household and a shop and not afraid of hard work." She paused, feeling her flush returning, then continued. "I am prepared to make you a good, faithful wife and to bear you children."

Nicholas's expression didn't soften. "Are you trying to sell yourself to me for a workhorse or a brood sow? Surely, you don't think those are my only reasons for marrying Alyssa. I *love* her. I love her blonde beauty and grace. Her sweetness. Everything about her!"

The words he left unsaid hurt more than if he'd spoken them. *And you're not beautiful, Kate Shaw. Not particularly graceful or sweet. You're tall and red-haired and I never gave you a second look.*

She wanted to fling his unsaid words back in his face. Declare that nothing about *him* appealed to *her*, either. But that wasn't true. Something had stirred inside her the first time he'd come into the shop.

But he'd been instantly captivated by Alyssa's deceptively sweet smile and beauty.

Suddenly, Kate's own anger surfaced. He had every right to be furious with her and Alyssa, but just the same, she couldn't humbly accept his open scorn.

Sell herself to him, indeed! Maybe she wasn't beautiful, but everything she'd told him was true. She'd been ready to make Nicholas a good wife. She shot another glance at him. He looked as black as the storm clouds swirling above them, ready to continue his diatribe.

She took a deep breath, drawing herself up and gathering the shreds of her pride about her. She'd give him no chance to do that. She kept her gaze steady on his, raised her chin a bit.

"You have no cause for concern, Nicholas Talbot. I wouldn't marry you now if you were the last man left alive on God's green earth!"

A dark-skinned woman stopped and stared their way, her mouth open. Kate pressed her lips together, wishing she'd kept her voice down. She didn't want Nicholas's servants to hear them quarreling.

Nicholas blinked and backed up a step. "That is, indeed, a swift change of mind, mistress," he said coolly. "Only a moment ago you were begging me to wed and bed you."

Kate barely restrained herself from stamping his booted foot with her own. "I was *not* begging you. I merely explained the situation and offered you another choice. Which I have now withdrawn."

He lifted an arrogant brow. "Oh? So you have passage money for your return to Devon?"

Kate opened her mouth to tell him that of course she did, then common sense won out over her temper, and she closed it again. She shook her head. "No. I will not go back to England. I'm not a fool. I can take care of myself. I will find work."

She also had a second plan that she had no intention of revealing to him. Maybe she wasn't a beauty like her sister, but she was sure she could find another man to wed here in this Maryland Colony. A better choice than she would have back in Plymouth. But that was a last resort to be used only if all else failed.

Nicholas glanced around him deliberately, slowly. In spite of her anger, Kate's glance followed his as the strangeness of these new surroundings swept over her again.

But this time the realization didn't fill her with excitement. She'd imagined the ship docking at a city, with her pick of shops in which to find work if Nicholas rejected her.

But instead it had sailed down the huge bay called the Chesapeake, then entered a wide river with deep water creeks running off it. No sun warmed the wintry day and the lowering sky hung over a dark wood that grew close beside the gardens, stretching away to the left as far as she could see.

Across the creek, there was nothing but more trees with bare black limbs, only an occasional tall green tree towering over the shrubs.

Never mind. It couldn't be too far from some town or city. She lifted her chin a little higher. "I'm sure I can find employment in the city of Baltimore."

He laughed shortly and with no amusement. "Baltimore consists of a few houses and taverns. There are no towns or cities close by. Do you plan to seek employment as a tavern wench or doxy?"

Kate's temper flared again at his words and tone. Before she could stop herself, she stepped forward and slapped him hard across the face.

Nicholas grasped her hand with his own before she could withdraw it. For a moment he held it pressed tightly against his reddening cheek.

With a jolt, Kate realized they were standing close together and Nicholas had a most appealing masculine smell about him. His hand, even through her glove, felt hard and strong, the heat of his touch radiating up her arm. The old attraction she'd felt for him resurfaced with a rush of warmth that left her breathless.

Despite his arrogant attitude, despite her own repudiation of him only a few moments ago, it wouldn't be wholly a bad thing to be married, bedded with this man.

Mortified at her thoughts, knowing how he felt about her, she stepped back and Nicholas moved her hand very slowly away from him.

"Don't ever do that again," he warned, his eyes gleaming.

"Since I have no intention of seeing you after today, that shouldn't be hard to manage," she answered in kind, glad the servants had gone aboard the ship and no one seemed to have witnessed the scene just past.

"Are you planning to stow away on the *Rosalynde* for your return voyage to Plymouth, then? That might be a long wait, as this is her last trip until spring."

His eyes raked her from the top of her head to her damp, slippered feet. "Also difficult to manage, since you're considerably more than a slip of a lass."

Even while her mind accepted his statements as true, her palm tingled with a renewed urge to slap him. On the other cheek this time! She half-lifted it, and Nicholas instantly reached out and pinned her hand to the side of her cloak.

"What did I just tell you about that?"

Again, against her will or wish, she was very much aware of his touch, his warm, hard strength. Humiliation flooded her face with heat. She'd been a fool to come here! She'd done a stupid, ridiculous thing, leaving herself open to his contempt.

She had to get away from him.

"Oh, you wretch!" Kate jerked her hand loose from his. Lifting her cloak, she whirled about and half-ran up the oystershell road. In a moment she heard Nicholas's steps behind, closing in fast. Irrational fear swept over her. She *wouldn't* let him lay hands on her again!

Wildly, she turned left, leaving the lane and zigzagging across the gardens. She heard a muttered curse and a thud and realized Nicholas must have stumbled and fallen, giving her a short reprieve.

Kate increased her pace until finally she reached the woods, with its tangled growth of underbrush as far as she could see. A path loomed ahead and she took it. A short way into the wood, the path forked. She took the right, then moved off the path and blindly pushed her way through the mass of growth as fast as possible.

Behind, she heard Nicholas crashing through the underbrush, and more curses, then the sounds faded away. Triumph filled her. He must have taken the left turning! He'd lost her! But a few minutes later, the triumph turned to uneasiness.

She was the one who was lost.

There were no paths in the woods surrounding her.

She'd never had much sense of direction, and she had no idea how to find the path she'd left behind.

She'd been born in Plymouth and lived there all her life. Her family were thorough-going town-dwellers. She hadn't even walked in a woods alone before. And never one without well-marked paths.

The uneasiness increased. She might wander for days and not find a house or people. And what about wild animals? Or possibly hostile Indians?

Kate stopped where she was before panic could claim her. She took a few deep breaths to calm herself. All right, she'd done another supremely foolish thing, just because she'd let Nicholas provoke her. Now, the sensible thing to do was stay put.

In a few minutes he'd be bound to realize she'd taken the other fork. He'd retrace his steps and take the left path and find her. Oh, but how he'd gloat and scold!

Kate took a step forward before she could stop herself, then ordered her feet to quit walking.

She knew her personality was an odd blend of quick-tempered impulsiveness and practicality. Most of the time, common sense curbed her temper, ruled her behavior. Only sometimes did the other side of her nature take over—usually when she'd been goaded past thinking into anger.

As had happened now. How could she have forgotten she and Nicholas had angered each other so easily when he'd courted Alyssa? How could she have believed for a minute that they could marry, live together in peace?

Again, she berated herself for not seeing what a hare-brained plan she and Alyssa had concocted. But her younger sister had never truly loved Nicholas, Kate thought. She'd been too young to understand what love meant. Now, with John Latton, it seemed she did.

Nicholas's letter and passage money had taken Alyssa by surprise. It had been so long, she'd thought Nicholas would never send for her, she'd wailed to Kate. She didn't even remember Nicholas's face!

So, since Alyssa had no intention of giving John up, the plan hadn't seemed completely unreasonable. Men in the Colonies married women they'd never seen all the time to have a helpmate and mother for the children they wanted and needed. On the *Rosalynde* alone there had been half-a-dozen women coming to meet and marry equally unknown men.

And Kate and Nicholas weren't strangers by any means. Since he couldn't have her, Alyssa had said, then he would no doubt accept Kate as a substitute with good grace.

Of course, he'd be broken-hearted about losing her, Alyssa had gone on, not without a certain amount of satisfaction in that thought, Kate remembered. But he'd get over it and he and Kate would get along just fine.

Ha! *Why* had she listened and believed her sister's specious argument? Kate scowled and kicked at an inoffensive rock by her foot. *Why* hadn't she found out more about opportunities for employment in the Maryland Colony? *Why* had she assumed everything would work out?

She knew why. She'd turned a deaf ear to her doubts because she'd wanted so passionately to get away from Plymouth, from the shop, from everything about her dull, predictable life. With no promise of it ever getting any better. Nicholas wanted and needed a wife and she wanted and needed a chance at a new life.

Look where her wishes had gotten her.

Not yet half an hour off the ship and she and Nicholas had argued violently, he'd insulted her in every way possible and refused even to consider having her as his wife. She'd found there was no work to be had. And she was penniless. During the voyage, the small amount of coin she'd brought had been stolen from her cabin.

She'd given up the security she'd had in England for nothing. Now, she was cold, hopelessly lost in a thicket, and forced to wait for Nicholas to rescue her.

A new, worse thought invaded her mind.

What if he couldn't find her? What if she'd strayed farther from the path than she'd thought? What if he didn't even try? After all, he was *very* angry.

That possibility didn't even bear thinking about, so she quickly dismissed it. Of course he would. No matter how angry, he was a good, decent man.

Wasn't he?

The kitten in her pocket mewed plaintively, and she again comforted it with strokes and soft murmurs. For the first time in her adult life, she felt helpless, with no way to turn. It was a feeling she hated with every bone in her body, every breath she took.

A large, cold drop of water plopped on her nose, then ran down her face, followed in a moment by another. On top of everything else, it was raining. Kate shivered, fear and despair sweeping over her.

What was she going to do?

Chapter 2

"Damnation!" Nicholas swiped at a raindrop that had landed in his eye. More drops followed, and he swore again. He stopped making his way along the path and listened. He heard nothing except birds twittering and the rustling of small woods creatures. Where had the foolish chit gotten herself to?

She was behaving like an idiot, but he felt chagrin just the same. In his anger and shock he'd taunted her, made her plight out to be worse than it was.

Baltimore was bigger than he'd told her and there were other towns closer—Chestertown, for one. He also well knew that some women in the Maryland Colony ran shops—even owned them. She might be able to find employment without much difficulty.

But Kate Shaw, as she'd always managed to do, had gotten under his skin. Her pert assumptions that he'd marry her in place of her lovely sister had mightily annoyed him. He hadn't been able to resist taking her down a peg or two. He wasn't a piece of property to be traded about between sisters!

"Sweet Jesus!" he rumbled at the thought of wedding the tall, carrot-topped wench. The idea was so outrageous it nearly took his breath away. And he didn't for a minute believe it was his sweet Alyssa's idea. His dark brows drew together. No, it couldn't be.

Alyssa's—admittedly infrequent—letters had assured him of her undying love and devotion, her eagerness to journey to the Tidewater to become his bride.

Kate must have had a hand in Alyssa's defection, he thought darkly. He remembered she'd been very lukewarm when he and Alyssa became betrothed.

Kate must have encouraged this John Latton. He was only a sniveling boy, Nicholas recalled, whose father had owned a bakery a few doors down from the Shaws.

His frown deepened into a scowl. *Kate* must have taken advantage of a weak moment in Alyssa and suggested this plan.

But why? Despite her avowed willingness to marry him, he was positive she'd not made the arduous journey across the Atlantic because of some secret affection. Then, a cynical smile curved up one corner of his mouth.

Ah, yes. That last letter he'd written. Telling of his prosperous plantation, his fine manor house, his splendid tobacco crop.

His face warmed. He'd boasted a little, he admitted. It had been a fine manor house, true enough. But it had not been wholly—

He stiffened, his thoughts breaking off. *That* was no bird. It was a stifled cry. God's breath! Had she fallen and hurt herself? Encountered a snake not yet holed up for the winter?

But at least the sound had oriented him to her whereabouts. She'd taken the other turning. He wheeled and made his way back to where the paths forked and then took the right himself. Yes, there was a piece of her gray cloak caught on a bramble thorn. He plucked the piece loose, looking at it disapprovingly.

Dark, dull gray. Naturally, she wouldn't choose a bright, pretty color. Alyssa would have. He pictured his would-be bride in a sky-blue cloak, matching her eyes, smiling bewitchingly up at him.

Nicholas scowled, tossed the scrap of fabric aside, and stomped his way along the path. Yes, he was furious with Kate, but he couldn't leave her here. The sensible thing was to take her home with him today. And tomorrow arrange for her transport to Chestertown. He could spare a few coins to tide her over until she found a job.

She'd run the greengrocer shop well, he recalled. She had a sensible head on her shoulders. She'd kept the books, too. Her father had often left the entire running of the business to her. She'd also done the housework and cooking for her family. If she couldn't find a position in a shop, she could hire herself out as a housemaid. She wouldn't starve.

He wished he could find someone as capable for a house-keeper. The last two bondwomen in that position had been slovenly and lazy. So much so, he'd sold their bonds. The one now in residence, that he'd taken from field work, was little better. A sudden, surprising thought entered his mind. He could let Kate work for him. She was a good worker and he was in dire need of someone.

Especially now that, due to Kate's scheming, he would have no bride.

Anger washed over him again at that thought. No, of course he wouldn't take her into his house! He walked faster, pulling his cloak more snugly around him to shut out the cold rain still falling. He didn't want to be reminded of her perfidy a dozen times a day!

Off to the side he caught another glimpse of gray fabric. So, she'd veered from the path to mislead him. By now, he'd wager, she was wishing she hadn't.

He heard another noise. One he couldn't identify. It was an animal sound, almost like a cat's meow, but not quite, followed by a voice, its tones comforting.

Nicholas left the path and moments later came around the trunk of a huge oak tree and stopped.

Kate stood a few feet away, her hooded head wet with rain, something small and furry nestled against her cheek. He felt a sudden flash of compassion as he realized all the wetness on her face wasn't caused by rain.

She was crying. She was afraid.

Impulsively, he took a step forward to let her know he was here, to comfort her. Kate raised her head and saw him. She stiffened, her hands folding protectively over whatever she held as if she feared his doing it harm.

Nicholas's compassion vanished. No reason for him to feel sorry for her. She'd brought all of this on herself. She should have minded her business and stayed in Plymouth! She should have sent Alyssa to him!

He strode closer, until again, as a few minutes ago, they were only a few feet apart. Now he saw what she held. A tiny scrap of a kitten.

"Did you pick that up in the woods here?"

Kate shook her head, relief that he'd found her, mixed with surprise at his words, sweeping over her.

"No, it was one of the kittens from the ship's cat. It would have been drowned. I kept it hidden in my cabin. I was going to—"

She heard herself babbling and abruptly stopped. He'd caught her off-guard. She'd braced herself for his anger and scorn for her headlong flight instead of a question about the kitten she'd rescued.

"Not that it's any of your affair," she added, sharply, because he was still frowning, still angry. No doubt he'd soon begin to berate her. She felt a big-enough fool—she didn't need him telling her.

"It *is* my affair if it's going to be living on my property," Nicholas said, then clamped his mouth tightly closed, as if appalled at his words.

"Why would it be living on your property?" Kate asked suspiciously.

"You need work and at present I require a housekeeper. Besides, you are indebted to me for your passage here. If you work for me, I can take it out of your wages until your debt is fulfilled."

Oh, now she understood. He didn't care if she starved or froze to death here in this dark wood in the cold rain, but he wanted to get his coin back—any way he could.

She'd be damned if she'd live on his plantation and work for him! She lifted her head. "No. Take me back to the *Rosalynde* and I will sail with it until it reaches a town. No matter what you say, I'm sure I can find employment. And I will pay my debt to you as soon as possible."

He raised one dark brow. "The *Rosalynde* isn't going anywhere now. It's staying anchored in the creek until spring."

She stared at him, dismay filling her. Was there no way to escape him? "Surely there will be small craft coming and going. On my journey here I saw many such sailing on these waters."

"Do you have the coin to pay for more journeying?"

Kate swallowed. She had no coin at all. Moreover, as Nicholas had just reminded her, she was his debtor. Neither had she any prospects of employment.

Other than becoming Nicholas's housekeeper.

No! She wouldn't. Then, she remembered she'd seen a sloop bobbing at anchor. "Your own boat could take me— and you could add that to my debt."

Something flickered in his dark eyes, then he shook his head, the gesture very positive.

"No, that isn't possible."

Kate's anger rose again. He owned this magnificent estate, had all those servants and slaves working for him, and yet was so miserly he wouldn't even help her get to a town?

Why was he so set on her staying here? When he couldn't stand the sight of her, why was he hindering her at every turn? Then the answer came to her, increasing her resentment.

He was determined to humiliate her because she'd presumed to take her sister's place as his wife. That was why he insisted she work as his housekeeper, why he wouldn't help her leave here.

She pressed her full lips together. She wouldn't allow him to get away with it. She'd talk to Morgan Lockwood, the *Rosalynde's* captain, and explain her predicament. He was a friendly man and seemed reasonable. Surely he'd help her. Impulsively, she took a step forward, her chin high, then stopped.

Wait a minute, she cautioned herself. Don't do anything else stupid today. Do you want to throw yourself on the captain's mercy? Explain how you took Nicholas's money and came here for your own selfish reasons? Do you truly believe he'd be sympathetic to your problems?

Carefully she put the kitten back in her pocket and pulled the the wet cloak around her cold body, repressing a shiver. No matter how she hated it, she had no choice, she finally admitted, except the one Nicholas had given her—at least for the time being.

"I accept your offer of employment," she told him, her voice cool. "But only until I pay back the passage money."

And then what would she do? She pushed the thought away. She'd worry about that when she had to.

Nicholas nodded. "Agreed. Now, come along." He turned and strode out of the thicket, not waiting for her.

Kate hastily followed, not trying to catch up, just keep him in view. Apparently he had no more wish to walk alongside her than she did him.

Finally, they reached the path and then came out of the dark wood. Kate let out a relieved breath, even though, here in the open, they had no shelter from the rain, which had settled into a cold drizzle. The sky was completely overcast now, gray and dreary.

Nicholas hadn't turned once to see if she'd kept up with

him. Now he strode across the gardens to the oystershell path leading to his mansion and started up it.

She increased her pace. He had the manners of a clod, and she was glad he'd refused her offer to wed him. Alyssa had been very wise to reject him in favor of John.

In spite of her black mood, she couldn't be unaware of the beauty of the plantation. The gardens, outlined in several kinds of evergreen shrubs, would be lovely in the spring and summer, and the mansion grew more imposing the closer they came. It was built of brick, a large three-story center section flanked on either side by smaller wings.

And—how odd! The front door of the house faced this way, instead of the road which Kate assumed must be on the other side. Ahead of her, Nicholas slowed and then stopped, finally waiting for her to catch up.

Kate deliberately slowed her own steps. Let him wait. She wasn't going to trot obediently up to him like a trained dog.

Nicholas turned and gave her an impatient glance. "Hurry up. I'm getting soaked."

So was she. Kate decided she was only spiting herself and walked faster. Together, silently, they walked up to the beautiful entrance. The massive door swung open before Nicholas could turn the knob.

A young, attractive woman stood framed in the doorway. Her golden-brown hair was carefully arranged, and she wore a pink silk dress. Her pretty mouth curved in a warm smile. But the smile seemed somehow sad, even though her brown eyes glowed with welcome.

"Nicholas! Come in! And this must be—" Her voice faltered as she fully took in Kate's appearance. "Alyssa," she finished, a little doubtfully.

Embarrassment hitting her anew, Kate abruptly realized how she must look. Her cloak was wet and torn in several places, her hair, straggling and soaked, hanging outside her hood. She had scratches on her face from the underbrush she'd encountered in her headlong flight which burned and tingled.

She and Nicholas stepped over the threshold into a wide hall. A graceful stairway rose to the right. The hallway stretched the full depth of the house, and at its end was another entrance very much like the one they'd just come through.

"Devona, this is Kate, Alyssa's sister. She'll be staying at Lydea's Pride for a while," Nicholas said, his words clipped.

Kate, her embarrassment growing, waited for him to say something else, to explain the situation, but he didn't. The other woman showed no hint of the surprise and confusion she must feel at Nicholas's unexpected announcement. She gave Kate a wide smile and stepped forward, placing her hand on Kate's arm.

"I'm Devona Aldon. I've missed Lydea so much. It will be wonderful to have you at Lydea's Pride."

Relieved at her warmth and tact, Kate smiled back. She liked this pleasant, friendly woman on sight, even though her words were puzzling. "It is so nice to make your acquaintance."

Devona must be a relative of Nicholas, since it appeared she lived here and acted as hostess. But who was Lydea and why had Nicholas named his plantation for her?

A noise on the wide stairway drew her glance. Three little girls, one with light-brown hair, the other two with chestnut hair and obviously twins, clattered down the steps, chattering and giggling.

Reaching the bottom, they hurried over to where the others still stood. There couldn't be more than a year between the twins and the other girl, Kate thought, giving Devona a sympathetic glance.

This woman certainly must have her hands full with three children so close together in age. Did her whole family live here, then?

Alyssa had never mentioned Nicholas's saying anything like that in his letters. Of course, Alyssa hadn't said much of anything about Nicholas's letters, except to hint they mostly contained rapturous words of love and undying devotion and how hard he was working for their future.

The brown-haired girl walked to Devona's side, sliding her arm around the woman's waist and smiling up at her. The twins, who were dressed in identical sky-blue gowns, stood as if rooted to the floor, staring at Kate in what appeared to be fascinated amazement.

No wonder. Kate forced a smile, resisting the urge to push her hair back under her wet hood. How she longed to be told which room would be hers and to go there and change. Of course, she realized, her trunks were still down on the dock. Or would a servant have brought them up by now?

One of the twins tore her brown-eyed gaze from Kate, directing it to Nicholas.

"Cousin Nicholas," the girl asked, "where is the beautiful, blue-eyed, yellow-haired angel who will be your bride?"

Chapter 3

Kate felt Nicholas stiffen beside her. She knew her face was reddening again and refused to glance his way.

Cousin Nicholas? Then Devona must indeed be his relative. And the child's tone had been odd, almost as if she were glad Alyssa wasn't here.

The silence grew, becoming more awkward by the second. Finally, Nicholas said, his voice strained, his words almost the same as the ones he'd used to explain Kate's presence to Devona. "This is Alyssa's sister, Kate. She will be staying on the plantation for a while."

And again, he'd explained nothing.

'Oh, where are my manners?" Devona said. "Come into the drawing room, do! We'll have tea. But first, you both need to get out of those wet cloaks. Daisy!" she called, and at once an attractive, dark-skinned young woman appeared from the room to the left.

"We must be going," Nicholas said. "This rain does not look as if it will let up and my supplies are loaded in the wagon."

Confusion swept over Kate. What did Nicholas mean?

Did he have *another* manor house somewhere on his vast plantation? Could he really be that wealthy?

Devona looked uncertainly from Kate to Nicholas, opened her mouth as if to say something, then closed it again and nodded. "Of course." She turned to the servant girl, still hovering nearby. "Daisy, please bring the girls' cloaks."

Daisy nodded and left, reappearing a few moments later with brown cloaks which she helped the twins don.

Devona smiled at Kate again. "I'm expecting to see a great deal of you! I'm sure you'll have lots of wonderful gossip to tell me about England! And of course, Becky loves to have Emily and Celia come for visits."

"Come along, girls," Nicholas said briskly. His eyes briefly met Kate's, and his face tightened before he turned away.

She didn't need any reminders that he hated the sight of her, Kate thought, stung. Her confusion growing, her mind whirled with unanswered questions.

Devona wasn't the twins' mother. Whom did they belong to, then? Another cousin of Nicholas's who lived in the second manor house?

The kitten in Kate's pocket, which she'd almost forgotten during the last few minutes, chose that moment to pop its head up and mew loudly. Kate recognized that particular sound. It meant he wanted food—now.

The twins, who'd started to follow Nicholas, stopped, their round eyes wide as they stared at the kitten. Then the one who'd spoken before looked at Kate. "Why do you have a kitten in your pocket?"

Again, Kate was puzzled at her tone. The child sounded almost hostile. Kate managed to find a smile. "I brought it with me from the ship," she explained.

"Cousin Nicholas will make you put it in the barn," the other twin said. Her voice merely sounded very positive of this fact, with no trace of the near-hostility Kate had heard in the other girl's voice.

Nicholas stopped in the doorway, frowning, as his glance rested on the kitten. "I said, come along, girls," he repeated, turning away again.

Her kitten was *not* going in any barn, Kate vowed, glaring at his broad back.

She saw wide-eyed expressions on the twins' faces, as if they couldn't believe anyone would dare to glower at their cousin. Even at his back.

They were afraid of him, Kate decided. How despicable to make two children cringe at his every command! The change in Nicholas wasn't for the better and went deeper than looks.

She managed a smile as she turned to Devona. "I do hope to see you again."

"We will make sure of that," the other woman answered warmly.

As their glances met, Kate again saw something sorrowful in Devona's brown eyes, in her smile. Kate's intuition told her all wasn't as serene with this woman as her apparent lighthearted friendliness would indicate. Kate shook off the thought. She was reading a lot into a glance. No doubt because of her own situation.

Nicholas already strode down the path leading to the dock, the twins hurrying to keep up with him. *She* wouldn't scurry down the path, Kate thought darkly. She was too tired and he might as well learn that, despite their bargain, she wasn't going to be at his beck and call like one of the indentured servants.

But the misty rain continued to fall, although it had slackened, so she walked briskly. Still, Nicholas and the girls arrived at the docks a full minute or so before she did.

By the time she got there, Nicholas was bent over a wooden-sided farm wagon containing crates and boxes. Two horses stood patiently in front, their reins tied to a tree.

On the *Rosalynde's* deck, workers unloaded crates and

boxes similar to the ones on Nicholas's wagon. Kate looked around for a carriage, but saw none. It still wasn't brought around? And Nicholas had been in such a hurry.

Planks were set across the wagon for seats. They looked hard and uncomfortable. She felt sorry for the servants who'd have to drive this conveyance to Nicholas's other manor house.

Nicholas finished inspecting his goods, untied the horses, then, holding the reins, climbed up on the front plank and sat down. The twins scrambled after him, sitting on the one behind. Nicholas turned and gave Kate an impatient glance. "Do you need help?"

Kate's mouth dropped open as she spied her trunks amidst the boxes and realized why there was no waiting carriage. *This* was to be their conveyance!

"Of course not," she snapped. She climbed awkwardly up beside the twins and sat down on the plank seat. It was just as hard as it looked.

Nicholas clucked to the horses, and they went around the curved driveway toward the other side of the house. Kate's smoldering gaze fastened on Nicholas's straight back, his broad shoulders. His thick, waving hair was caught back with a leather thong.

Again, she felt that unwanted pull of attraction and furiously pushed it aside. How could she still feel this way about a man who'd made it abundantly clear he wanted nothing to do with her?

He was treating her abominably and all she'd done was offer to take her sister's place . . . to be his wife and help-mate. True, she'd used his money for her passage here, but of course she'd intended to pay that back if they didn't marry.

Kate conceded Nicholas had every right to be wrathful. But why was all his anger turned on her? *Alyssa* was the one who'd jilted him.

Indignation, mixed with hurt pride, rose up inside Kate at the memory of his scornful rejection. He'd always been somewhat arrogant and cocksure, but five years had made him into a hard, cold man.

And he had to be taking them in this horrible wagon to wherever they were going just to further humiliate her.

She should have stayed in Plymouth. At least there she had work she knew how to do capably and enough income to live. Most importantly, she'd had no one telling her what to do. She should have stayed and remained a spinster.

Here, she felt certain, Nicholas would make her life as miserable as possible, no matter how unjustified his anger. He was proving that with each passing moment.

And she couldn't go back to England even if she found a ship. She not only owed Nicholas, she had no money for the return passage. And Alyssa and John now ran the shop. There was no place for her.

Anger at herself swept over her. Why on earth had she agreed to this plan? she asked herself again, and the answers she'd given herself earlier no longer satisfied her.

Alyssa, of course, had assumed Nicholas's prosperity had been the deciding factor. No longer having to worry constantly about making enough money to survive was appealing, of course. Kate wouldn't deny that.

But it hadn't been the real reason behind her decision. Leaving a dull, predictable life in England for a new, exciting one here in the Maryland Colony hadn't been, either.

So what had?

Long-suppressed emotions welled up inside her, struggling for release. Frantically, she pushed them down, but they would no longer remain hidden.

And Kate finally admitted what had made her do this thing that was so contrary to her practical nature.

More than hurt pride and indignation at Nicholas's unjust anger were bothering her. Looking at the back of his head, her face flamed as if he could read her mind.

She'd desired Nicholas.

She'd wanted him since the first day he'd come into the

shop. But she'd never thought she had a chance of getting him so she'd pushed the forbidden desires deep inside, not even letting them surface when Alyssa had proposed this plan.

Instead, she'd told herself it was a sensible idea, one that would solve everything. Alyssa and John could have the shop, and she'd create a new life in the New World. If Nicholas didn't want her as a wife, then that was fine. She'd find a job and make her own way.

But she'd been lying to herself. She hadn't truly believed she'd have to do that. She hadn't expected Nicholas's angry, bitter rejection.

What had she thought? That he'd grown away from Alyssa over the years? Just as Alyssa had grown away from him? That he'd sent for her only out of a sense of obligation? That he might even be relieved and happy for Kate to step off the *Rosalynde* instead of Alyssa?

Incredulity at her naïvete swept over her. Oh, what a fool she'd been! She, who'd always prided herself on her common sense, her firm grip on reality.

Of course, Nicholas should be angry with her. How would she feel if she were in his shoes? Furious, disappointed, and tricked.

And broken-hearted.

Because it was clear Nicholas's love for Alyssa hadn't faded over the years. Not at all. If anything, it had grown. Kate's absurd dream world had dissolved into mist, like the cheerless day surrounding her.

She tightened her mouth and sat up straighter on the hard plank seat. All right. She'd gotten herself into this impossible situation. Alyssa had not forced her. And there was no going back, so she'd just have to make the best of it.

At least she'd been spared the ultimate hurt that Nicholas was enduring. She'd wanted him—still wanted him, she knew, in spite of everything that had happened.

But her heart wasn't broken. She didn't love him as he loved her sister.

One of the twins giggled at something the other had said, penetrating Kate's black mood, even lightening it a little. There were some bright spots, she told herself firmly. She wouldn't be here forever, subject to Nicholas's scorn. As soon as her debt was paid, she'd leave, find a job somewhere, as far away as possible.

But while she was here she hoped the twins would be a part of her life. Kate liked children—these two would help her sojourn here. And maybe their mother would also be a congenial woman, like Devona.

Probably she'd made too much of the few words the one girl had said to her, and her tone, because she was exhausted. No doubt Nicholas had talked much of Alyssa's fair beauty, and the twins were understandably surprised that she hadn't come as expected.

And thank God, the rain had stopped. Maybe they could all dry off.

Reaching the front of the house, Nicholas guided the horses down the long driveway, with huge trees growing on either side, then turned left onto a rutted, dirt road.

The wagon jolted, making Kate bounce on the seat. A twinge of pain moved up her backbone. She hoped this other manor of Nicholas's wasn't far away.

The road was narrow, trees and underbrush growing closely on either side, with no houses or buildings of any kind along the way. And they had it completely to themselves. She'd gotten her wish—everything was as different from Plymouth as could be.

But somehow the surroundings, combined with the overcast day, filled Kate's heart with renewed melancholy in spite of her avowal to make the best of things.

And the rigors of the long sea voyage were finally catching up to her. She felt as if she could sleep for days. The kitten had gone to sleep again, and the twins huddled together, whispering to each other. Kate found her heavy eyelids closing, her head moving downward until another jolt would awaken her.

Finally, after what seemed hours and the heavy gloom of the day had darkened to an even more dispiriting twilight, they turned into another tree-lined, oystershell-covered lane.

Relief filled her tired and aching body, her troubled mind and spirit. At last they must be arriving at their final destination. Soon, surely, she'd be shown to her room and she could go to bed.

Whatever duties Nicholas expected of her, they'd have to wait until tomorrow. She could do nothing more today. Her eyelids drifted shut again.

"Get out of here, you good-for-nothing beasts!"

Nicholas's shout jerked her awake. Kate sucked in her breath.

The wagon had stopped at the inside curve of the same kind of circular driveway as the other manor house.

But instead of another imposing brick structure, in front of them stood the burned-out remains of what must have once been such a place. Now, only tall chimneys and some brick walls attested to that fact.

In the dusk, the ruined building looked almost ghostly. Kate suppressed a shudder as she stared at it. Where were they?

Nicholas jumped down from the driver's seat and went tearing off, passing the ruins, his dark-blue cloak flapping as he ran. Kate's bewildered gaze followed him. What appeared to be a cottage stood at some distance behind where the mansion had. A couple of large animals, which Kate couldn't identify in the dim light, seemed to be rooting at the ground near the cottage.

Without breaking stride, Nicholas grabbed up a long stick from the ground and brandished it at the animals, who ran, squealing loudly at his approach.

"What is he doing?" Kate asked the twins who were in the midst of sliding off the wagon seat.

One of them shot Kate a look made up of equal parts of near-dislike and agitation. "He's chasing Alfreda and Mordred!" She turned abruptly away. "Come on, Emily, we have to stop him!"

"Wait!" Kate said. No, she hadn't imagined the earlier hostility in the one twin's voice. "Why are we stopping here? Where are we?"

The girl, who must be Celia, Kate realized, and the leader of the two, jerked her head around and gave her another of those unsettling glances. "We live here with Cousin Nicholas." She pointed at the cottage ahead of them.

"You mean your whole family lives on Nicholas's plantation?" Kate asked, her puzzlement growing.

Celia's mouth tightened as she shook her head. "Lydea's Pride is *our* plantation and Cousin Nicholas is our family now. Our mama and papa are dead."

Shock spiraled through Kate. "Oh, I'm so sorry! I didn't mean—"

Celia didn't wait to hear Kate's apologetic words. She grabbed her sister's hand and they went running after Nicholas, obviously intent on trying to stop him from his rout of the animals.

Kate stared after them, trying to make sense of what Celia had said. The kitten popped its head out of her pocket, again giving her his hungry mew.

"Just be patient," she told him, absently, temporarily comforting him with strokes. "We'll soon find you some food."

She stiffly got down from the makeshift wagon seat and, passing the ruins of the house with a shudder, followed the running twins.

Reaching the other building, she saw it was, indeed, a shabby frame dwelling . . . where the twins and Nicholas lived.

If that were so, there could be no manor house on this plantation like the one Nicholas had so glowingly described in his letter. Moreover, if Celia told the truth, and Kate saw no reason to doubt her, the plantation didn't even belong to him, but to these two orphaned children.

All the puzzling things that had happened today suddenly made perfect sense. Devona had welcomed them so warmly because that was *her* beautiful house, not Nicholas's.

And he hadn't brought them here on the jolting farm wagon merely to annoy her. It was probably the only conveyance he owned! No wonder he'd told her he couldn't take her to a town on the sloop she'd seen. It didn't belong to him, but to Devona and her husband.

Nicholas wasn't the wronged party in this farce after all. Obviously, he'd lied about everything in order to have Alyssa for his wife.

The twins had flung themselves at Nicholas, each one holding onto a knee, successfully preventing him from hitting the large squealing animals, which Kate now recognized as rotund pigs.

He glanced up at her approach, the frown she'd seen on his face almost constantly since she'd debarked from the *Rosalynde* once more firmly in place.

Kate folded her arms and glared at him, all her exhaustion and resentment sparking in her hazel eyes. To think that she'd been feeling so sorry for him only a little while ago!

"And you actually had the gall to accuse *me* of hoodwinking *you?*"

Chapter 4

Nicholas's scowl mixed with bafflement. He stared back at Kate, momentarily ignoring the entreaties of the twins. "What in bloody hell are you talking about?" he demanded.

"You know exactly what I'm talking about and you should be ashamed of yourself for using such language in front of two innocent children."

He did feel a little abashed for that, but he'd be damned if he'd let her see it. He also knew he was overreacting to the pigs' getting loose because he was so angry at Kate, at losing Alyssa.

"I have no idea what you mean, and the language I use is my own affair."

Kate's expression darkened. "Why did you lie to my sister? 'A prosperous plantation, a stately manor house,' indeed."

Nicholas recognized the quotation as coming from his last letter to Alyssa. His mouth curled. So he'd been right—Kate had only wanted to marry him because of his supposed wealth. He'd been prepared to tell Alyssa, of course, but he couldn't talk about it now, not in front of the twins. And he owed Kate no explanation—not after what she'd done!

"It appears all your treacherous work was wasted," Nicholas said, his voice hard.

"What?" Kate demanded.

"Your conniving to make my sweet Alyssa break her troth with me and arrange another with that sniveling John Latton so that you could take her place."

Kate's mouth dropped open, her face draining of color. "I had nothing to do with Alyssa's decision."

Her words were firm, but her voice wasn't, Nicholas noted. His conviction that Kate had been behind his beloved's defection strengthened. He silently cursed his impulsive offer of employment.

"I will never believe that," he told her coldly. "Alyssa loved me truly—as I loved her. As I still love her."

Kate's face whitened even more.

Nicholas pressed home his advantage. "Then I gather your only reason for coming here was to become mistress of a large, prosperous plantation. I suspected as much, and you've given me the proof with your words just now."

Kate stepped back, renewed shock and anger flooding over her.

Somehow, he'd turned her words around, made it appear that *she* was completely in the wrong, he the innocent, duped party. And now she understood why he was so angry at her. He thought she'd persuaded Alyssa to break her troth. How could he believe such things of her?

And there was no way she could defend herself. On the surface, it did appear she'd come here for the reasons he'd just stated. He'd never believe his supposed wealth wasn't her sole reason for making this journey.

He'd never know the true reason. She'd make sure of that.

So she wouldn't make the futile effort to try to convince

him she was innocent of his accusation. She raised her chin. "Think what you will. You always do, anyway."

Her glance went to the twins, standing side by side. Their brown eyes were wide as they gazed upon the two arguing adults.

Kate's conscience smote her and she smoothed out her frown and smiled at the girls. One twin smiled back, the other didn't. Kate turned back to Nicholas.

"We should both be ashamed for airing our private problems in front of these innocent, helpless children."

"Innocent? Helpless? Just wait until you get to know these imps. And now, I've wasted enough time." He turned and brandishing his switch, started after the pigs again.

"No! Cousin Nicholas," Celia wailed, following him, Emily close behind her. "Please don't hit Alfreda and Mordred!"

He gave them an irritated glance. "As I've told you often enough, you do not bestow names upon animals which will soon be your food."

At that callous remark, Emily burst into tears, sobbing as she followed Nicholas and her sister.

He was an absolute brute, Kate thought indignantly. He stepped up his pace, and the pigs, who'd been happily rooting at some plants growing near the house, squealed again and scooted through an opening in a wooden fence where a rail had been knocked down. Safely through again, they loped off toward a large building in the distance.

A barn, Kate surmised, watching Nicholas and the twins following the animals. As they approached the building, a big Negro man came out of it and walked toward them. Did Nicholas have only one worker?

No wonder, in spite of his obvious dislike for her, Nicholas had offered her a job as his housekeeper. No, not offered—he'd known she was forced to take the job to survive.

Or was she?

The sudden thought made her catch her breath. How

could she now believe anything he'd said? He'd probably invented all those things he'd told her.

This very minute, the *Rosalynde* could be sailing up the Chesapeake, heading back to England. Failing that, there might be many places at a reasonable distance from here where she could find a job.

Kate pressed her lips together. She'd have it out with him tonight, just as soon as these children were fed and put to bed.

She inspected the cottage while she waited for Nicholas and the twins to return. Even in the growing dusk it looked dismal. A coat of whitewash would improve its looks immensely. And scrubbing its filthy, cobwebbed windows. She grimaced. If the outside looked this bad, what must the inside be like?

In a few minutes, Nicholas came back, trailed by the girls. His boots and cloak were splashed with mud, as were the twins', and his scowl was still in place.

She remembered the smile he'd worn while waiting for Alyssa to get off the ship. That smile had melted her, even though she'd known it was meant for her sister.

And it was an excellent thing it hadn't lasted. She didn't want any tender feelings toward this man! How could she ever have desired him? Have thought she could spend the rest of her life with him?

"You might have gone on inside and begun making yourself useful," Nicholas said, his words clipped. "It's late and we're all tired and hungry."

So she'd been right! He *didn't* have any more servants. "Then, I'm to be the maid and cook as well as the house-keeper?"

Nicholas gave her a sardonic glance, his dark eyes hooded. "You may name your various duties as you please. At the moment there's no one in the house to help. Tucker just told me the bond servant who did household work has run away with my joiner."

He turned and strode to the door, grasping the latch

and swinging it open. It creaked on rusty hinges, sending a shudder down Kate's spine. She peered around Nicholas's shoulder, wary of what would be revealed.

The outside appearance had indeed been prophetic of the interior, she saw at once. The door opened directly into one large room which stretched the length of the structure. At the left, a door stood ajar, revealing a narrow, steep staircase.

A rough settee and several equally rustic chairs occupied this part of the room. The furniture had clothes and other objects heaped on them. On the right side, a fieldstone fireplace took up most of the wall, its stone hearth dirty and covered with ashes. A crane was suspended inside the chimney, from which a large, black cooking pot hung. An oven for baking was built into the left side.

A table and chairs sat against the back wall. A stack of unwashed dishes stood on the table.

The floor of rough boards was scratched and dirty, and all manner of odds and ends were scattered here and there. It looked as if no one had picked anything up or cleaned this house in days—even weeks.

Nicholas stood in the doorway for so long that Kate shot a glance at him. His face looked stunned, as if the sight of the disorderly room were as shocking to him as it was to her.

Finally, he went on inside, Kate and the twins following. He shrugged out of his wet, muddy cloak and carelessly flung it across a chair back, then went across to the hearth and began to build a new fire.

Kate took a deep, indignant breath and let it out. Why, they were living little better than the pigs he'd chased! These poor children! She started to berate him, than glanced at the twins, who were standing just inside the door in their own wet, muddy cloaks.

No, she wouldn't get into another row with him now. Not in front of the children. And besides, she needed to tend to them.

"Here, let me help you with your cloaks, girls," she said, smiling at the two. "We'll hang them up to dry."

Both of them stared at her in surprise, then one gave her a tentative smile in return as Kate aided her in sliding the damp garment off her shoulders. Emily, no doubt. Turning to Celia, she found the girl staring at her intently, a wary expression in her eyes. Thankfully, the cloaks were heavy and the girls' gowns dry beneath.

"Are you cold?" Kate asked, and both of them shook their heads in unison.

Kate hung their garments on pegs by the fireplace, where a welcome crackling of burning wood and tendrils of heat were making themselves felt.

A new insight had just hit her. Celia hadn't wanted Alyssa here—and she didn't want her, either. It would take some doing to win the girl over . . . but it could be done.

Kate brought her thoughts up short. But of course, *she* wouldn't be the one to do it. She'd be gone from here once she'd made Nicholas admit he'd lied to her about everything. No matter what he said, she'd insist he arrange for her to be taken to a nearby town tomorrow.

But she had promised to stay, she thought uncomfortably as she removed her own cloak and hung it on another peg. Of course, that was before she'd discovered Nicholas had lied to Alyssa. Things were different now.

She glanced at him. He still knelt before the fire, adding a couple of logs to its growing flames, seemingly indifferent to the others in the room.

How could she leave these two children with such an uncaring, incompetent man? Who'd not only lied about what he possessed, but who was letting the twins' plantation go to wrack and ruin.

An indignant face suddenly stuck itself out of her cloak pocket and gave an insistent mew, reminding Kate of her own charge. She scooped the kitten out and placed it on the floor, where it looked around curiously, its little tail stuck straight up into the air.

At once both twins squatted beside it. One reached out a tentative hand and smoothed down its head, and then the other, after a glance at her sister, followed suit. Kate smiled at their rapt attention. Celia, like her sister, obviously loved animals.

"Animals are not to be indoors."

Nicholas's voice startled Kate, making her jerk her head up. She hadn't even realized he was watching. She gave a disdainful glance around the disheveled room.

"I'm sure one tiny kitten will mess it up fearfully. After all, it is *so* neat and clean."

Nicholas's brown eyes narrowed. "That isn't the question. We do not allow animals in the house. This one must stay in the barn."

Kate reached down and scooped up the kitten, holding it against her green gown. "This one must stay with *me*," she said firmly.

Their glances met and clashed, neither giving an inch. Finally, Nicholas got up from his crouching position and Kate realized with chagrin that once again they'd been arguing heatedly in front of the children.

"I will make sure he doesn't leave my room during the night. Where am I to sleep?"

He pointed toward the stairway. "Up there. And see that you do. Now, we're all famished. Do what you can about getting some supper." He turned and left the house.

She supposed she'd won this skirmish, Kate thought, barely restraining herself from making a face at his stiff, retreating back.

But it was only one.

Was she going to stay, then? Her stomach rumbled loudly, reminding her that she, too, was very hungry. Her decision could wait awhile.

She put the kitten on the floor again between the two girls. "Do you want to watch him while I cook supper?"

Both twins nodded eagerly and Kate heaved a silent sigh

of relief that, at least for the moment, Celia seemed to have forgotten her animosity.

Kate scooped the stack of dirty dishes into a wooden tub standing by the fireplace, then headed for a door near the table and chairs, hoping it was a larder. Her guess had been correct, she saw, dismay filling her at the almost-bare shelves revealed as the door swung open.

A cloth-wrapped bundle contained the end of a loaf of bread, growing stale and hard. That would have to do for supper. She lifted the tightly fitting lid of a large crock on the floor. Only a layer of fat told her it had once contained cooked meat. Two crates held a few potatoes and onions. A wooden bin held flour, another a coarser ground substance. She looked in vain for milk, butter, meat, or other vegetables.

The front door opened behind her and a loud thump reverberated through the house. Kate whirled to see her trunks on the floor and the door closing again behind Nicholas.

She hurried to the door and snatched it open in time to see him lift a crock from the bed of the wagon. He handed her the crock then turned back to lift another one.

Kate hastily set the icy cold crock on the table and took the other, which she put beside it.

Nicholas came inside with a cloth-wrapped bundle. "Here's fish left from breakfast," he told her. "I brought all this down from the springhouse. Beginning tomorrow, I'll expect you to fetch the food."

She burned to tell him that tomorrow she wouldn't be here for him to order around like a servant, but with effort she held her tongue. Time enough for all that later.

"Don't worry about that." She kept her voice civil for the benefit of the twins, who were still entranced with the kitten. Celia—at least she thought it was Celia—had found a string and was drawing it along the floor and the kitten was pouncing on it. Both girls giggled in delight.

Nicholas glanced their way, and for a moment his face softened. Then, he turned abruptly away and went back to the wagon, bringing in two sacks, then left again, springing up into the driver's seat and clicking his tongue to get the horses started.

Kate watched as he headed toward the building she guessed to be a barn, then closed the door against the evening chill and examined the first crock.

Thick, golden cream crowned the milk the crock held, and the smaller one contained deep-yellow butter. Her mouth watered and her stomach rumbled again, drawing Celia's curious glance.

Kate smiled at her. "Are you hungry?" she asked and was rewarded with a blank stare. "Supper will soon be ready," she said to them both.

Sighing, Kate turned away, finding a bowl and cup on a shelf. She skimmed back most of the cream, then dipped a little of the milk underneath into the bowl.

"Here you are." She set the bowl down before the kitten, who, after a suspicious sniff, began lapping it up eagerly.

One twin giggled. "Edward is very hungry," she said, giving Kate a sweet smile.

Edward? Kate remembered Nicholas's recent admonition to the twins about naming animals. Well, this one certainly wasn't to be used for food!

She smiled back at the girl, who must be Emily. "Yes, he is. Edward is a nice name. Which one of you thought of it?"

Emily pointed at her sister. "Celia did," she said.

Another quick glance at Celia revealed only a slight frown, so Kate merely nodded and turned away to start cooking supper.

To her surprised relief, the large pot suspended from the crane was scoured and clean. She added more wood to the fire and found a wooden pail of water which she poured into the pot, then added cut-up potatoes and onions.

She sniffed the fish, which had been filleted into neat, boneless slices. It smelled fresh and her stomach rumbled again as she cut it into chunks and laid them on a pewter plate awaiting their turn to be added to the stew pot. A small, covered crock on a shelf yielded salt, another pepper.

Supper cooking, she investigated the contents of the two sacks Nicholas had brought in. One contained more of the coarse ground substance, the other, flour.

She'd set bread to rise tonight for tomorrow, but that could also wait. She sliced the remains of the loaf from the larder, approving of its texture. Someone who knew how to mix a proper loaf had baked this. Nicholas? A wry smile turned up her mouth. No, she hardly thought so.

How she longed for a hot cup of tea! After searching the shelves, she located a tea caddy behind a crock on the shelf over the table. It didn't smell very fresh, but it was *tea*. At the moment, that was all that mattered.

A pretty porcelain teapot with a design of pink roses and green leaves sat on the shelf, too. It looked incongruous among the homely pewter and wooden dishes beside it. Kate dusted it off with a cloth she found on a peg and put it on the table.

She became aware of eyes on her and glanced over at the twins. Celia stared at her, brown eyes opaque, mouth in a straight line. "That was my mama's teapot," she said.

Her voice trembled, in spite of her stony countenance, Kate noticed, her heart softening even more toward these two waifs.

The door opened and, out of the corner of her eye, she saw Nicholas enter.

Kate ignored him. She smiled at the girls and nodded. "It's beautiful," she said softly. "I'll be very careful with it."

Nicholas paused just inside the door. As he listened to her gentle cadences and saw the curve of her generous

mouth in profile as she smiled at the twins, something
inside his stormy heart softened in response. He'd never
before heard her speak in such a manner. Working in the
greengrocer shop, she'd always been brisk and business-
like, friendly to her customers, but not overly so.

And as for the other times, when he'd been sitting with
Alyssa . . .

Thinking of those times, the momentary softness evapo-
rated. No, she'd never left him and Alyssa alone for an
instant. She'd acted more like a martinet maiden aunt
than an older sister.

And now he knew that had been a deliberate ploy . . .
all part of her scheme to see that he and Alyssa never wed,
that Kate take her place.

Or *attempt* to.

He strode across the room to deposit more wood on the
dusty hearth. No matter how much she smiled and spoke
sweetly to the girls, she was a cold- hearted, scheming
wench. Since she'd gotten short shrift from him, her new
plan must be to win them over.

Despite what she'd told him down by the *Rosalynde* and
her knowledge that his circumstances were not now as
he'd described them in his last letter to Alyssa, he had no
doubts she still wanted to wed him.

Kate was no fool. She had to know she'd be immeasur-
ably better off as his wife than trying to earn her own living
as a shop drudge.

As he added another log to the fire, his mouth watered
involuntarily at the savory aroma drifting up from the pot
on the crane. Good cooking wouldn't entice him into
marriage, he vowed. Nothing she could think of would!

But now that his anger had cooled a bit, he had to admit
he needed her help. But only temporarily. He'd allow her
to stay over the winter, until the tobacco was shipped in
the spring and his new crop of wheat safely planted. The
care of the twins and the house, in addition to other tasks

which he'd require of her, should amply repay his expenditure for her passage.

And give the saucy wench time to become a bit humble for what she'd tried to do.

Of course, nothing would give Alyssa back to him. It was too late for that. His heart hardened more as he glanced across the room to see Kate walking toward him, holding a platter of cut-up fish.

He moved aside so she could add it to the pot simmering over the fire, watching her slim, deft hands perform the simple task. Her movements made the fabric of her plain, green gown tighten across her full breasts.

Nicholas jerked his glance away, but not before, to his own incredulous disbelief, he felt the reaction to that sight in his lower regions. He turned and headed for the door again, stepping over the blasted kitten in the middle of the floor.

"Supper will be ready very soon now," Kate called after him as he jerked the door open.

"It will keep," he told her brusquely. "I have work to do."

Outside, he stood shivering in the chill November wind. In truth, he'd done all the evening chores, with only the help of two almost worthless indentured servants and Tucker, his black freedman, who did more work than both of the bond servants put together.

Nicholas let out a pent-up breath and headed for the barn again. Now, on top of everything else, because of the wily wench, he was shut out of his own house and hearth. Ignoring the fact he'd left of his own volition, his mind's eye gave him the picture of Kate's rounded form, bending over the fire.

Damnation! He hurried his steps, savagely kicking a stick out of his way. He'd been too long without a woman, being faithful to his anticipated bride.

No longer. There were plenty of willing tavern wenches in Chestertown. Many a time, they'd given him glances of blatant invitation. As soon as possible, he'd take one—or maybe several of them—up on that.

And come spring, he'd transport Kate Shaw to Chestertown and good riddance!

Chapter 5

It would serve him right if she let his supper get stone cold!
Kate thought, dishing up the fish stew for herself and the
twins. Did Nicholas have to make it so painfully clear at
every opportunity that he found her presence impossible
to tolerate?

"Let us eat our meal," she said, making her voice light
and pleasant. She was gratified when both girls came
promptly at her bidding and sat down on either side of
the rectangular table. At least Celia's aversion to her didn't
extend to everything. It seemed she'd eat Kate's cooking.

Fifteen minutes later she was certain of that. Both girls'
bowls were empty, wiped clean with the somewhat stale
bread, which Kate had thickly spread with the sweet golden
butter. They'd also drained their mugs of milk.

Emily gave her a shy smile. "That was very good."

Kate included solemn-faced Celia in her smiling return
glance. "Thank you." Celia had eaten well. That was a
good beginning. Beginning? her mind asked her. You are
staying, then?

She ignored that and, pushing back her chair, rose and

began clearing the table. It had grown dark by now and she'd lit a half-used tallow candle sitting on the shelf over the table. She'd put water to heat in another pot over the fire while supper cooked, and now it steamed its readiness for the cleanup. After carrying the tub of dirty dishes to the hearth, she ladled hot water over them.

Edward had settled down for a nap by the fire, but came to eager life, twining around her ankles, mewing his desperate need for food. Kate ladled a bit of stew into his milk bowl and he lapped it up, his whole body quivering with delight, then went back to sleep.

Emily clapped her hands together, laughing. "He's so funny!" she said gleefully. She glanced at Kate. "Is Cousin Nicholas going to let you keep him in the house?" Her mouth opened in a wide yawn, and she rubbed her eyes.

"Yes, he will stay in my room," Kate said, her voice firm and positive. Let her, indeed! Maybe Nicholas Talbot was lord and master to these children, but not to her. "And now, I think it's time you two were in your beds for the night."

Emily nodded. Celia frowned. "Cousin Nicholas doesn't make us go to bed this early," she announced, her voice as firm as Kate's had been.

Kate took a deep breath. This was her first test of wills with the girl. If she let Celia overrule her now, it would be twice as hard the next time. And never mind if there would *be* no next time.

"It's bedtime," she repeated, gently but firmly. "Come along, girls, and show me where you sleep."

In a moment, Celia's defiant gaze dropped and she led the way upstairs. Emily walked behind her sister and Kate brought up the rear, holding the candle aloft as they climbed the steep, narrow staircase. A narrow hall had three doors opening off it.

"This is our bedchamber," Celia said sullenly, stopping at the first door on the left.

It was a small room, sparsely furnished with a bed and

chest. On top of the chest sat a white pitcher and basin. A few garments hung on pegs. Threadbare muslin curtains hung limply at the small, dirty window, and the white-washed walls were smoke-blackened and smudged with fingerprints.

Tomorrow, she'd do something about that, Kate thought.

Celia walked into the room and sat down on the bed, her arms folded across her chest. Emily followed, glancing uncertainly from Kate to her sister.

"Come, girls, you need to wash up before bed," Kate said briskly, going to the chest. Both girls looked surprised at her command, and Kate's lips tightened. Yes, these girls certainly needed to be taken in hand.

Emily cast a quick look at her sister and Kate saw the slight head-shake Celia gave her. Relieved to find the pitcher nearly full of water, Kate poured some in the basin and took a washing cloth from a peg over the chest.

The twins gazed at her with wide, solemn eyes, but didn't budge. Celia's hold on Emily was enough to make the other girl disobey, too. Kate got their nightdresses from the foot of the bed where they were tossed carelessly, inside out.

"Come now, let's get this over with." Kate folded her own arms across her chest and let her gaze rest on Celia, hoping she looked more certain of their obedience than she felt. She desperately wanted to get these two settled for the night and go to bed herself. She was trembling with fatigue.

The girl returned her gaze and kept her arms folded for what seemed like forever to Kate. At last a huge yawn overcame her, and her eyelids drooped.

"Come on, Celia," Kate said, softening her voice. "We're all very tired."

The girl raised her hand to smother another yawn and widened her eyes, trying to keep her lids from drooping again. Then, to Kate's relief, she got up from the bed and walked to where Kate stood, Emily behind her.

They were old enough to wash themselves, but not tonight. Kate scrubbed both girls' faces and hands with dispatch and had them into the nightdresses and tucked under their covers before Celia thought of any more delaying tactics.

"I'll hear your prayers now."

Another surprised glance passed between the sisters. But this one was mixed with something else, Kate thought, something akin to pleasure. As if the bedtime prayer ritual were one they'd missed. Sadness for their orphaned state swept over her again. She wondered how long it had been since they'd lost their parents, and under what circumstances.

In unison, they repeated a simple prayer, and Kate gave their covers a final adjustment. She thought about kissing them good night, feeling Emily would be receptive, but then decided against it.

"Good night, girls," she said, knowing her smile was soft and gentle.

As she'd expected, Emily smiled back. "Good night, Kate," she said sleepily. "I'm glad you've come to stay with us."

Kate felt a tug at her heartstrings at the child's words and tone. Her glance fell on Celia.

The other girl's face was unsmiling as she stared back at Kate. "I'm not," she announced. "Cousin Nicholas isn't either." Her glance dared Kate to dispute that last statement.

She couldn't, of course. It was clear Nicholas detested the sight of her. And she him, she told herself firmly. After today's events, the unwanted physical attraction she'd long felt for Nicholas had surely died.

Kate picked up the candle and left the room, pulling the door partly closed behind her. The bedchamber next to the twins obviously belonged to the man in question.

The narrow bed was rumpled and unmade, quilts and sheet flung back as if Nicholas had gotten up in a terrible hurry. A shirt was draped across a bedpost, and other personal items lay scattered here and there. This window was also dirty, with a ragged curtain. Kate's lip curled in disgust as she turned away.

The third room, its door open, was across the hall. This one had to be hers, since Nicholas had said she was to sleep upstairs. She opened it, then, as the flickering candlelight revealed the interior, released her pent up breath in a weary sigh.

A thick film of dust covered the floor. A battered bed, pieces of straw sticking out of holes in its ancient mattress, sat underneath the dirty, curtainless window. Discarded furniture, in various states of disrepair, lay here and there, also covered with dust. Obviously, no one had used the room as a bedchamber in a long time.

Fighting her dismay, she reminded herself none of this was important tonight. All that mattered was falling into that bed, as uninviting as it looked, and getting some sleep. But she had to clean up a bit, first. She heaved another sigh as she headed for the hall again.

Walking past the twins' room, she stopped and peered around the corner of the door. Both girls were asleep, Emily curled into a ball on her side, Celia lying on her back, her arms outstretched, her hands closed into fists. Even in sleep, she looked unhappy. Truly, the two needed a great deal of love and care.

But she couldn't furnish it. Kate pushed down the sympathy she felt and quietly went back downstairs. She realized her vacillation with herself had ceased.

No matter what she'd agreed to, she couldn't stay under the same roof with Nicholas. Not after discovering he blamed her for Alyssa's defection and that he'd lied to her sister.

And if that weren't enough, they couldn't talk to each other five minutes without fighting!

Edward was still napping. And Nicholas hadn't returned from wherever he'd gone. The fire was nearly out and she was sorely tempted to let it be. Nicholas deserved to eat a cold supper for leaving so rudely after she'd cooked a hot meal.

Her better nature won out, however, and she added another log to the fire, then scooped up the kitten and carried him outside. To her relief, he at once went off behind a bush and scratched at the ground before performing the act for which she'd brought him outside.

Kate glanced around while she waited. There was yet no sign of Nicholas. Not that she wanted to see him, of course. She only wished he'd come in and eat so she could finish cleaning up the kitchen.

She'd left her cloak inside and shivered at the chill wind. The night was clear now, the earlier clouds and rain gone. Stars shone brightly and coldly in the black dome overhead, a half-moon lending more light to the night scene.

She could see the tall brick chimneys of the burned house ahead, looming against the night sky like stark and lonely sentinels. When had it burned? And why hadn't someone pulled the ruins down? She shivered again, not from cold this time, scooped up the kitten, and went back to the cottage.

Inside again, Kate looked at the disorderly room. No matter how tired she was, she couldn't go to bed without cleaning up a little. She quickly picked up clothes and other items and piled them on the settee. Finding a broom leaning against the hearth, she swept the floor, then tidied the kitchen area.

There, that was sufficient. Apparently Nicholas intended to stay out all night. Very well. It was no concern of hers. She was going to bed. But first she had to find some bedding and clean her bedchamber a bit.

A wooden chest in the corner yielded a quilted bed covering and a rough sheet. She'd make do without further search for a pillow, she decided, picking up the bedclothes, the broom, a dusting rag, and finally the kitten, and heading upstairs again.

Kate made swift work of the broken furniture, piling it in a corner, then attacked the dusty floor. Two sneezing fits and half an hour later, the room was clean enough to sleep in.

The rough bed was neatly covered with the sheet, the covering turned back ready for her to slip underneath it. A pitcher of water and a basin she'd found in the kitchen sat on a backless chair. The nightdress she'd taken from one of her trunks lay across the bed. At the foot lay Edward, curled into a tiny ball and purring contentedly.

So tired she was almost staggering, Kate pushed the door of the room closed. It slowly swung open again, and she saw the latch was broken. What did it matter?

She was sure she needed no barricade to prevent Nicholas from invading her room. She smiled derisively at that thought, then unbuttoned her dress and pulled it over her head. In her chemise, she crossed to the makeshift wash stand.

She'd also found a sliver of soap and towel in the kitchen and smiled with weary pleasure as she washed away the travel grime from her face and arms. Lifting her hands to her head, she took down her long hair and brushed it out, preparatory to braiding it for the night.

Her arms still over her head, Kate heard a muffled thump from the doorway. She turned quickly, her heart thumping to match the sound she'd just heard, in time to see Nicholas straightening himself. Her trunks sat just inside the doorway, and Nicholas had a peculiar expression on his face.

Kate grabbed her wrapper and hastily pulled it around her. "It's customary to knock on a person's door before barging in," she snapped.

Nicholas stared back, in his mind a vision of how Kate had looked a moment ago. Standing in that long, white undergarment, her bare shoulders gleaming in the candlelight, her shining red-gold hair loose, reaching almost to her waist. Her hair was still down, still shining, although she'd put on her wrapper.

"The door was open," he finally said, frowning at the slightly hoarse tone of his voice. He told himself sternly to dismiss that unwanted image. "The house is on a slant; this door always opens itself."

Kate's eyes narrowed as she pulled her robe tighter around her. "It wouldn't if you'd repair the latch. I've never seen such a mess as this room was in."

Nicholas's frown deepened at her tone and words, the vision of Kate in dishabille effectively banished. As if all he had to do was spend valuable time repairing a door to heretofore unused room. And he didn't have to explain himself or his actions to her, he reminded himself. "Some-day, I may see to that, mistress."

Her chin came up at his brusque reply. "That will be nice for whoever takes on the responsibilities for this household after I leave tomorrow. And for tonight, I will be sure to put a chair under the knob—that is, if I can find any with a sound back," she added, glancing at the pile of discarded furniture in one corner.

Surprise went through Nicholas at her first statement, his certainty that Kate still wanted to wed him faltering. He gave her a narrow-eyed glance. Her determination and annoyance appeared to be real, and he couldn't keep her here against her will. Soon enough, she could find out, if she had a mind to, that there was work she could do in Chestertown.

And she had a right to be annoyed, he reluctantly admit-ted. Damn Clarissa to hell for not cleaning the house before she ran off with Rupert! She wasn't much of a housekeeper, and he'd let things slide, busy as he'd been with the plantation work.

But this morning he'd given her explicit directions, determined that Alyssa would at least come home to a neat and clean cottage, if not the manor house she deserved and expected.

He pushed those thoughts aside. He had to give Kate some sort of an explanation, he had to be civil at least until he found out her intentions.

"My bond servant was supposed to have cleaned the cottage. But not this room. Alyssa would have shared my bedchamber, since I'd planned for us to marry today."

He saw her odd, greenish eyes flicker at that remark, her mouth tighten. Damnation! Why had he said that? If he wanted her to stay, he wasn't going about it in the right manner.

And he did want her to stay. When he'd come in a few minutes ago, the big, newly neatened room had welcomed him. His bowl of food waited, still warm, on the hearthstones. The fire was crackling, and a savory aroma lingered in the air.

He'd fully expected Kate to leave him a cold supper— if she left him any at all. The food had been excellently cooked and seasoned, too. He'd wished for a second bowl.

He took a deep breath, once again banishing the erotic remembrance of Kate as she'd looked a few moments ago. If she were truly in earnest about leaving, he must change her mind. As much as he hated to admit it, he truly needed her now.

"We must talk," he said, making his voice and tone polite. "Will you come downstairs?"

She stared straight at him for several heartbeats of time, then finally nodded. "All right."

He turned and left the room, hearing her light footsteps on the bare wooden stairs coming along behind him. Somehow, he liked that sound, he realized, then hastily pushed the thought away from him. He wanted her to stay, true, but purely for practical reasons. The less he saw of her, the better.

"Your supper is on the hearth," she said when they'd

reached the kitchen. A lone candle flickered on the mantel.

"I found it." He paused, starting to tell her how good the food had been, then, as a new thought occurred to him, caught back his words.

Perhaps she had no real intention of leaving. She'd certainly followed him down here with alacrity. Maybe her words upstairs were only a ploy to get him to beg her to stay. His certainty grew.

Yes, that must be it.

So he wouldn't praise her cooking. That was just what she wanted him to do . . . so that she could further her scheme of enticing him into marriage.

But he did have to tell her what had happened here. There was no getting around that.

"Sit down," he said, pointing to one of the kitchen chairs. He had a sudden vision of his sweet Alyssa sitting there, smiling up him . . . if not for Kate.

He noticed a tinge of color on Kate's fair skin as she stiffly obeyed him, almost as if she'd read his mind. He seated himself across the table from her and took a deep breath.

He wasn't looking forward to the next few minutes. Even after all this time, he could still scarcely bear to talk about what had happened that terrible night.

"I owe you an explanation," he said, his voice sounding pinched and remote to his own ears.

"Yes, you do," she agreed, her voice also subdued.

"I gather that you have talked with the girls."

"Only a little. They told me their parents were dead, this was their plantation, and that they lived here with you—their cousin."

"All that is true. Or at least partially so. My cousin Philip and I were partners, and our land adjoins. We were in the process of legalizing the partnership when Philip and his wife Lydea died six months ago in the fire that destroyed the manor house we shared. This happened after I'd sent Alyssa the letter with the passage money.''

Cold sweat broke out on his forehead. "I woke and smelled smoke. I tried to save all of them. After I'd gotten the girls out, I went back, but it was too late.''

Kate swallowed, surprise and shock sweeping over her. So he hadn't been lying after all when he wrote Alyssa that letter. She owed him an apology.

"I'm very sorry. Is that how you got the scar?" she asked before she thought.

He looked at her for a long moment, the mark on his forehead livid, then nodded. "Yes.''

Grief was in his face, along with something else. Guilt. He was still anguished over his inability to save Philip and Lydea.

"Why didn't you tell me all this before?" she asked, her voice softened, sympathetic.

As she watched, he recovered himself, obviously regretting letting her see his raw emotions. One corner of his mouth tipped up in a lopsided, half-mocking smile.

"As I recall, you didn't give me much chance to do so.''

She felt her color returning with a rush, staining her cheeks and throat pink. Oh, she'd always loved his smile no matter how she tried to deny it.

"I don't recall it that way at all," she answered. "You merely accused me of being a fortune hunter and left it at that.''

Nicholas studied her in the dim light of the dying fire and one flickering candle. She would stay now even if she'd intended to go. And if it had been merely a ploy, then of course she would. Either way, he had her where he wanted her. He should feel triumphant.

But he didn't. Instead, his negative feelings toward Kate had ebbed, replaced by something else he couldn't define.

"And I'm sorry about that," he said, hearing his own softened voice in bemused wonder. No, he wasn't sorry;

he still believed that—didn't he? His mouth curved into another smile—not a mocking one this time.

"You didn't try very hard to explain," Kate said. She swallowed again, his smile making a slow heat begin somewhere inside her.

How could Alyssa have given up this man for that boy she professed to love? The thought took her unaware, made a shiver of alarm go down her spine. She quickly moved her gaze away from him, focusing it on the gleam of the pretty teapot she'd carefully washed and dried and returned to its place on the shelf.

The sight of the everyday object steadied her. The teapot had belonged to the twins' mother. A woman who was now dead, along with their father. These poor waifs had lost everything—even their home. Another shiver moved down her back—of compassion and sympathy this time.

These children needed her, now that Alyssa would not be their substitute mother. She could not imagine her sister taking on such a responsibility in any case. It was really better all around that Alyssa had changed her mind. Someday, Nicholas would realize this. But not now.

No, in spite of his softened mood, he was still full of anger because he'd lost the girl he wanted to marry. Kate moved her glance back to Nicholas, jolted to see his eyes fixed on her, an odd expression on his face.

He didn't appear angry. She didn't know what that look meant.

His chestnut hair gleamed richly in the firelight; his velvety dark eyes seemed full of mysterious secrets. He'd taken off his coat and stock, which left him in a plain white shirt and dark breeches. The breeches strained against his hard thigh muscles; the unbuttoned shirt revealed curls of thick chest hair.

"I warrant we both said things we didn't mean," she heard herself say.

"Yes." Bemused, Nicholas watched her mouth as she said the soft, conciliatory words. Her voice had a pleasant

throaty quality that he'd never noticed before. He leaned
toward her, clenching his hands into fists at his sides.

Her hair still cascaded down her back, some strands
waving over the front of her dressing gown. How he wanted
to run his fingers through that red-gold mass.

He was deeply shocked at that thought, even while he
couldn't deny it.

"I believe we did say things that were perhaps too
harsh," he answered, his own voice softened until he barely
recognized it.

He leaned closer, gratified that she didn't retreat, but
only looked at him, her mouth parted as if in invitation.
Nicholas rose from his chair, walked the few feet separating
them.

The log broke apart in the fire, flaring briefly in a blaze
of sparks, lending new luster to Kate's hair, her white
throat. Her strange, greenish eyes were softened, that full,
pink mouth softened, too.

Kate also rose. Nicholas reached for her, pulling her
towards him.

She came, willingly, lifting her head to his lowering one,
ready for his kiss.

Chapter 6

The first touch of Nicholas's mouth against her own was still dreamlike, soft and sensuous. His lips moved on hers, stroking, caressing, and she responded with movements of her own, instinctively pressing herself closer to him.

Her nostrils flared at his masculine scent, compounded of the things that bespoke the outdoor life he lived. The tang of the wind and rain, a smoky blend of tobacco and hearth fire, and an indefinable something that was all his own.

Desire whispered inside her, urging her to deepen the kiss, to press herself even more ardently against him. She sighed into his open mouth. "Nicholas, oh, Nicholas . . ."

Kate's sweet breath fluttering against his lips further stiffened Nicholas's already hard nether regions. Jesus, but she felt wondrous in his arms! How could he have thought her cold and unwomanly? He lowered one hand to press against her backside, urging her closer to his inflamed body.

His tongue made a darting foray into her mouth, and he was rewarded with her gasp as she opened her lips to him. Nicholas drew in his breath, feeling his heart tumbling faster and faster inside his chest. He tightened his hand on her backside and scooped her up into his arms, never releasing her lips for a moment.

He was already on the second step of the steep staircase when a loud scream rent the quiet of the night.

The shocking sound broke the spell that held them in its grasp.

Nicholas stopped, one foot on the third stair, the other still on the second. He stared into Kate's wide eyes for a second, then lowered her to the step above him so abruptly she staggered, only her hand darting out to the wall preventing her from falling.

"Wh—what?" she asked, shakily. Even as she formed the question, she realized one of the twins had made that sound.

"It's Celia; she has bad dreams," Nicholas muttered, the lips that had given her such sensuous delight now pressed into a thin line, his brows drawn together once again in the familiar frown.

Incredulous shame flooded over her in a wave of a different kind of heat than that which had just aroused her. Oh, how could she have let Nicholas kiss her, hold her—almost take her up to his bed! Worse, she'd *encouraged* him. Her own lips and arms had been as eager as his.

She'd behaved like the tavern wench he'd sneeringly told her she might have to become to support herself.

Nicholas brushed by her and disappeared into the twins' bedchamber. Kate stared after him.

She still wanted Nicholas. Today's events hadn't killed her desire, after all. What was more startling, more dangerous, was that he also desired her.

Oh, she couldn't stay here. Not after what had just happened between them. She took a few deep breaths and smoothed down her tumbled hair and rumpled skirts until she calmed a little.

She couldn't stay, but while she was here she'd do what

she could for these children. To that end, she followed him up the stairs. Pausing outside the twins' bedchamber, she glanced inside.

Nicholas sat on the bed, Celia's arms locked tightly around his neck as she sobbed into his chest. Emily sat up beside her sister, rubbing her sleep-filled eyes. "It's all right now," Nicholas murmured, stroking the child's tumbled curls.

His tone was softened until Kate hardly recognized it. And it held a note of barely contained desperation. He was in over his head with the twins. She walked quietly to the bed and stood beside Emily, smiling as the girl gave her a surprised glance.

"The fire, it's after me! It already got Mama and Papa!" Celia sobbed into Nicholas's chest, her words muffled but intelligible.

Kate's heart twisted as she realized the child must be reliving the most horrible event of her young life.

"Does she have these nightmares often?" she asked, avoiding Nicholas's eyes.

"Too often," he said tightly, wishing Kate would leave the room, wishing she were anywhere but here. Back in England where she belonged!

As he'd thought, she'd never truly wanted to leave.

He couldn't believe he'd let her entice him into her arms . . . after telling himself he'd resist her wiles, no matter what they were. And what could be more effective than luring him with her body? Yet he'd almost carried Kate to his bed. If Celia hadn't screamed when she had . . .

Praise God she had! How could he have wanted to bed Kate, the perfidious witch who'd made his sweet Alyssa betray him? But even as he protested, he was aware that somewhere deep inside, a small part of him wished the interruption had never occurred.

Wished that even now, he and Kate were locked in each other's arms on his bed.

He quickly turned back to Celia. "It's all right," he said

again, then clamped his mouth tightly closed, as if in so doing he could shut out his traitorous thoughts and feelings. All he needed was a woman to bed, and he'd soon enough tend to that.

He considered his dilemma. No matter what had happened a little while ago, he still needed Kate to stay here. Out of the corner of his eye, he watched as Emily reached out and grasped Kate's hand and smiled up at her.

Already, in these few short hours, Emily was growing fond of Kate. Celia would soon be won over, too, because both of them badly needed a substitute for their dead mother.

He'd had every expectation that woman would be Alyssa. He tried to picture Alyssa here with him, helping comfort his young cousin. In a moment he realized he couldn't do it. The image wouldn't form itself in his mind no matter how he tried to make it.

It was just as well, since that was not to be, he told himself, pushing down the surprise and discomfort he felt at his failure. Another thought occurred to him.

Why was he willing to leave his two young cousins to the care of a woman whose motives he so deeply distrusted?

He had no logical answer to that. He only knew that as far as the twins were concerned, he had no doubts Kate would take excellent care of them. And she was a good cook and housekeeper. She'd done more to restore order to the house in a short time this evening than his bond servants had managed to accomplish in months.

A niggling doubt wormed itself into his mind. Could it be possible he was wrong about Kate's motives? That she actually did want to leave? If that were so, she'd be even more set on going after what had happened between them a few minutes ago.

He quickly dismissed the thought. No, she'd journeyed across the Atlantic to become his bride, resorting to malicious trickery to bring that to pass.

The doubt returned. But that was before Kate discovered

his prosperity had been destroyed in a few swift blows of fate. Maybe learning that *had* changed her mind about the desirability of becoming his wife. But then, why would she try to entice him? Another notion, even more disturbing, insinuated itself into his mind.

Maybe she'd been as spellbound as he, had truly desired him as he'd desired her.

Appalled at these errant thoughts, he pushed them violently aside. He was dithering like an old woman. Thinking nonsense.

Of course Kate wanted to stay, to further her own ends. To a penniless woman, any kind of a marriage was more advantageous than remaining single. . . .

And if she stayed the winter, assumed the household chores and looking after the twins to repay her passage, he could use his remaining funds to hire another man or two for field work, buy the seed he would need to plant the wheat crop in the spring. . . .

She must stay, as she'd agreed to do. To that end, he'd force himself to behave civilly toward her, no matter how he felt. He'd never mention this incident tonight and would avoid being alone with her. Not that he'd ever again desire her, he hastily told himself; he'd take care of that problem, but just the same . . .

He gave Celia one last pat and gently laid her back down on her pillow, relieved to see the wild fear had left her eyes. "Go to sleep now. You will have no more bad dreams."

He fervently hoped that was true. Most of the time the child had only one such episode during a night. He pulled the quilt up around her neck and smiled at her again.

Kate watched his movements, heard his gentled voice. She'd been wrong. He cared for his young charges. But she itched to smooth the bunched quilt under Celia's chin, fluff up her pillow, give her the extra measure of comfort of a woman's touch she sorely needed.

Instead, she smiled at Emily as the girl slid back down beside her sister, then hesitantly turned her smile on Celia.

Instead of smiling back, which Kate had hoped for, the girl frowned and turned away from both adults, closing her eyes.

Kate straightened. "Good night girls," she said for the second time that evening. Steeling herself, she glanced at Nicholas.

He stood by the bed, his face expressionless, looking toward her. Then he nodded, civilly enough.

"Good night, Mistress Kate. I will see you in the morn."

Kate nodded in return, pushing back memories of the kiss, the embrace they'd shared so short a time ago. Had that dream-like episode actually happened?

"Good night, Master Nicholas," she answered, her voice as cool and controlled as his. She turned and headed for her own bedchamber across the hallway.

She pushed the door closed, forgetting the broken latch. A few moments later, as she sank down wearily upon her lumpy straw mattress, she heard a whisper of sound and glanced up in time to see the door swinging slowly open again.

Nicholas was standing in his own doorway, directly across the hall. He was turned toward her, one large strong hand on his door latch.

Kate's startled glance met his own unguarded one, and something passed between them. Something akin to what had happened down by the fire. Then, Nicholas closed his door.

Kate stared at the expanse of dull-green painted wood now facing her instead of Nicholas's face. She pushed herself off the bed and hurried to her door, holding it shut while she maneuvered the back of a kitchen chair missing half its rungs under the latch.

"There, that should do it," she muttered, dusting off her hands and going back to the bed.

Edward awoke and stretched, glancing at her hopefully.

"It's a long time until morning," Kate told him as she

pulled off her wrapper and folded it into a makeshift pillow.

Her candle was guttering. Kate blew it out, then lay down on her back, grimacing as she realized the mattress left a great deal to be desired.

Too exhausted to be more than dully surprised, she realized she'd changed her mind again. In spite of tonight's incident, she'd stay here until spring. These girls truly needed her.

And if she were going to be completely honest, she *wanted* to stay here. Something about the twins drew her, and something about this place did, too, in spite of its current desolation.

It had nothing to do with Nicholas, she insisted to a doubting part of her mind. Nothing at all.

So she would stay—for now, she amended. Her tongue came out and slid along her lips. They were still slightly swollen from Nicholas's kiss, and she could taste his elusive but definitive scent. Lifting her hand, she scrubbed it firmly across her mouth, then settled down on her side.

That episode had been no dream, she admitted, as she stared, wide-eyed and sleepless in spite of her fatigue, into the darkness of the room.

Of course there was no danger of any repetition of such a scene. She rued it deeply and she knew Nicholas regretted their actions even more strongly than she. But still, she would take care that they weren't alone together on any future occasion.

Because, as she'd realized a few minutes ago, what had transpired tonight had made it achingly clear to her that the old attraction she'd felt for him hadn't died.

She turned over on her other side, trying to ignore the fact that her flesh still felt the imprint of his.

If Celia hadn't cried out, Nicholas would have carried her to his bed. They'd be there this very minute, deep in each other's arms.

And afterward, it wouldn't have meant a thing to him.

She would have given herself to a man who could never love her. He'd already made that abundantly clear. He still loved Alyssa. Worse than that, he blamed Kate for Alyssa's defection.

Oh, she'd been a fool, Kate admitted—and more than once.

But no more. From now on, she'd give Master Nicholas Talbot the widest berth possible. She turned again, trying to block out the thought that insisted on presenting itself.

In this small cottage, seeing each other a dozen times a day, it would take some clever maneuvering indeed to keep her distance from him.

Chapter 7

A rough little tongue and an insistent mew woke Kate. She sat bolt upright in the lumpy bed, staring out the dirty window with dismay. How late was it? The sky was still overcast, so she couldn't judge by the sun.

"But you're telling me breakfast is long overdue, aren't you?" she asked the kitten, throwing off the covers and putting her bare feet on the cold floor. She hastily found her slippers, glad there was a tiny fireplace in the corner. She'd make use of that before long.

She poured last night's water into the slop jar, added more from the pitcher and hastily washed. After arranging her hair into its coil on her nape, she again donned her green gown. Then, scooping up the kitten, she removed the chair from under the door latch and opened it.

Nicholas's bedchamber door stood open, revealing an empty room as disordered as it had been yesterday.

Hurrying past the twins' door, she saw to her chagrin that it, too, was unoccupied. She'd never been a slug-a-bed. She'd planned to be up before Nicholas, to cook him a hot breakfast of porridge before he left for his morning chores. She'd made a bargain with him, and she'd keep it to the best of her ability.

And stay away from him otherwise. Her mind shied away from thoughts of last night's unfortunate incident. It was over and done with. It wouldn't, couldn't happen again. Best not to dwell on it.

Reaching the bottom of the stairs, she saw the twins were not downstairs. Neither was Nicholas. He'd built a new fire; but other than an empty pewter mug on the table, there was no evidence that he'd cooked any breakfast, either for himself or his cousins.

She hurried to the door and flung it open, relieved to see Celia and Emily skipping rope in front of the cottage. Both were fully dressed in another pair of identical gowns; but their hair was in disarray and one of them, at the moment she didn't know which, had her dress buttoned wrong.

Today was much warmer than yesterday, the bitter wind gone. The hazy overcast was yielding to the morning sun. Edward squirmed, mewing his urgent need to be released. Kate put him down and he scampered off to the side and began frantically digging in the soft dirt under a bush.

The twins stopped their rope-skipping and glanced at her. She ascertained their identities as one of them gave her a smile and the other's mouth fixed itself into a straight line. Celia's aversion to her hadn't changed overnight. Had she actually supposed it would? Kate smiled at both of them.

"Cousin Nicholas was most unhappy that you were still abed when he left for the barn," Celia said, a smug note in her voice.

Kate forced the smile to remain on her face. "I'm sorry I overslept and you had no breakfast when you awoke. I will soon have porridge ready for you."

Both twins looked surprised at her words. "We don't eat breakfast until later . . . until Cousin Nicholas finishes the morning chores," Celia informed her, the smug note intensifying. "And when he returns, he will expect far more than porridge."

"Oh. Then I will need your and Emily's aid in telling me what to prepare," Kate countered. Maybe an appeal to Celia's superior knowledge would soften the girl's attitude.

In that she was disappointed. Celia merely smirked, but Emily nodded. "Yes! We will help you." Celia gave her sister a disapproving frown, and Emily's eager smile faded.

Celia wasn't content with showing her dislike for Kate at every opportunity. She was determined Emily do the same. Kate's exasperation grew. The child dearly wanted a good spanking!

Then, a memory of Celia's frightened, tear-stained face last night flashed across her mind and her irritation faded. No, she didn't. Celia was scared and lost and alone. What she needed was abundant love. And fight her as she was sure the girl would, Kate vowed to try to get behind the surface hostility and reach the vulnerable child beneath.

"When does Nicholas return from the barn?" she asked mildly. "Should we begin our breakfast preparations now?"

Emily cast a wary glance at her glowering sister, then straightened her small frame and looked at the eastern sky, as if gauging the time. "Yes, we should," she replied, her voice serious. "Cousin Nicholas has a great appetite."

Kate felt encouraged by Emily's show of independence. At least it appeared she had one ally here in this strange land.

Edward, finished with his business under the bush, walked over, announcing his own readiness for the morning meal with a loud, insistent meow as he wrapped his small frame around Kate's ankles.

Emily laughed. "Oh, Edward! Are you hungry, too?"

"Yes, he is." Kate scooped him up, gratified to see that, in spite of herself, Celia's mouth had also relaxed into a smile. The kitten might prove to be a help in overcoming her hostility.

"Now, girls," she said, her own smile including Celia, "you need to show me where the springhouse is."

This time Emily avoided looking at her sister when she nodded. "Come along," she said, her voice a trifle wary but determined. "It will take all of us to bring back what is needed."

She led the way up the lane they'd come down last night, toward the burned house, Edward frolicking along behind. Kate's aversion to it had intensified after hearing Nicholas's story. Celia lagged behind, too, at first, then caught up with them.

Behind the ruins stood a frame structure positioned over a sparkling spring. This must also be the source of the household water. Emily flung open the door and Kate moved up beside her.

The air inside the building smelled damp and mossy and was so cold Kate shivered. Shelves were built along the bottom in the cool water. Kate recognized the crocks she'd used last night on the shelves, along with other containers.

Celia walked up beside Kate. "Cousin Nicholas will want meat, as well as spoonbread and vegetables," she said officiously. "Here, we will show you." She walked over and picked up a new crock.

Kate smiled at her bent back, relieved that the girl had apparently decided to help her instead of fighting her at every move.

A few minutes later, the supplies for the morning meal were in the cottage. "You had best get the spoonbread begun," Emily said.

"And what is spoonbread?" Kate asked. "We don't have such a dish in Plymouth."

"You don't know what spoonbread is?" Emily asked, her brown eyes wide with surprise. "I'll show you how to prepare it."

"No, *I* will do that," Celia quickly put in, giving her sister a hard stare. "You can put the table to rights."

Emily opened her mouth to protest, then closed it again. "All right," she said, turning away, her voice subdued.

Kate was so relieved Celia had made such a turnaround and was actually being helpful, she decided not to press the issue. She'd make it up to Emily later.

"Spoonbread is made from cornmeal," Celia said. "It's very simple to prepare."

Kate decided she was right when, a few minutes later, the dish was simmering over the hearth fire in a smaller pot than the stew kettle. Simple and rather odd, requiring an enormous amount of milk and water. But Celia had assured her the liquid would thicken during the cooking.

She'd learned cornmeal was the coarse yellowish-white grain in the pantry and in the sack Nicholas had brought in last night. It was ground from maize, not the barley, wheat, or oats she'd known as corn in England.

A chunk of beef was sliced and cooking in another pan, as were cut-up potatoes and turnips from the root cellar she'd been introduced to underneath the cottage. Kate was pleased to discover an array of winter vegetables stored there.

If today's breakfast were any indication of the size of Nicholas's appetite, there would be need of everything in it before spring gardens could produce fresh vegetables.

"There! Everything seems to be in order." Kate smiled at the girls. Celia gave her a smug smile and Emily a rather wan one. The girl seemed awfully subdued, Kate noticed. Probably because she'd let Celia coach her in the spoon-bread preparation.

The door was opened to the morning sunshine and Edward, replete with a dish of milk, napped in a patch of it streaming across the worn, stained floorboards.

She'd get this room thoroughly scrubbed as soon as breakfast was finished, Kate vowed. She glanced up at the sound of footsteps to see Nicholas standing in the doorway, the sun striking glints off his rich chestnut hair. He wore a white shirt that was clean but in need of ironing and the same dark breeches he'd worn yesterday.

Fight it as she might, memories of last night washed over her. Of his strong arms enfolding her. His hard body against her own, his warm lips moving on hers . . .

Their eyes met before Kate quickly glanced away, her heart beating faster than it had before Nicholas's arrival.

"Is breakfast ready?" he asked, coming into the room. He glanced at Kate's head, bent over the pot she was stirring, and was transported back to last night, to those dream-like moments when he'd held her in his arms.

Nicholas shook his head to clear it. Damnation! He swore silently, forcing the unexpected, unwanted vision away.

"Indeed, it is," Kate answered, her voice brisk and casual. "Girls, you may sit down now."

The twins quickly seated themselves. Too quickly. Something in their manner alerted him. He gave them a suspicious glance. Emily smiled at him, but Celia's smile was more like a smirk. What had they been up to?

He dismissed his thoughts and smiled back at them. Kate was in charge now. And he was sure she was capable of that task. He sniffed the air of the room and counted the number of vessels on the hearth, surprised and pleased that she'd cooked such a substantial meal.

He hadn't expected it. Not this first morning. He'd remembered her family's normal breakfast at home in Plymouth was merely porridge. He supposed the twins had told her what to prepare.

"I see you've already learned that here in this country, men labor early and hard and they must eat heartily," he said, sitting down at his usual place.

Kate put several bowls of food on the table and seated herself. "Celia told me you had a very large appetite," she answered.

Was there a hint of amusement in her voice? He supposed he had sounded a trifle pompous to hide the way the sight of her had affected him.

Obviously, the sight of *him* had not upset *her,* he noted, proving she'd only been pretending her passion of last night. So! He'd been right in all his suppositions.

After saying grace, he picked up his eating utensils, knowing he should feel relief at that confirmation, annoyed with himself that he didn't.

The beef slices were smothered in a savory gravy, he saw, his mouth watering at the wonderful aroma. And the potatoes and turnips were juicy looking, with their own enticing smell. He was chewing appreciatively on a large bite of beef and gravy when Kate put another dish beside his plate.

It was a pewter bowl, he saw, filled with a watery-looking mixture. He frowned at it, then glanced up at her. "What is this?"

Kate gave him a surprised look. "Why, it is your spoon-bread, of course. The girls tell me you must have it with every breakfast."

Nicholas picked up his spoon and dipped it into the bowl, then sipped it, instantly making a face of distaste. The unappetizing concoction was practically water and was so salty he made a grab for the mug of ale by his plate.

After washing the taste away, he gave Kate an astonished glance. "Are you trying to poison me, woman? This is the most abominable dish I have ever tried to eat!"

Kate stared at him, then dipped her own spoon in the bowl and took a taste. Her eyes widened.

She forced herself to hold his glance, not turn her eyes on Celia. The girl had roundly tricked her, Kate had to admit. No wonder she'd insisted on giving her the directions for the spoonbread instead of allowing Emily to do so. Though when she'd managed to sneak the salt in, Kate had no idea.

"This is a new dish for me. I promise you tomorrow it will be cooked properly," Kate told Nicholas, her voice even and controlled. "And you seem to be finding the rest of the meal to your liking."

Behind her, she heard an exhaled breath. Whether Celia was relieved or disappointed at Kate's reaction, Kate had no way of knowing.

What she did know was that Celia still disliked her. All the helpfulness this morning was only an act to try to get Kate off on the wrong foot with Nicholas . . . as if that hadn't already happened.

" 'Tis a most simple dish to prepare," Nicholas said, ignoring her jibe. He lifted another bite of meat and gravy to his mouth.

Kate clenched her teeth and whisked up the offending bowl, sorely tempted to pour it on his head.

Taking the bowl to the cooking pot, she poured its contents back in. As she sat back down, she glanced at Celia to find the child's wide-eyed glance on her.

Kate swallowed her anger. She wouldn't react as the child expected. Instead, she gave Celia a level look, then moved her gaze to Emily. That twin had a stricken expression on her face as she stared back at Kate.

Emily had known what her sister was up to, Kate realized. That's why she'd been so subdued all during breakfast preparations. It appeared that Emily had quite a way to go before she was free of her sister's domination, after all. Not that she'd want Emily to tattle on Celia, but . . .

Looking after these children was going to prove quite a challenge. Kate ate a bite of turnip, relieved it tasted all right. It seemed the spoonbread was the only dish Celia had ruined.

She glanced at the twins again to see that neither of them were eating. They were still staring at her. Kate smiled again. "You'd best eat your food, girls," she said mildly, "before it gets cold."

Nicholas glanced up from his almost-empty plate, turning his gaze from his young kin to Kate. Celia was looking at Kate as if she expected the woman to jump down her throat.

That was odd. And Emily looked like a scared little hare.

That wasn't so unexpected. Emily was far too timid, especially since her parents' terrible death. Celia bullied her, he knew. What he didn't know was how to stop it. He'd scolded the child often enough, to no avail.

He glanced at Kate. Maybe he'd been a trifle harsh with her about the spoonbread. After all, the rest of the meal was passing good. More than that. Could his wrath have perhaps put the notion of leaving in her head once more?

She didn't look as if she had any such idea. Her profile was to him and he noted the smoothness of her brow, her straight short nose, her full lips, and firm chin.

Aye, it was a firm chin, indeed. And oft tilted skyward. Indicative of the hard, determined nature that had served her well as she schemed to destroy Alyssa's love for him so that Kate could journey here instead. No, she had no desire to leave Lydea's Pride. She knew she was better off here. That had only been a ploy, he reminded himself.

He pushed back his heavy chair. It scraped on the rough plank floor, the sound making all three female faces turn in his direction. He stood up and cleared his throat.

"For your first breakfast, you did well. I will expect my dinner in the midafternoon."

She raised her brows. "And I imagine by that time you will have worked up another surpassingly large appetite?" she asked, her voice low and pleasant.

Or was it sarcastic? He couldn't tell with the woman. "Yes." He inclined his head. "Good morn, Mistress Kate. Cousins."

Nicholas squared his shoulders and walked across the room. He had been civil with the wench, he told himself, just as he'd sworn to be last night. And surely that was all she could expect from him.

As Nicholas reached the doorway, Edward awoke from his nap and reached out a desultory paw toward Nicholas's trouser legs, claws extended.

Nicholas glanced down, breaking his stride, stumbling and swerving to avoid falling upon the kitten. He righted himself and jerked his head around toward Kate. "I thought it was agreed that this animal was to remain in your bedchamber or outside."

She raised those curving brows of hers yet again. "Edward was outside until a few minutes ago," she said. "And it was only agreed that he would spend the night hours in *my* chamber."

Again, she hadn't raised her voice, but he could tell this time that she wasn't pleased at his words. Good, he thought, realizing *he* was pleased to know that he'd ruffled her serenity.

Civil. He had to be civil, he reminded himself. He took a deep breath and erased the frown from his face. Without another word, he walked around the kitten and out the door.

Kate looked after him. She drew in a deep breath and let it out in an exasperated sigh. Oh, he was an irritating man! How could she stay here and keep up a pretense of civility for—how long would it be? At least five months, she supposed. Perhaps longer. When did spring come to this Maryland Colony? This Tidewater land?

Well, she would stay. She'd decided that last night, she reminded herself. It was hard to remember in Nicholas's presence that she owed him anything. But she did.

And she was a woman of her word. She'd stay. And she'd clean this cottage until it sparkled, too, she vowed. And without delay. By the time Master Nicholas came striding back in his lordly way for his dinner, he'd have to scrape his boots on the doorsill before she'd allow him to enter.

She turned to the girls. They'd finished their breakfast, she saw. She found a wooden pail and poured the so-called spoonbread into it. "Celia," she said pleasantly, "you and Emily may take this to the pigs."

Celia looked horrified at this suggestion. "Oh, don't make us do that. It will make Alfreda and Mordred ill!" She clapped her hand over her mouth and gave Kate a stricken glance.

Kate looked gravely back at her until the girl dropped her gaze. "Perhaps it will. Then you shall pour it into the bushes somewhere away from the cottage."

Celia nodded. "Come along, Emily," she mumbled, picking up the pail.

Kate watched them go, both unusually silent as they stepped over the doorsill. Edward stretched widely, then decided to follow them. He disappeared around the sill, his short little tail sticking straight up. Kate turned back to the kitchen, feeling as if she'd won this skirmish.

But a skirmish didn't make a war, she knew. And before she left here, she had a feeling she'd be waging war on more than one front.

And she wouldn't win all the skirmishes—or the battles, if it came to that. But she'd try to do her best and when she left here . . .

Her thoughts came to a skidding stop.

When she left here, what? Celia would be fond of her? Would no longer have the horrible nightmares? Emily would be able to stand up to her sister as she should? Both children would be healed of their emotional wounds from losing their parents in such a terrible way?

And what of Nicholas? By the time of her departure, would she have convinced him that Alyssa's decision to marry John Latton was entirely of her own making? That Kate's only sin was to offer to take her place?

Would she have gotten over her desire for Nicholas? How could she expect to do that when she would be seeing him so often, when they'd be sleeping only a few feet apart from each other?

"You are biting off a very large piece, Kate Shaw," she told herself as she began to clear the table. "Are you sure that you will be able to chew it?"

Chapter 8

Kate glanced across the barnyard, relieved to see the twins engrossed in hand-feeding corn to the dozen geese, who were loudly honking and jostling each other. They were beautiful birds, and she'd gotten over her fear of them after Tucker showed her how to spread her arms, flapping them a bit and hissing as she advanced on the geese.

She'd felt like an idiot, but to her amazement they'd at once retreated and never again had she to watch her ankles for fear of their sharp attack. The geese never chased the twins, maybe because they always had a handful of corn when they approached the fowl.

A pleasant breeze drifted by and the sun shone down. The weather had been warm and agreeable for several days now. And though she knew it wouldn't last, since it was December, she enjoyed it fully while it did.

She turned back to Tucker, the freed Negro who, she'd discovered in the two weeks she'd been on Lydea's Pride, was Nicholas's right-hand man. On his part, Tucker seemed almost to worship Nicholas. And not only because Nicholas had given him his freedom.

Tucker had followed her glance. He smiled, his teeth flashing very white against his dark skin. "Them little mites have been through a heap o' trouble."

Kate nodded. "I know. I try to help them, but Celia resists me at every turn."

Tucker nodded. "That girl holds everythin' in. Don't let nobody see how she really feels. She always been like that."

He had keen perception, Kate had also discovered. For lack of anyone else, he'd become her friend—almost her confidant.

She certainly couldn't talk to Nicholas. He was never around long enough for that. Up before first light, back for his hearty breakfast about ten, then back to the barn or the fields until his equally large dinner in midafternoon. Now, he was in one of the tobacco curing sheds, inspecting the leaf, Tucker had said.

Of course she was glad that Nicholas was seldom around. It made avoiding being alone with him much easier.

Since that shocking incident the night she arrived, they'd never been alone, and spoke only of necessary things. He was polite enough, but hardly friendly, apparently satisfied with the job she was doing. Although since he seldom spoke a word of praise, she had to only assume that was true.

Of course it was, she told herself, or he would certainly have told her so. Nicholas could never be accused of not letting his complaints be known.

She'd learned to make excellent spoonbread since that first ghastly morning. Celia had played no more tricks on her, but Kate watched her with a wary eye. As she'd just told Tucker, the girl still held herself aloof.

Emily, on the other hand, seemed truly to like Kate, although the girl had a hard time trying to juggle her behavior to suit both her sister and Kate. But she was gradually coming out of her timidity, Kate was glad to see.

Celia's nightmares hadn't ceased—but Kate left the

comforting of the girl to Nicholas. The second night she was here, Celia had again wakened screaming. Kate had hastened to her, only to have the girl scream even more loudly, demanding Nicholas, who sleepy-eyed, and with clothes pulled on hastily, stood in the doorway.

Kate had felt the rejection keenly. Averting her eyes from Nicholas's unbuttoned shirt, which reminded her too strongly of that night when some kind of spell seemed to have possessed them, she'd stepped aside. From then on, she didn't arise when Celia's screams began ... although she lay rigidly in bed, silently urging Nicholas to hurry to the girl.

The bad dreams didn't come every night, for which Kate was deeply thankful. Several times a week was exhausting to all of them. And Kate knew Celia must be tortured by these memories while awake to have them bother her so much while she was sleeping.

But there was little Kate could do. She'd tentatively, tried talking to the girls a few times about their past, their former life with their parents, but Celia had brusquely rejected those efforts, too. Emily seemed much less affected, but she still followed her sister's lead in most things.

All Kate could do was wait until the child was ready to confide in her about the terrible experience, her deeply felt grief. And that time might never come, Kate well knew. In the spring, she'd be leaving here, and she'd probably never see any of these people again.

The thought made a cold feeling go through her. She brushed it aside. Of course, it would be for the best. Nicholas would find another woman to wife, thereby giving the twins a mother.

She wouldn't worry about it. Today, she had other problems: The journey to the Aldon plantation to celebrate Devona's birthday. She'd be delighted to see the warm, friendly woman again—but not the other houseguests who'd be there, wealthy planters who lived along the river.

"What that heavy sigh for, mistress?" Tucker asked,

flashing his white smile at her again. "All this work around here gettin' you down?"

Shaking her head, she returned his smile. "No. I'm used to hard work. And now I finally have the cottage in good order. The twins help a lot."

She glanced at him, biting her lip. "I'm dreading the visit to the Aldons'," she admitted.

"You'll do fine," he assured her. His face changed. He leaned forward. "If you happen to see Daisy, would you tell her hello for me?"

Kate remembered that first day. Daisy. Devona had called that name, and a pretty Negress had appeared. So Tucker was interested in her. She nodded. "Of course I will," she assured him.

Tucker's face darkened as he caught her curious glance. "Daisy and me ought to be married," he muttered. "We would be, too, 'cept Master Aldon won't let us."

"Why not?"

Tucker shrugged his massive shoulders. "He don't like it that Master Nicholas freed me and the other slaves Master Philip had here. He think that settin' a bad example, going to cause trouble with his people."

Kate's eyes widened with surprise. Apparently Nicholas must hate the institution of slavery as much as she did.

She hadn't known that. In fact, she knew very little of how Nicholas felt about anything . . . since they were never alone or had occasion to talk to each other about personal things.

She knew he'd changed—grown harder and colder. But it appeared some of the changes had been for the better. Back in Plymouth all his talk had been of making his fortune in the New World.

"Nicholas freed all the Negroes?" she asked, suddenly wanting to know more.

"Yes'um. And them ungrateful people left him, wouldn't work for the wages he could afford to pay. Most of them shiftless 'dentured folk do the same. And just when he need them the worst, too. After losing last year's 'bacca crop at sea and that bad storm takin' down the wharf and outbuildings and 'most ruinin' the boat.''

Kate's surprise deepened. That first night Nicholas had only told her about the tragedy of the fire. He hadn't mentioned these strokes of bad luck that had befallen him.

It appeared none of the plantation woes were due to any mismanagement on his part. Some people, of course, would say he'd used poor judgment when he freed the slaves. But she couldn't. She admired him for that action.

She'd faulted him unjustly, blamed him for things beyond his control. And Nicholas hadn't tried to enlist her sympathy, had only told her what he had to, and no more.

Kate felt ashamed of her self-righteous condemnation of him that first day. And he truly needed her help here now. He toiled harder than any worker. . . .

Pulling herself out of her reverie, she smiled at Tucker again. ''I'll be sure to tell Daisy you asked after her. I hope it all works out for you and her eventually.''

''No way it can, 'less Master Henry change his mind, and I can't see him doin' that. He a hard man, Master Henry is.''

''Maybe Devona could talk to him,'' Kate ventured.

A smile that held no amusement touched Tucker's mouth. ''Ain't *no* chance of that,'' he said, his rich voice very positive.

Henry Aldon must be a hard man with his wife, too. Might that account for the glimpse of sadness Kate had seen in Devona's soft brown eyes?

Kate rose. ''I'd better be going. I have to finish the twins' gowns and get us ready for the trip tomorrow.''

''Miss Emily tell me she gonna have a gown different from Miss Celia's.''

''Yes. I think it will be good for the girls not to dress alike all the time. And that way I can always tell them apart.'' She grinned at him.

Tucker threw back his head and laughed, the rich sound making Kate's spirits rise. "That a good idea, for sure! You have yourself a grand old time, mistress, you hear? You been workin' mighty hard. You need a couple days rest."

"I'll try," Kate told him. "Come along, girls, we have to go back to the house now."

They came, grumbling a bit at having to leave the barnyard, so much more fascinating than the cottage.

On the walk back, Kate frowned at the neglected look of the plantation, the unused or damaged outbuildings. The spinning and weaving shed was empty; the blacksmith shop's roof had fallen in.

Yes, Nicholas had indeed had a run of very bad luck, and he was doing all he could to rectify things. She felt a new softness toward him, and the thought made her stomach tense.

She didn't want that. It was too dangerous for her. All she wanted was to pay her debt to him and then leave this place.

The wharf was now repaired, as was the sloop. More's the pity, thought Kate. She'd rather ride on the rattly wagon, over the horribly bumpy roads, than journey on the small sailboat to the Aldons'. Not only had she never taken such a trip before, even though she'd always lived in a seaport, it would mean a time of being in Nicholas's presence, at very close quarters.

No, she dreaded this visit in many ways. She'd be glad when it was over.

Thank God the good weather had held and the dark, murky water was calm and smooth, Kate thought, as she huddled on the sloop's side seat. At least her stomach wasn't giving her any trouble, as she'd feared it might.

And so far, the trip had been uneventful. The nearness to Nicholas she'd been so concerned about had turned out to mean nothing. He was far too busy handling the craft to pay her any heed—not that she'd expected him to.

He didn't even like her, she reminded herself . . . despite that night they'd kissed so passionately. He merely tolerated her because he needed her help and she was doing a satisfactory job for him. He still mourned his lost love and still blamed Kate for the fact Alyssa had abandoned him.

Would God Alyssa had kept her promise! *She* had no desire to foist her presence on a man who wished she were someone else. How she wished her sister were here instead of her.

Or did she? Did she truly want to be back in Plymouth wrapping vegetables for customers day after dreary day? With nothing to look forward to other than withering up like a dried prune and running the shop until she died? Or enduring a marriage that would take away her independence?

Wouldn't she rather be here, out in this pleasant weather, on board this boat, with two children she was growing to love more each day?

The twins sat across from her, perfectly at ease in the small craft, chattering to each other, their excitement at this outing high.

They'd pleaded to bring Edward, but Nicholas wouldn't hear of it. Kate could understand this, but she hadn't want to leave the kitten alone, either. Finally, she'd taken Edward to Tucker, who'd promised to keep an eye on him and let the kitten sleep in his cabin the night they were gone.

She glanced across at Nicholas, who handled the tiller with accustomed ease. He looked very handsome today in a gold waistcoat with a deep-blue frock coat over it. His breeches were a soft dove gray, and the silver buckles on his black shoes gleamed from polishing.

However, the splendor of his person seemed incongruous with his present task. The thought lightened her mood and made her lips curl in a tiny smile.

"This excursion is not to my liking," Nicholas said, breaking the silence. "There is much work to be done at the plantation. I've half a mind to turn about."

"Cousin Nicholas!" Celia said, echoed by Emily. "It will be such fun! We can't do that!"

No, they couldn't, Nicholas admitted. He wouldn't insult Devona by not attending her birthday celebration, and Henry Aldon had insisted they come, even volunteering to send his carriage. Nicholas had refused that offer. A man had some pride; and the battered sloop, newly repaired, was still seaworthy.

Kate said nothing, even though he was certain she shared his young cousins' sentiments. Why wouldn't she want to get away from her drudgery for a little while of being waited on by servants, eating food others had prepared? She had no stake in Lydea's Pride. Why should she worry about its precarious financial state?

He wondered what caused her amusement. Something to do with him no doubt, as she was looking directly at him, those odd eyes of hers going over him from head to foot.

Her blue-green gown deepened the color of her eyes, and she'd arranged her hair in a much more becoming manner, tendrils escaping on the side, as if accidentally. He'd wager it wasn't accidental at all, but carefully calculated for effect.

Was Kate expecting to meet some eligible male at this soirée? He frowned, making some adjustments to the single sail as the wind shifted.

The idea didn't set well with him, he admitted, discomfited by that reaction. Of course it didn't, he told himself hastily. If she did, perchance, meet a man who was interested in marriage, her new husband might pay her debt and she could leave before her allotted time was up.

He didn't want that. The cottage was clean and neat;

he always had fresh, mended clothing, and the meals were on time and tasty. She kept the twins reined in, too.

But there shouldn't be too much chance of Kate's leaving. Even though he supposed there would be several unmarried males of good family there—Morgan Lockwood, the *Rosalynde's* captain, for one.

Kate was no beauty. She was too tall, and most men wouldn't care for red hair and green eyes, preferring instead the kind of pale blondeness Alyssa possessed. He frowned again.

By all rights, the woman sitting across from him should have been Alyssa, smiling adoringly up at him. He wondered darkly if she'd yet wed her simpering new suitor. No doubt she had. John Latton would not want to wait long for his lovely bride.

That thought made him give the tiller too sharp a turn and the boat tilted, causing spray to come over the side.

Kate clutched at her skirts, the amused expression leaving her face. Nicholas felt a moment of satisfaction since he was positive that look had been at his expense. Kate didn't care for this boat, but she was a good sailor, he had to admit. She'd not been sick or complaining.

"No, we will not return," he said finally. "We have come too far to turn about."

"Oh, good. Thank you, Cousin Nicholas," the twins chorused.

Kate hid another smile. The girls' relieved tones didn't ring quite true. They'd known Nicholas didn't intend to go back to Lydea's Pride even though it was obvious he looked forward to this event no more than she did. After two weeks she realized Nicholas's oft-times gruffness with the twins had nothing to do with his feelings for them.

No, she knew he loved them deeply. And after today's talk with Tucker, she understood his moods better. He was working himself half to death to try to save the plantation. And he had to fear he might lose the battle. Small wonder he sometimes sounded abrupt.

Of course that insight did nothing to explain his attitude toward *her*. Nicholas's civility didn't quite hide his resentment of what he believed she'd done to him.

Kate pushed down the pain that knowledge gave her and watched as he furled the sail almost in as the Aldons' wharf came within sight. The sloop glided gracefully toward it. Two Negroes on the wharf grabbed Nicholas's thrown line and made the craft fast to a piling.

Nicholas stepped out and offered Kate his hand. Kate hesitated. She hadn't touched him since that first-night incident. She'd gotten into the boat by herself; she could surely get out unaided, too.

The twins got to their feet, and the boat tilted. Kate swayed, and her insides quivered. Without thinking she lifted her hand to Nicholas's waiting one. His large hand held hers in a firm, warm grip, allaying her moment's fear. A strong urge to leave her hand in his assailed her.

To do more than that. To move toward him . . .

Exasperated with herself, she stepped up onto the wharf, then quickly slid her hand out from his. "Thank you," she said primly, not quite looking at him, then turned back to Celia and Emily.

Nicholas helped the twins up, still feeling Kate's slim, strong hand clasped within his own, his mind going back to that night by the fire when he'd come so perilously close to taking her to his bed.

She'd done nothing to encourage him these last two weeks; and on his part, he'd gone out of his way to avoid being alone with her. And yet, with one touch, the hunger that had possessed him that night had swept over him again.

Damnation! How could he still have this yen for Kate's body? He knew the answer to that.

Because he was still without a woman.

He'd been entirely too busy since Kate's arrival to go to Chestertown to find a willing tavern wench. And up until yesterday, when the sloop had finally been repaired, he'd had no way to get there.

The sloop was in good condition now. And things were getting caught up around the plantation for the moment. He could get away for a day.

Within the fortnight, he vowed, he'd make that journey and be plagued no more by thoughts of Kate's warm lips, her willing body against his own.

Chapter 9

"Master Nicholas! And Miss Emily and Miss Celia!" Daisy, the pretty Negress Kate had seen the first time she'd been here and the woman Tucker loved, had opened the ornate garden door for them today.

She smiled warmly at Nicholas and the twins. Her smile for Kate was warm, too, but a trifle uncertain as if unsure what to call her.

"This is Mistress Shaw," Nicholas said, his tone reserved but polite.

Relief went through Kate. At least Nicholas apparently was going to treat her with courtesy, unlike on her first visit to this household.

"Good day, mistress," Daisy said, nodding. "Come along into the drawing room. Master and Mistress Aldon are there."

"You are wrong, Daisy. We are here," a cool, controlled masculine voice said; and then the owner of the voice stepped out of a room across the hallway, Devona clinging to his elaborately frock-coated arm.

No, Kate corrected herself. The man, who must be Henry

Aldon, was instead holding onto Devona's arm, pressing her close against his side.

If she'd thought Nicholas splendidly dressed, his attire was nothing compared to this man's. Atop his head was an elaborate wig, powdered to a snowy whiteness.

His waistcoat was of scarlet; his frock coat, a sky blue. His breeches were a pale fawn, and the silver buckles on his shoes twinkled with inset stones. And he was at least twenty years older than Devona.

"Good evening," Devona said, including all four of them in her greeting. "Henry, this is Mistress Katherine Shaw."

Devona's voice was warm, as was her smile, but again Kate caught that sad look in her brown eyes. She, too, was expensively and attractively dressed, her gown of lemon yellow very flattering to her coloring. Her light-brown hair was arranged in a stiff-looking way which, although the height of fashion, didn't seem to fit the woman's personality.

Henry released his wife's wrist and took Kate's hand in his, bowing formally to her. His touch felt cold and bloodless. "It is my pleasure to make your acquaintance, Mistress Shaw." His odd, very pale, blue eyes met hers.

Kate inclined her head. As her glance fell on Devona, her eyes widened. The woman's wrist held the distinct imprint of her husband's fingers. Devona's skin didn't look that fragile. Henry must have been holding her in a hard, hurtful grip to have caused those angry red marks.

Relief swept over Kate when he freed her hand. She hated its cold, bloodless feel and was shaken by his look. It, too, was cold and penetrating, as if he could see all the way through her clothes.

She didn't like this man, she decided instinctively. She didn't like him at all.

Devona smiled again, laying her slender hand on Kate's sleeve. "We're so glad you could come. You are the first guests to arrive, so we can have a nice visit before the others get here. Let us go into—"

"Mistress Aldon, where are your manners?" Henry interrupted, his cold voice precise and disapproving. "I'm sure our guests will want to be shown to their chambers to freshen up before the festivities."

He'd spoken to Devona as if she were a child to be admonished, Kate thought, appalled.

Devona's hand fell away from Kate's sleeve. "Oh, yes, of course. How thoughtless of me."

The other woman's voice had gone wooden, but her face remained serene, except for that sadness in her eyes. Henry Aldon's words had served no purpose other than to humiliate his wife. As Devona had said, it was still quite early. There would be plenty of time later to prepare for the evening.

Kate felt someone's glance and turned to see it was Nicholas, shaking his head just the tiniest bit. As if he were warning her to hold her tongue. Of course she would—did he think she was totally without common sense?

But in spite of all the sharp words they'd exchanged, Nicholas had never struck fear and loathing into her heart as Devona's husband had done in only a few minutes. Now, she understood what Tucker had meant.

"Daisy!" Henry said curtly, and the girl, who'd been standing at a discreet distance behind their group, started and moved forward quickly.

"Yessir," she answered, her voice subdued, all friendliness gone.

"Take our guests up to their chambers," he commanded.

Kate walked beside Nicholas up the beautiful staircase, her mood darkening. Now, in addition to feeling out of place with these wealthy Tidewater planters' families, it appeared she would have to endure an evening and another day watching Henry mistreat his wife.

Anger shot through her. Men *owned* their wives! By law, they could treat them any way they chose. Of course, she knew in practice that was modified. Usually, anyway, she amended.

But it was obvious Henry did exactly as he pleased. She felt eyes on her again. Nicholas, of course. No doubt, being a man, he thought Henry's behavior perfectly all right.

Kate jerked her head around to glare at Nicholas. His brown eyes stared into hers with sympathy. As if he understood her concern—even shared it. Her anger melted in her astonishment, and for an instant she felt completely in tune with him.

"Here is your bedchamber, Mistress Shaw." Daisy stopped before a door. "Is it all right if the young misses share it with you?" she asked, her voice apologetic. "The house will be very full tonight."

Kate forced a smile and nodded. "Of course," she said, turning to the twins. "Come along, girls." She walked into the room, the twins following, not glancing at Nicholas again, still bemused at that moment of oneness she'd felt with him.

As she'd expected, the bedchamber was large and expensively furnished. The four-postered bed was adequate for all three of them. Celia would have no nightmares tonight, Kate hoped. What if she had to try to find Nicholas to soothe the child?

Kate turned and hurried to the door again, in time to see Daisy open the door to a bedchamber across the wide hallway and usher Nicholas inside.

At least he'd be close by if the need arose. Her worry eased, Kate walked back to where the twins still stood in the middle of the room, staring at her. She smiled at them. "Isn't it a lovely room?"

Emily smiled back, but Celia, of course, didn't. The girl turned her head, making a deliberate survey of the mahogany furniture, the Persian rug on the highly polished floor, the rich wine-colored draperies at the wide windows.

Her glance returned to Kate. "We used to have a bed-chamber nicer than this." Her tone was matter-of-fact.

Kate swallowed. This was the first reference the child had made to the life she and her sister used to have. Was this a breakthrough? How should she answer her? Finally, Kate nodded. "I'm sure you did. Would you like to tell me about how it looked?"

"It had blue curtains and bed coverings, and—" Celia's voice broke off. She looked at Kate for a moment, then turned to her sister. "Come on, Emily, we must unpack our trunk."

Kate pushed down her disappointment. Maybe that was a beginning. She watched the two girls as they bent over the trunk, absorbed in removing their nightdresses and combs and brushes.

When they finished, Kate removed her own things, thankful they were only to stay the night and return to Lydea's Pride tomorrow after breakfast. Most of the other guests, the twins had informed her, would be staying for another day or two, since some of them would be coming from long distances.

Oh, how she dreaded this evening! How could she fit in with this group of wealthy planters' families? She was sure to be roundly snubbed since her family background was merely that of small merchant. Some of these families had lived in the Maryland Colony since its earliest beginnings. They were its aristocracy.

Glancing in the gilt-framed mirror over a chest, she smoothed her hair and pinched her cheeks to give them color, then ran her palms down the skirt of her blue-green gown. It had been the height of fashion in Plymouth, so it should do very well. Alyssa had insisted she buy it before she left. In case Nicholas wanted to take her on a wedding trip.

Kate smiled wryly at that thought. Her sister wouldn't get the letter she'd written soon after her arrival until the *Rosalynde* sailed again for England in the spring. Not that

Alyssa would be excessively perturbed that Kate and Nicholas wouldn't be marrying.

No, Alyssa, as always, would be too engrossed in her own life, her own plans, to spare much time or sympathy for anyone else. Where had she gone wrong, Kate wondered, in rearing her younger sister? True, she'd indulged her because their mother had died when Alyssa was so young. But that didn't account for Alyssa's total self-absorption, her blithe selfishness—

"Miss Kate!" Emily's agitated voice interrupted her meandering thoughts. The girl trotted over and stood looking up into Kate's face, tears in her brown eyes ready to roll down her round cheeks.

"Celia says we won't get to stay for the opening of Miss Devona's gifts. That we'll be sent upstairs with Becky, like babies, as soon as supper is over!"

Kate glanced at Celia in time to catch a smug smile on her face. At Kate's glance, she quickly wiped it away, presenting her usual blank countenance for Kate's inspection.

Kate smiled reassuringly at Emily, although inside she felt as unsure and uncertain as the girl. "Don't worry about that now," she soothed. "It's a long time until supper. We're going downstairs soon and you and Celia and Becky will have a nice visit."

Kate sighed as she smoothed the girls' gowns—Celia's a pale pink, Emily's light green. They'd turned out well, and Emily, at least, seemed happy to be dressed differently than her twin. Celia hadn't said a word of thanks; Kate hadn't expected her to. But she'd seen the girl preening in the one wavy old mirror the cottage possessed.

Oh, she hoped the evening wouldn't be a total disaster!

Nicholas, seated across the long, splendidly outfitted dining table, watched Morgan Lockwood tilt his head as he listened attentively to something Kate, who sat on his right, said, then smile widely.

What had Kate said that was so amusing? The chit certainly had never tried to make entertaining conversation with him during the many meals they'd shared the last fortnight.

No, she'd said scarcely a word that wasn't absolutely necessary. Of course, he conceded, he had been as silent with her. But that was different. Women were the ones versed in social graces, such as making men laugh at their sallies.

His frowning glance collided with Kate's smiling one. Apparently, she found Lockwood as congenial a dining partner as he did her. And why not? The man was handsome and personable. His tales of his voyages on the *Rosalynde* seemed to fascinate her. Of course they would.

Kate had made the arduous journey to the Tidewater expecting to become the mistress of a fine plantation. Why would she be interested in Nicholas's day-to-day worries and problems in trying to bring Lydea's Pride back to full prosperity?

And she looked deuced attractive, he had to admit. Under the glitter of the candles in the crystal chandelier overhead, her pale skin shone like alabaster, her hair glowed with a life of its own, and those eyes of hers weren't at all cat-like tonight. They had taken on the same blue-green luster as her gown.

"I hope we shall be seeing more of you now," the pretty young woman on his right said, smiling at him.

He knew to what she was coyly alluding. News traveled fast on the Tidewater, he thought, irritated. Everyone here knew his long-awaited bride hadn't arrived as expected.

Mistress Wilson had given him attentive glances ever since they'd come to the table. He hadn't returned them because of her foolish simpering and giggling. He hated silly women! But anything was better than letting Kate think he cared about her behavior. And it was either the silly girl or the triple-chinned dowager on his left.

He jerked his glance away from Kate and gave the woman a warm smile. "I'm very busy with plantation work at present."

Kate's smile died as she stared at Nicholas's averted profile. She'd felt a moment of satisfaction when she'd seen him take in the fact that Morgan Lockwood, the *Rosalynde's* handsome captain, seemed to be finding her conversation absorbing. Even witty. She'd not had much chance to get acquainted with him during her voyage here since the rough crossing had occupied most of his time and attention.

Of course, Nicholas wasn't being neglected by his table partner, either. Georgianna Wilson was hanging on his every word and move. Annoyance swept over Kate as she watched the girl make an idiot of herself. She firmly brushed it aside. What Nicholas Talbot did or did not do was no concern or interest of hers.

Hadn't she told herself that he'd find another woman to take Alyssa's place? If Mistress Wilson were setting her cap for him, it was only to be expected. After all, he, too, was a handsome man. And even if his plantation had fallen upon hard times, Nicholas still had the land and the potential to recoup his losses. He was still very eligible.

And it would be a good thing, too, she stoutly told herself. The twins needed a mother. A *real* mother, one who'd be there for them permanently.

Not like herself, who'd be gone with the spring flowers.

Yes, Nicholas could look out for his own interests. She had enough to occupy herself with tending to her temporary duties. And planning for her own future.

Which wouldn't involve trying to interest any of the available men at this table. No, she intended to find a job in Chestertown and be independent, but she was glad of their interest. It was flattering and did a great deal for her self-esteem.

Maybe she wasn't beautiful like Alyssa—she'd never claimed to be—but Morgan wasn't the only single male who'd cast an interested glance her way since the late supper began. And even a few of the married ones. Including Henry Aldon.

At that unwelcome thought, Kate looked down the table to where Devona sat. Kate blinked in surprise as she saw the woman's glance fixed on her. Surely, Devona didn't think Kate was encouraging her husband's roving eye.

Then, Kate realized Devona's look wasn't for her, after all, but for the man on her right. As unobtrusively as possible, Kate half turned toward him.

Morgan's blue eyes, his handsome face, as he gazed back at Devona, held an expression Kate hadn't brought to them in the hour they'd exchanged pleasantries at this table. Not that she wanted to. No, even if he were one of the most handsome men she'd ever seen, he stirred nothing inside her. He might as well be her brother.

But what if Henry Aldon saw that glance of burning ardor?

Alarm hit Kate as she remembered the red marks on Devona's wrist. If Henry thought his wife was dallying with his ship's captain, what might he do to her in retaliation?

She turned fully toward Morgan, her only thought to divert his attention. "Did I tell you the story about old Mr. Murgatroyd?" she asked, her smile bright.

For a moment his face froze, then his handsome features rearranged themselves into polite interest and he looked down at her, returning her smile.

"No, I don't believe you did. Do tell me. Your stories are very entertaining."

"Well," Kate began, noticing his eyes had an unfocused look, as if his thoughts were still back with Devona. "Mr. Murgatroyd had an ancient bulldog, and the animal would eat nothing but fresh vegetables that he had to arrange a certain way . . ."

As she finished the story, Kate stole a glance to the other

end of the table, where Henry Aldon was engrossed with a strikingly beautiful woman seated on his right. Kate didn't think he'd seen the glance that had passed between his wife and the man who captained the *Rosalynde* for him.

But maybe other people had . . .

Kate gave herself a mental shake, stopping her crazily meandering thoughts. What was the matter with her? None of this was her concern. She'd seen other flirtatious glances passing back and forth here tonight. And it probably meant nothing. Henry Aldon might not care a whit.

But that hadn't been a flirtatious look. It had been far more than that. She glanced again at their host.

A frosty smile on his face, he looked up in time to see her staring his way. The smile changed into a smirk and Kate felt her face flame.

Oh, lord, the abominable man thought she found him irresistible. She turned quickly away, jerking her attention back to Morgan.

Her peripheral vision caught Nicholas staring at her again, surprised disapproval on his face. Her cheeks reddened even more. Now, even Nicholas thought that!

Her almost-smug mood of a few moments ago faded. She'd only been fooling herself. She was out of her element here, as she'd known she would be. She didn't know how to flirt and had no desire to learn. Her gown was passable, but she'd seen more than one woman look her up and down, then mentally dismiss her as of no importance. And there had been a few slightly raised eyebrows when she'd been introduced.

Until tonight, she'd not given any thought to the propriety of living in Nicholas's house with no other adult females present. She'd been too busy coping with all the new things she had to learn, keeping up with the daily work.

But clearly other people had—or certainly would now. Oh, how she longed to be back at Lydea's Pride! Tending the twins, preparing a simple meal, talking to Tucker. She wished that she, like the twins and Becky and the other children who'd come, had been fed their supper early, then banished upstairs.

"I hear that you intend to try planting a wheat crop this spring," Morgan said.

What was he talking about? Kate came out of her fog of misery to see he was speaking to Nicholas. With relief she saw the dazed look was gone from Morgan's eyes and his glance was now firmly on Nicholas.

And no wonder he'd turned his conversation elsewhere, Kate thought. She must have been sitting there like a bump on a log for the last few moments.

Nicholas nodded, his brow smoothing out from its frown. "Yes, I am." His voice had a slight edge to it, Kate thought, as if he expected to have to defend his decision.

"Most of the Tidewater planters still believe that the only profitable crop is tobacco. Including my father," Morgan said.

"What about yourself?" Nicholas asked.

Morgan shrugged. "I don't have an opinion. Since I have no intention of ever becoming a planter, it doesn't concern me. I'm very happy with my present occupation."

Something in his tone belied his words. He wasn't as unconcerned as he wanted to appear, Kate thought.

Nicholas gave him a wry smile. "I imagine your father doesn't feel that way . . . since you're the only son he has."

Morgan shrugged again. "He can always find someone to run the plantation for him. Now, let's talk about wheat, not me. I'm interested in your opinions."

"Wheat is going to be the coming crop," Nicholas said, his voice firm with conviction. "Tobacco is difficult to cure, and it wears out the land. There's only so far these plantations can expand."

"But is growing wheat profitable?" Morgan asked. "That has to be the major concern."

Nicholas nodded. "Naturally, it does. And yes, wheat can be very profitable. Did not you hear of John Stevenson's coup?"

"No. Tell me about it."

Nicholas's face grew animated. He leaned farther across the snowy, damask-clothed table. "He bought up a thousand barrels of wheat and sold them in New York for a great profit. What the German settlers in the western part of our colony are doing, we can also do—to our own great benefit!"

His last words rang out during a sudden lull in the conversation. Several heads turned their way.

"So our excellent Maryland leaf isn't good enough for you anymore, Talbot?" Henry Aldon's voice, half-amused, half-superior sounding, came from the head of the table.

Nicholas's jaw tensed. Slowly, he swung his head toward his host. "Of course it is. That has nothing to do with my decision. We Tidewater planters need to diversify in order to survive and prosper."

"I've always grown tobacco! I'll never grow anything else," a florid-faced man three seats down from Kate said.

"As have I." Henry Aldon's icy-blue eyes stared at Nicholas.

"I've heard about that most successful deal Stevenson pulled off," another planter put in. "There may be something in what young Talbot says. 'Bacca does wear out the land."

This was Nicholas's dream, Kate realized. His dark eyes shone with enthusiasm, and he spoke well and fluently. He knew a great deal about this subject.

Impressed, she leaned forward, forgetting her worries about Devona and Morgan, forgetting her own misery of a few moments ago on several different fronts, and listened as he expounded eloquently on the growing of wheat.

Chapter 10

Devona quietly opened her bedchamber door and just as silently closed it. She stood in the hallway, leaning against the wood panels, listening. All was quiet in the big house. Quickly, almost fearfully, she glanced at the door next to her own.

Even though she'd expected that door to be closed, relief swept over her to see it was.

Thank God Henry had partaken so freely of the supper wine! That overindulgence had sent him off to sleep as soon as the festivities ended and everyone adjourned to their bedchambers . . . saving her from having him come through the connecting door to share her bed.

Not that he would have stayed longer than to satisfy his lust. No, he never spent the night with her, for which she was devoutly thankful. His possessiveness did not include one ounce of real love and caring.

The wine had had the opposite effect on her. She'd lain wide awake, staring at the dark ceiling, until she could stand it no longer. She'd go down to the library and read for a while.

Did she dare bring a book upstairs with her? It would be such a luxury to prop herself up in the wide bed and read until her eyelids became heavy.

But then she'd have to hide the book from Henry and slip it back into its place on the shelf before he noticed its absence. She well remembered the rage he'd flown into when they were first married and he'd found her greedily devouring the contents of the well-stocked library.

He'd taken the book from her hands, read the title aloud. The *Iliad*, indeed, he'd sneered. Who was she trying to impress with her knowledge? Only he was here. No guests.

If she were bored, had nothing to occupy herself with, she could pick up her long-neglected embroidery. Tinkle a dainty tune on the spinet he'd had brought from England at such great expense for her enjoyment.

She'd been in tears long before his tirade was over, begging his forgiveness, apologizing for upsetting him. Her tears had gratified him and so had her bowed, repentant head. He'd kissed her tears away, called her his little foolish mouse, and had made love to her that night with such a ferocious passion she'd had bruises for days.

She'd lain awake that night, too, long after Henry had gone back to his own bedchamber, trying to convince herself that his anger and his treatment of her were her own fault. That if she were very careful not to annoy him in any way, he'd never again fly into such an irrational rage.

Walking silently down the curving, beautiful staircase, Devona's mouth twisted at the naïve young girl of ten years ago.

Like her parents, she'd been dazzled when Henry Aldon, of the wealthy Aldons, had chosen her—Devona Miller, her family only farmers making a meager living. Henry had wooed her with impeccable courtesy and soft words. She'd had no idea of the beast that lurked within him until that day in the library two weeks into their marriage.

Now she knew all too well. Knew that no matter how

zealously she tried to watch her every move so as not to arouse his anger, eventually he would explode with it.

Today he'd been just on the edge of an eruption. She could see it in his tense jaw, the iciness of those pale eyes she'd learned to fear and hate. She'd tried to avoid him, but that had been impossible. He'd made her pay for that when Nicholas and Kate had arrived. Absently, she rubbed her wrist where the red marks had now turned to bruises. Usually, Henry was careful not to hurt her where it showed.

She stepped off the last step onto the Persian runner and walked down the wide hallway to the library. The knob turned easily and silently under her hand. Naturally. Henry would have nothing in his perfect house that didn't work perfectly.

She pushed the door open, went inside, and pushed it closed again. Unerringly now, after many a nighttime sojourn in this room, she walked toward the mantel, reaching for the silver candlestick that sat there.

The tall candle lit, she picked it up, heading for the shelf she wanted, then froze. Standing by the long windows was the indistinct figure of a man. She felt her heart lurch, then begin pounding in her chest.

Oh, God, no, it couldn't be Henry! The figure turned and looked at her.

"Devona," Morgan Lockwood said, his voice soft. "What are you doing down here?"

She backed up, the candle flame wavering in her shaking grasp, remembering that naked look they'd exchanged tonight at the supper table.

How it had frightened her. How it still did. "I only wanted a book," she said quickly, hearing the tremble in her voice. "I'll get it and go."

She turned blindly to the nearest shelf, grabbed a volume at random, and started to leave the room, still holding the candle. Her hand on the doorknob, she felt his warm touch on her shoulder, burning through the fabric of her wrapper and nightgown. She shivered and frantically tried to turn the knob, to escape from here before . . .

Her fingers, slippery with nervous perspiration, slid on the knob, and she was unable to turn it. Morgan gently turned her around to face him.

"What are you afraid of? Do you think I would hurt you—as that bastard does?" His face tightened with the last words.

Devona stared up into his face. His blue eyes had darkened until they appeared almost black in the flickering candlelight. His sea-tanned skin, his black hair, all combined to give an effect of darkness.

She shivered again. "Let me go," she pleaded. "I *must* go now."

Morgan's hands dropped from her shoulders. He stepped back. She saw he was controlling his anger with difficulty.

"I can't stand watching you with him," he said between his teeth. "I want to kill him, and then pick you up in my arms and carry you far away from this place."

She gasped and pushed herself against the door.

Oh, she must get out of here! Now! She turned and grasped the knob again.

She'd known, of course, that Morgan was attracted to her. Any woman is aware of such things. But until tonight, he'd always been careful not to give her those glances unless he was sure no one else could see.

And he'd never said a word to her. Not a word. Why had he chosen tonight to break his silence?

Her hands slipped on the knob, and she felt tears coming to her eyes. Sometimes, Henry awoke in the middle of the night after drinking too much wine. Sometimes, he came to her bedchamber on these occasions.

Oh, what if tonight were such a time! Her bruised spirit quailed at that thought. Finding her not in her bed, he'd without fail come looking for her. And if he found her here—in the library with Morgan, with the door closed . . .

A sob escaped her aching throat. She grappled with the slippery knob even more frantically. And she felt Morgan's hand on her shoulder again.

"Here, wait," he said in her ear, his heart almost breaking at her fear. "I will open the door for you, little love. Never fear."

Again, he turned her to face him and tenderly wiped away the tears on her flushed cheeks. With the greatest effort he'd ever expended, he kept himself from pulling her into his arms as he'd ached to do since the first moment he'd seen her three years ago.

He managed a smile and gently pushed her away from him. "There, go back to bed. Hurry, now. It will be all right." He hated how she needed that kind of reassurance, hated how he'd seen Aldon break her spirit more each day.

How could anyone want to dim that radiance she gave off so naturally, like the sun or the stars and moon.

He watched her scurry off and swore a violent oath to himself. Somehow, he'd make Henry pay for what he'd done to Devona.

And someday he would have her for his own.

Chapter 11

Kate turned over, careful not to wake the sleeping twins, one on either side of her, thankful to at last be in bed. The evening had seemed interminable . . . especially the late supper which had lasted for hours.

Henry Aldon had finally allowed the festivities to come to an end after his wife had opened gift after expensive gift. It was obvious Devona was embarrassed by her husband's lavish show of wealth, but Henry had shown no signs of noticing or caring.

After that one revealing glance at the table, Morgan and Devona hadn't even looked at each other, thank God. And in spite of that look, Kate felt nothing was going on between the two. True, she knew neither of them well, yet something in her bones told her they were both too honorable for clandestine meetings, a sordid affair. And her intuition was most often right. She hoped it was this time.

She and Nicholas had carefully avoided even a chance of another exchange of glances, too. Although she *had* enjoyed listening to him talk about his plans for growing wheat.

So had Georgianna Wilson.

Kate ignored that wayward, pointless thought, yawned hugely, and closed her eyes. Now all she wanted to do was sleep. Thank goodness they were going back to Lydea's Pride tomorrow morning.

And she'd managed to give Tucker's message to Daisy. The young Negress had smiled, then looked sad and given her the same message to take back to Tucker. Kate wished there were something she could do for the pair, but didn't know what it could be. Tucker was free, but Daisy wasn't. Henry Aldon was, indeed, a hard, cruel man, she thought indignantly.

That thought made her think of Devona again. She'd liked to have had a chance to talk to the other woman, get to know her better, but that didn't seem likely to happen this time. Not with all the other guests here. Maybe Devona would visit them, Kate thought drowsily. When her husband wasn't with her. . . .

An hour later Kate sat bolt upright, the hair standing up on her neck at Celia's first half-strangled cry. Quickly, she rolled over, pulling the child against her, trying to soothe her, but afraid she couldn't.

A few moments later, she knew she couldn't. She'd have to get Nicholas. She slid off the bed, grabbed her wrapper, and hurried to the door. She opened it, then drew in her breath. Nicholas, his shirt unbuttoned and hanging outside his breeches, stood just outside, his hand lifted toward the knob.

Some other noise alerted Kate. She glanced into the hallway to see Devona walking toward them from the direction of the stairs, her head down. She looked up just then and froze, a startled look on her face as she saw the tableau Nicholas and Kate presented. Quickly, the expression faded as Celia once more cried out.

Not looking at Kate, Nicholas hurried to her vacated

spot on the bed and gathered Celia against him, patting her back as he always did and murmuring reassuring things.

Devona had reached Kate's doorway by now. "Can I do anything?" she asked, concern evident on her pretty face, in her soft voice.

"No," Kate answered, forcing a smile. "When Celia has these bad dreams, only Nicholas can comfort her."

Devona nodded. "He told me about them. I was hoping by now she'd have gotten over them. If you're sure there is nothing I can do, I'll go on to bed."

An odd, self-conscious look came over her face. She held up a book and gave Kate a smile. "I couldn't sleep, so I went down to the library for a book. Well, good night again."

"Good night." Kate stood for a moment in the doorway, watching the other woman walk to her bedchamber farther down the hall and enter. Either Henry was a very sound sleeper or he and his lovely wife didn't share the same bedchamber.

And that hadn't been only surprise on Devona's face when she saw Nicholas and Kate. That look had held another element. Guilt?

Had she, after all, met Morgan somewhere?

Kate turned back into the room and closed the door. No, she still didn't believe that—her instincts couldn't be that wrong. There had to be some other explanation. She wished again she could talk to Devona alone because her intuition was telling her something else. The other woman badly needed a friend.

Emily, apparently so exhausted nothing could rouse her, still slept soundly. Nicholas was being very careful to keep his eyes on Celia, and away from Kate.

She felt her face warm. Did he always have to make it so abundantly clear that he wished she were anywhere but in his presence?

She wouldn't look at him, either. But as if drawn by a magnet, her gaze strayed back to the bed. Her glance settled on Nicholas's bare, muscled chest. The whorls of silky chestnut curls shone in the candlelight. What would it feel like to run her fingers through them? His arms, still gently holding his small cousin, were strongly muscled, too.

Those arms had held her once, pressed her close against his hard, warm body. . . .

Forcibly, Kate moved her gaze away. She wouldn't look at Nicholas again! She'd keep her eyes fixed on the mahogany highboy across the room, her mind on how wonderful it would be to get away from here tomorrow, back home.

Home? Did she actually think about Lydea's Pride as that, now? After only two weeks and under the impossible circumstances? How could she?

She forced those thoughts away, too. Celia was quiet now, thank God. Kate hoped they hadn't roused the people sleeping in the rooms all around them. Her glance strayed to the bed again, in spite of her resolutions.

Celia's heavy eyelids were closing. Carefully, Nicholas eased her down on her pillow, as always saying what seemed to be the magic words, "You'll sleep well now. The dream won't come back tonight."

The child nodded drowsily, then—her eyes completely closed—sighed and turned on her side. In a few moments, her regular breathing signified she was again asleep.

Nicholas turned away from Celia.

Kate snapped her gaze back to the highboy.

Nicholas let out a relieved sigh himself and got up from the bed. God, but he was tired. He'd put in what amounted to a full day's work before he'd sailed the sloop here, a tiring job in itself, and he'd thought the evening would never end.

Frowning, he realized he was deliberately concentrating on anything but the fact that Kate stood only a few feet away.

Why should that concern him? She slept across the hallway every night. She sat across the table three times a day.

Why should the fact they were in this strange room together affect him in any way?

He knew why. Ever since he'd helped her out of the sloop this afternoon, he'd remembered her touch, wanted it again. Nicholas set his jaw and drew his brows even closer together. He raised his head and glanced at Kate. With a fixed stare, she was looking across the room at something.

Nicholas turned his head that way. For some reason, she seemed to be totally absorbed in the massive highboy standing against the wall.

He should be glad she was staring at the furniture instead of him. He *was* glad, he told himself hastily, pushing down a new thought. Could she be having the same trouble as he?

"I think Celia will sleep the rest of the night now," he told Kate, his voice stiff.

She slowly moved her gaze toward him. "Yes. She always does," she agreed coolly.

No matter how their voices sounded, once their glances met, neither seemed able to look away.

Kate wore the same wrapper she'd worn that other night, down by the fire. Her hair was in one thick braid which hung over her left shoulder. The flickering candlelight lit red-gold gleams in it. Her eyes were that strange sea-foam green again, just as they'd been that other night. . . .

Nicholas felt a cold trickle of sweat slide down his back. And they'd looked at each other like this that time, too, and then . . .

He wrenched his gaze away from her, appalled. Was she some kind of a witch that she could so easily arouse these feelings in him? When he didn't even *like* the wench?

When she'd cheated him of the woman he'd planned to wed?

That thought stopped whatever was going on inside his traitorous body. He raised his glance to Kate again, knowing it was safely cold now.

"If she wakes again, I'll probably hear her. If not, you can fetch me."

Kate shook her head, as if to clear it of cobwebs. That strange feeling had stolen over her, just as it had the night down by Nicholas's hearth. If he hadn't spoken then, she thought, they'd have moved together. Just like that night.

Her face warmed. Of course they wouldn't have. Considering the way Nicholas felt about her. And she him. With the twins sleeping not three feet away.

She gave Nicholas a firm, unsmiling glance. "Yes, of course, I will."

Nicholas turned and walked to the door. He opened it and left, pulling it closed behind him.

Kate jerked off her wrapper, blew out the candle, and climbed into bed. Emily pressed against her on one side, and Celia the other. The bed, which previously had been ample for the three of them, now seemed entirely too narrow.

Her nerves were raw, on edge. She knew sleep would be long in coming this second time around. Lying on her back, she futilely tried to suppress the shocking thought that insisted on surfacing.

She wished it were Nicholas beside her, his hard arms holding her tightly against his warm, naked body here in this strange bed.

Chapter 12

Kate looked across the rough-hewn table, transformed now with a snowy cloth and a centerpiece of holiday greenery. The cottage looked and smelled festive, she thought, smiling at the twins. They'd helped her festoon evergreen branches over the mantel, over furniture, and every other conceivable place that would hold or contain them.

Emily smiled back, a warm and loving smile. Celia gave Kate her usual blank look, then to Kate's surprised pleasure, a tiny hint of a smile turned up the girl's lips.

Nicholas was expertly carving a turkey into juicy-looking slices. A platter of steamed oysters and clams sat beside it, along with bowls of gravy and winter vegetables.

The dinner seemed bountiful to Kate, but Nicholas had said in the old days, when the plantation had many slaves and workers, they cooked slabs of beef or a whole pig over a pit. She'd seen that he longed for those days to come again.

"Pass me the plates, please," he told Kate, his glance sliding quickly away from hers.

His voice was a trifle brusque, she noticed. As if this

Christmas dinner was a strain for him. No doubt he was thinking that, instead of Kate, it should be Alyssa sitting at his table.

Kate handed him Emily's plate, trying to keep a pleasant expression on her face for the girls' sake.

Nearly two weeks had passed since their visit to Aldon Manor. Busy, work-filled days, with Nicholas putting in longer hours than ever.

But he'd managed to find time for a trip to Chestertown in the sloop. He'd not invited her or the twins to accompany him. Of course she wouldn't have gone; she didn't need another time of being confined to the small quarters of the boat with a man who didn't want her company.

But it would have been thoughtful of him to have asked. And why would she expect Nicholas to exhibit thoughtfulness toward her? Other than treating her with a distant civility, he hadn't thawed a bit since that day she'd arrived and he'd discovered Alyssa wouldn't be his bride.

For which he apparently still blamed Kate.

Maybe he even blamed her for that night when some unaccountable spell had seized them, when they'd moved into each other's arms as if it were the most natural thing in the world. . . .

Kate quickly pushed those thoughts away. Natural it might be, since they were a healthy man and woman living together in this small cottage, but it could lead to nothing but disaster and heartbreak for her.

However, she needn't fear it would ever happen again. Nicholas gave her a wide berth, and she him. Whether he still felt lust for her, she didn't know. What she did know was that she couldn't trust her own body. Even a mere touch from him, such as when he'd helped her off the boat at the Aldons', affected her foolishly.

Today, in honor of Christmas, Nicholas had taken pains with his appearance. His chestnut hair was freshly smoothed back and neatly tied at the nape of his neck with a russet thong. He wore his best gray breeches, and his shirt, though almost threadbare, was also his best one.

He looked very handsome and appealing. She hastily turned her attention to her food, relieved when it was time to serve the flaming steamed pudding to excited ooh's and ahh's from the girls. Even Nicholas seemed impressed.

She cleared up quickly, the girls helping with no urging because, as soon as that was done, it would be time for the Christmas gifts.

Soon they were seated around the hearth, for the weather had turned cold, a true winter nip in the air now. It even looked like snow, Nicholas had said.

He looked startled when she handed him a package, then, in a moment, uncomfortable. "Thank you," he said, then sat holding the package as if he didn't know what to do with it.

The twins had no such problems. They opened their two gifts from her—lace collars she'd tatted for their new dresses and dolls pieced together from the leftover fabric scraps—with squeals of pleasure. Even Celia unbent enough to show her excitement.

Nicholas's gifts to his cousins were identical gold lockets. Where he'd gotten the coin to purchase such expensive gifts, Kate didn't know.

The girls thanked both of them, gave Kate handkerchiefs they'd laboriously stitched and embroidered with her initials and Nicholas a pen wiper, which was also obviously of their own manufacture. Then they hurried upstairs, giggling, to try on their new finery.

They left Nicholas and Kate alone in an uncomfortable silence, Nicholas still fingering his unopened package from Kate.

Finally, he turned to her. "I did not get you a holiday gift," he said. "I had no thought you would give me one."

She hadn't planned to. After all, Nicholas had made it crystal clear from the beginning that she was here on little more than a servant's basis. And only temporarily, at that. Which suited her fine, of course.

But it was Christmas, and the joy and good will of the season had made her feel generous. So, in the evenings, after the twins were in bed and all the work done, she'd made two shirts for him, using one of his old ones for a pattern.

"Do not trouble yourself about that," she assured him. But deep inside she recognized the feeling that coursed through her as disappointment. Perhaps she had thought he might give her some token of the season.

He looked again at the package, then opened it. When he drew out the shirts, his expression changed to surprise. "Where did you get the cloth?"

"Folded away in the corner cupboard."

"Oh." Nicholas fingered the soft fabric, then cleared his throat. "I can certainly use these," he said finally. "Thank you."

Kate felt warmth course through her as Nicholas spoke the two simple words. He'd spoken them so seldom to her. And it was obvious he felt embarrassed about not giving her a gift. "You are welcome."

The silence grew. The fire crackled and spat; a gust of wind rattled the windowpanes, and excited giggles drifted down the staircase.

Damnation! Nicholas saw that, in spite of her denials, Kate was annoyed because he'd neglected to buy her a Christmas gift. Even if he'd thought of it, he had no money. He'd sold his only silver shoe buckles in order to get the twins' lockets.

No, Kate wasn't annoyed, he decided. She was hurt. Disappointed.

That made him feel worse. Why on earth should they exchange gifts? They were nothing to each other. Were they? Kate was here only because of dire necessity. If the foolish chit had stayed in Plymouth where she belonged, she wouldn't be here, working like a bound servant.

If she hadn't guilefully persuaded Alyssa into breaking her troth with him . . .

His thoughts stopped revolving in their well-worn, familiar groove.

How had Kate managed to execute that feat? he wondered for the first time.

In spite of his efforts to avoid her, he'd seen a great deal of Kate these last weeks. She was strong-willed, true. He'd always known that. Also stubborn and full of pride. He'd also been aware of that.

But in her day-to-day activities, caring for the twins, doing the work around the cottage, he'd seen no evidence of wiliness. In fact, he admitted, ever since he'd first met Kate, all those years ago, she'd been very straightforward.

And time hadn't changed that. Why, the day she arrived, she told him she'd come to be his wife with no simpering or blushing stammers whatsoever.

Of course, he amended, there were those few minutes here by the fire that first night. When she'd tried to entice him to take her to his bed. To further her scheme to marry him.

Or had she?

Was it possible that she'd been as caught up in passion as she'd appeared? For a moment that night, he'd considered that possibility—but had at once dismissed it. Now, for some reason, he couldn't do that so easily.

The thoughts were so surprising that he looked over at Kate with new eyes.

She wore the same blue-green gown she'd worn to the Aldons' party. And her hair was pinned demurely at the back of her neck. But as usual, one or two shining, unruly locks had come loose at the sides and curled around her ears. Her cheeks were pink; her eyes had taken on that sea-foam shade he found so distracting. She looked—pretty.

Too much so. Nicholas had to acknowledge that his breeches were becoming too tight in certain places.

Damnation! What was wrong with him?

He'd made his planned trip to Chestertown a few days ago. Visited his favorite tavern. A comely serving wench had made it abundantly clear she would not be at all averse to having him in her bed for the evening.

He hadn't been able to go through with it.

He frowned fiercely as he thought of that time. It had been blasted embarrassing and annoying! And now he was right back where he'd been before. He still wanted Kate. He wanted her with an intensity he could never remember feeling before.

Not even for Alyssa? he asked himself, appalled. And had to admit that was true. Not ever. Not for any woman had this bedeviling passion manifested itself.

"Cousin Nicholas! Kate! Look at us." Emily came running down the stairs.

Abruptly Nicholas came to himself, aware he'd been sitting, staring at Kate, in a brooding silence. And Kate was looking at him, too.

Emily, with Celia close behind, came to a stop between Kate and Nicholas. Her new locket bounced on its chain around her neck, her lace collar was already slightly awry, Kate saw, relieved the girls were back in the room.

Nicholas had been looking at her so oddly, as if he'd never seen her before. It had made her uncomfortable, made that unwanted desire she could not seem to keep from feeling surge up inside her.

Turning away from his intent gaze, Kate reached over and straightened Emily's collar. "There. You both look very nice." She smiled at the twins.

Emily smiled back. Celia, of course, didn't. But, like her sister, her eyes were wide with excitement, her cheeks flushed.

"You do, indeed," Nicholas agreed, looking at his young cousins with those same new eyes he seemed to have acquired in the last few minutes.

He spoke the truth. They'd both gained some needed weight since Kate had arrived. And Emily was blossoming by the day. Even Celia seemed to be gradually coming out of the shell of grief and fear she'd built around herself after the night of the fire.

As always, when he thought about that terrible night, remorse hit him like a hammer. If only he'd woken sooner, gone back in one more time to try to save Philip and Lydea. If only . . .

No! He forced his futile thoughts to stop their frantic scrambling in his brain. It was long over and done with. No help for any of it now.

All he could do was try to build this plantation up again to its former prosperity so the twins would have some kind of a future, security.

Nicholas took a deep breath and rose. "All three of you look so splendid, I must go and change into one of my new shirts."

He smiled at the twins, then at Kate before heading upstairs, carrying his shirts.

Kate stared after him, feeling her breath coming faster, trying to deny how Nicholas's words and brief smile had affected her.

It didn't mean a thing, she told herself. He was merely trying to be pleasant because it was, after all, Christmas. And she'd given him a gift and he hadn't reciprocated. He no doubt felt a bit uncomfortable about that.

A knock sounded on the cottage door. Emily flew to answer it. Could it be the Aldons? Kate wondered. Before she'd left there from the visit on Devona's birthday, the other woman had told her they'd be out to visit sometime during the Christmas festivities. Or maybe only she would. Henry was always so busy.

Oh, Kate hoped it was only Devona! How she'd love to see the other woman. But not her husband.

It was neither. Tucker stood in the doorway, his big, tall frame slightly stooping to fit beneath the sill. Behind him, Kate glimpsed one of the farm carts, piled high.

He swept off his knitted cap and grinned at Kate. "A good Christmas to you, mistress," he said.

"And to you. Come in, Tucker," Kate invited, getting up from her chair.

Tucker and the two bondmen had already been given their extra food and tobacco rations and bright new shillings. The twins had gone with Nicholas yesterday to distribute these. Kate had made shirts for each of the men out of some blue homespun she'd also found in the cupboard, taking special care with Tucker's. She hadn't given them out yet.

Tucker nodded, then grinned at the twins. "I believe I need help with some o' this stuff," he told them.

Both girls were eager to oblige him. They pressed through the doorway as he turned back to the cart. "Oh, it's a dollhouse!" Celia said, awe in her voice.

It was, indeed, Kate saw, coming up behind. The biggest one she'd ever seen. Tucker must have been working on this for months.

"It's wonderful," Kate told him, hearing the awe in her own voice as the three of them brought the structure in and set it on the floor.

Both twins knelt before it. Emily reached inside one of the tiny rooms and brought out a wooden doll which looked remarkably like herself.

"I likes to whittle," Tucker said, modestly, his white teeth flashing in a gratified smile at her words of praise. He went back to the cart and returned with his arms full.

"Here, I made this for you, Mistress Kate." He handed her a cedar box.

Kate took it, the smell of the aromatic wood filling her nostrils. Carvings of flowers were artfully arranged on its hinged lid and trailing down the sides.

She felt tears come to her eyes. Blinking them back, she gave Tucker a radiant smile. "Thank you. It's the most beautiful thing I've ever owned."

His smile widened. "You're mighty welcome." In his

other hand he held a carved eagle; its fierce beauty almost took her breath away.

Kate heard Nicholas on the stairs, and then he came into view, wearing one of the new shirts. To Kate's relief, it fit perfectly, making his outdoor-tanned skin look even darker in contrast to its whiteness.

Their glances met. "Look what Tucker made for you," she said, her voice unsteady.

Nicholas drew his breath in sharply. Kate looked so softened, so vulnerable. He hadn't seen her that way since that first night when he'd heard her reassuring Celia about how careful she'd be of the teapot that had belonged to the twins' mother.

And, just as it had that night, something inside him softened, too, in response.

He walked to where they all stood, just inside the door. He took the proffered gift and stood holding it. "It's magnificent, Tucker," he said quietly. "And I know just where it belongs."

Holding the eagle carefully with both hands, he walked across the room and set it in the center of the mantelpiece, then stood back.

Kate nodded in agreement. "Yes, that's the perfect place."

Uncannily realistic, the carved bird overlooked the room as if it were guarding the cottage and its inhabitants. It reminded her of Nicholas, she thought, as he turned toward her . . . its proudly raised head, its fierce glance.

But at the moment, Nicholas looked remarkably unfierce. The expression on his face made her heart thump in her chest, her breathing grow fast again.

"Edward! Be careful! You're going to mess it up," Emily wailed. "Miss Kate, stop him!"

Kate gave her attention to the dollhouse, relieved for an excuse to turn away from Nicholas. The kitten was trying to wedge its fast-growing body into one of the minuscule rooms. Kate grabbed him and pulled him out. He protested all the way, a tiny chair and a doll who looked like the twins coming with him.

She placed him on the floor. "Edward," she scolded, carefully keeping her eyes on the offending feline. "That house isn't for you to play with. Do you understand?"

Of course, being a cat, Edward merely yawned and ignored Kate . . . then again leaped toward the dollhouse.

Nicholas caught him before he landed. "You are not to do that," Nicholas said mock-sternly, holding him by the scruff of the neck but with his hand supporting the kitten.

"Cousin Nicholas! Stop! You'll hurt him," Celia said urgently, tugging at Nicholas's sleeve.

"No, I will not." Nicholas still held Edward's now meekly curled up body, looking the kitten in the eye before gently lowering him to the floor.

Kate bit her lip to hold back her amusement, positive the kitten would immediately make another attempt to get in the dollhouse. But instead, he turned and went stalking off to the hearth, where he curled up and lay down as if he'd never had any interest in the twins' gift.

Tucker chuckled. "That old cat know when he met his match."

"Yes," Kate agreed. "I guess he does." She braved another look at Nicholas. He was again inspecting the eagle. And the hint of a smile turned up the corners of his mouth.

For the first time, he'd accepted the kitten as being a part of the household, she realized. Not just a nuisance he had to step over all the time, but a living creature that he was, if reluctantly, a bit fond of.

This Christmas Day was turning out to be full of surprises. She went to the cupboard and got out Tucker's shirt and gave it to him.

He stood looking at it, running his gnarled fingers across the tiny, careful stitches. "Thank you, mistress," he told her, his eyes glistening.

Kate smiled back. "You are certainly welcome. That can't begin to repay you for the work you put in on my gift."

"I wanted to do it—all of it," Tucker said. He straightened. "I'd better be gettin' back to my house," he said.

"How is Nellie?" Nicholas asked, turning his attention from the bird on the mantel. "Does she show any signs of calving yet? I'm afraid it may snow tonight. You did put her inside the barn."

Tucker nodded. "Yessir, I did. Can't tell about her. She actin' a little tired. I'll keep a close watch on her tonight," he promised.

"Yes," Nicholas agreed. "I want you to. She's getting too old to calve. This will be her last one, and it may be too much for her."

Tucker nodded again. "She pretty old, but I think she do all right this time."

"I hope so. Come and get me if there's any trouble."

Another knock sounded on the cottage door. This time it had to be Devona. Kate hurried to answer it, but now her emotions were mixed. She'd like a visit with Devona, but overriding that feeling was another, stronger one.

She wanted to send the twins outside to play and be alone with Nicholas.

Pushing down the thoughts, Kate opened the heavy door, and another feeling added itself to the jumble inside her. Disappointment.

Devona and Becky did, indeed, stand on the doorstep. But Henry stood there, too.

Chapter 13

Kate moved back a step. "Come in, come in." Behind her, she heard Nicholas's step.

"Welcome, Aldon, Devona, Becky," Nicholas said, his voice hardening on Henry's name.

He felt as she did about the two people, Kate thought, remembering that moment of shared awareness at the Aldons'. He was no happier than she to see Henry.

Devona gave them both a warm smile and hugged the twins. They hugged her back, then took Becky with them to admire the wonderful dollhouse.

"You're just in time. We were about to have a glass of wine," Nicholas said.

Henry stared at Tucker, his expression haughty, as if he couldn't believe the field worker had actually been welcomed into Nicholas's house. Then, his gaze traveled around the humble room and his look didn't alter. Kate's indignation began rising.

"I'd better be gettin' on back," Tucker said.

He was plainly uncomfortable now that the Aldons were here, Kate thought. There was an edge to his voice, too.

No wonder. Henry was, out of mere spite, keeping him from the woman he loved and wanted to marry.

"You be sure to come and get me if Nellie starts calving," Nicholas again reminded Tucker.

"I'll do that, Master Nicholas." Tucker smiled at Kate and Devona, his expression blank as he looked at Henry, then left.

Kate took their cloaks and soon, all four of them were seated around the blazing hearth with glasses of wine in their hands. Kate smiled at Devona again.

Here they were, she and Nicholas seated on one side, the Aldons on the other, for all the world like two happily married couples.

But that was only an illusion.

Although Henry sat close to Devona, his hand resting possessively across her arm, they weren't content with each other. Devona feared him, and contentment was an emotion totally foreign to Henry's nature, Kate thought.

As for her and Nicholas, they weren't even friends. Were they? No, of course not. He still believed she'd caused Alyssa's defection. Didn't he?

Her sureness of that wavered. Something had happened between them a few minutes ago, but she didn't know just what it had been.

"Shall we drink to a prosperous new year?" Henry asked, his eyes gleaming as he looked at Nicholas. "I have every expectation of it being another such a one as the last."

"Of course," Nicholas replied. His smile looked forced, but he raised his glass with the others. "To a prosperous new year for us all!"

Kate saw a muscle flex in Nicholas's jaw and heard the tight control in his voice. He detested Henry Aldon, she fully realized for the first time. She couldn't blame him. Henry was a detestable man. And it was obviously all Nicholas could do to be civil to him when the man was so blatantly taunting him.

Her glance caught Devona's. She looked uncomfortable,

almost embarrassed, holding her arm rigidly, as if longing to pull it out from under Henry's hand.

A wave of sympathy for the woman's plight swept over Kate. She wouldn't exchange places with Devona for anything!

Maybe she had no money, was living here as little more than a servant, but it wasn't forever. In only a few months she'd have her debt to Nicholas paid and be independent again, working in a shop in some nearby town.

Still another emotion, strangely like regret, added itself. Was that truly what she wanted? To leave here.

Of course it was. She pushed the disquieting thoughts aside and smiled at the other woman. ''See what Tucker made for me?''

She handed Devona the exquisitely carved box, feeling a moment of satisfaction. Now, Henry would have to let go of his wife's arm.

Devona slipped her hand out from under her husband's restraining hold and took the object. ''It's beautiful,'' she said, turning the box to admire it from all angles.

''You accepted a gift from that darkie?'' Henry's voice was full of incredulous disgust.

''I most certainly did,'' Kate said coolly, her glance at him even cooler. ''Tucker is a talented man, and it's a beautiful piece of work.''

Surprised and pleased, she saw Nicholas's mouth curve upward in a small approving smile at her words; but almost before they were out, Kate wished she'd bitten her tongue. She didn't want to do anything that would further prejudice Henry Aldon against Tucker, make him even more adamant about not letting Daisy and Tucker marry.

Trying to soften her expression, she held Henry's cold gaze, even though she had to restrain a shudder.

To her relief, a knock sounded at the door again and Emily ran to open it. Tucker once more stood outside, the shoulders of his dark jacket covered with white powder.

It was snowing! Excitement built in Kate. Snow was rare in Plymouth. She'd never seen a heavy fall of it.

Nicholas was already on his feet. "What is it, Tucker? Is Nellie calving?"

"Yessir, I think so, Master Nicholas. And she seem real tired. 'Fraid she gonna have a bad time o' it."

Grabbing his cloak from its peg, Nicholas turned to his guests.

Henry also got to his feet, reaching for his own cloak. "I'll go with you. Maybe I can be of some help."

Nicholas's nod looked reluctant. "All right, come along." He smiled at Devona. "I'm sorry to have to leave."

"Of course, you must go," Devona said, smiling back. "We all know and understand that plantation matters must come before visiting."

As Nicholas closed the door behind them, Kate felt her excitement build. She turned back to Devona, a wide smile curving her mouth. "Shall we go out and walk in the snow?"

Devona looked startled and a little perturbed at the idea of their walking in the falling snow, like children. She glanced at the closed door as if expecting Henry to come back inside and forbid her, Kate thought. Oh, damn the man! How she hated him.

Then Devona's pretty mouth curved into as wide a smile as Kate's. "Oh, yes! Let's do that."

The three girls elected to stay inside and play with Edward and the dollhouse. At least for the moment. Kate felt like a girl again, escaping adult restraint. She and Devona slipped on their cloaks, pulled the hoods up snugly, and found their gloves.

Outside, it was like a fairyland. Snowflakes danced in the gray winter afternoon light, reflecting a dozen different colors. Kate felt exhilarated, free and happy in a way she hadn't for a long time.

Devona must feel the same, Kate thought, glancing at her. Her face was lifted to the sky, and snowflakes glistened on her cheeks. Impulsively, Kate held out her hand. "Come, let's run."

The other woman turned a startled face to her, then grinned and took Kate's hand. Holding up their cloaks and skirts, they ran up the lane toward the ruins of the burned house. Finally, warm and laughing, they stopped by the springhouse and leaned against the door.

"I've never seen snow like this," Kate said, still looking with wonder at the falling flakes, heavier now. "We have bad storms and sleet and ice in Plymouth, but not much snow."

Devona smiled at her. "I grew up on the Tidewater, but we don't have many heavy snowfalls here, either. This may not last long."

"Oh, I hope it does! I hope it snows and snows all night and all day tomorrow—" Kate broke off, laughing. "That sounds like Celia or Emily, doesn't it?"

"It may sound like you. We don't know each other very well." Devona gave Kate another smile and looked as if she wanted to say something else. But didn't.

"I'd like to know you better," Kate answered, wondering how far she dared go. She'd love to admit how she felt about Devona's horrible husband. "I'd like for us to be friends."

Devona's face looked blank for a moment, then her smile widened. "Oh, yes, I'd like that, too. Very much. I don't have any true friends. And I don't see much of my family."

"Do they live far from here?" Kate asked, feeling her way into this fragile new friendship.

"No. Only on the other side of Chestertown. It's just that Henry . . ." Her voice trailed off, and a sad look wiped away the smile.

Taking a deep breath, Kate decided to take a chance. "Henry doesn't like for you to visit them?"

Devona looked at Kate for a long moment. Then she

nodded. "No, he doesn't. It's been several years since I've seen my mother and father."

Shocked anger filled Kate. Before she could stop herself, she blurted out, "That's terrible! Why don't you visit them whether he likes it or not?" The moment she'd said the words, Kate realized how stupid they sounded. "I'm sorry. It's none of my business and I know you can't do that."

"No, I can't," Devona answered simply, her voice sad. Then she gave Kate a direct look. "You don't have to pretend you like Henry. I know you don't. Most people don't."

"Including you?" The words hung in the snow-filled air. Appalled, Kate couldn't believe she'd said them aloud.

But Devona didn't look shocked. She stared at Kate, her eyes glistening. "No, I don't like Henry. I hate him."

Her last words were so soft Kate barely heard them. But she knew she'd heard correctly. Kate swallowed, longing to put her arms around Devona, to tell her to come back to the cottage with her, that she'd never have to spend another second with Henry.

But she didn't do or say either of those things. "How bad is it?" she finally asked after a long pause. "Does he . . ."

Devona's mouth twisted. "Yes, he hits me—usually not where it shows. But that isn't the worst. He belittles me, tries to make me feel as if I'm nothing, can do nothing, without him. My family is poor—he never lets me forget what I came from."

Sympathy and pity, mixed with anger, swept over Kate. She clenched her hands into fists, raging against the laws, both legal and assumed, that said a woman was her husband's property.

"There's got to be something you can do," she said, even though she knew there wasn't.

"No. If I leave him, go back to my family, he'll only come after me. I tried that once. My family thought I was crazy to leave a man who'd given me everything I could possibly want. And then, there's Becky." Her mouth twisted again. "If I try to leave him again, he'll see that I lose her."

Oh, God. Kate's throat ached. She searched for something to say, some scrap of comfort to give.

Devona reached out and touched her arm as if to ease Kate's mind. "Enough of this. It's Christmas. I shouldn't have said all that. I'll be all right. Let's walk back to the cottage and talk about you and Nicholas."

Kate knew Devona was right. They'd just said things to each other people don't usually confide except after years of friendship. Now, they did need to change the subject—but not to the one Devona had suggested.

"There's nothing to talk about. Nicholas detests me."

Kate paused, remembering how Nicholas had smiled at her before he went upstairs to change into the shirt she'd made him. And the look they'd exchanged when he had come back down.

Hadn't she thought something fundamental was changing between them today? But there was no reason to believe that. No doubt they'd just been caught up in the spirit of the season.

She'd given Nicholas a gift and it had touched him. That's all it was. All it could ever be.

"He thinks I persuaded Alyssa to break her troth with him," she continued, "so I could take her place. I'm only working here until the spring, until I pay for my passage money. Then I'm going somewhere to find a job."

"I think you're wrong," Devona said. "I can see something else in his eyes when he looks at you."

Kate glanced at her. Devona had confided in her; now she owed it to the other woman to be just as open. "He feels lust, but he hates feeling that. He fights it."

"That emotion can lead to deeper ones," Devona said, an odd note in her soft voice. "And what about you? Does Nicholas attract you?"

Kate's smile held no amusement. "Yes. Since the first

time I saw him," she admitted. "And although I did come here to be his wife if he'd accept me, I *didn't* persuade my sister to find another!"

"I would never believe that of you," Devona agreed, gravely. "I don't think Nicholas truly does, either. He's only angry and his pride is hurt."

Kate stared at her. Could that be true? And if so, could Nicholas now be changing his mind? Could that be what she'd seen in his eyes earlier today?

Don't be a fool. Don't leave yourself open to more hurt, her inner self cautioned. She shook her head. "No, it's more than that."

Devona looked as if she were trying to hold back a smile at Kate's last emphatic words. She tucked her hand in the crook of Kate's elbow. "We'd better be getting back to the cottage. It's snowing harder."

"Yes," Kate agreed, forcing her mind off Nicholas. The snow was staying on the ground, she noticed, not melting. Maybe she'd have her wish for a deep snowfall. And her slippers were entirely inadequate for this, as were Devona's. Their feet would soon be wet as well as cold. "We'd better hurry," she said.

"There are Nicholas and Henry, returned from the barn," Devona said as they neared the cottage, tension coming into her voice.

The two men stood before the cottage door, waiting for them. A small shiver went down Kate's spine as she looked at Nicholas.

How *did* she feel about this man? How did he feel about her? Had something subtly changed between them today? No, of course not! She pushed her erratic thoughts away again, concentrating on Devona.

Was she afraid Henry would scold her because they'd walked in the snow? Or did she just dread being in his presence again?

Henry's cold, pale-blue eyes were fixed on his wife. Kate

decided she wouldn't give him a chance to humiliate Devona as he had at her birthday celebration.

"Isn't this wonderful?" she asked, pasting a bright smile on her face as they reached the men. "I persuaded Devona to walk out in the snow with me. I've never seen such a snowfall in my life."

Not giving either of the men a chance to reply, she turned to Nicholas. "Didn't the first snowfall after you came here surprise and delight you?" she asked him, her smile still bright even while she searched his eyes and face for a hint of that different something she'd seen there earlier.

"I suppose it did," Nicholas answered.

All Kate saw in his brown eyes was surprise at her uncharacteristic sprightliness. She tried to ignore a stab of disappointment.

"And how is your poor cow doing?" she chattered on. "Has she had her calf?"

"No. Not yet. I must go back in a little while. Now, we'd better go inside. You and Devona are shivering with the cold."

Nicholas opened the door and stood back as the women entered, then followed after Henry.

"Oh, I do hope that all will be well with her and her baby!" Kate said, holding her wide smile, even though she felt as if her face might crack.

She turned to the girls, still absorbed in the dollhouse and the kitten. "Edward likes Becky," Kate said, beaming at the girl, who was pulling a string for the kitten to pounce on. Out of the corner of her eye she saw Henry's frown. He'd not be silent much longer.

She turned back to Devona, who was giving her a bemused look. "Come, we need to warm our feet," she told the other woman, taking her hand and leading her to the fire.

"Devona, we must leave," Henry said, his voice peremptory as he came up behind them. "We have stayed too long already."

Henry sounded as if he'd conferred a great honor on Nicholas's household by coming here. "Oh, do you have to go?" Kate asked, turning her false, bright smile on the man she detested. "Why don't you stay here until tomorrow?"

Saints preserve her! Why had she suggested that? Where would she put them if they accepted her offer? Becky could sleep with the twins. Their bed was wide enough. And she supposed Devona and Henry could have her room, which she'd finally gotten livable.

But somehow she couldn't picture Henry in her narrow bed with its straw mattress. Her smile widened at that thought, holding genuine amusement now.

Henry's haughty frown deepened. "We could not possibly accept that offer."

He sounded as if the very suggestion of staying in the cottage were unthinkable. Kate would love to have kicked him.

He lifted his head and looked at his wife again. "Come, Devona," he said imperiously.

"Of course," she answered, her voice subdued, the pleasure that had been in it when she and Kate ran laughing through the snow extinguished.

Kate's heart filled with futile anger for her. Oh, how she wished she could do something, get her away from this man!

Devona turned to Becky. "Come get your cloak."

"Oh, I want to stay the night with Celia and Emily!" Becky abandoned the kitten and hurried to her father, the twins behind her. Laying her hand on his coat sleeve, she looked up into his face with a coquettish smile that was much too artful for a child her age. *"Couldn't* I, Papa?" she coaxed.

Henry's face didn't soften an iota as he looked down at his daughter. "No, of course you may not stay here,

Rebecca.'' His words were hard and cold, too, each one sounding like small pellets of ice.

You'd think his daughter had suggested spending the night in one of his slave's cabins, Kate thought, annoyance sweeping over her. He was trying to make Nicholas feel even worse about his change in fortune, she guessed.

She glanced at Nicholas to see that muscle working in his jaw again and wondered how he could abide the other man's patronizing manner.

"I will allow Celia and Emily to visit you soon," Henry added loftily, as if conferring a great favor.

Becky tilted her head and again gave him that horribly sly, coquettish glance from under her lashes. "Oh, thank you, Papa! You are so very kind to me."

Henry leaned down and took her chin between his fingers. His icy glare probed her eyes. "You must never forget, Rebecca, that you can never argue with my decisions!" His voice cracked like a whip as he released her and straightened.

Becky moved back a step and quickly shook her head, her eyes widening in fright. "Oh, yes, Papa! I will always remember that. Always." Her voice quavered.

The girl's chin bore the red imprint of her father's grip, Kate saw, shocked by the unfolding scene, so horribly reminiscent of the one she'd witnessed on Devona's birthday.

Henry's thin mouth curved into a cold, self-satisfied smile that was somehow infinitely worse than his arrogant frowns. "See that you do. Now, come, we must go."

A chill went down Kate's spine. No wonder Devona felt she could do nothing about Henry's treatment of her. She couldn't leave her child with him. Henry would soon break the girl's spirit completely. Or turn the girl into some kind of monster. Already, it was obvious the relationship between them wasn't healthy.

Kate glanced at Devona in time to see a look of anger and hatred flash across the other woman's smooth features.

She walked to the pegs on the hearth where their cloaks hung and silently removed them.

At the door, Devona turned and impulsively hugged Kate. "We do want the girls to visit soon," she said, her smile including both Nicholas and Kate.

"Oh, yes, Cousin Nicholas, we would like to do that," Emily said. Celia said nothing, but Kate could see she, too, wanted the treat.

"We shall see," Nicholas said.

His voice was as cold as Henry's had been, Kate thought. But there was a world of difference. She would never fear Nicholas. Neither would the twins.

"I will walk with you to the wharf," Nicholas continued. "I need to check on Nellie."

He turned to Kate, and she saw the frustrated anger sparking in his brown eyes. As well as something else— wasn't there? Absurdly, Kate felt her heart skip a beat.

"I don't know how long I will be," he said. "Don't wait supper for me."

"All right." She and the twins stood in the doorway and watched all of them leave. The snow was still coming down, she saw, but not as hard and fast as before. But already there was a thin layer on the ground and coating the bushes and trees with a fairytale splendor.

It was beautiful, but somehow the magic had gone out of it for her. Devona turned for one last wave, and Henry turned, too; but the look he gave Kate wasn't fond or even friendly.

Today, thank God, there had been no trace in his manner of the interest in her he'd exhibited at Devona's birthday celebration. She decided he'd merely had too much wine that evening and was flirting with every female whose glance happened to cross his.

Kate waved back, then closed the door against the rising wind. But there was something else in Henry's glance just now that upset her almost as much as the look he'd given her at the party.

He seemed to recognize that she and Devona were becoming friends. And he didn't like that idea. No, he wouldn't. A man such as he would try to keep Devona isolated, with no family or close friends. No one who could be on her side.

She and Devona would have to be careful about showing the warmth they felt for each other, Kate realized, or Henry might very well not let Devona come here again. Or invite Kate and Nicholas to their plantation.

"It's getting late. We will soon have to begin to think about supper," she told the twins. Nicholas had said he didn't know when he'd return from the barn, but she'd keep his food warm. He deserved a hot meal after spending long hours with the cow.

A memory forced its way into her mind. That first night she was here, when Nicholas had come in late for his supper because he was so angry with her. Begrudgingly, she'd kept it warm for him.

She wouldn't begrudge doing it this time. And it had nothing to do with the way she and Nicholas had looked at each other this afternoon, as if each were seeing a different person.

Of course it didn't.

But no matter how she tried to keep them at bay, other memories from that first night surfaced. Had Nicholas really pulled her into his arms, kissed her, started to carry her up the stairs?

The episode had seemed so dream-like—maybe it *was* only a dream. . . .

The feel of his warm hands on her body, his mouth moving against hers came back to her as if it had taken place only a few moments ago instead of nearly a month.

Kate's fingers smoothed across her tingling lips.

No, it hadn't been a dream. It had been all too real.

And no matter how late Nicholas came in, she would keep his supper hot for him . . . a cup of cider warmed.

And she would be there to give it to him.

Chapter 14

Nicholas shook the still-falling snow from his cloak and stamped his feet on the threshold to clean his boots. Through the cottage's small, clean window he could see a flickering candle on the table. Kate must have left it for him.

Kate. He liked the sound of her name, saying it over in his mind.

He opened the door and stood, transfixed. Kate was at the hearth, adding another log to the fire. The tender curve of her neck and shoulders sent a shaft of longing through him. He tried vainly to ignore it, push it aside.

Today, tonight, something was different between him and Kate. It had started being different when he'd accepted her Christmas gift and gone upstairs to put on one of the beautifully stitched shirts.

He still regretted not giving her a gift. But there was no help for it. He had nothing to give her, and even if he had, the too-late gesture would only be embarrassing for them both.

He pushed the door closed and walked across to the

hearth, the cozy warmth and order of the big room closing in around him.

How different the room looked than it had that first night he'd brought her here. Now it seemed like a home, even though it was simple and plain, the first dwelling that Philip had built for Lydea, with nothing of the burned manor house's grandeur.

And it was all Kate's doing. She'd worked tirelessly to achieve and maintain this order and peace, going far beyond what was necessary to honor their agreement.

He hung his damp cloak on its peg, very conscious of Kate so near to him.

"How is Nellie?" Kate finally asked into the growing silence.

Nicholas turned toward her. She wore the same white wrapper of that first night, buttoned primly to its high neckline. Her hair was confined to one thick, shining braid hanging down her back. As usual, errant red-gold tendrils had already escaped.

The longing intensified. "She and her heifer calf are doing fine," he answered, a smile of relief that all was well with them curving his mouth.

Kate's return smile was relieved, too. "Good. I saved your supper."

She picked up a pewter plate from its place near the fire and placed it on the table, her slender hands quick and deft. With the movement, her braid swung over her shoulder, leaving the back of her bent neck bare.

He wanted to cross to her, to kiss that vulnerable white nape. He wanted that so strongly he had to press his feet into the floor to keep them still.

Finally, she straightened, moving back from the table. Her expression didn't match her movements of a moment ago. Her face looked young and unsure.

And very lovely.

"I'll go up to bed now," Kate said. But still she stood, as if waiting for something from him.

Nicholas crossed the room and seated himself before his steaming plate. "Thank you," he told her, hearing the softened tone to his voice. It occurred to him that she had not had to wait up. He could have found his food.

He glanced at her, feeling the increased rhythm of his heartbeat. "Why don't you stay and have a glass of wine with me?"

After a moment, she nodded. "All right."

She went to the shelf and took down the bottle from which they'd drunk the toast with the Aldons earlier. She poured two glasses, put one in front of his plate, and sat down across from him with the other.

A faint, pleasant flowery scent wafted across to him. His heartbeat quickened again and he made fast work of the plate of food. Finished, he lifted his head and allowed himself to glance at her.

She was looking at him. Pink came to her ivory cheeks. He raised his glass. "Shall we drink to Nellie's successful calving and to not having Henry here for the night?"

Her eyes widened, then she smiled as she raised her own glass.

"That was an impulsive offer on my part. I confess I couldn't imagine Henry sleeping in my chamber."

"Nor could I," Nicholas agreed, smiling back.

Kate was still sleeping in the room with all the bits of broken furniture pushed to one corner. He needed to move them out of her bedchamber. He'd do that tomorrow. At the thought of Kate in bed, his breath came faster.

His body urged him to push back his chair, move around the table, and gather Kate into his arms. He swallowed. "You and Devona seem to get along with each other well," he said, congratulating himself on keeping the conversation light and ordinary.

"Yes. I like her very much."

Kate set her glass on the table, her stomach quivering. She could no longer pretend she'd stayed downstairs only so she could tidy up when Nicholas finished eating. She'd stayed because she wanted to be alone with him, the twins safely asleep upstairs.

Now, looking at him across the table, the cottage dim and intimate in the flickering candle and hearth light, she knew she'd done a dangerous thing. Whatever negative feelings she'd felt for Nicholas had been transmuted into something else entirely.

And his face again wore that odd expression, like this afternoon, almost as if he'd never seen her before. And her own face must look different, too, reflecting her feelings.

Because all her old desire for him had returned.

Nicholas pushed back his chair and stood. He held her gaze still with that heart-stopping expression in his dark eyes, then walked around the table until he stood behind Kate's chair.

She felt his warm breath on her neck and shivered, then drew in her breath as he moved her chair out and his hands settled themselves on her shoulders, gently squeezing. "Kate," he said, as if that were the first time he'd ever pronounced her name.

Kate rose and turned into his embrace. His hands slid down her arms, even through the wrapper leaving a trail of fire where they touched. His head lowered toward her uptilted one, slowly, ever so slowly, and she knew the promise of heaven was in his lips. She moved closer to him again, lifting her face toward his.

Nicholas's hands curved gently around her face, and as his mouth found hers she opened to him. Exultation filled him. She was as eager for their lips to join as he. Her mouth was sweeter than honeycomb. He was drowning in her sweetness. He never wanted to let her go.

His heart thumped, hard, and he swept her close against his also rapidly hardening body. Finding the buttons at the front of her wrapper, his hands fumbled with the tiny fastenings.

Kate moved his hands aside and unbuttoned the wrapper

to her waist, hearing his sharp intake of breath as the garment fell away from her breasts.

No man had ever gazed upon her naked breasts before, and she'd thought none would until her marriage bed. But this did not seem wrong, even though she and Nicholas were far from marriage.

It seemed right and inevitable that it should happen. Now, like this.

Nicholas lowered his head; his hot mouth found her breast, and his tongue teased her nipple until she thought she might faint from the pleasure of the sensations his touch aroused. Kate pulled his head closer to her aching flesh. She trembled with the need building deep within her for something she'd never experienced, yet knew she'd yearned for from the first moment she'd seen Nicholas all those years ago.

His hand moved to her spine, slipped lower until it cupped her bottom. With no apparent effort, he lifted her, just as he had that other night here, holding her easily. His mouth left her breast; his head raised. His brown velvet eyes were glazed with passion as they looked down at her. Once again he found her lips, his tongue lightly circling, then at her own hot response, closing over them, taking possession.

"Kate," he breathed into her mouth. "Let me love you."

Even as he said the words she'd longed to hear, even as her mind formed her own tremulous agreement, Kate stiffened, the dream-like feeling fading.

Yes, this was like that other night. Too much so.

And not again would she blindly melt into his arms as if they were bewitched and had no choice in what they did. Not again would she be left afterward drowning in humiliation.

Kate pushed her hands against his chest. "Let me down," she told him. She had to know the answer to the question burning in her heart before this went any further.

His eyes blank with disbelief, Nicholas lowered her to the floor.

Pulling her wrapper around her, she moved back from him, then lifted her chin, her look straight and unflinching.

"Do you still believe I persuaded Alyssa into breaking her troth with you so that she could wed John Latton?"

For a moment Nicholas couldn't take in what she'd asked. All he could think about was how much he wanted to kiss her, hold her, carry her up to his bed. He moved forward again to implement that wish, then the sense of what she'd said finally penetrated.

There Kate stood, looking just as she had on the wharf when she'd said she'd come to marry him. She wouldn't be moved, either. Not until he answered her question.

He thought about it, his brow furrowed, trying to be honest, to separate how he really felt from the answer she wanted to hear ... the answer he wanted to give her so that once again she'd come into his arms.

He realized he didn't believe that anymore. He'd always known Alyssa was spoiled and willful. It had been part of her charm. Why, he could no longer remember.

He looked back at the woman standing so straight and tall before him.

"No, I don't. I was angry. My pride was hurt. I couldn't believe Alyssa would do that to me. But now, yes, I can accept that she grew tired of waiting, found someone else. She was very young when I left Plymouth."

Kate's expression didn't dissolve into softness as he'd hoped it would. She merely nodded. "And are you sure your anger toward me has gone?"

Again, Nicholas searched his mind and heart. "Yes," he answered, his voice firm and sure. "It has fled."

Something else had fled, too, he realized. His overwhelming, reckless desire. He still wanted Kate badly, but now he knew that he must not take her.

The answers Kate demanded were for her own benefit,

but those moments when he'd stopped touching her, had thought instead of felt, had saved him from making a terrible mistake.

She pulled her wrapper tighter around her gloriously pink-tipped breasts . . . which he still wanted to kiss and fondle all the night long. And more than that. Much more than that.

And that was exactly what she wanted him to do, just as she had that other time, so similar to this one, when Celia had cried out and stopped their lovemaking before it could lead to the ultimate act.

Yes, of course it was! his still inflamed body told him. *She wants you just as you want her.*

Maybe Kate did truly want him. Maybe she had that first time, too. But she wanted something else more. Just as she always had. She'd proven that just now with her questions.

A woman didn't make an arduous ocean voyage in hopes of marrying a man only to give up her plans at the first setback.

He'd refused Kate, but then taken her into his home, where he had to see her, be with her, sleep only a few feet away from her every night. He'd put her in a perfect position to wear his defenses down so his physical desires would make him bed her.

Then, of course, she'd expect him to wed her.

He'd be morally obligated to do so. Which she well knew. Kate was no fool. Her plans were simple but shrewd. *What's wrong with that?* his body demanded. *You need a wife and you can't have Alyssa, so why not marry Kate?*

Because she wouldn't be marrying him for love, his mind answered. She'd never pretended that. Even that first day she'd told him calmly and coolly that she'd make him a good wife. Bear him children.

He wasn't yet ready to settle for only that. Even if desire did flame between them, desire wasn't enough. He'd loved

Alyssa. Maybe he still loved her, although she'd proved faithless.

His mouth pressed together as he stared at Kate. "It almost worked, didn't it? You very nearly had me carrying you to my bed."

Kate stared at him with what appeared to be astonished anger in her eyes.

"Are you again pretending you were reluctant? That I tried to seduce you?" she asked hotly. "What is the matter with you, Nicholas Talbot?"

"Nothing is wrong with me, Mistress Kate. I am just not so desperate to have a woman in my bed that I will let you hoodwink me into marriage."

"What are you talking about? You told me you no longer blamed me for what happened with Alyssa."

He nodded. "I don't. But even if you didn't persuade Alyssa to break our troth, you were ready and willing to take her place. You know this is a valuable plantation and will someday be rich and prosperous again. In any case, marriage is always better for one in your position than spinsterhood."

Kate's hand shot out and slapped him hard across the face.

Nicholas grasped her hand in his and lowered it. "I told you never to do that again."

She glared at him. "And what do you intend to do about it? Hit me as Henry does Devona?"

The silence was charged between them. The fire hissed, a small, sleepy noise came from Edward, then Nicholas shook his head.

"Do you really believe that of me? No, I would never hit you back, but I demand you cease your schemes and plans."

Kate gasped in outrage. "My plans and schemes, as you so elegantly phrase it, are only to fulfill my obligations to you and to leave here as soon as possible."

They stood, angry glances fixed on each other.

Nicholas was the first to turn away. He banked the fire and then picked up the candle.

He bowed, mockingly, and with a sweep of his arm motioned toward the stairs.

" 'Tis time to go to bed. After you, mistress.''

Chapter 15

Devona heard the sound of horse hooves behind, fast approaching, and stiffened, disappointment filling her as she reined in her mount from a canter to a walk. She'd anticipated this ride alone in the early-morning briskness, even though she hated the sidesaddle and longed to ride comfortably astride as men did. Now it would be spoiled.

Henry must have felt better, well enough to ride. When he caught up, he'd scold her in his cold, hard voice about riding out alone, an action he'd expressly forbidden her to do.

She straightened, pushing her true feelings deep inside as she'd long ago learned to do in her husband's presence, showing him only a docile, calm facade, ready to accede to his every wish. But it wasn't Henry who drew in his mount alongside her own.

It was Morgan.

Her breath quickened as she gave him a sideways glance, taking in his muscled body in his well-tailored riding habit. His black hair caught gleams of morning sunlight. What was he doing here? She hadn't seen him since the night of her birthday celebration.

At the thought of that time in the library, she felt her cheeks warm. Oh, how many hours since then had she lain awake, reliving those few minutes?

"You must leave," she said quickly, urgently. "If any of the servants saw us . . ."

"Only Riggs and Daisy know I'm here," he assured her. "And they are as safe as the grave."

"Nothing is safe where Henry is concerned. He's turned the slaves and bond servants against one another. He pays them all to spy and tattle."

Even as she spoke she was amazed at herself. She'd never told a living soul about Henry. Now, within a few weeks, she'd told both Kate and Morgan.

"There will be nothing for anyone to spy and tattle about, Devona," Morgan answered. "We are only riding along this woods path and talking, nothing more."

When he'd arrived half an hour ago to discuss a business matter with Aldon, Daisy had told him the man was sick in bed with the ague and Mistress Aldon was out for a ride.

At the stables, only a Negro slave, Riggs, was in attendance. With no questions, no sidelong glances, he'd saddled the gelding Morgan used. Riggs hated his master, Morgan well knew. Even if he and Devona were truly arranging a clandestine meeting, Riggs would never tell.

"And just to make sure, I took the other bridle path, then doubled back this way," he further assured her, his lips tightening as he listened to himself. "But I hate all this! I want to be able to see you openly."

Devona stared at him as if he'd lost his mind. No wonder. It had been a stupid thing to say.

"I'm sorry," he apologized. "I know that's impossible, but at least I can be with you, talk to you, look at you for a little while."

His eyes devoured her slim figure in its blue-gray riding

habit, her golden-brown hair pulled back, her brown eyes soft and warm. But filled with apprehension.

God, but he loved this woman! Why had fate brought them together when they could never truly be so? Remembering his vow that night when they'd encountered each other in the library, his mouth twisted.

If he had any sense, he'd resign his position as Henry's ship captain, go far away from the Tidewater, never to return. But he knew he'd never do that. Not as long as he could sometimes see Devona.

He watched as she fought a silent battle with herself. Finally, she looked over at him, her mouth curving in a smile.

"All right, we will ride together for a little while," she said. "And we will talk together as friends do."

Morgan fell in beside her, elated at her words. "I owe you an apology for what I said that night in the library."

He paused, glancing over at her. Her profile was to him, her small straight nose, her strong rounded chin.

"I'm not in the least sorry for *what* I said," he continued. "I meant every word of it. But I know I frightened you— and that I regret."

Her head turned quickly toward him. Her full lips, that he so longed to press his own against, tightened. "I don't want to talk about that. Or my marriage. Not ever again."

"All right," he agreed. He'd yield to her wishes. At least for the time being. "Then what shall we talk about?"

Her mouth relaxed into a smile. "We can talk about you," she answered. "I know very little about you."

He shrugged. "There isn't much to tell. You know my father owns a plantation on the Western Shore."

She nodded. "Yes, and that even though you are the only son, you chose to leave it and become a sea captain." She tilted her head and looked at him inquiringly. "Why did you do that? Did you so much dislike plantation life?"

He shrugged again, feeling his gut tighten. "No. What

I disliked was my father's arbitrary ways. He would give me no voice in how the plantation was run.''

"And you wanted to make some changes?"

"Yes," he said tersely, not wanting to talk about this any more than she did her marriage. But he guessed he owed it to her to let her know something about his background. "You heard the argument at the table the night of your birthday celebration. So many of the Tidewater planters are completely opposed to change of any kind. They'll go on growing tobacco as long as they have an acre left of arable land."

"And do you, too, want to try growing wheat as Nicholas does?"

"I don't know what I'd like to do. But we need to diversify, I know that much. The days of growing only tobacco are numbered."

Devona nodded. "I can see that. Henry will never change, either. He just wants to use the land up and never return anything to it. Wheat-growing sounds as if it would be a good venture."

He glanced at her, surprised. "You sound as if you've given this some thought."

Her face pinkened. "I have. I've read about it, and I've listened to the talk around the table."

Morgan's surprise deepened. Along with his respect for her. There appeared to be depths to this woman he loved that he'd never suspected. His heart twisted. What a woman she could be if she were freed from Henry!

"So you never plan to return to your plantation home?" she asked in a moment.

"No," he answered. "There's nothing there for me."

"But someday you will have to take it over. When your father gets old or sick or—"

"Dies?" he finished, his voice ironic. "No, even that will make no difference. Father has an overseer who suits him perfectly. Handles things exactly as he wants them done. He's already more of a son to him than I've ever been."

They rode on in silence. Devona was obviously perturbed by what he'd told her. "Don't worry about all that," he said finally. "I've gotten over it long ago. I chose my road in life many years back."

She gave him a swift, sideways glance. "And you never miss the home you grew up in? Never wish it would be yours someday?"

The knot in his gut tightened. "Yes, of course I do. Naturally. But my life is to my liking. It's exciting and adventurous. I've been to many places most people can only dream about."

He'd been telling himself this since he was twenty and had embarked on this seafaring, nomadic life. And he'd felt genuine excitement and enjoyment in his travels.

But that was before he'd met Devona.

Now, he'd give it all up in an instant if he could have her for his own. He'd take his savings and buy another plantation somewhere here on the Tidewater and install her as its mistress. Or maybe they'd leave here. Go somewhere far away and start over again.

The silence was even longer this time as they rode on. But finally, she glanced at him again. "Someday, you will marry and have your own family," she said, her voice steady and calm. "Has your father made no provisions for that?"

He drew in his breath. He'd hoped she wouldn't think of this. But of course she would. "Yes. If I marry and give him a grandson, he will leave everything to me."

This time he didn't wait for the silence to drag out, for her inevitable next question.

"No, I will never marry until I can have you for my wife," he told her, his voice rough with feeling. "I will never sire children except with you."

She gave him a startled, agonized glance from those doe-like eyes, then reined her mare and with one fluid motion turned back on the trail toward the stables.

Morgan watched her go, not trying to catch up, cursing himself for failing to curb his runaway tongue. He would have had the bittersweet pleasure of her company for a while longer if he had.

He stuck his feet in his mount's sides and cantered on up the trail, his mood dark and brooding. Henry was twenty or more years Devona's senior. In his late forties, Morgan guessed. Not a young man by any means. Most men didn't live too much longer than that.

Morgan's mouth twisted again in a mirthless grin. But the bastard was hale and hearty, in robust health. He might very well outlive Morgan. Easily that could happen. More than once the *Rosalynde* had nearly gone down in a storm. One day he might not be lucky.

Why did the evil people in this world survive and prosper? What was that term? "Flourish like the green bay tree?"

Somberly, he at length turned his mount and headed back the way he'd come. By now Devona would be back in the splendid manor house her husband had provided for her. Probably she'd already be upstairs, tending to his needs.

At the thought of her in Henry's bedchamber, bent over his bed, Morgan's jaw tightened until a sharp pain pierced his face.

If he had any sense, he would give up this hopeless love once and for all. Leave here and make a new life for himself somewhere far away.

But he knew he wouldn't do that. Couldn't do that. He was bound here by silken, invisible strands that held him more firmly than the ropes that tied the *Rosalynde*.

Chapter 16

Kate picked up the heaping basket of mending and sat down by the hearth. Outside, the twins jumped rope and giggled, Edward, now a long-legged adolescent cat, with them.

It was an early afternoon in late January. The twins' lessons were done for the day, dinner just over, kitchen freshly tidied, Nicholas in the barn.

At that thought, her mouth tightened. Since the night when Nicholas had again almost taken her to his bed, he'd avoided her like the plague. And she him. She'd give him no further chance to accuse her of scheming to wed him.

Her face flamed as, as dozens of times before, she thought of that night. How could she have allowed herself to be so humiliated? And for the *second* time—this one even worse. Nicholas had said in scathing words what he'd only put into a glance before.

Why had she thought he'd truly changed during that magical Christmas Day? Even though he no longer blamed her for Alyssa's defection, she'd neglected to ask him the important question.

Did he still consider her a conniver, a person not to be trusted?

Obviously he did. Probably always would.

Oh, how she wished she'd not offered herself to him in marriage that day she'd arrived. Why hadn't she just told him she'd borrowed his passage money? That she planned to find work at once and pay him back?

Why had she been so blind to all the other facts that must be faced? Such as the undeniable one that they always struck sparks off each other whenever they were together. A situation that could never lead to a happy, placid marriage.

She knew the answer. She'd wanted Nicholas. God help her, in spite of all that had happened between them, she still wanted him. Maybe he still wanted her.

That didn't matter.

The two regrettable scenes had happened only because they were living in the same house. And Nicholas, being a man, had physical needs.

As did she. But that wasn't as far as it went with her. Despite everything that had happened between them, she was falling in love with him.

A film came over her eyes for an instant and she pricked her finger with the needle. A bright-red drop of blood stained the shirt she held. Nicholas's shirt. One of the new ones she'd made him as a Christmas gift. Already he'd managed to snag the sleeve and tear it.

Flinging the shirt back into the basket, she stood and walked to the window. The twins still skipped rope, deftly avoiding Edward's leaps at the enticing moving object.

Celia's bad dreams had become further and further apart these last weeks. And more than once she'd returned Kate's smiles. The girl seemed well on the way to getting over her parents' deaths, even if not fully accepting Kate.

Right after Christmas, Kate had started the twins on lessons. Nicholas had given them a surprised look the first day, but said nothing. He even seemed to approve. Aside from learning how to run a plantation home, Kate knew the Tidewater girls were only taught how to play the harpsichord, to embroider, to make interesting conversation. To be entertaining, in short.

She felt they needed more. Her own ability to read well and to cipher had stood her in good stead. And even if they never needed these things, why waste perfectly good minds? The twins were bright, eager to learn.

Of course, they still preferred the out-of-doors and spent as much time at the barn as she'd allow. Nellie's calf was thriving, and Alfreda and Mordred had not been slaughtered.

Tucker told her Nicholas had decided to keep them as sow and boar to start their own broods of piglets. It seemed Nicholas was more softhearted than she'd thought.

But not with her. And that was fine! All she wanted was to leave here, leave this man that she'd been a fool to think she could ever get along with.

A movement down the lane from the wharf caught her attention. She peered out the window for a better look, then her eyes widened. Several women were walking toward the house. As they came closer, Kate recognized them as guests at Devona's birthday celebration.

And Mistress Georgianna Wilson was tripping along in the forefront of the group. Visitors? Guests? Oh, Lord, they were dressed in splendid afternoon gowns, and here she was in her old cotton work dress, looking for all the world like the servant she, in truth, was.

Kate's hands flew to her head and she hastily smoothed down her hair. There was no time to change. They'd just have to take her as she was. She took a deep breath and drew herself up, then opened the cottage door before Mistress Wilson had time to knock.

"Good afternoon, ladies," Kate said, a pleasant smile on her face. "Won't you please come in?"

Mistress Wilson gave Kate a superior smile as she looked the other woman up and down. "Good day, Mistress Shaw." She came inside, four women behind her.

The twins, their eyes round with interest, rope-skipping forgotten, followed.

Georgianna looked around the cottage, her brows raised. Whether at the humble furnishings or at the fact it was in order, Kate didn't know. Or care, she assured herself.

"Won't you please sit?" Kate asked cordially, even though she felt far from sociable. "I will make us a pot of tea."

One of the other women, whose name escaped Kate for the moment, gave her an unsmiling look as she settled herself in a chair. "We have come to see both you and Master Talbot," she announced. "Since he doesn't seem to be about, it's best you send for him."

An uneasy feeling swept over Kate at the woman's words and curt tone. What was this all about?

"Celia, Emily," she said. "Go fetch your cousin from the barn."

Kate busied herself with the tea preparation and they all waited in awkward silence until the door burst open.

Nicholas, scowling impatiently, the sleeves of his shirt rolled up, revealing his tanned muscled arms, his chestnut hair disheveled, entered, the twins trailing him.

"Good afternoon, ladies." He stood with his legs planted firmly apart just inside the door. "I am sorry but I have little time for visiting."

Mistress Rogers, the woman who'd bidden Kate send for Nicholas and the one who'd stared the hardest at Kate at Devona's dinner party, straightened and gave him a severe look.

"We have not come for a social call, Master Talbot. What we have to say concerns the entire community. So I believe you should sit down. This matter may take some time."

Instead, Nicholas folded his arms across his chest. "I prefer to stand, Mistress Rogers."

The woman sniffed and drew herself up haughtily. "Very well. It is the consensus of the community that it is

4 FREE BOOKS

These books worth almost $20, are yours without cost or obligation when you fill out and mail this certificate.

(If the certificate is missing below, write to: Zebra Home Subscription Service, Inc., 120 Brighton Road, P.O. Box 5214, Clifton, New Jersey 07015-5214)

Complete and mail this card to receive 4 Free books!

YES! Please send me 4 Zebra Lovegram Historical Romances without cost or obligation. I understand that each month thereafter I will be able to preview 4 new Zebra Lovegram Historical Romances FREE for 10 days. Then if I decide to keep them, I will pay the money-saving preferred publisher's price of just $4.00 each...a total of $16. That's almost $4 less than the regular publisher's price, and there is never any additional charge for shipping and handling. I may return any shipment within 10 days and owe nothing, and I may cancel this subscription at any time. The 4 FREE books will be mine to keep in any case.

Name _____

Address _____ Apt. _____

City _____ State _____ Zip _____

Telephone ( ) _____

Signature _____ LF0797
(If under 18, parent or guardian must sign.)

Terms, offer and prices subject to change without notice. Subscription subject to acceptance by Zebra Home Subscription Service, Inc.. Zebra Home Subscription Service, Inc. reserves the right to reject any order or cancel any subscription.

4 BOOKS FREE!

A $19.96
value....
absolutely
FREE
with no
obligation to
buy anything,
ever!

ZEBRA HOME SUBSCRIPTION SERVICE, INC.

120 BRIGHTON ROAD

P.O. BOX 5214

CLIFTON, NEW JERSEY 07015-5214

unseemly for you and Mistress Shaw to be living here in this cottage alone. It is quite shocking.''

Kate couldn't hold back the smile that curved her mouth upward. Out of the corner of her eye, she saw Georgianna give her a disapproving glance.

These self-righteous women couldn't possibly be further from the truth if they believed she and Nicholas shared the same bed. Of course, maybe they were only concerned with appearances. And she should have been expecting this after the glances she'd gotten at the Aldons' party.

But they didn't know Nicholas very well or they'd never have come here and said such things, she thought, as Nicholas stiffened and his jaw set.

"We are not alone here," he clipped out. "My cousins also share the household."

Mistress Rogers drew herself up taller. If possible, her expression became even more disapproving. "That is not good enough," she pronounced. "For propriety's sake, two young children do not make the situation acceptable."

Nicholas returned her stare, his jaw muscle twitching. "And pray tell," he said, his voice quiet, his words enunciated carefully, "just what do you ladies feel should be done to rectify the problem?"

The women looked surprised and gratified at his words, obviously not recognizing them as sarcasm. These women were in dead earnest, Kate realized, dismay and embarrassment replacing her momentary mirth.

"You must either marry this woman or she must leave your household," Mistress Rogers said, giving Kate a dismissing look that plainly expressed what she felt Nicholas's choice would be.

Georgianna gave Kate an even more telling look, then simpered at Nicholas, preening for him.

The silly little goose! Did she really think Nicholas had an eye for her? But maybe he did, Kate thought, her feelings changing into anger. How would she know? After all, he'd made two more trips in the sloop these last weeks. And said not a word when he returned about where he'd been.

Kate's glance fell upon the twins, standing off to the side, their brown eyes wide, their mouths slightly open. Her anger turned on herself for not thinking to have them stay outside. But then, she hadn't dreamed why the women had come here. She still could hardly believe what they were saying.

Ignoring the women, she walked over to the twins. "You girls go outside and play," she told them softly.

Emily's lower lip trembled. "You're not going to leave, are you, Kate?"

Leave? Kate stared at her. Up until that moment, she hadn't thought this through. But if the fact that she and Nicholas were sharing the same quarters had these women, the wives and daughters of the neighboring plantation owners, so up in arms that they'd come here to force this issue . . .

She managed to find a smile for Emily. "Go on outside now. It will be all right."

Celia's lips were pressed firmly together and her expression was stony. What did that mean? Kate wondered. Probably that she wouldn't care at all if Kate left, she thought, her mood darkening.

The girls went outside. Kate closed the door behind them and turned back to the group. Nicholas stood exactly as before, his arms folded across his chest, feet planted firmly, jaw muscle still moving.

"So that is what all of you have decided, is it?"

His voice was even more ominously quiet, more precise, Kate noticed, tensing. It couldn't be long now before the explosion.

Mistress Rogers nodded regally, a satisfied look on her hawk-nosed face. "Yes. We are pleased that you are being reasonable about this. Of course, we all realize," she glanced at her colleagues, who nodded, "that the obvious, the only sensible course of action is for Mistress Shaw to depart."

Leaving the field clear for Georgianna. Kate's simmering anger headed toward the boiling point. These women couldn't have made it clearer that they found her completely unsuitable as a prospective wife for Nicholas.

"Reasonable. Yes, I am trying my utmost to remain so," Nicholas said. He unfolded his arms and strode to the door, jerked it open, then held it wide.

He made a large, sweeping bow, which Kate thought even these obtuse women had to recognize as mocking, then straightened.

"I would advise all of you to depart and leave me to manage my family and my household as I see fit. I believe I am still capable of doing so without your or anyone else's aid."

Mistress Roger's mouth made a round O of surprise and shock. "I cannot believe that you would speak to us in such a fashion." Stiffly, she rose, clamping her mouth shut, outrage showing in every rigid feature.

The others followed suit. All of them marched to the door, heads and color high.

Mistress Rogers paused just over the doorsill and delivered a parting shot. "You cannot flout convention in this manner and set such a terrible moral example for your two innocent young cousins."

"Good day, *ladies,*" Nicholas said between his teeth, his brows drawn together in a ferocious scowl. "Go!"

They scuttled. The twins came back inside and Nicholas closed the door with a resounding slam.

Kate, standing by the table, bit the inside of her lip. She couldn't decide whether to laugh or cry.

Not for an instant could she deceive herself that Nicholas's actions had been made as a defense of her virtue. No, he was merely furious that the women had dared to enter his home and try to tell him what to do.

Nicholas strode to the hearth and stood before the fire,

underneath the carved eagle. Kate was startled at how closely he resembled the bird at the moment.

He looked across at her. "I'd like a mug of ale."

Kate decided that she would, too, even though she usually left the ale alone. It was so much stronger than what she'd sampled in Plymouth.

But she felt shaken by the episode just past, and she dreaded the next few minutes. She poured the ale into two mugs and gave Nicholas his.

She looked at the twins, standing just inside the door. "Celia and Emily, please go up to your chamber for a few minutes," she said, hoping they'd give her no argument.

More subdued than she'd ever seen them, they quietly did as she bid.

Standing a few feet from Nicholas, she took a large swallow of her ale, wincing as it slid down to her stomach.

"They were right, you know," she said, then took another large swallow. "This situation should not continue. We are not setting a good example for the twins. I—"

"What? What?" Nicholas jerked his head up to stare at her. "Did you put these busybody females up to this little trick?"

His lips tightened. "Ah, yes, I see it now. What a clever scheme, Mistress Kate. Did you really think you could *force* me into wedlock since your plans to entice me into wedded bliss haven't worked?"

Kate was so surprised, so stunned at his accusation, she could only stare back at him, openmouthed. Then, a rush of anger filled her. She slammed the ale mug down on the table so hard the contents sloshed out onto her fingers and returned his glare with one equally fierce.

"I have had enough, more than enough, of your conceited, pompous accusations!" she told him. "If you would have had the courtesy, which I know is quite beyond your capabilities, to let me finish my sentence, you would have learned that I have absolutely no wish to wed you! How many times do I have to tell you that before you will believe it?''

Nicholas blinked, taken aback at Kate's outburst. This last month had been so tension-filled, he felt ready to explode. Twice more, he'd made the trip to Chestertown to the tavern, with the same results as before.

At these thoughts, he frowned again at Kate. Damn the wench! Why did she plague his waking thoughts, disturb his sleep and dreams? He wanted no woman but her. Yes, he would admit this—though not to her. But he would not marry her!

And if she thought she could force him into it, she was wrong!

His thoughts came to a skittering stop. Did he really believe what he'd just said? The accusations he'd once again made? Or was he merely venting the anger he felt at the stupid, prattling women who'd butted into his affairs?

Kate was still giving him that challenging look.

"What I planned to say had nothing whatever to do with marrying you, Nicholas Talbot. I am going to leave here. That is the only thing to do. Perhaps I have not fully worked out my passage money, but when I have secured a position, I will send you part of my wages every week until you deem the amount is sufficient.''

There was a sudden clatter on the stairs and then the twins burst into the room. Both ran to Kate and pulled at her skirts, one on either side. "You're not really leaving, Kate, are you?" Emily asked, her voice trembling.

"You can't leave," Celia added. "We won't let you go."

Kate swallowed as she looked from one to the other. A suspicious brightness stood in Celia's eyes, and Kate felt answering tears threatening to overflow her own. Over these last few months, she'd earned Celia's respect, but she'd despaired of ever winning the child's affections. Now, it seemed, she had.

Loneliness swept over her. She didn't want to leave here, in spite of the bittersweet misery living in the same house with Nicholas brought. She'd miss the twins terribly. She'd miss Devona, too. And once gone, she was sure she'd never see any of them again.

"I must," she answered Celia softly. "I—we—I shouldn't be here," she floundered. "It isn't seemly." Most of all, she'd miss Nicholas, jackass though he was.

Celia gave her a glare to rival her cousin's. "We don't care what those old busybody women say! We want you to stay."

"Why can't you marry Kate, Cousin Nicholas?" Emily asked, leaving Kate's side and coming to his. She looked up at him. "Then, there would be no problem."

Nicholas heard Kate suck in her breath at his young cousin's words. He glanced at her, to see her face flushed, her breast heaving. As usual, wisps of her shining hair had come loose at the sides. Her eyes had taken on that sea-green shade that bothered him so much.

His breeches were tightening.

He eased his stance so his embarrassing condition wouldn't be obvious. Damnation! What was he going to do about this woman? If he had any sense at all, he would tell her to go. He would take her to Chestertown in the sloop himself. Help her find employment.

But he didn't want her to leave any more than the twins did. Neither did he want to wed her, even though he very much desired to take her to his bed.

Frowning at his dilemma, he put his hand on Emily's shoulder. He forced a smile, or maybe it was a grimace. "You are too young to understand these matters," he told her. "People do not marry each other merely for convenience."

The hell they didn't! Why was he saying these pompous things? Because he couldn't admit to the girls that he lusted after Kate—but didn't find that a strong enough reason to marry her? She wanted to marry him because of what he could ultimately offer her. That was the only reason she'd come to the Tidewater. In spite of her denials, he still distrusted her motives.

His scattered thoughts came to a stop.

Or did he?

Confusion swept over him. The woman standing before him was not playing a role. Even he didn't believe Kate that good an actress.

No, he couldn't convince himself of that, or that she had anything to do with what had happened a few minutes ago. She was truly willing to leave here, leave these children he knew she'd grown to love, because she thought it was the right thing to do.

And he needed her. What would he do with Emily and Celia if she left now? How could he give up the order and harmony she'd brought to his life?

But on the other hand, if she stayed, how much longer could he keep resisting his ever-increasing desire to bed her?

"Celia's right. I don't give a fig for what those women think," he heard himself say. "I want you to stay, Kate. All of us need you. We don't want you to go."

Chapter 17

Kate stared at Nicholas, her anger deflated by his swift change in mood. Had her impassioned self-defense caused it? Or the twins' tearful intervention?

And here were the twins, right in the middle of everything, as usual. "Emily, you and Celia should go back upstairs."

"Let them stay," Nicholas said. "They can hear everything we say anyway and they are also concerned in this matter."

She supposed he was right. She took a deep breath and looked at him again. "How can you ask me to stay when only a few moments ago you were accusing me of trying to force you into marriage?"

Nicholas looked uncomfortable and lifted his mug for a swallow of ale. "Perhaps I spoke out of turn."

Kate's eyes widened, her bewilderment turning into amazement. "Do I hear you aright?" she inquired. "You are actually admitting you might be wrong about something?"

Celia, still standing beside Nicholas, giggled. Emily, at Kate's side, followed suit.

Nicholas frowned at all of them. "I am saying that I would like for you to stay here, Kate," he said. "That is all."

"I will be leaving in another few months in any case," Kate pointed out.

"Not unless you want to. You were to stay here until spring to repay your passage. You may stay on indefinitely if you wish. I will pay you the wages you could expect to make as a shop worker."

"Oh, yes! Kate, please do stay!" Celia said urgently.

Kate looked down at her earnest little face, bemused. Now that Celia had let down her guard, it seemed that she was going to hold nothing back. Warmth flooded over Kate, making her smile.

Celia smiled back. So did Emily, who clapped her hands. "Oh! You are going to stay. I can tell you are!"

Kate's gaze met Nicholas's, and the warm feeling intensified.

For the first time since she and Nicholas had met six years ago, discounting those two incidents when his eyes had been full of lust, he was looking at her candidly, without that spark-filled friction that had always been between them.

"As soon as possible, I'll hire a woman to help you with the work," Nicholas said, beyond surprise now at what he was saying. He supposed these thoughts had been in his mind for some time. Otherwise, he couldn't be speaking them so easily.

He smiled at Kate, uncomfortably realizing how infrequently he'd done that.

Kate smiled back. Whatever had caused Nicholas's abrupt about-face, he was offering her what she most wanted. And what she most dreaded. What would give her the most pleasure. And the most pain.

"I don't give a fig what those women think, either," she said. "I will stay. At least for a while."

"Good." Relief went through him, mixed with disquiet.

He had solved one of his problems, for the time being anyway.

But Kate's decision to remain here had left him with another. The one causing his breeches to pull most embarrassingly in his lower regions . . . the problem that had given him many a restless night and would continue to do so.

But, given all that, he still wanted her to stay.

He cleared his throat. "I am glad that's all settled. Now I must go back to the barn." He turned and left.

Biting her lip, Kate watched him go, wondering if she'd made the right choice, after all.

"Are you going to stay here forever and ever, Kate?" Emily asked.

"Of course she is," Celia said, her voice very positive, as only Celia's could be. "She just said so. Come, Emily, we did not finish our game. And Edward is waiting for us."

Linking hands, the two girls went back outside.

Kate dumped out the remainder of the ale, then settled at the window again with her mending basket. Her hands froze on Nicholas's shirt as she saw the bloodstain and remembered what had caused it.

She'd just let herself admit, for the first time, her love for Nicholas. And how hopeless it was, because he would never love her in return. Maybe she was a fool, but she didn't feel that despairing now.

Nicholas had backed down from his accusations about her scheming to wed him and truly appeared to feel he'd been wrong. And that was ironic, wasn't it? She got up to rinse out the bloodstain before it set and ruined the shirt.

Because he was absolutely correct in his assumptions that she would gladly marry him.

If the circumstances were different.

She'd come to this Tidewater country to make him a good wife, to bear him children. But that had been only to fulfill her part of a bargain she'd proposed they make with each other.

Now, she was just as willing. Now she would marry him purely because she loved him.

If only he also loved her.

She returned to her seat and threaded her needle again. Only an hour ago she'd felt that could never happen. But in that hour, Celia had given over her love and trust to Kate. Nicholas had admitted he was wrong about his accusations. He'd asked her to stay on here even past the time of her indebtedness.

What other miracles might also happen, if she only waited for a while?

Kate removed the pewter plates from the supper table. "It seems passing quiet with the twins gone, does it not?" She heard the tautness in her voice and wondered if Nicholas did, too.

Two weeks had passed since that afternoon when the women had descended upon them. In the interim, Nicholas had made obvious efforts to be cordial. So had she. The atmosphere in the cottage when they were all together for meals and in the evenings had lost the kind of watchful tension it had held before.

Celia's newly revealed trust had lasted. She'd not rebuilt the barriers between herself and Kate. And the nightmares seemed to have gone for good. It had been weeks now since she'd had one.

That afternoon, Henry had sent his sloop to pick up Celia and Emily to stay the night and the morrow. The girls had been full of excited chatter as Kate helped them pack their small trunk for the long-anticipated visit.

Now that Kate knew what an unhappy household the Aldons' was, she felt reluctant to let them go. But it was none of her affair. Nicholas seemed to have no hesitations, and she felt sure the twins would be well treated. It was only his own family that Henry treated so abominably.

Kate's stomach tightened as it always did when she thought about the situation. And her own inability to help.

Kate had walked with the girls to the wharf, seen them off, and stayed to visit awhile with Tucker, trying all the while not to think about the undeniable fact that she and Nicholas would be alone in the cottage tonight.

It should make no difference. They'd been alone together every night since she'd come here, after the twins were asleep in their bedchamber.

But now that the time had arrived, she knew it did make a difference.

One kind of tension might have left—that consisting of distrust—but the other, the crackling physical tension between her and Nicholas, was still very much in evidence.

Nicholas sat at the table, finishing his ale. He glanced up at her. His dark eyes gleamed in the candlelight, telling her nothing of how he felt.

"Yes, the twins do keep it lively here."

Edward stood on his hind legs and put his front paws on Nicholas's thigh, meowing. Nicholas glanced down at him, then back at Kate.

"And it seems we are not the only ones to miss them."

"No."

Kate smiled again, hoping it hid her nervousness. Nicholas and Edward had become, if not exactly friends, polite acquaintances the last few weeks. Another thing to be happy about.

Her glance met Nicholas's and held. Kate shivered. His eyes seemed to probe her own. She turned away and quickly set about cleaning up the remains of the meal. Her back felt warm, as if Nicholas's glance were boring into her.

When she dared look his way again, she let out her breath in mingled surprise and what felt suspiciously like disappointment.

Nicholas was settled by the hearth, reading a book on wheat-growing. By now he should have it committed to memory. He was obviously prepared to spend this evening

as he always did. The absence of the twins, the fact he and
Kate were truly alone together, meant nothing to him.

Her face heated. Had she expected him to sweep her
off to his bed? Or take himself to the barn to avoid temptation? Did she think he'd been waiting, longing for this
opportunity?

A fresh surge of embarrassed color flooded her face.
She lifted her chin. She, too, would spend the evening as
she often did, going over the plantation accounts, a job
she'd recently taken on.

A few weeks ago, Nicholas had asked her to explain the
system she and her father had used in the shop. She'd
tried, but Nicholas hated paperwork. Kate rather enjoyed
it, so she'd volunteered to set up his accounts on this
system.

The kitchen tidied, Kate settled in her chair by the
hearth, ledger in hand. Edward stretched in front of them
before the fire, reconciled to the absence of his two favorite
people.

Every noise in the quiet cottage seemed exaggerated.
The fire hissed and popped. Kate was acutely conscious of
each rustle as Nicholas turned the pages in his book, of
her own small sounds as she scratched with her quill upon
the paper.

Finally, she closed the ledger with a snap. The sound
seemed loud to her oversensitive ears. She glanced across
at Nicholas.

He'd looked up at the noise. Again she could see nothing
in his dark eyes, on his handsome face, except perhaps
mild curiosity.

"How do the accounts look?" Nicholas hoped his voice
sounded calm and cordial, giving no indication of his inner
turmoil. *Kate* certainly felt no such disturbance. He should
be relieved. And of course he was.

She smiled. The curving of her full lips revealed a dimple
he'd never noticed before at the left corner of her mouth.

Somehow, it changed her whole appearance, softened her face.

"Good," she answered. "You have quite enough to purchase your wheat seeds."

Her voice was low and agreeable, pleased to tell him this good news. Why had he always remembered it as too firm, with none of these amiable tones he now detected?

He smiled back. In talking about the subject dear to his heart, he could keep his mind occupied, maybe forget his physical turmoil.

"That is, indeed, excellent news. I have high hopes for this crop. My neighbors will all be watching and waiting. If 'tis successful, that may persuade them to try something besides tobacco."

"And if it isn't?" Kate asked. She concentrated on their conversation, trying to ignore the way Nicholas's hands, outdoor browned, flexed and then relaxed on the book he held. Or how curly chest hair peeped out of his shirt where he'd unfastened the first few buttons in the cottage's warmth.

Nicholas shrugged. "If it fails, it will only make them more set in the old ways, more convinced than ever that tobacco is the only safe crop."

He didn't mention the most important result if his experiment with wheat-planting failed. But Kate knew. He would be in desperate shape.

Even if the current tobacco crop, winter-curing in the sheds, brought a good price in England, those profits would have to go to pay debts owed to the London factor and to keep the plantation going.

And, of course, there was no assurance tobacco prices would be good or that the crop would make it safely to its destination.

"Planting is such a hazardous way to make a living. I always thought our greengrocer shop was risky enough, but that was a sure thing compared to planting!" Kate leaned forward, her expression earnest.

Nicholas swallowed. The bodice of her blue gown pulled against her breasts, outlining their rounded curves in a most unsettling manner.

He nodded, forcing his eyes away from that delectable sight to a spot a few inches to the side of her face. "Yes, it is. One has to love plantation life to be able to endure it."

"As you do," she said softly.

Nicholas moved restlessly in his chair. He placed his open book on his lap to hide the undeniable fact that his body was responding in its usual way to Kate's presence. The very air of the cottage seemed filled with tension.

He couldn't stand another hour of this.

"I think I will go on up to my chamber," he said. Abruptly, he stood, forgetting his book. It slid off his lap onto the floor with a resounding thump.

Kate also rose. Her ledger made the same trip as Nicholas's book.

Edward leaped up and backed away, hissing at these threats to life and limb.

"Oh, how clumsy of me!" Kate bent to retrieve the ledger.

At the same instant, Nicholas reached for the book he'd dropped.

His hand closed over Kate's much smaller one. A charged tingle swept up his arm, as if he'd never before touched her, never felt her warm, smooth flesh beneath his own.

For a long moment he didn't move. He left his hand where it rested, enjoying the contact, the intensity of the feelings.

"I'm sorry. I'll just get the ledger." Kate heard the high, alarmed note in her voice as she tried to move her hand from under Nicholas's. When his hand had covered hers, a jolt had traveled up her arm.

Like touching lightning. And that was strange. Because

he'd touched her before, in a much more intimate way than this.

His hand didn't release hers. She glanced at him, her head tilted sideways, peering at his bent-down face. Her heart jumped in her chest because Nicholas's face held an odd, bemused expression.

She knew, then, that, like her, he'd only been pretending to be at ease this evening. And all during those weeks since that second time he'd almost carried her up to his bed.

Just as she had.

He still wanted her. As she wanted him.

At last, Nicholas moved his hand, picked up his book, and straightened.

Feeling his eyes on her, Kate closed the ledger, which had fallen open as it fell, then righted herself. She kept her eyes downcast.

"I believe I will stay downstairs a bit longer and catch up on the mending," she said. "Good night."

Her gaze was on his muscular legs in his tight black breeches. His feet, the metal buckles on his shoes twinkling in the firelight, remained firmly planted in front of her.

"Kate, look at me!"

No, she wouldn't look at him. For if she did, she would be lost. Instead, she'd walk away, get her mending, act as if this were an ordinary night like all the others before it.

She half-turned, and felt his hand on her arm. Again that jolt shot through her, and she gasped as he turned her to face him.

The intensity on his face frightened her, made her draw in her breath again.

"Let me go," she said breathlessly. "Please."

"Do you truly want me to do that, Kate? If that is what you wish, I will."

Kate knew he would. But she also knew he didn't want to. Any more than she wanted him to. And his question meant much more than what it appeared. If she admitted she wanted his touch, she knew as well as she knew her own name that tonight wouldn't end as those other two times had ended.

"No," she said. "No, I don't want you to do that."

She stopped and looked at him fully for the first time that evening. His dark eyes held depths she'd never before suspected. His mouth was slightly open, and she shivered, remembering the feel of his lips covering hers, taking hers.

"I want you to kiss me, hold me."

She heard his sudden intake of breath, saw a brief flare of light in his eyes before they again returned to that velvet darkness.

"Then that is what you shall get," he said hoarsely, pulling her toward him until her breasts were crushed against his hard chest. "All the long night long, my darling Kate, that is what you shall get."

He lowered his face to hers. She lifted her own to meet him. In the instant before their mouths touched, caught fire from each other, Kate had one clear, rational thought.

Whatever this night led to, she would take it and not be sorry or look back in regret.

Chapter 18

Kate's lips were warm and smooth beneath his own, as they'd been those other times he'd kissed her ... her rounded body as delicious as he remembered as he pressed her against him.

Her mouth was open enough to tantalize. He slid the tip of his tongue inside, his breath coming faster.

Kate opened to him, welcoming his probing tongue. As he plunged into that beckoning, honeyed space, mimicking those other movements, that other opening, he so desired from her, his body hardened with an instant swiftness.

All the pent-up frustrations of the past weeks and months swept over him, making his breathing harsh, his mouth crush hers, as his body was crushing hers against his hard chest.

God, how he'd wanted this—wanted her!

How had he waited so long? Why? All the reasons that had seemed so logical were swept from his mind the instant their hands touched and set them afire.

Now that he finally had her in his arms again, he never wanted to let her go.

She wore a day gown instead of the wrapper she'd had on those other times. It buttoned down the back, he soon discovered. The fastenings were too intricate to try to undo standing here beside the hearth.

And tonight he wanted no repetition of those other botched times. No, they must both understand what they were about—and consent to it.

His mouth left hers, and he drew back, looking down into her eyes. They'd darkened into an even more stirring shade than the sea foam—almost jade.

"I want you, Kate," he whispered, his avid gaze roaming over her face, her soft white throat. "I hunger for you. But you must understand what this means. Once we are upstairs in my bed, there will be no turning back."

"Yes," she whispered with no hesitation. Her lips still throbbed from his kiss, her body from his touch. And now her heart flamed with his words. "I know. I want you, too. I've always wanted you."

One part of her mind was shocked at her plain speaking, her revelations to Nicholas of her deepest feelings, of how long she'd desired him. But another part, the stronger one, pushed her on.

And this was the part she listened to.

She heard the hiss of Nicholas's indrawn breath as his arms went around her again to lift her as he'd done before.

"No." She stepped back, wanting nothing to be the same as those other times. "Let us walk up the stairs together," she said, her voice soft but firm.

His eyes darkened even more as he stared at her, then he nodded, as if he understood exactly what she meant by her request: That they were equal, together in this, sharing it all, taking full responsibility for everything that happened between them this night.

"All right."

He left her for a moment and carefully banked the hearth fire, then picked up the candle from the mantel and held it aloft.

"Let us go," he said, for all the world, Kate thought, as if they were a long-married couple going up to bed together.

The staircase was so narrow they either had to walk very close together or one in front of the other. Again, as if reading her thoughts, Nicholas took her hand and they walked side by side up the twisting flight, their bodies touching. With each touch and bump, Kate felt her heart beat faster, the blood warm in her veins.

At last they stood before Nicholas's closed door. He turned the knob and pushed the door open, and they walked into the bedchamber together.

The room looked far different than the first time she'd seen it. A blaze in the tiny fireplace welcomed them, and thanks to her ministrations, the room was neat and clean.

And the bed, spread with a colorful patchwork quilt, seemed to fill the room, to assume an importance far beyond its ordinary appearance.

Kate stiffened as she looked at it, her resolution faltering. What was she doing here? They hadn't talked, hadn't settled the things that still stood between them. She didn't belong here! She half turned to leave, only to be brought up short by Nicholas's hand falling on her shoulder.

She raised her head, knowing her expression must reveal her near-panic. Nicholas gazed down at her, and the look on his face stopped her tumbling thoughts and half-formed fears.

His dark eyes burned into hers, searing away her doubts until all that was left in her mind and heart was the love and desire she felt for him.

He placed the candle on the mantel, then came back to her. She moved into his arms as if she'd done that, too, a hundred times before, parting her lips in anticipation of his kiss.

Nicholas did not make her wait overlong before his mouth covered hers, his lips moving across hers, leaving heat behind wherever he touched.

"Oh, God, Kate," he whispered, his warm breath fluttering inside her mouth. "I have wanted you so long . . . from the first night you came here."

And what else? she burned to ask him. *Is there more to the feeling you have for me this night than the need of a man for a woman?*

But she didn't. She shied away from that. Maybe she didn't really want to know the answer.

Instead, she pressed her lips more firmly against his. She wrapped her arms around his waist, pushing her body against his until there were no more disturbing thoughts left in her mind to plague her.

Only feeling.

She felt his hands on her back, his fingers fumbling with the buttons of her gown, then the air cooling her flesh as the garment fell away from her shoulders into a heap at her feet, leaving her in her thin, cotton chemise. His hands, leaving fire where they touched her skin, slipped it off, too. She stood naked before him.

"You are so beautiful," Nicholas said.

The flickering flames behind her made her skin glow like alabaster, made the tips of her breasts as pink and fragile appearing as rosebuds beginning to open.

Created tantalizing shadows in the red-gold silkiness between her legs.

He hardened even more with a rapidity that startled him as he tore at his own clothing. Moments later, he, too, stood naked before her.

Kate stared at him, taking in every aspect of his male splendor: his strong body, well-muscled from the hard physical work he did every day, bronzed from the waist up, the curly mat on his chest catching gleams from the fire. Her gaze followed the hair as it narrowed and tapered, followed it still lower.

Her eyes widened as her glance at last came to rest on that portion of his anatomy that was pure, jutting male. She felt her heart racing in her breast. She'd known, of course, from pictures, paintings, what a naked man looked like. But the reality was far more than she'd bargained for.

"Well? Will I do?"

His voice was amused, yet there was a touch of anxiety in it, too, Kate thought. That evidence of his vulnerability, his wish for her approval, erased the last trace of her doubts, her fears. She smiled at him and held out her arms.

"Oh, yes, you do very well, Nicholas," she said, gasping softly as he pulled her against him.

If she'd thought their earlier embraces had ignited a fire between them, this, with their bare flesh meeting, melting together at every point of contact, made her feel as if she were truly on fire, incandescent with it.

"We are burning, burning," Nicholas murmured against her throat. He lingeringly, hotly, kissed his path down it, lower and lower until he reached her breast. His trembling increased when at last his mouth closed around that delicious rosebud nipple; his tongue laved it, teased it until he felt Kate writhe against him.

"Enough," she said hoarsely, pushing at his head.

Nicholas gave a low, satisfied laugh. "Oh, no, my sweet. We have only begun."

He raised his head, and once again his lips found hers in a deeper kiss. Their mouths and bodies locked together, he lifted her enough to clear the floor and carried her to the bed.

He stripped back the quilt and laid her between the sheets, where her gleaming body sank down into the feather bed, and he came down beside her. He was wildly aroused, more than he could ever remember being in his life. He didn't know how long he could wait.

Lying on his side, he pulled Kate to him so that his hardened length was fully against her, his aroused manhood pressing against her silky nest of curls. He felt her gasp into his neck as the tip penetrated a tiny bit.

One hand found her rounded buttocks and pressed her

even more firmly to him, while with the other he caressed her breasts, alternately kissing her mouth and her breasts until again she began to writhe against him.

"Are you ready for me, love?" Nicholas asked, his voice low and vibrant, rumbling warmly against her ear.

"Oh, yes," she breathed, glorying in the feel of their bare flesh meeting, pressing. Yes, she was ready for the ultimate joining, even though she'd never before experienced it.

Gently, he rolled her onto her back, then moved over her, supporting himself above her with his hands and knees. His eyes stared into hers, the dim, flickering light of the fire and the one candle darkening them even more.

The intensity of that dark gaze, his hard muscled body towering over her, frightened her, and a frisson moved down her spine.

What was she doing here, on this bed, letting a man who, up until very recently, had deeply distrusted her, make love to her? How had this come about?

Then, Nicholas lowered his head; his warm, seeking lips found hers again, and the moment passed. Kate opened her mouth to him, opened her body to him; and as his tongue found hers and thrust deeply inside, his manhood found the secret place between her thighs and made its own entry.

She cried out as he filled her, and she felt something inside her give way with a small, sharp pain.

Nicholas stilled, lying upon her, then raised his head and looked at her. A strange expression was in his dark eyes: Concern, mixed with something else she couldn't identify.

"Are you all right?" he asked.

The pain had stopped. Kate smiled at Nicholas, curved her hand around his neck. "Yes! I am fine." Drawing his head down to hers, she kissed him with a woman's full passion.

His answering kiss was hard and possessive. He gathered

her into his arms and thrust inside her again, gently this time. The pain had gone; Kate felt nothing this time but pleasure. Then, they were caught up in the rhythm that was older than time, moving together as if they were two parts of one whole.

A coiling heat built deep inside her, spiraling out from that core until it seemed to fill every part of her. The intensity grew until she thought she must surely burst from it; and when she could stand it no longer, she seemed to break apart into a million different pieces.

Wonderingly, she came back to herself. She felt Nicholas thrust inside her, harder and deeper than ever before; then he collapsed upon her breast, his breathing harsh and loud.

She held him to her, the sense of wonder still strong within her.

So this, then, was the act that happened between men and women in the dark, secret nights . . . that she'd often thought about, wondered about, told herself could not be so important as it was made out to be.

Now, she knew how wrong she'd been. She'd never dreamed that somewhere, hidden deep within her, lay coiled that secret heat, those feelings that were unlike anything she'd ever before experienced.

Nicholas raised his head and looked at her. Again with that odd expression in his eyes. "I'm sorry. I should have been more gentle. I didn't know that you'd never—that is, I wasn't thinking," he floundered.

Still caught up in the glory of what had just transpired between them, Kate had no idea what he meant, what was causing him this awkward embarrassment. Then, in a flash, she understood.

The other part of that look he'd given her, both during their lovemaking and now, had been surprise. Embarrassed heat flooded her own face.

He hadn't expected her to be a virgin.

The lingering wonder disappeared as if it had never been, replaced by the worst pain she'd ever known.

"There is nothing to be sorry about," she said, tightly, shrinking into herself, drawing away from him as much as she could. "I suppose it is I who should be sorry for my lack of experience."

Oh, Jesus, why had he said that? Nicholas castigated himself. She'd misunderstood him entirely. All he'd meant was that, in the glorious heat of their passion, he'd forgotten her virginal state.

He felt exceedingly foolish at that admission since her innocence was the reason he'd not made love to her before. Since she and Alyssa were from a respectable family, possessing Kate would make him honor bound to marry her.

At that thought of his lost love, he felt a twinge of what might have passed for guilt. Three months ago, he would never have believed that he'd be lying here in bed with Alyssa's sister.

And enjoying every second of it, wanting more.

Mother of God, but he'd never before experienced anything like what had happened between him and Kate! He'd never even known it was possible to feel as he'd felt.

"I'm sorry," he said again, moving off her to lie on his side facing her. "I didn't mean that as it sounded."

"And what other way could you mean it?" Kate asked, hiding her hurt, covering it with indignation. " 'Twas quite plain what you said."

Suddenly, she was very conscious that she was lying, completely naked, in Nicholas's bed. That she'd let him make passionate love to her, that she'd returned the love-making with every bit as much enthusiasm as he'd shown.

And now she knew, as she'd feared, that all it had meant to him was the slaking of his lust. Only a little while ago, she'd told herself she'd take whatever this night had to offer, would not regret anything that happened.

But, she'd been wrong. More wrong than she could have dreamed.

Tugging on the top sheet, she moved toward the edge of the bed. All she wanted now was to gather her clothes and flee to her own room across the hall.

Nicholas reached for her. "Don't go, Kate," he protested. "We must talk about this."

His hand grabbed empty air as she scrambled off the bed, taking the sheet. She flung it around her, then snatched up her gown and chemise from the middle of the floor and ran to the door, slamming it behind her as Nicholas reached it. The door caught the sheet, pulling it off her.

Abandoning it, Kate ran across the hall and into her room. She grabbed the broken chair and pushed it under the still-unrepaired door latch, then went to her bed. She sat a moment, anger and pain still flooding over her, and then reached under her pillow for her nightdress.

Out in the hall Nicholas stood, as naked as the day he was born, in his hands the sheet Kate had left behind, listening to the sounds from her bedchamber, knowing what they meant.

Damnation! Did she think he was an uncivilized barbarian? That he'd force himself in if she didn't bar his way? She must.

Anger at himself creased his brow into a frown.

How had the most wondrous thing that had ever happened to him ended like this? And so soon afterwards? And what could he do to make things right between them?

The hall was chilly. Absently, Nicholas wrapped the sheet about him. What did he mean by making things right? Did he now intend to ask Kate to marry him? As he knew he should.

Yes, most assuredly so.

He had taken a virgin from a respectable family. The older sister of the woman he'd been betrothed to for five long years. Only weeks ago, he'd warned himself that if he gave in to his lust, these were the consequences he would have to face.

And that was why he hadn't given in—until tonight. He

had had no wish to wed Kate. Only to bed her. Because she didn't love him. Because he didn't love her.

Did he still feel this way? Did she? If so, why had their lovemaking been such a sublime experience, at least to him? Far beyond the physical. Lost in thought, Nicholas let the sheet slip until he realized his backside was cold. He wrapped up again.

He didn't know. All he was sure of was that he certainly had the most intense desire to bed her again. Often. And that could not be unless they wed. No, he'd not skulk around in his own house seeking Kate's favors.

Even if he would, he had no reason to think she'd be agreeable to such an arrangement. Even though she'd enjoyed the lovemaking. He had no doubt of that. She was a lusty wench, even if this were the first time she'd ever been with a man.

If he married her, his bed would no longer be cold; his nights would be full of repetitions of what had gone on there this eve. At that thought, he felt his manhood rise, pushing up the sheet draped across his middle.

He listened, but heard no more sounds from Kate's chamber. She must have gone to bed. There was no sense standing here in the drafty hall. No use knocking on her door. Not tonight.

By tomorrow she'd have calmed. They could talk. He'd explain what he'd meant and again apologize. He'd ask her to marry him. And surely, she would accept. After all, her only purpose in coming to the Tidewater had been to wed him. He had no reason to believe she'd changed her mind.

But as for tonight's events, he could not, in good conscience, blame Kate for seducing him into taking her to bed.

Even if her motives were still to entice him into wedding her, she'd not handled that part of it very cleverly, running off in offended wrath so soon after.

No, he'd been as willing as she. They'd simply been

drawn together by the strength of their desire for each other.

He heard a noise on the stairs and glanced over. Edward poked his head over the top step, then made his way to Kate's door where he scratched for admittance.

Nicholas's spirits brightened. Maybe she'd open the door to get her cat and they could still talk this out tonight before the twins arrived home.

Edward scratched again and meowed loudly. Nicholas heard the scrape of the chair being removed from under the door, and then it cautiously opened.

"Come, Edward," Kate said and the half-grown kitten scuttled inside.

She glanced up to see Nicholas standing before his open door. Behind him she saw the rumpled bed in which only a few minutes ago she'd lain in his arms. Embarrassed heat flooded over her again.

Why was he standing there like that with the sheet half falling off him, his bare chest exposed, his strong legs, his . . .

Kate drew her breath in, pushed the door closed, and firmly replaced the chair under the latch.

Edward wrapped himself around her ankles, purring loudly, and she absently stroked him. Nicholas had not only looked handsome and appealing and a little ridiculous, he'd also looked unhappy . . . as if he felt as miserable as she did about the outcome of the night.

Doubts assailed her. Maybe she should have stayed and talked this out with him.

Talked *what* out? Nicholas had made it crystal clear in what light he regarded her and what they had shared.

To her, what had happened between them had been a wonderful, magical experience.

To Nicholas, it had been nothing more than the kind of thing men found with women they paid for their satisfaction.

And it was her own fault. From that first night, she'd

come willingly into his arms, needing no urging. She couldn't say with any truth that he'd seduced her. Both the other times when they'd not fulfilled their passion, she hadn't been the one to stop them.

Nicholas had.

Her face flamed in the dark night. Small wonder he'd thought her no maiden. She'd been a fool again. The biggest fool imaginable.

Yes, in spite of her many warnings to herself, she'd fallen into the trap that had been yawning for her ever since that first night she'd arrived here. And the pit was deep, the sides slick, with no footholds to help her scramble out.

Now that she and Nicholas had made love, now that she knew how wonderful lovemaking was, would she be able to resist him the next time?

She knew the answer to that.

Her mind was no match for her traitorous body. It had managed to convince her brain that tonight was inevitable. That she wouldn't regret whatever came of it. She smiled wryly, her heart paining her.

She'd regret it all the rest of her life!

And there was only one solution. The one she'd known from the beginning. She must leave here. No matter what she'd promised the twins. They would probably never understand, but she couldn't help it.

She'd stay until Nicholas got his wheat crop in the ground, until he had a little money laid aside to hire a woman to care for Celia and Emily.

Then she would go to Chestertown. Or farther away than that would probably be better. Never again see these three people who had come to mean more to her than anything in the world.

And she would leave her heart behind her when she went.

Chapter 19

Devona opened the library door, then stopped just inside, her heart slamming in her chest. Henry sat behind the big desk, papers spread before him. She hadn't known he was here. She'd thought he'd left for the day long before. But her husband's presence hadn't caused her physical reaction.

Morgan was in the room, too, standing by the big window overlooking the lawns, just as he'd been the night of her birthday celebration. And now, for the same reasons, she was as afraid as she'd been then.

She nodded at Morgan, not making eye contact, but even that brief glimpse was enough to make the blood rush through her veins as she remembered the last time she'd seen him. The day she'd been out riding and he'd found her.

Oh, the things he'd said! That he'd never marry, never have children except with her. She felt her face redden and hoped Henry didn't notice.

She looked at Henry, making her gaze as bland as possible. She had no business in his library, his pale, cold gaze told her.

"I—I wanted to see if new candles were needed in here," she said. She'd come to read, thinking Henry gone and Becky and the twins happily playing.

"You know my housekeeper tends to that, as well as all the other details of keeping my house in order," Henry said, his voice as icy as his eyes.

My housekeeper. *My* house. Henry never missed an opportunity to show her how unimportant she was to him. Purely an ornament. And a vessel in which to satisfy his lust.

"Of course." With loathing, Devona heard her own voice, dead and dull. "I will leave you two gentlemen to your business. Good day, Morgan."

She gave Morgan the tiniest smile possible to be polite, her gaze trying to slide over him, to make her escape as fast as possible. She drew in her breath at the expression on his face.

His blue eyes were fastened intently on her, blazing with feeling. A muscle moved in his cheek, signaling his tension.

Oh, God, had Henry seen that look? She jerked her gaze away and quickly left the room, afraid to glance at her husband again. She hurried upstairs to where the three girls were playing in Becky's bedchamber and stayed to join in their game.

Listening tensely, in a few minutes she heard the library door open again, then the massive approach front door open and close. Then the sound she dreaded most. Henry's feet on the stairs.

In a few moments, he stood in the doorway, his face impassive. Becky looked up from her game, her pretty face taking on the artful, beguiling expression which Devona so detested.

"Oh, Papa!" Becky said, jumping up and coming over to slip her hand in his. "Thank you for allowing Celia and Emily to visit. We are having such a grand time. Must they go home tomorrow? Couldn't they stay another day?"

Henry gave her a condescending glance. He patted her head. "No, Rebecca, that will not be possible this time."

Becky stuck out her lower lip and looked up at him from under her lashes. "Oh, please, Papa."

Henry's look hardened; his voice turned to ice. "Rebecca, you are forgetting all our lessons. I have already told you *no*. That is the end of it."

The child's face changed, the smile wiped away, a fearful look coming onto it. "Yes, Papa," she whispered. "I promise I won't forget again." Her shoulders drooping, she went back and sat down beside the twins.

Devona clenched her hands into fists at her sides. Henry was turning her daughter into the kind of female he preferred. Indulged precisely as far as he wanted to go, and no further. Making sure she learned his word was law. By the time she was grown, she'd be fit to marry no one except another man like Henry.

"Devona, come with me."

Her heart lurched at Henry's tone. Was he angry because she'd invaded his sacred library? She hoped it was only that and he hadn't caught the look Morgan had given her.

If he had, what would he do? What might he have already done? Ordered Morgan out of the house? Relieved him of his command of the *Rosalynde*?

She followed Henry to his bedchamber, fear and dread growing with every step. She stood just inside the door, waiting. Henry closed the door and seized her arm in such a hard grip Devona cried out. She muffled it instantly, not wanting the girls to hear.

"I saw that dying calf look Lockwood gave you," Henry said silkily. "Why did you come to the library, Devona? I wasn't expecting Morgan. He had no appointment. Did you think I would be safely out of the way and you could meet your lover?"

His hard fingers bit deeper into her arm.

She bit her tongue to keep from crying out. This was

even worse than she'd feared. Of course, Henry *would* think something like that!

She shook her head.

"Of course not," she said, forcing her voice to remain low and seemingly calm. "I did not see any look your captain gave me except polite friendship."

He grasped her other arm and pulled her around so that she was facing him.

"Look at me!" he commanded. "Now lie to me again if you dare."

Swallowing, Devona moved her head up. Henry's face was a mask of controlled fury. Fear seized her in a harder grip than that of her husband's hands.

"I do not lie," she said, her voice trembling. Even while hating that sign of weakness, she realized it would work to her advantage if she broke down. Henry loved her complete humiliation and subjugation.

"Then why did you come to the library? Surely you do not expect me to believe the excuse you offered. And not for a book, I hope. You know we discussed that long ago. I won't allow you to waste your time on useless literary pursuits. That is not the reason I married you—for your intelligence."

He made it sound as if she possessed none at all, but Devona's fear was too great now to care about any of that. She would sacrifice her reading, one of her few pleasures, if that would relieve his suspicions.

"Yes, I was after a book," she said. "I often come to the library to read."

Please, she prayed, let him take the bait. Let him believe me and forget about Morgan, not punish him for something he hadn't done.

Henry's icy stare bored into her, making her shiver. "Now, that is a pretty confession, is it not? After all these years, I find you've been disobeying me. From now on, I must lock the door when I am out of the house and give

my housekeeper the key. With express orders not to give
it to you.''

Her fear was still so great that what he said didn't even
bother her. He'd accepted her story. Maybe it would be
all right and he wouldn't pursue this any further.

But she was wrong. A frosty smile curved his mouth.

''I believe what you have said because it is not in your
nature to be deceitful. But that has nothing to do with the
fact my captain gave you such a look as men give only to
the women they are bedding.''

Her heart froze in her chest. She knew her expression
was stricken, would damn her in his eyes. Even if his accusations were false, the feeling he'd detected in Morgan's
look was all too real.

She shook her head. ''That is ridiculous. How could that
be? I am never out of this house alone.''

''I see you are not denying the charge,'' Henry said, still
in that low, silky voice which was worse than if he'd shouted.
''Only trying to convince me there was no opportunity.''

''That isn't what I meant,'' Devona floundered, digging
herself in deeper, as he intended her to. ''Morgan has
never touched me.''

''That may be true,'' Henry said in a moment. ''You did
not return his yearning look, I was happy to note. Perhaps
all this is on his side only. After all, Lockwood is only a
pup! Not a real man as I am.''

Henry pulled her closer to him, putting a rough hand
under her chin to tilt her head up so that her eyes had to
meet his.

Then his head lowered, he pressed his mouth to hers
in a hard, hurtful way, crushing her lips, grinding them
beneath his own, forcing her to open her mouth so that
he could plunge his tongue deep inside.

With a tremendous effort of will, Devona kept from
gagging, from crying out again. She endured the kiss, and
finally Henry released her, pushing her back from him
until she staggered and nearly fell.

He gave her a sneering, satisfied smile. He never seemed to notice that she didn't, couldn't, respond to him. Her subjugation always seemed to be enough.

"I don't intend to do anything about this," he told her. "Not at present. Lockwood is too capable a captain to discharge for this reason. Let him moon over you if he likes. I will enjoy seeing his unrequited desire."

Henry's face lost its smile. "But if I ever see you returning one of those looks, if I ever see him touching you, that is a different story. Then I will see to it that he never again finds a ship to captain. I will ruin his name, his reputation, everywhere. Do you understand me? Do you believe me?"

Devona nodded, her throat too dry to speak. Oh, yes, she understood him. She believed him. He could and would do exactly as he threatened.

"Good. Now you had better get back to the children and play your little games with them."

"Of course," Devona answered, her voice wooden. She turned and left the room, knowing Henry watched her with satisfaction.

Knowing that tonight he'd come to her bedchamber. He would hurt her to prove once again how manly he was.

Her spirit shrank at that prospect, and she shuddered with anticipated dread. But, as she had so many other times, she pulled herself together.

She could endure. She must—for Becky's sake.

Chapter 20

Kate hurried to get breakfast finished before Nicholas came in. She'd like to dish it up, leave it for him, then go back upstairs, but his breakfasting time varied—he might be another half hour.

She had no intention of talking to him about what had happened between them. An almost sleepless night hadn't changed her mind about that.

It would be too dangerous to talk to him, to let him near her. Before she knew it, in spite of her anger at both herself and him, he'd have persuaded her to share his bed again.

And if she did that, soon she'd be no better than that delegation of women had thought her. That *Nicholas* thought her.

No, she had to leave here, the sooner the better. How would she get through the interim, seeing Nicholas every day, every night? She'd spend no more evenings sitting around the fire with him, she decided. That way lay nothing but trouble. A noise at the door made her raise her head.

Nicholas came inside. Their eyes met and Kate felt her

skin redden before she quickly glanced away. Memories of last night washed over her. How wonderful, magical, that time between them had been!

Why couldn't he have shared her deepest feelings? Why couldn't he have truly loved her?

"Good morning," she said, a catch in her voice. She quickly turned back to the hearth to begin dishing up the breakfast.

"Good morning." Nicholas walked to the hearth and hung his cloak on its accustomed peg, giving Kate a wary, sideways glance. Her profile looked set and firm and her color was heightened. Not good signs.

He cleared his throat. "Kate, we have to talk about last night."

She carried a dish of vegetables to the table, then glanced at him. "No, we do not," she said, her voice as firm as her expression.

Nicholas's glance traveled over her, remembering how she'd looked when she stood so gloriously naked before him. He'd lain awake most of the night reliving their time together. Even now his body hardened at these erotic thoughts.

He'd spent the morning pondering while he worked. There was no reason to believe that Kate had grown to love him. Or he her. But they most assuredly got along well together in bed. A short while ago, he'd thought that not enough for marriage.

But that was before he'd possessed Kate, known the full delight of their lovemaking.

Yes, he would ask Kate to marry him. He'd do it now, this morning, while they were still alone. Their feelings would deepen as they grew to know each other. Didn't that often happen between married couples?

"We must," he insisted. "We cannot leave things as they were. We have to—"

"We don't have to do anything," Kate interrupted. "Come, sit and eat your breakfast before it gets cold."

She turned back to the hearth. A moment later she gasped as Nicholas's warm body pressed against her back; his firm hand removed the pot from her hand and deposited it on the hearth.

"Oh, yes, we do." He turned her to face him. As she'd feared, she felt herself weakening as the warmth of his hands traveled up her arms. Turning her head to the side, she tried to avoid looking at him.

But one hand left her arm, cupping her chin, tilting it up so that she had to. His brown eyes were troubled looking, with dark circles under them, as if he'd slept no better than she.

"Kate, I did not intend to insult you in any way last night."

Kate fought the weakness his touch engendered. Another few minutes and she wouldn't care what he said or what she answered. All she'd care about would be his arms around her, his lips on hers.

She twisted out of his grasp.

"How could you think what you said would not insult me? It would insult any woman!"

"But all I meant was I had forgotten you were a virgin. I did not want to—"

"You did not want to take a woman to bed who might obligate you in any way. I well know this. You've told me enough times how averse to marriage with me you are. And I've told *you* the same!"

"No! That's not at all what I was going to say. You aren't listening to me. You're twisting my words. Are you trying to make me angry?"

Kate heard the frustration in Nicholas's voice, knew he was holding onto his temper with effort. And she also knew he was right. She *was* trying to make him angry.

Because anger was her only defense against the way he made her feel.

Her unreturned love for him.

The last thought strengthened her resolve. "That is

never a difficult task to accomplish, is it? Almost anything seems to anger you."

His face hardened. He released her chin and stepped back.

Good. Let him become angry and storm out. If he were wrathful with her, she need not fear her weakness with him.

"I see you are determined to misunderstand everything I'm trying to say."

Kate shook her head. "No. You haven't said anything yet that is possible of misinterpretation."

"Damnation, woman! You are enough to try the patience of a saint!"

Kate tilted her head, putting a falsely cool smile on her mouth. "And we both know that under no circumstances would you ever be mistaken for a saint."

With a visible effort, Nicholas calmed himself. "All right. Have it your way for the moment. But we are going to talk, Kate Shaw. And soon. Don't forget that."

She turned away to resume dishing up the breakfast. Finished, she headed back upstairs, her head erect, her spine very straight.

Frowning fiercely, Nicholas watched her go, then seated himself. He looked at the steaming bowls on the table, his usually hearty appetite gone. Kate was sorely upset. Surely, she hadn't meant all of what she said—that she wouldn't consider marrying him. He must give her time to calm down.

But not too much time. Damn it! She *was* going to listen to him!

He pushed his chair back and left the table, and then the cottage.

Kate reached the top of the stairs, realizing she was waiting to hear Nicholas call her back or come after her. She stalked into her bedchamber and smoothed the bed.

Was she such a fool she couldn't stick with any sensible decision regarding Nicholas?

It was a good thing he hadn't come after her. She might very well have given in again since her feelings for him were so strong.

Finished with tidying, she glanced out the half-open door into Nicholas's chamber across the hall.

The bed was still tumbled, the bedclothes half on the floor.

Her face flooded with color as again, for the dozenth time, she relived those moments in Nicholas's arms.

She hurried across the room and closed her door, then put the broken chair under the latch. There! She'd wait until he left for the barn again before she went downstairs.

And if his room got tidied today, it would be by Nicholas, not her.

"Devona! I was hoping you'd come, but not really expecting it."

Kate gave the four people on the doorstep a wide smile and stood aside to let Devona and the three girls enter, her heavy heart lifting a bit.

She'd indulged in a frenzy of housecleaning since breakfast to try to keep her mind off Nicholas, with the result that the cottage shone. A fresh cloth covered the table; a bowl of catkins and snowdrops rested in the center.

"Neither was I." Devona smiled back, removing her cloak. She glanced at the girls, already engrossed in the magical dollhouse, then lowered her voice. "Henry was called away to Chestertown on business."

"I'll make tea," Kate said, getting down the pink-flowered teapot, her happiness in seeing Devona dampened. Devona had dark circles under her eyes as if she'd slept little, and Kate had glimpsed a dark mark on her neck, like a bruise.

"That would be nice," Devona agreed, hanging her cloak on a peg.

A few minutes later, the girls outside, they sat across from each other at the table. Kate poured the tea, and as Devona took her cup, their glances met. Kate drew in her breath at the look in the other woman's eyes. A frightened, desperate look.

"What's wrong?" Kate asked without stopping to think. "Tell me."

Devona swallowed visibly. Finally, she nodded. "I have to tell someone. I can't stand it otherwise. And I trust you, Kate."

"I hope so," Kate answered. "As I would trust you."

"Henry saw Morgan looking at me yesterday," Devona said in a rush, then paused. "I know that sounds ridiculous, but Morgan . . ."

It was Kate's turn to swallow. So what she'd been so afraid of had happened. Should she reveal her awareness of the attraction between Devona and Morgan? Yes. It would do no good to dissemble now. Devona needed help and comfort.

"I understand," Kate said. "I—couldn't help but see something like that at your birthday celebration."

Devona gasped, her eyes widening. "Oh, I'd never thought . . . did anyone else see?"

Kate didn't know, but her friend needed no more worries. "I don't think so."

Devona took a large swallow of tea, then lowered her cup. "Nothing has happened between us. And nothing ever will. But of course, Henry isn't sure of that. He's threatened to ruin Morgan if I so much as look at him. And with Morgan the captain of the *Rosalynde* . . ."

She paused, looking down at her cup.

"He'll be at your house often," Kate finished.

"Yes." She glanced up at Kate, her expression anguished. "It's an impossible situation! I don't know what to do!"

"Is Morgan aware that Henry knows?"

"I don't think so. Confrontation isn't Henry's way. Not with other men, anyway. He'd rather keep this secret until he can realize some advantage from revealing it."

It was, indeed, a bad situation. Kate took a long swallow of her own tea to delay her answer while she tried to think of something reassuring to say. Nothing came to mind. Devona was very intelligent. She couldn't be fooled with false reassurances.

Finally, Kate looked over at the other woman. "I don't know what to say except you must somehow warn Morgan that Henry knows."

Devona nodded, her expression despairing. "And that will be impossible! From now on, Henry will be watching me like a hawk. When he finds out I came here today, I'll pay for it." Her hand went to her throat, fingering the dark mark on her white skin.

Inwardly, Kate winced at the thought of the lovely woman sitting across from her suffering more abuse. "Do you trust Daisy? Could you give her a note to slip to Morgan?"

"I trust Daisy, but I'm sure from now on, when Morgan comes to the house, Henry will be waiting for something like that."

"Maybe I can do it," Kate mused. "I could ask Nicholas to invite Morgan to supper."

And how would she explain that to Nicholas? Never mind, she'd think of something. Devona had to have help! "Why don't you write a note and leave it with me?"

The other woman's face lightened as hope rushed in to replace the despair. "Oh, that's a wonderful idea. I'll do it right now."

Kate rose and found her a sheet of paper from the precious sheaf she'd brought with her from Plymouth. She watched as Devona hastily scrawled a few lines, folded it, and then handed it to Kate.

"I'll seal it tonight," Kate told her, slipping the missive safely into her deep apron pocket.

She poured more tea, feeling a bit awkward. Did Devona want to talk further about this? Confide in her about her feelings for Morgan?

Devona reached across and patted Kate's hand as if reading her mind. "I think I love Morgan," she said simply. "But I will never tell him so. That would only make things worse. And besides . . ."

She paused, her soft features firming, hardening, then gave Kate a wry smile. "I don't know if it would make any difference now even if I were free. After Henry, I'm not sure I could ever trust any man again."

"Oh, Devona," Kate said, softly. "I'm so sorry. I don't know what to say."

"There's nothing to say. Or do. And now, I've talked about my own problems long enough. What about you? You look like me—as if you didn't sleep much last night and something is worrying you. Would you like to talk about it?"

Kate blinked in surprise. Apparently her own face was as transparent to Devona as the other woman's had been to her. And yes, she, too, needed a confidante. But how could she tell Devona her problems? Why not, though? Who better than Devona, who'd not judge her, condemn her for anything?

"Nicholas and I made love last night," Kate said, her words as rushed as Devona's had been. No, *she'd* made love, she amended silently. Nicholas had merely enjoyed her body.

Devona smiled. "I'm so happy to hear that. I felt you two were right for each other the first day I saw you. Of course, I don't know what your sister is like, but I believe you and Nicholas belong together."

Kate shook her head. "No, that's not true." She swallowed. She may as well be as honest as Devona had been. "I love Nicholas, but he feels only lust for me."

"How can you be sure? I've seen how he looks at you."

"I'm sure. He was . . . surprised I was a virgin. He

expected me to be experienced! He wasn't prepared to deal with anything but a night's romp.''

And the promise of future repetitions. But she couldn't bring herself to admit this.

''Oh.'' Devona's smile faded. ''But don't you think if you two talk it out with each other . . .''

''No! There's nothing to discuss. He as much as said he'd never have taken me to bed if he'd thought of me as any different from some tavern wench he'd pay for his satisfaction.''

Kate couldn't help the angry bitterness in her voice. But most of the anger was directed at herself for willingly putting herself in this position, for being such a fool as to go to bed with Nicholas when she'd always known he didn't love her.

Devona patted Kate's hand again. ''Kate, I still think you're wrong. I know what lust and only lust, without any kind of love, is like. That is what Henry feels for me. Nicholas does not look at you as Henry does me.'' Her voice was very positive.

Kate could not repress a shudder at the thought of Henry being compared to Nicholas. No, of course Nicholas didn't look at her like that, but . . .

''If he cares for me, why didn't he tell me so? And why did he say those things?''

Devona's pretty mouth twisted. ''Who knows why men do things? Sometimes I think they are past all women's comprehension. I understand Morgan not a whit better than I do Henry. He's vowed to love only me—never marry and sire children except with me.''

She put her hand on her mouth and glanced at Kate. ''Oh, I shouldn't have said that! But I am so afraid Morgan may do something truly rash. Something that will get him killed by Henry.''

Now Kate reached over to touch Devona's hand where it made a fist on the tablecloth. ''I know how you must feel, but I believe Morgan can take care of himself.''

Devona heaved a sigh, forcing a smile as she glanced across the table at Kate. "You are no doubt right, and now that we've both poured out our souls to each other, shall we talk of more pleasant things?"

The door opened suddenly. "Mama! Come out and watch me skip the rope!"

Devona's smile became natural as she rose. "Shall we go outside for a while?"

"Yes." Kate got up, too, and followed her new friend outside. The day was warm and pleasant. It didn't seem like the middle of February. She was constantly amazed at how fast the weather could change here in this Tidewater country.

They sat together on a small wooden bench outside in the sunshine, talking of everyday things, and watching the three girls play.

No one seeing them would have suspected Devona lived a secret life of sadness and fear. Or that Kate's heart felt close to breaking over Nicholas. She shifted and heard the crinkle of paper.

The note to Morgan in her apron pocket. She was about to deliberately deepen the intrigue surrounding Devona and Morgan and Henry.

The thought scared her, but she'd do anything she could to help Devona. As she was sure the other woman would help her if she could.

Pain twisted inside her. No one could help her now. She'd gotten herself into this situation of her own free will, knowing she was risking all.

But she hadn't known how much her heart could ache!

Chapter 21

At the sound of horse's hooves, Nicholas raised his head from his repairs on the weaving shed.

Who could that be? Any of his acquaintances coming here would have traveled by boat.

A swarthy, dark-haired stranger on a bay gelding, dressed in black breeches and a tan coat, rode toward him, pulling up a few feet away.

"Good day," the man said, giving Nicholas an affable smile.

"Good day," Nicholas replied warily, although he didn't know why. The man looked harmless enough.

He dismounted and walked to where Nicholas stood by the shed, smiling as he glanced about him. "Place seems to have gone downhill a bit since last I was here."

Nicholas gave him a surprised look, his hand still grasping the hammer he'd been using. "I don't believe we're acquainted."

There was something about this stranger that made him uneasy, although he couldn't put a finger on the reason.

"No, we're not. I'm Bradford Hayes. Lydea's brother."

A jolt shot through Nicholas. He stared at the other man. He knew Lydea had a brother who'd left home a long time ago and hadn't been heard of since. She'd thought him dead. But his name had been Bradford, Nicholas remembered.

And although this man didn't resemble Lydea, that didn't necessarily mean anything. Nicholas had never seen her parents. They'd been dead for years when he came to the Tidewater.

He stepped forward, extending his hand. "I'm Nicholas Talbot, Lydea's husband Philip's cousin."

The man who'd said he was Lydea's brother grasped Nicholas's hand briefly, then released it.

Nicholas didn't like his handshake, either, although again he didn't know why. The other's grip was firm enough.

Nicholas took a breath, his forehead clammy.

"I'm sorry to have to tell you that your sister and her husband both perished in a fire that destroyed the manor house nearly a year ago."

Time didn't make talking about the tragedy easier, nor help assuage his guilt.

A shocked, grieved expression spread over the man's face. "Then I'm too late! I stayed away from my dear sister too long!" He lowered his head to his outspread palms, his shoulders shaking.

Nicholas watched him, wondering why he couldn't believe the other man's grief was real. But then, what proof had he offered that he was truly Lydea's brother? Other than giving the right name and seeming to be familiar with the plantation?

Finally, the man raised his head. Tears ran down his face. His very dark eyes looked wide and shocked and grief-stricken. He reached inside his coat, and when his hand came back out, it held a small black book.

"I carried this with me all during my travels," he said, his voice shaking. "Even during my stretch with old Iron

Head Forbes, when our unit was ambushed by bloody savages near Ft. Duquesne. Lydea gave it to me the day I left. She was only a child, then. She wrote our names inside.''

He held out his hand and Nicholas took the volume, seeing it was a well-worn Bible. He opened the scratched leather cover, and the inscription leaped out at him, faded but clearly legible.

To my beloved brother, Bradford. Carry this wherever you go. And come back home safely. With all my love, Lydea.

Nicholas stared at the words so long they blurred before his eyes. Lydea had often helped with the plantation accounts so he was very familiar with her handwriting. This was indisputably hers. Finally, he handed the Bible back to the man.

To Bradford Hayes, Lydea's brother.

''I'm sorry you never saw her again,'' Nicholas said. The man had proved his identity. Why couldn't he warm up to him?

Hayes carefully replaced the Bible in his coat. ''You can't know how sorry I am. Are there children of the union between your cousin and my sister? Have I any family left?''

Another shock traveled over Nicholas. This was the twins' uncle. A man much closer to them in blood ties than himself. With more of a claim to them if he chose to press the issue. Especially since Nicholas had never been appointed their legal guardian, but had just assumed the duty.

''Yes, there are two girls, Celia and Emily, twins, eight years old,'' Nicholas answered finally. ''Let's put your horse in the stables and go to the house so you may meet your kin.''

As they walked to the cottage, Nicholas's thoughts were sorely jumbled and disturbed. This man, he realized, not only could claim the twins, but also his share of the plantation. More than that.

Since the partnership agreement papers had burned

in the house fire, Hayes could contest Nicholas's claim. Perhaps successfully.

But Hayes had been gone for years, without even so much as writing to his sister. He'd apparently been involved in the French and Indian Wars, and who knew what else. He wasn't likely to want to stay here in this quiet backwater place.

But he was certainly giving the plantation a once over, his brows raising at the empty buildings, the absence of workers.

Nicholas's eyes narrowed. "We've had a run of bad luck. The last tobacco crop was lost at sea and a storm damaged many of the buildings."

Hayes turned to Nicholas, giving him a sorrowful look. "So that is why things are so run-down. I'm sorry to hear that. But I'm sure you're doing all you can to bring my dear nieces' plantation back to its former glory. I am so eager to meet my only living kin."

A warning signal went off in Nicholas's head. Something in the man's tone had sounded mighty possessive. And as if he, Nicholas, were merely a servant here. He'd better let him know how things stood.

"Of course I'm doing all I can to look out for the twins' future, but the plantation is also half mine," he said, keeping his voice even. "I was an equal partner with Philip and Lydea."

Hayes nodded, his expression unchanging at this information. "I understand. Of course. Why else would you still be here?"

Instead of reassuring him, Hayes' words put Nicholas more on the defensive. "I'd be here in any case to take care of my young cousins."

The other man gave him a sad smile. "You have performed an unselfish and noble task. But now that I am home again, your duties and responsibilities will be eased."

Nicholas stiffened. Hayes' last words left no doubt that

he meant to stay. And despite his conciliatory tone, something told Nicholas he also intended to take over.

That would never happen! And Nicholas didn't intend to let this man settle in without trying to find out more about him.

The twins were outside the cottage, playing with Edward. They stopped when they saw the two men, their eyes wide with interest.

Nicholas drew in his breath, hating what he must say. "Celia, Emily, this is your uncle Bradford, your mother's brother."

Hayes hurried toward the twins, holding out his arms to them. "My dears, come and give your old uncle a hug!"

To Nicholas his words sounded falsely hearty. For one thing, the man was far from old. He must have been quite young when he left to start on his wanderings.

The girls looked surprised and hung back for a moment, then moved forward and allowed him to pull them into the circle of his arms.

"What a pretty pair you little girls are," he said.

His smile was too fond, almost doting. Wasn't he overdoing things a bit? Nicholas knew he should feel ashamed of himself for these thoughts. The twins were all the family Hayes had left. But he couldn't.

Nicholas heard a noise from the cottage and turned to see Kate standing in the open doorway, wiping her hands on her apron. She wore her everyday green cotton dress and her hair was a little mussed, those tendrils that couldn't stand confinement curling around her ears. Her face was rosy, her odd eyes very green.

She looked delectable.

They still hadn't settled the misunderstanding from the night they'd spent together. Nicholas quickly veered his thoughts away from that. The thought of those moments when Kate had been in his arms made his body warm, something inside him soften.

Devona had brought the twins home yesterday and had

stayed for dinner, so there had been no chance to talk then. In any case, he'd planned to wait a bit, after his and Kate's quarrel. Last eve, Kate had avoided his glance during supper and retired to her chamber when the meal was over and the kitchen restored to order.

But today he'd planned to linger after dinner, send the twins outside, persuade Kate to listen to him. To agree to marry him.

Now, with this stranger here, obviously intending to stay, everything was changed. Damn the man!

"Kate, this is Bradford Hayes, Lydea's brother," he told her.

He saw the startled look in her eyes before he turned to Hayes. The other man was giving Kate an appreciative glance, Nicholas saw, displeased.

"Hayes, this is Mistress Katherine Shaw, who's—" He paused, floundering as he sought a way to describe her presence here in his household.

He couldn't say *my future wife,* not when he hadn't even proposed to her yet. "—helping out around here," he finished lamely.

Hayes stepped forward and gave Kate a sweeping bow. "Mistress Shaw, I am most honored to make your acquaintance," he said, smiling at her.

"And I, yours." Despite her embarrassment at Nicholas's awkward introduction, Kate smiled back, dipping a curtsy.

Nicholas hadn't known what to call her position in the household. How about My Woman For one Night? Or My Would-be Mistress? she asked him silently. Now, *that* would have made this man's dark eyes pop out.

What was Lydea's brother doing here? Kate hadn't even known such a person existed. Nicholas had never mentioned him, nor had the twins. And Nicholas's jaw muscle twitched; his mouth was set—he wasn't happy about the situation.

"Dinner is ready," she announced, turning to Bradford

with another smile. "You are very welcome to share the meal with us."

"Thank you, mistress," he answered. "I would be more than happy to do so. If the appetizing aromas wafting out the door are any indication, you are, indeed, a most accomplished cook."

Kate blinked in surprise, her smile widening. "Thank *you*, sir," she answered. "Let us hope you're not disappointed."

She led the way inside and served the meal, glad that she'd cleaned the cottage so thoroughly yesterday. She wasn't ashamed for a stranger to be seated at the snowy-clothed table, with its still-fresh centerpiece.

While they ate, Bradford held forth with tales of the French and Indian Wars, in which he'd been wounded. The long, newly healed scar on his arm attested to that. He complimented her lavishly on the meal, exclaiming over every new dish he tasted.

Which was more than Nicholas did. No, his glowering looks were almost as bad as that first day she'd arrived. What ailed him? She knew he was still determined to talk to her, still wanted her to share his bed again, and that her avoidance of him kept him angrily frustrated. But this was something more than that.

She wouldn't think about Nicholas. That way lay only trouble. She turned her attention back to the stranger. Bradford was not only well-spoken, but a good-looking man, with his black hair and nearly black eyes, his dark skin and muscled body. More than once, she caught his gaze on her, openly admiring. It was nice to be admired, even if she weren't the least interested in him.

"Will you try some of the oysters?" she asked, gratified when he handed over his plate with alacrity. She gave him a generous portion, returning his smile and watching as he took a large bite.

"This is ambrosia, Mistress Kate!" he proclaimed, his rich voice rolling over the syllables.

Keeping his eyes on his plate, Nicholas fumed at Hayes's absurd behavior. Flattering Kate until she blushed like a strawberry! And the man's grief for his sister seemed to have dissipated very easily and swiftly.

Nicholas glanced across the table, managing for the first time since the meal started to catch Kate's eye. "Bradford will be staying on," he told her. "It will be necessary for you to move in with the girls and give him your chamber."

There! See how much she liked the boasting knave when she was turned out of her room to accommodate him.

"Oh, I cannot take your chamber, Mistress Kate," Hayes protested. "If there is no room for me in the house, I'll sleep in one of the haylofts. Many a time I did that as a boy."

Nicholas wondered what the man would do if Kate agreed to that suggestion. Turn around and head out of here to find another war in which to fight and brag about afterward?

"I wouldn't think of such a thing," Kate assured him. "The girls' chamber is large. There will be ample room for all of us."

She gave Hayes another warm smile and Nicholas's stomach lurched. What was wrong with Kate? Why was she taken in by this man's oily flattery, his equally overdone smiles?

Nicholas's thoughts abruptly stopped their roiling, surprise replacing his anger.

Why was he feeling, acting like this? Why was he so upset over Kate's behavior? One would think he was a jealous, possessive husband!

Kate's husband he was not, although he planned to be. Soon. And of course, he would expect Kate to be faithful. That went without saying. And this emotion he felt must, indeed, be jealousy.

The idea mightily displeased him. He'd never considered himself the jealous type. And it had made him rashly offer Kate's room to Hayes to pay her back for enjoying the man's attentions.

An action Nicholas now regretted. He frowned darkly.
He didn't want the man here at all. And he especially
didn't want him sleeping across the hall from Kate. But
this was his, Nicholas's, fault. Nothing he could do about
it now.

"Good, then that is settled," he said finally.

"Let me give you another portion of beef and gravy,"
Kate urged Hayes.

"I would be most happy to partake of that."

Hayes passed his plate again. He glanced at the twins,
sitting side by side across from him. "My nieces are very
fortunate to have you here to care for them."

Nicholas's frown deepened. The man wasn't missing any
opportunity to ingratiate himself with Kate. And everything
he'd said was true. Kate *was* a wonderful cook and a loving
companion to the twins. Nicholas had long known that,
even though he'd told Kate little of how he felt.

Another thing he now regretted.

Surely, she wasn't truly attracted to this stranger sitting
across from her. No, he couldn't believe that. More likely,
she was only pretending, deliberately trying to make Nicholas
las jealous. If that were her aim, she'd roundly succeeded.

With an effort, he erased his frown, replacing it with a
smile. "Yes, we are all very fortunate to have Kate here."

Surprise shot through Kate at his unexpected words, the
smile that had replaced his frown. "Thank you."

What had suddenly come over Nicholas? A few moments
ago he'd been as black as a thundercloud. Now, he was
echoing Bradford's words of praise.

Maybe it would be a good thing to have this man here
for a while, Kate thought as she gave him another generous
serving and handed the plate back.

In only a few minutes, his presence seemed to have made
Nicholas appreciate her more than he had in all the time
she'd been here. And what did she care about that? She
wouldn't be here much longer. It didn't matter how Nicholas
las felt about her.

Oh, what a liar she was!

She cared, too much. Every time she looked at him, she remembered the night they'd shared. Remembered his hands and lips caressing her, loving her . . .

No, not loving her.

All the loving had been on her part. And that was why she must leave. But no matter how far away she went, how much time passed, she'd knew she'd never be free of the memory of his touch, the memory of that night.

She'd never, ever be free of wanting, loving Nicholas.

Chapter 22

"Oh, how I used to tease your mother!" Bradford said. He chuckled richly, smoothing back Emily's hair. The girls sat at his feet before the hearth.

"Were you mean to her?" Celia asked.

Her voice sounded hesitant, yet eager to hear more, Kate thought. She glanced up from her ledger, from her own seat before the fire. Celia's face looked eager, too, as she leaned forward in rapt attention.

No wonder. Lydea's brother seemed to have an unlimited supply of stories about when he and Lydea were children together, here on this plantation.

Evenings after supper had fallen into this pattern since Bradford arrived a few days ago. All of them sitting around the hearth, she occupied with mending or the accounts, Nicholas reading, Bradford holding forth.

The twins couldn't get enough of the stories, especially Celia. He was an accomplished raconteur, making his tales come alive, Kate admitted grudgingly.

Grudgingly? Yes. She couldn't deny it. Nor understand her reaction, either. Bradford had fitted into the household as if he'd always lived here, instead of being away for more than fifteen years.

Maybe that was what bothered her. After such a long absence, shouldn't he have had some problems adjusting? Especially since he'd apparently left because he wanted no part of plantation life.

But maybe he'd only wanted to sow some wild oats before he settled down. Whatever his reasons for leaving, he obviously intended to stay now that he was back.

He was a good looking man, too. Kate's speculative glance rested on his laughing face as he gave the twins all his attention. He turned his head just then and his glance caught hers.

She saw an appreciative gleam in his almost-black eyes as he smiled at her. Kate smiled back, although she felt uncomfortable. That way he had of looking at her bothered her, too, although she couldn't in all conscience complain about it. It couldn't even be called flirting; it wasn't that overt.

But once in a while she caught something else behind the charming smile, something predatory gleaming at her out of his eyes, like a wild animal might look at you.

Right before he devoured you.

Kate let out a gusty sigh at her imaginative flights of fancy. As she turned back to the accounts, her eyes collided with another pair—this time Nicholas's.

Her heart skipped a beat at that contact, even though Nicholas certainly wasn't giving her a charming smile or appreciative look. He wasn't smiling at all. His mouth was set in a straight line.

Ever since Bradford's arrival, Nicholas had been exhibiting all the symptoms of an acute case of jealousy. But, of course, that wasn't possible since he didn't love her. Most likely it was only male pride involved, of which he had aplenty.

Nicholas suddenly stood. "I need to go check on the sow," he said. "I think she's coming down with an ailment.

Kate, will you come with me, since you have a good deal of knowledge about home remedies.''

Kate's glance turned into an amazed stare. What was he talking about? She'd never even looked at the farm animals when they were ailing, let alone tried to dose them with anything. Recovering herself, she shook her head. "I don't know—"

"You cured the twins' coughs very quickly not long back," Nicholas interrupted.

"Oh, well, but I know nothing about the animals," she protested.

"That doesn't matter. Sick creatures are sick creatures, human or animal. Come along with me."

His voice sounded as if he didn't intend to take no for an answer, and a suspicion began to form in her mind. Did Nicholas want to get her out of the cottage, alone with him? She tried to dismiss the notion as she reluctantly arose and laid the ledger on the table. After all, if he still harbored that intention, he'd had opportunity before now.

And she didn't want to be alone with him. Oh, yes, she did, she admitted, but it was too dangerous for her.

"Is Alfreda sick?" Emily asked as her cousin's words penetrated the spell Bradford had been weaving. She scrambled to her feet along with Celia.

"Let Emily and me come, too!" Celia said.

Nicholas shook his head as Kate plucked her shawl from its peg. "No, no, you girls stay here. I'm sure it isn't anything serious."

The twins said no more, but Kate saw their worried looks. Alfreda was due to pig soon, and the girls went out to feed her choice tidbits every day and to check on her progress.

Kate gave them a reassuring smile, but they still looked worried, she thought, following Nicholas to the door.

Behind her, a chair scraped on the floor. "Do you need me to come along?" Bradford asked. "I haven't dealt with a sick sow for a while, but . . ."

Nicholas gave him a quick glance. "No, that isn't necessary."

Relief spread across the other man's face as he settled back down into his chair. "Then I'll just stay here with my nieces."

Hayes never let a chance pass to mention his relationship with the twins, Nicholas thought, letting Kate precede him out the door. He closed it behind them with more force than necessary. And the man professed such interest in the running of the plantation, yet avoided work whenever possible. Nicholas's inquiries in Chestertown had produced nothing. No one had seen the man prior to his arrival at Lydea's Pride. He certainly appeared to be Lydea's brother.

Yet Nicholas still distrusted him.

Nicholas's coat-clad arm brushed against Kate's shawl, making him want to move closer to her so that more than their clothes touched.

Damn! But he wanted her. This last week had been agony, and tonight, watching those almost leering looks Hayes gave her, he'd decided he must not delay longer.

Whether Kate's temper had cooled or not, he must talk to her. Quite obviously the man considered Kate unattached and ripe for the taking. Nicholas's mouth firmed.

That wouldn't be true after this night!

Hayes had told Nicholas he planned to stay here, taking over his share of the plantation. What beyond that wasn't yet clear. If he tried to obtain legal guardianship of the twins, Nicholas intended to fight him every way he could. And maybe he'd lose. But one thing he knew.

Hayes wouldn't get Kate, too!

They were going to talk this whole thing out. He would make Kate listen to him. He would tell her that he wanted and needed her in his life and that she must marry him. Although he had no reason to think she'd grown to love him, surely that declaration would move her.

Nicholas gave her a sidelong glance, wondering why

he'd ever thought her unattractive. Maybe Kate didn't have Alyssa's blonde prettiness, but she had something far better. True beauty—and not only physical. Kate's beauty shone from deep inside her. She was good and kind and generous. She had a temper, too, he admitted. But then, so did he.

"What appears to be the trouble with Alfreda?" Kate asked into the silence.

Her voice sounded strained. He wondered if she'd rather have stayed with Hayes. She seemed to like the fellow well enough. Maybe too well. Uneasiness hit Nicholas. Had he waited too long to declare his intentions? No! He wouldn't let himself entertain such thoughts.

"It's difficult to say exactly," he hedged, moving closer. He didn't want to scare her off, but the temptation to stop right here on the path, beneath the stars and the moon, and crush her into his arms was almost overpowering.

In truth, there was nothing wrong with the sow, a fact he hoped wouldn't anger Kate so much she wouldn't listen to him when she found it out. "She just, uh, seems not to be as sprightly as she should."

Kate shot him an exasperated glance. "You most likely wouldn't be sprightly either if you were soon to give birth."

Nicholas blinked at her plain-speaking, but then smiled. That was one of the things he enjoyed about Kate. Unlike most of the silly young Tidewater women he knew, there was no artifice to her.

"That's probably true," he conceded, gratified that her expression softened into a smile, too. They'd almost reached the barn and he began worrying about how he was going to handle this. Pretend the sow was truly ailing for a while longer, he decided. That would no doubt be best.

The full moon shone through the big barn doors Nicholas had left open, revealing Alfreda lying on her side in the cow stall that had been converted to her use.

Soundly and contentedly asleep.

"See, does not she appear to be having trouble with her breathing?"

Kate moved up beside him to look over the top of the stall. Gazing down at the somnolent animal, her suspicions about Nicholas's motives in bringing her out here grew. If ever an animal looked to be in perfect health, this one did.

"I see nothing wrong with her."

They were standing so close together her sleeve touched his. Part of her wanted to move away and another part wanted to move nearer. Much nearer.

"Perhaps I was wrong," Nicholas said. "But I would not want anything to happen to her. The girls would be broken-hearted."

Kate tried to concentrate on his words, to ignore his nearness and that they were alone together in the night, in the shadowy barn which smelled of animals and sweet hay.

"Remember that first night I arrived?" she asked him. "You stopped the wagon and went tearing after the pigs and the twins chased after you. I thought you were so mean!"

He gave her a surprised look, even while relief coursed through him. Maybe she wouldn't be angry, after all. Maybe this wasn't going to be as difficult as he'd thought. But he still had to go slowly.

"You did? Just because I was trying to get the pigs back to the barnyard?"

She nodded. "Yes. Of course, that wasn't the only thing that had happened . . ."

Her voice trailed off and she looked uncomfortable. No, Nicholas thought, that certainly wasn't all that had happened that first night. He'd been so angry and his pride badly hurt. But even with all that, he'd kissed Kate, taken her into his arms. Had some part of him, even then, known that someday, not too long in the future, he'd want to marry her?

Nicholas abruptly realized there was no way to ease into what he planned to say to Kate. No way to lead up to it. He had to plunge right into the middle.

"Kate, there is nothing wrong with the sow," he said into the silence. "At least as far as I know. I wanted to get you away from the others. You know we have to talk. We can't leave things as they were that night. . . ."

Now his own voice trailed off and he squirmed inwardly, remembering how they'd left things. But he also remembered how she'd felt in his arms, so soft and warm. Nay, not warm. Burning hot, she'd been. And he, too. And over and above that, he'd felt something else.

Contentment. A feeling that they belonged together.

He thought he saw the same feelings, the same memories, on Kate's face as he looked at her, but then her features firmed and she moved away.

"I don't see that we need to talk about anything. Both on that occasion and another one, you expressed yourself and how you felt about me rather completely."

"No, I didn't," Nicholas said, moving toward her. She backed up again and he followed until they were in front of an empty stall. "You wouldn't let me."

Alarm shot through her. He was too close. And just as she'd feared, his nearness was making her forget all the reasons she must not give in to him. Desperately, she tried to concentrate on them, but there was only one that mattered.

He didn't love her.

That knowledge made pain knife through her, giving her strength. "You got what you wanted from me once," she said tightly. "But that doesn't mean it will happen again."

As she'd hoped, a spark of anger glowed in his brown eyes. Anger was her only defense against him.

"I thought the feeling was mutual. You seemed to enjoy our—" He paused, then continued. "—experience as much as I did."

The knife twisted deeper. He couldn't bring himself to call what had happened between them lovemaking. Of course not. Because, just as she'd always known, it wasn't that to him.

She let her lip curl, hastily lowering her eyes. He'd read the truth there. She wouldn't be able to hide it.

"That doesn't matter," she said dismissively. "I'm going to leave here. Just as soon as my debt is fulfilled and you have someone to care for the twins."

"So the pleasure we found together meant nothing to you?" Nicholas asked, moving closer. "You can leave here without a backward look?"

Kate sucked in her breath at his words, his tone. Her plan was turning on her. That spark in his eyes hadn't been ire. Instead of angering him, she'd hurt his masculine pride in his sexual prowess. Still not looking at him, she shrugged.

"Of course I'll miss the twins," she said, ignoring his first question, trying to draw his attention to her answer to the second. "I've grown to care for them. But now they have their uncle. He seems to be fast winning their affections."

She heard Nicholas's sharp intake of breath at her last words. But then his hands, hard and warm, settled on her shoulders.

"Look at me, Kate," he demanded, just as he had that other night. "And tell me you felt nothing when I held you in my arms."

The warmth of his hands was spreading through her shoulders, down her arms, taking her, as his evocative words were also doing, back to that magical night. She couldn't meet his eyes and tell him those lies.

She kept her head down, and one of his hands left her shoulder and cupped her chin, gently tugging upward. Slowly, Kate's head lifted.

Nicholas's firm-featured face was only inches from her own. She smelled his scent from the hand that still securely held her chin, blended with the fragrance of the sweet hay around them.

Languid heat began spreading inside her, making her forget the reasons she mustn't let this happen again, persuading her it was all right to lift her head, part her lips. . . .

Let him pull her into his arms and cover her mouth with his. Oh, yes, this was right. It was so sweet. So wonderful. How could she resist him?

"Oh, God, Kate," Nicholas rumbled into her mouth, his body hardening, his fierce desire for her flaring again, just as it had those other times when she'd been in his arms.

Desperately, he tried to hang onto rationality, the fact that they hadn't settled any of the problems between them. But Kate's sweet mouth moving beneath his own, her soft warm body against his, swept all thought away. He plundered her mouth, then moved lower, trailing a rain of hot kisses on her tipped-back neck.

The stall door behind her moved inward with the sound of creaky hinges. Kate staggered and fell into a pile of fresh hay, Nicholas coming down half on top of her, his mouth never leaving hers.

The stall door closed again and the hay rose up and enveloped them like a warm feather bed, making a dark, secret nest. Kate's body felt so hot beneath his own, even through her clothing. Her heat inflamed him further, if that were possible.

He tried to slow down, not rush this, but his body urged him on. And Kate's kisses, her movements, were as urgent as his own. Feverishly, Nicholas pushed her skirts up, fumbled with his breeches. Kate moved her thighs apart and Nicholas entered her, swiftly and hotly.

She gave a moan of pleasure and moved with him, her breath heavy and panting, as was his own, until finally, as he plunged within her, with one final hard thrust, he felt her quivering with release as his own release came deep inside her.

He collapsed on her breast, feeling her rapidly beating heart, in tune with his own, gradually slow. Again, that sense of deep contentment filled him. Kate felt so right in his arms, as if she'd always been there. He wanted to keep her there forever, never leave this enchanted place.

He rolled to his side, bringing her with him, holding her close against him as his own heart slowed, as his contentment brought a pleasant drowsiness. He hadn't slept well lately. Scarcely at all. He'd been strung up so tight he couldn't relax. But now, in the afterglow of their lovemaking, in the shadowy, warm stall, his tired body slept.

"Wha—what?" Nicholas felt himself being roughly shaken and shook his head to clear it. Then gazed up into Kate's snapping green eyes as she bent over him, her hand on his shoulder.

"Wake up. I'm not going back to the cottage alone." She straightened and stood stiffly erect.

He still felt traces of that drowsy fulfillment, but obviously Kate felt nothing of the sort. What was wrong with her? He searched his mind. No, he'd said nothing out of the way this time.

He hastily adjusted his clothing, noticing that Kate averted her eyes, and stood, brushing bits of straw and hay from his garments.

He reached for her hand to have her move quickly back, snatching it out of his reach.

"Don't touch me!"

She sounded almost hysterical. Confused, Nicholas stared at her. "What is the matter with you?" By all rights, she should still be lying on the fragrant hay, snuggled warmly against him, as satiated and drowsy as he. Instead, here she stood, spitting at him like a cat.

"What do you *think* is the matter with me?" she demanded. "Once again, I've let you have your way with me! And in a barn stall!"

Nicholas frowned. "I don't care for your choice of words.

You did considerably more than that. You gave every appearance of enjoyment.''

His frown deepened as he remembered what she'd said earlier. "Or is this another incidence of your memory failing you, Kate?"

She looked abashed, then firmed her mouth. "No, it is not. I am ashamed of myself. I was raised to be respectable, Nicholas, as well you know. Not tumble in barns like some tavern wench."

Hot color flooded her face. "So, whatever you think of me, I deserve it. If not earlier, then certainly now."

Nicholas heaved a great sigh. He ran his hands through his disordered hair. "So we're back to that, are we? Kate, don't be a fool. Listen to me. All this is very simple to straighten out. You must marry me."

She stared at him, her face blanching of color. She stood like that for what seemed forever to Nicholas as he waited expectantly for her answer.

"Oh!" she said finally, her voice even more outraged than before. "So now you think you must do the honorable thing, do you, Nicholas Talbot? Had your way with the wench twice, so now you must marry her!"

"Will you stop saying those asinine things?" Nicholas roared. "Of course I feel obligated to marry you. I am a decent man!"

"And I am a decent woman, despite what you may think of me!" she roared back. "And you don't need to make the supreme sacrifice of wedding me to salve your delicate conscience!"

She jerked around and marched to the door, leaving Nicholas staring after her. As his anger slowly seeped away, chagrin replaced it.

Damnation! Again, he'd said all the wrong things, told Kate nothing of how he felt.

No wonder she'd been so angry. But then, she'd been no more sensible than he. And he still didn't know if she were merely angry with him or if it went deeper than that.

He still didn't know how she felt about him—or he, her. That they had a most powerful physical craving for each other was obvious. That was what caused most of the problems between them at present.

He wasn't sure how he felt about her and, for all he knew, she could despise him.

Outside the barn, Kate smoothed her hair and took deep gulps of the fresh night air. Humiliation flooded her again. She'd like to kick Nicholas!

He'd looked so smug and superior—so, so *reasonable*—when he made her that offer of marriage! Just as if she were a hysterical child he must calm! And then stood there with that expectant look on his face, positive she'd fall at his feet in gratitude!

Well, why had she expected anything else from him? Hadn't that pig-headed brain of his, from that very first day she came, held only one thought? That she desperately wanted to marry him? That she'd go to any lengths to secure that objective?

She firmed her lips and, hoping her hair and dress wouldn't reveal what had just transpired in the barn, hurried back to the cottage.

Once there, she hesitated, smoothing down her skirts again, pulling her shawl over her shoulders, then opened the door. Bradford stood by the hearth, his hands behind him, studying the eagle on the mantel.

The twins were not in evidence. Gone on to bed, she thought, relieved. As would she, right now. She closed the door and came into the room.

Bradford turned toward her. "And how is the pig?" he asked, his eyes making a lazy survey of her from head to foot.

"Nothing serious, I think," she said, swallowing at the knowing look she seemed to see in his dark eyes. She couldn't stand it if he guessed what had happened between her and Nicholas!

"But Talbot is staying with her?" Bradford persisted, and now she seemed to hear something sly and knowing in his voice, too.

Kate's spirit quailed. Yes, there was definitely something there that seemed to say he knew exactly what had gone on in the barn, why her hair was mussed, her clothes not as tidy as when she'd left.

"Only for a little while," she answered. "I am going to retire. Good night." She headed for the stairs without looking at him again.

"Good night, Kate."

His voice lingered on her name, insinuatingly, and her teeth clamped together.

She gained the tiny hall and let herself into the twins' darkened bedchamber as quietly as possible.

"Is Alfreda all right?" Celia's anxious voice said out of the dark.

Kate's hands were already busy on the buttons of her gown. "Yes, she's fine," she answered, forcing her words to come out evenly, not show her agitation. If she did, Celia, who was very sharp about such things, would pounce on it and be sure Kate was lying about the health of her pet.

"Good," Emily's sleepy voice said. "We were worried about her."

Kate slid out of her gown and shift and found her nightdress hanging on its peg. As she carefully eased herself to her usual position between the twins, she heard the cottage door open, then close.

She tensed. Nicholas. She heard a rumble of voices as he and Bradford talked, then in a few moments, steps on the stairs. Nicholas? Or Bradford?

Her tension increased. She truly didn't expect Nicholas to come barging in here, did she?

Of course not, but just the same, relief made her muscles

weak when the steps didn't even pause outside this door, but went on to the one across the hall.

Her old chamber. So it was Bradford, after all. What was Nicholas doing? Standing by the fire? Congratulating himself that he'd managed to do the honorable thing, and wouldn't have to go through with it after all? Preening because once again, she'd fallen into his arms like a ripe piece of fruit?

Kate changed positions, trying to turn off her whirling, chaotic brain. How could she have gotten herself into such an untenable position? Why had she ever come to this Tidewater country? Why hadn't she stayed in Plymouth where every day was the same, predictable and dull and safe.

Because, even then, she'd loved Nicholas Talbot, she admitted to herself. Yes, she had. She'd loved him from the first moment she'd seen him.

And that was why she hadn't protested Alyssa's decision to break her troth. That was why she'd gone along with her sister's ridiculous scheme. Why she'd staunchly kept telling herself those weeks before she sailed here that things would work out. That Nicholas would get over his love for Alyssa. That he'd accept Kate as his wife.

Oh, the irony of it! Nicholas had, indeed, only a few minutes ago, asked her to wed him.

But never, by word or deed, had he said that he loved her. Or that he no longer loved her sister.

Chapter 23

Damn it! Where was the bloody fool? They were supposed to meet deep in the woods, off the riding trail.

But this trail kept going on forever with no end in sight. And he was tired of riding. He'd never liked it that well, anyway.

Suddenly, he saw someone ahead, off to the side, half hidden by bushes, and reined sharply. "There you are! Thought you'd changed your mind."

"How are things going?"

"Smooth as silk. Talbot hates my guts, but he's accepted me as Lydea's long lost brother. Having that Bible did the trick. That, and my acting ability."

"No, my telling you what to do every step of the way was what did it. You'd have done nothing but come here and look for a handout if not for me."

"Say now! That's about enough of that. If I hadn't known Hayes, found out all about his family and this Godforsaken plantation, it wouldn't have worked in a million years. I've even got the wench on my side." He licked his lips and grinned slyly. "Won't be long now until I have her in my bed."

"Stay away from her. It will only complicate matters."

"Wait a minute. My private life is my own affair. You stay out of it. If I want to have a little fun on the side, I'll do it."

They stared at each other, gazes locked.

"Don't worry. I won't tell her anything but the lies I need to tumble her."

"See that you don't. Now listen closely. We're ready for the next step. I want you to go hunting with Talbot tomorrow."

"Hunting together? Why? I get enough of him without that. You didn't tell me I'd have to work my guts out here. That this stupid Talbot had freed all his slaves and now he works harder than any of them."

"We haven't time to fight with each other. Stop whining and listen to me. You must persuade Talbot to come out here with you."

"Why? I don't understand this."

"You don't have to understand. All you need do is bring him here. I'll handle it from there. After tomorrow, neither of us will have to worry about Talbot."

"What do you mean? You planning to do him in?"

"I told you not to concern yourself."

"Now, wait a minute. Nothing was said about murder when we made our agreement. I'll have naught to do with that. If this is what you intended all along, I'm leaving. Right now."

"Fine. Go. Be the feckless fool you've always been. Starve awhile longer. Give up your one prospect for a life of ease and plenty."

Another silence fell as they stared at each other.

"Even if you pull the trigger, I'll be blamed. As well you know."

"No one will think it anything but an unfortunate accident. Hunting accidents happen all the time. What would *you* have to gain by killing Talbot? The entire community knows you're Lydea's brother, come home to stay. And to lay claim to the estate. Talbot would have far more reason to kill *you*."

"Why do you want him dead?"

"Alive he can cause us much grief. Contest your claim to the property. Try to get the courts to demand more proof of your identity than an inscribed Bible and your tales of the old days with your sister and her family."

"I don't like this. I've got a bad feeling about it."

"You don't have to like it. Only do as you're told. Tomorrow morning at first light."

"That will be a delightful way to start the day." He watched as his partner melted back into the underbrush. No, he didn't like this business. Too many things could go wrong. He had to go along with it, though. He'd come too far now to leave, to give up this chance of a lifetime.

But he was tired of being bossed around.

After tomorrow, he'd have some leverage on his side. Something he could hold over his partner.

Then he'd see who ran things.

Nicholas tramped along through the woods toward the duck blind. He hadn't particularly wanted to go hunting with Hayes, but they could do with some wild birds on the table. And maybe the two of them could become better friends.

Friends? Nicholas glanced at the back of the other man's dark head. As usual, he was meticulously, almost foppishly, groomed, even if they were only going to sit in the chill early morning fog with no one else around. Nicholas knew he was fooling himself. They could never be friends. He disliked the man, distrusted him, for no good reason other than instinct.

And the stalemate with Kate wasn't helping his temper any. Since that episode in the barn two nights ago, she'd had nothing to say to him, avoiding him as much as possible.

Damnation! What was he going to do about it? Let her leave here when her debt to him was paid? If he had any sense, he'd do just that. Because obviously, they'd never be able to get along. Except in bed.

Aye, there they pleased each other surpassingly well! And *Kate* pleased *him* in many other respects, too, he'd finally realized. He liked her spirit, her kindness—her essential goodness. She would make an excellent wife, as she'd promised the first day she arrived. And a loving mother to the twins.

And he was fully prepared to make her a good husband. But apparently, *he* suited *her* not one iota—except, he amended again, physically. His proposal of marriage had insulted her even more than the words she'd taken such offense to earlier.

Nicholas frowned. His brain told him to let her go. There were other women here in the Tidewater who'd make him adequate wives. *Adequate.* He hated that word. He didn't want any of them.

He wanted no one but Kate.

And, he admitted, he still intended to have her. He heaved a sigh, knowing that again he'd have to wait until her temper cooled. And then he would guard his tongue, his temper, and give her a proper proposal. The kind he supposed every woman wanted.

On his knees if he had to, he granted, reluctantly. He could do that. What he hated was the blasted waiting! He'd already done too bloody much of it!

They'd almost reached the blind by now. Nicholas moved closer to Hayes to tell him so, and then he heard a sound off to the side, a crackling of dried leaves, and turned quickly.

From behind him, a musket shot cracked in the early-morning stillness.

Nicholas whirled. What was Hayes doing? There was nothing to shoot at yet.

Then he saw that the other man clutched his arm, blood

seeping from between his fingers. His gun had fallen at his feet. A look of stupefaction was on his face.

Disgust swept over Nicholas. The idiot had shot himself! "How bad is it?" Nicholas asked, not able to conceal his irritation.

Hayes's expression changed from surprise to anger. "I don't know," he grated.

One would think the man would be embarrassed, rather than angry, at this display of total ineptitude. Especially since he was a former soldier.

"Here, let's get your coat off and take a look." Nicholas helped him ease the coat sleeve from the arm. The bullet had scraped a shallow tunnel. "Only a flesh wound. "How in hell did you manage to do that? I didn't even see you load."

"I don't know." Sullenly, he struggled into his coat again and turned to Nicholas. "I guess that ends my hunting for the day."

"Yes, you need to go back and bandage that. But now that I'm here, I think I'll stay and try to get a bird or two."

Hayes nodded. "Kate can help me."

A spasm of jealousy shot through Nicholas. He well knew Hayes had been smelling around Kate ever since he came. He'd welcome a chance to get her alone.

"On second thought, I'd better go back, too, in case your wound is worse than it looks. You might need my aid."

Hayes's expression became tinged with surprise at Nicholas's offer. "I'll be fine." He picked up his musket and began walking back the way they'd come.

"Just the same, I'll come along." Nicholas fell in beside him.

At the cottage, Kate was predictably horrified at the sight of Hayes with blood seeping down his sleeve onto the hand which still clutched his arm. She found cloth for bandages and carefully washed the shallow wound. The twins stood nearby, wide-eyed with interest.

Nicholas watched her slim, nimble fingers, feeling their gentle touch on his own body, trying not to think about how much he wished she were touching him. It would be worth getting shot to have Kate touch him like that!

She carefully avoided looking at him, he noted, just as she had these last two days. She was still angry with him. His warm feelings mixed with a surge of determination.

When she went to the door to throw out the pink water from the basin, he followed. Instead of waiting for Kate to move, he squeezed alongside her.

"We're going to straighten this mess out. You can't avoid me forever," he told her in a low voice as he passed.

Nicholas felt her start. Damnation! He hadn't phrased that well. Not like the oily, well-spoken Hayes would have.

He went on by, reluctantly leaving her with the other man. But the twins were there, too. Not much the man could do with those two present and completely absorbed in whatever was going on, he tried to reassure himself.

Kate stirred the dinner pots, hoping everyone would come in soon so that she could get the kitchen cleaned and go outside. She'd discovered some overgrown flower beds trying to come to life outside the cottage and she wanted to weed them.

"And why are you bothering when you'll be gone before most of them bloom?" she asked herself aloud.

The thought of leaving sent a sharp stab of pain through her midsection. But leave she must.

Nicholas would shortly be planting his wheat crop. And he would have enough coin left over to buy another bondservant to do the housework and care for the twins. She hadn't discussed the exact date of her departure with him yet, but she would, and soon.

She hadn't discussed anything with him of a personal nature. As she'd vowed, she'd done her best to stay away from him since their encounter in the barn the night before last. Since his humiliating offer of marriage.

We're going to clear up this mess. You can't avoid me forever, he'd said this morning.

Ha! Wasn't that a pretty speech? The only way to clear up the mess they'd both made of things was for her to leave. As she planned.

"That stew does put forth a tantalizing aroma."

Kate jumped and whirled to find Bradford so close he could have touched her. "Don't creep up on me like that! You're supposed to be resting. How is your wound?" she prattled to hide her discomfort.

He gave her one of the smiles she found less charming with each day that passed. "It is much improved. The throbbing has ceased entirely."

Kate edged away from him. "And just in time for dinner, too."

She strongly suspected he was malingering, that he'd never felt much pain from the shallow bullet graze he'd inflicted upon himself this morning. He'd only wanted an excuse to get out of helping Nicholas with the never-ending plantation work.

"Yes, that is true. But your delectable cooking, dear Kate, is enough to raise a man from his deathbed."

"That was hardly the case with you, and I'm no better a cook than most."

She found his extravagant flattery less charming every day, too. She'd never been completely alone with Bradford before, she realized, and she didn't want to be now.

He closed the gap between them again, and Kate glanced toward the door, hoping for the others to arrive, but no one was in sight. She gave him a cool smile.

"Any minute now, the twins and Nicholas will be in for their meal," she said pointedly.

He smiled back, apparently not the slightest bit perturbed by her announcement. "Ah, yes, Nicholas. The cousin who stepped in and held everything together after the terrible fire that killed my dear sister and her husband."

Kate nodded, surprised at his words. "Yes, he did that."

"Did you never wonder what caused that fire?" he asked. "Or how it was that Talbot escaped completely unharmed?"

She gave him a sharp glance. Something in his tone bothered her. Some sly undercurrent. "No. I never did."

"*I* have, time and time again. I've lain awake of a night asking myself how this came about."

Now Kate knew there was something in his voice she didn't like. "Nicholas awoke first, and by the time he'd gotten the twins outside, it was too late to save the others."

"Yes, that is the tale that he tells," Bradford said smoothly.

Kate's eyes narrowed, not sure what he was getting at, but not liking the way this conversation was going.

"It's what actually happened," she corrected him.

His smile didn't waver. "Are you positive about that?"

She'd had enough of his sly innuendoes. "What are you trying to say?"

He quickly shook his head. "Nothing. I just find it passing strange that everything worked out so well for Talbot. Now he has this plantation with all its hundreds of acres."

Something cold hit Kate in the pit of her stomach. Once more she moved a step away from him.

"Half the plantation was Nicholas's anyway," she pointed out. "He and Philip were partners. And he doesn't have the other half. The twins do."

Bradford's smile still lingered as again he closed the gap between them. "No, you are forgetting *my* share. And yes, Talbot avows he was a full partner. How odd there are no papers attesting to that."

Kate considered backing up again and decided to stand her ground. "He and Philip were in the process of doing that when the fire happened. The papers burned."

"Another item about which we have nothing but Talbot's word. And he has also never legally become the twins' guardian.''

"If what you're saying is true, why didn't Nicholas let the twins die in the fire, too? That would have made it easier for him," she countered, probing for the weakness in his argument so that he'd falter and she could tell him what she thought of his nasty accusations!

He shook his head. "That wouldn't work because Talbot knew about me. He couldn't inherit unless it was proven I was dead and he had no idea where I was. But by becoming the girls' guardian, he could control the plantation until they were of age."

Kate stared at Bradford, cold sweeping over her again. She didn't want to listen to him, but what he said made a horrible kind of sense. Nicholas had always been very ambitious. He'd come here with nothing, and he'd worked like a slave for five years to achieve what he had.

And he passionately loved this plantation.

Enough to commit murder for it?

She recoiled inwardly from that thought, but others followed. She remembered the night Nicholas had told her about the fire, and the guilt she'd seen in his face because he hadn't saved Philip and Lydea.

Could it be possible he felt guilt for a different reason than she'd supposed?

Bradford sighed. "With every passing day, I find it harder to entertain the thought of leaving my dear young nieces to be raised by Talbot. And I find myself becoming more attached to this place where I was born and raised. I don't want to leave it—ever."

"Why are you telling me all these things?" Kate demanded, her voice shaking with her distress.

He looked at her and smiled again. "Why, my dear Kate? Because I thought that you might feel somewhat the same way that I do. That you might be sympathetic to my cause. After all, my blood ties with Celia and Emily are much stronger than Talbot's."

Bradford paused and moved another step nearer. "And also because I find you most personable—most lovely."

Before Kate realized his intentions, he put both hands on her upper arms and drew her to him, pressing his mouth against hers.

His hands were hard and muscular, much stronger than she'd expected. Kate struggled to get away from him, but his grip kept her arms down.

She couldn't escape, she realized, horrified and disgusted as his mouth crushed hers and his body pressed against her own.

Something crashed to the floor across the room. Bradford stiffened, then he loosened his grip, his mouth leaving hers.

Kate gasped for breath, then glanced toward the door.

A wooden pail which had been standing just inside the room was knocked over, a trickle of water running across the boards of the floor.

And Nicholas stood in the doorway, his face like stone. Their glances met—his filled with angry contempt. Then he whirled and left.

Horror swept over Kate. He'd seen Bradford force that kiss on her, but it must have looked to Nicholas as if she'd been willing! And how much had he heard of those terrible things Bradford had said? Her own words?

Fury at both Bradford and herself seized her. She turned back to Bradford, who was now standing a few feet away, a look of smug satisfaction on his face.

"Get out of here! Don't ever touch me again!"

He looked discomfited, but quickly regained his aplomb. The new smile he gave Kate had lost its charm, and the predatory look she'd glimpsed in his eyes before had strengthened.

"Why, Kate, I believe you're forgetting something. This happens to be my cottage. If anyone must go, it would have to be you."

She gaped at him, not believing her ears. "Are you telling me to leave?"

"Of course not. I'm only reminding you that *I* have every right to be here. Much more right than you and your lover do."

Kate swallowed, dismay and loathing and a touch of fear sweeping over her. Bradford *did* know what had happened that night. And he intended to force Nicholas out of here any way he could.

"I don't mind sharing your favors. And I don't want any dinner after all. My injury has become painful again."

He gave her a mocking bow and headed for the stairs.

Kate hurried after Nicholas. She had to try to explain what had actually happened here!

She saw him striding ahead of her, every line of his muscular body showing his outrage. Her stomach suddenly developed a hundred lumps. Oh, she dreaded the next minutes!

Apparently hearing her footsteps, Nicholas paused and glanced behind him. Seeing her, his face darkened even more and he increased his pace.

Kate broke into a run, relieved when Nicholas didn't do the same. Finally, she caught up to him and laid her hand on his arm. "Wait! We must talk."

She felt his warmth through his sleeve and realized the irony of her words. Now it was she instead of Nicholas who was insisting they must communicate.

He shook off her touch as if it were no more than an annoying fly. "Go back to your lover," he said coldly. "Maybe he will believe your lies."

Kate took a deep breath, biting back a retort. As she'd feared, Nicholas was jumping to conclusions. But getting angry in return wouldn't help.

"Bradford isn't my lover," she said evenly. "He forced himself on me."

Nicholas's mouth tightened. "It didn't look to me as if you were trying to escape his embrace."

"I couldn't! He's much stronger than I. Please listen," Kate begged.

"Now I understand your behavior in the barn the other night," Nicholas continued, as if she hadn't spoken. "Your pretense of outrage at my proposal. You'd decided that Hayes, not I, was now the good catch."

Kate recoiled, her eyes widening in shock. "How can you believe that?"

"How can I believe anything else?" he countered. "Marrying a prosperous plantation owner was your reason for coming to the Tidewater, was it not?"

"No! I came here to—" Her voice faltered. *She'd come here to marry Nicholas because she'd always loved him. But she couldn't tell him that.*

He stared at her, his face twisting. "I see you can't find words to deny that. But you had better be careful, Kate. Not all men are prepared to make you a marriage offer after sampling your charms."

"Oh!" Before her outraged cry had faded away, Kate slapped Nicholas. For the third time. "I hate you! You are the most despicable man I've ever known!"

This time Nicholas didn't grasp her hand or react with angry words to her action. He looked at her a moment longer, red marks standing out on his face, the scar on his forehead standing out, then turned and continued on his way to the barnyard.

Kate stared after him, tears of anger and frustration in her eyes, her hand tingling. Finally, she, too, turned and began walking back the way she'd come.

Waves of anger and humiliation swept over her. How could Nicholas have said those horrible, hurtful things to her?

But why was she surprised? she asked herself. Hadn't he always believed she'd come here for selfish, mercenary reasons? Despite his earlier denial, it was clear he still did and had interpreted the scene he'd just witnessed to fit that belief.

The cottage was quiet when Kate reached it. She sat down at the table, her knees suddenly weak from the ordeal just past. She groaned and put her head in her hands.

If he hadn't before, Nicholas now truly believed her to be no better than a trollop.

Nicholas strode toward the barnyard, his face tingling from Kate's slap, rage filling him. He wanted with all his body and soul to turn around and go back to the cottage, knock Hayes to the floor, and then throttle him. And throttle Kate, too.

Damn her for a conniving, lying female! Out in the barn with him only two nights ago and kissing Hayes in the kitchen today.

Nicholas had arrived at the cottage door in time to hear Kate ask Hayes why Nicholas hadn't left the twins to die, too. And Hayes had glibly answered with an all-too-plausible lie.

Kate had listened, never said she didn't believe his pack of lies. And then she'd let him take her into his arms.

Bitter anger and hurt swept over Nicholas.

What he'd heard had confirmed all he'd suspected about Hayes and his motives. He hadn't seen any authorities yet. He hadn't even been off the plantation since he'd arrived. But the man was merely biding his time before he pounced.

And that wasn't the worst of it.

Hayes would take the twins, too. He had to, to make his plan work. Even though Nicholas was sure that the man's show of affection for them was merely that—a show.

Hayes' accusations about the fire were so horrifying that Nicholas had a hard time taking them seriously. But he knew he must. If the man did go to the authorities, his word might have some weight. He'd woven a credible tissue of lies for Kate's ears—and she'd listened.

Perhaps other people would, too.

For the dozenth time, Nicholas told himself something

about the man didn't ring true. Although he certainly appeared to be Lydea's brother, come home at last, Nicholas deeply distrusted him.

Didn't believe he was truly who he claimed to be. But if he weren't, he'd left no trace of his real identity behind. And he knew all about Lydea's Pride and the family he claimed to be a part of.

He heard a noise on the path ahead and glanced up. Celia and Emily skipped along, coming toward him.

"Cousin Nicholas!" Celia cried. "Alfreda has had her piglets! Oh, they are so tiny!"

"Are you going to see them?" Emily asked, as excited as her sister.

Nicholas managed something that he hoped passed for a smile. He'd been out in the wheat fields all afternoon so had missed this awaited event. "Yes, I am."

"We will go back with you."

Emily took one of his hands and Celia the other. He felt the touch of their small hands with a pang of fear and anguish. They trusted him and he loved them. He would not give them up, or this place he loved, without a fight. The worst fight that Hayes had ever dreamed of.

As for Kate . . . pain pierced Nicholas's heart.

His first beliefs about her had been right, after all. She'd proved herself to be the deceitful wench he'd believed her when she'd arrived.

Hayes could have her. They would make a good pair.

Chapter 24

He waited in the same place he had before.

At last the bushes parted, and his partner slipped out.

"It's about time you showed up! Your aim was good, wasn't it?" He brandished his bandaged arm. "Or were you *trying* to hit me?"

"Don't be any more of a fool than necessary. Although, I admit at times you try my patience enough for me to shoot you."

"So, not even any apologies for nearly killing me? I know this may come as a shock, but I often feel that way about you, too."

"Enough of this. We have to replan. Did Nicholas suspect anything?"

He let out a bark of humorless laughter. "Only that I didn't have sense enough not to shoot myself!"

"Good. I'll have to figure out something else. Maybe a riding accident."

"Oh, no you won't. I didn't want to do this in the first place and I'm not getting involved with anything else."

"You'll do as I tell you. You understood that from the beginning."

"I've done a lot of thinking since this happened yesterday. I'm doing just fine on my own. Talbot doesn't like me, but he accepts me as Lydea's brother. The twins are becoming very fond of me and my tales of when their mother and I were children here. I'm beginning to believe them myself. I'm starting to feel that I belong here."

"You don't belong here, and you'll help me get rid of Nicholas. When you obtain control of the property, you will sell it in the best interests of the twins. To *me*. As we agreed. Then, you'll take your money and be on your way."

"The more I hear from you, the more I like my own plans better. I think I'll go along with them instead."

"And what plans might you have, you conceited clown?"

"Now, now. Don't lose your temper. If anyone should be angry, it's me. *I* didn't shoot *you,* remember?"

"Perhaps I should have finished the job. Get on with whatever you have to say!"

"All right, I will. It's very simple. I'm going to try to persuade Nicholas to leave here peacefully. I believe I can do that."

"And what if you can't?"

"Then, I'll go to the magistrate in Chestertown and see if they don't find it strange that Nicholas managed to rescue the twins from that fire and not Philip and Lydea. That should do it. I'll stay here on Lydea's Pride and enjoy life like these other Tidewater gentlemen."

"I won't let you do that! I've wanted this plantation for years. I *must* have it! *I* got rid of Lydea and Philip, you fool. I can get rid of you and Nicholas, too."

"What did you say? *You* started that fire?"

"Yes. But you'll never be able to make anyone believe your wild tales against either me or Talbot. I'll give you one last chance to reconsider before I—"

"Threats won't work now. You can't turn me in or you implicate yourself. And you have a hell of a lot more to lose than I do. I've done the work, taken all the risks. The fact is, I don't need you anymore."

"Yes, you do. I'll give you time to calm down and think this over. I'll meet you here this same time, three days from now."

"No. I've already thought it over. I've got a good thing here, and I'm going to enjoy the life of a country gentleman."

"You are a complete idiot. Nicholas is barely holding this plantation together. You hate to work. What are you going to do when you get rid of him?"

"Oh, I won't do anything drastic until he gets his marvelous wheat crop harvested. The money from that and the tobacco crop should give me plenty to buy some slaves to do the work."

"Three days from now. And you'd better be here."

His erstwhile partner melted back into the bushes and disappeared from sight.

"You'll be waiting a long time, my friend. A bloody long time."

"The master has gone to Chestertown," Daisy told Morgan. "Would you like to speak to the mistress?"

Morgan nodded, forcing a smile, trying to hide the fact he knew very well that Henry was not in the house. "Yes, I would. I'll wait in the library."

Daisy nodded, her dark gaze revealing only courtesy, not the curiosity he knew she must feel. "I'll go fetch the mistress."

Pacing the floor of the luxuriously appointed room, Morgan went over again in his mind how he was going to present his argument persuasively enough for Devona to listen. It would not be an easy task, he well knew.

He reached the window and turned back, then glanced up as the door opened and Devona stood framed in the opening. She wore a pink gown; her face was flushed.

His heart skipped a beat as his smile became genuine, warm. "Devona!" He hurried across the room to her.

She looked frightened and nervous. "What are you doing here?" she asked. "Didn't you get my note?"

"Yes. And that's why I'm here." He wanted so badly to pull her into his arms he had to clench his hands into fists and hold them rigidly at his sides.

"What do you mean? Don't you realize how dangerous this is? I can't stay here with you! I must go back upstairs and you must leave."

"Devona, listen to me. Hear me out. Will you do that?"

Her face tensed even more, but finally she nodded. "All right, but you must hurry."

Morgan crossed to the door and pulled it inward. It closed silently on its well-oiled hinges. He could see by Devona's expression she didn't want him to do that, but she didn't say anything.

Returning to her, he took a deep breath and let it out. "You can't stay here with him. You and Becky have to leave with me." He shook his head as her eyes widened, her mouth opened to protest. "You promised to listen."

She stared at him, then nodded. "All right," she said again.

"Can't you see you mustn't go on living with this man? Someday he'll hurt you badly. Maybe Becky, too."

Devona shook her head wildly, backing away from him. "No! You are saying crazy things. I—we can't do that. Henry is my husband. He will always be. I can't leave him."

Morgan's face tightened. "I know I can't legally marry you now, but we will be married in our hearts. I've saved my money. We can go somewhere far away where that bastard can never find us."

"You don't understand the way it is. You don't know Henry. He'd find us wherever we went. You must go away by yourself. Find another ship. But go!"

She turned toward the door. He couldn't let her leave him now. If he did, he knew he'd never see her again.

Desperately, he reached for her shoulders, turned her to face him.

Tears starred her lashes, rolled down her flushed cheeks. He felt the delicate bones of her shoulders beneath his hands, the heat of her body through the silk of her gown, and he was lost.

"Oh, God," he muttered. He pulled her to him, cradling her in the circle of his arms. He could feel her heart beating against his chest like a frightened bird's. His own heart contracted with sympathy, with love and desire.

She felt so right in his arms, as he'd known she would. They belonged together. He'd known that from the first moment he'd seen her. His hand found her chin, tilted her face up. He had to kiss her now. Nothing on earth could have stopped him.

He lowered his head, his lips found hers, and the fire long banked in both of them flared. Morgan pulled her tightly against him. He felt her arms slide around him, too.

"Now, isn't this a pretty sight."

Aldon's voice erupted into the room.

Morgan felt Devona stiffen against him, heard her gasp, then she pulled away from him. He let her go and turned slowly to face Henry.

The other man's face was tight with anger, his icy-blue eyes glaring. The door stood open behind him, and Morgan cursed himself for putting Devona in such a situation.

Why hadn't he been more careful? Hadn't Devona warned him Aldon would try to catch them together? And the irony of the situation was that, until only a moment ago, there had been nothing for him to find.

"Lockwood, of course you realize you no longer have a ship. And I'd advise you to find another occupation. Before I'm finished with you, no one in this colony or anywhere else will hire you."

"Henry, please be reasonable. This isn't what you think!" Devona moved to his side, her expression pleading.

He gave her a look of contempt. "I find my wife in the arms of another man, and you are telling me I am misinterpreting the circumstances?"

"I know how it looks, but this is the first time, the only time. . . . It will never happen again."

"That is the only sensible thing you've said. It most assuredly will not happen again. Now go upstairs to your chamber. I'll deal with you later."

Instead of obeying him, Devona held her ground. "I know Morgan must leave the *Rosalynde*. But don't ruin his chances for another ship!"

She choked down a sob and reached her hand to his shoulder, pleadingly.

He took her slender wrist in a hard, hurtful grip and pushed it off his shoulder. His other hand came up and slapped her across the face with so much force that she staggered and fell.

A red haze obscured Morgan's sight. Blindly, with a growl like an enraged animal, he flung himself upon Aldon, his fist connecting with the other man's jaw.

Aldon went down. Morgan stood over him, his face menacing. "If you ever touch her again, I will kill you."

Slowly, the other man got to his feet, his hand holding his jaw, a look of deadly fury on his face. Morgan heard Devona's gasp of fear, but he was long past worrying about anything now.

"If any killing is done, I will be the one who does it. And with the full support of the law on my side. Get out of here, Lockwood. Now. This instant."

Behind Aldon, in the hall, Morgan glimpsed Daisy, stupefaction on her face, as if she couldn't believe what was going on in this room.

Turning his head, he looked at Devona. She'd gotten to her feet and the deep red imprint of her husband's fingers spread across the whiteness of her face. Morgan knew that wouldn't be all she suffered. After he left, Aldon would take out his fury on her.

Morgan had never been so angry in his life. Or so determined. "No. I'm not going without Becky and Devona. I'll not leave them here with you."

A sharp bark of incredulous laughter came from the other man. "Are you an utter fool?"

"Perhaps, but I mean what I say. I'll not leave Devona to be abused by you any longer."

Aldon had backed up as he talked. Now he'd reached the massive mahogany desk. He jerked open a drawer and fumbled inside.

Before he'd completed the movement, Morgan realized his intentions and moved swiftly. As Aldon withdrew a pistol from the drawer, Morgan jerked it away from him and hit him again.

Aldon's head struck the floor with a resounding crack. This time he stayed down, obviously unconscious.

"Come on!" Morgan grasped Devona's hand. "Where is Becky? We must get out of here."

"She's upstairs," Devona said. She looked back at her husband. "We must see how badly he's hurt!"

"I don't care if he lives or dies, but he'll be all right. Come!"

Like a sleepwalker, she followed him into the hall.

Daisy still stood there, her dark eyes wide with shock, her hand over her mouth.

"Go fetch Becky," Morgan told her. "And don't dally."

The servant woman nodded. "Yessir." She hurried upstairs.

Morgan turned to Devona. "Now, do I have to pick you up and carry you out of this house or will you come with me willingly?"

Devona, her face white, the red imprints on her cheek standing out like stripes of paint, nodded. "I won't fight you. But where will we go?"

"I'll take you to a safe place to stay until I can get my affairs in order. Then we will go far away from here."

Devona checked the protest rising to her lips. He'd never

get away with this, never get away from Henry. She couldn't do what he wanted—and not only because of her husband. Even if that obstacle were removed, she wasn't at all sure she could ever give her trust, her life, over to another man.

Even Morgan.

But she knew she had to leave with him now or someone would be killed here today.

"Take us to Lydea's Pride," she told him. "Nicholas and Kate will let Becky and me stay, and we'll be safe there."

Daisy came down the stairs, Becky holding her hand.

Morgan gave Devona a warm, reassuring smile. "Everything will be all right. Let us go."

It could never be all right; but without another word, she followed him out the door.

Chapter 25

Kate, her arms full of soiled clothing, came out of Nicholas's bedchamber into the hall. She walked to her old chamber, where the door stood half open.

Bradford lay on the bed, his eyes closed, apparently asleep. His bandaged arm lay on top of the quilt. Kate curled her lip.

He hadn't gone out with Nicholas again today—his injury was paining him, he'd said. This was the third day since the accident and Kate was sure now he was only finding excuses not to work. The wound had been little more than a deep, wide scratch!

Nicholas hadn't seemed to mind not having Bradford's help, even appeared relieved. Studiously avoiding Kate's eye, he'd gulped his ale and left.

He was ignoring her as much as possible. A few times these last few days she'd looked up to find his glance on her. That had been worse. The fiercely scornful expression in his brown eyes had cut her to the quick, even while she railed at his stubbornness.

He still thought she'd welcomed Bradford's embrace.

Probably also thought she believed the other man's horrible insinuations about Nicholas's part in the manor house fire.

Of course she didn't! The doubt Bradford had put in her mind that day had been fleeting. Blindly stubborn and hot-tempered Nicholas might be, but he wasn't a murderer. She could never believe him capable of such a thing!

But she hadn't tried to talk to him again. He wouldn't listen, and what real difference did it make? She'd soon be gone from here. She resolutely pushed down the bitter sadness that knowledge gave her.

She'd be leaving soon and he wouldn't try to stop her. No, he'd probably help pack her trunks and take her away from here with dispatch.

The devil take all men! Unreasonable creatures, the lot of them. Not a one had any sense. Even Morgan, as good and kind as he was. He'd come by the cottage to see Nicholas yesterday, and she'd been alone. She'd run upstairs, found Devona's hidden note and given it to him.

He'd read it, then crumpled the paper, face darkened with anger. He had to get Devona away from her husband, he'd muttered. Now, like all cocksure men, who always thought they were right, instead of leaving her alone as he should, he was no doubt planning something that would get Devona in more trouble with her wretched husband!

Several pieces of soiled clothing were piled on a chair by Bradford's bed. Kate tiptoed in and over to the chair. She bent to pick up the clothes, her back to the bed.

A strong, hard hand clamped down on her shoulder. Kate's heart thumped in shock and she dropped the pile of clothing onto the floor.

"What's your hurry, Kate, me darlin'?" Bradford said, his voice low and strangely slurred.

She tried to squirm away from his grip, but couldn't. She shot a glance at the bed, then sucked in her breath. Bradford's eyes were half-open, and a sly grin curved his mouth.

"Let go of me!" she commanded, trying again to straighten up and escape.

"Why should I? I'd much rather do this." He jerked her backwards and she tumbled onto the bed, landing on her back half across him.

"Now thass better," he said, still in that odd, slurred tone. "Isn't it?" The hand on her shoulder slid down across her breast, squeezing as it went, still holding her firmly down. His other hand found the bottom of her hiked-up skirts and moved under, up her leg.

Alarm shot through Kate and she began to struggle in earnest. This was different than when he'd kissed her. He wouldn't be satisfied with only a kiss this time. He leaned over her and she recoiled as strong brandy fumes hit her nostrils.

He was drunk! That's why he was behaving this way. Real fear joined the alarm. She twisted, trying to dislodge his hand, bent her knees, then straightened them, her feet connecting with his throat.

Bradford gagged, then cursed, and pushed himself on top of her. "You li'l bitch! What do you think you're doin'? You know you want this as much as me!"

"No! I don't. Get off me. Let me go!" Kate stared up into his angry, drunken face, more afraid than she'd ever been in her life. He was a big man. His weight was holding her tightly against the bed.

"Like hell I will," he snarled. I've got you right where I've wanted you since tha' day I came."

Her skirts were pushed up almost to her waist from the struggle. Bradford reached a hand down to slide under them again, moving slowly up her thigh. He lowered his head.

Just before his mouth covered hers, Kate drew a deep breath and screamed as loud as she could. It was almost time for the twins and Nicholas to come in for breakfast. Please let Nicholas be nearby! Let him hear!

"Damn you!" Bradford clamped his mouth down on

hers, grinding her lips into her teeth until she could taste blood. She could scarcely breathe, let alone try to scream again. His hand pulled at her bodice, ripping it down the front, finding her breast, grasping it cruelly until tears came to her eyes.

Then, his horrible touch, his heavy weight were off her. Nicholas's muscled arm was hooked around the other man's neck, jerking him backward, off the bed. He landed on the floor with a jarring thud.

Nicholas stood over him, his legs spread apart.

Behind him, Nicholas heard Kate's sobbing breath of relief, and his heart contracted. God, how afraid he'd been when he heard her scream. All kinds of terrible pictures had sped through his mind as he took the stairs two at a time.

Everything else fell away. Their last bitter quarrel, the hurtful words they'd flung at each other.

If anything happened to Kate . . .

When he saw Hayes on top of her on the bed, a red haze of fury had blinded him. He'd been afraid he was too late, that this animal had already violated her. If that had happened, Nicholas would have killed him where he now lay on the floor at his feet.

"Get up and get out of here," Nicholas said. "I'll give you five minutes to be off my property."

Bradford sneered up at him. *"Your* property? Aren't you forgettin' some things? Such as the fact that I've more claim to this plantation than you?"

"If you don't get out of here, I'm going to knock you senseless, then tie you to your horse and send him off. Or do I have to do it now to show you I mean what I say?"

Bradford still glared defiantly at him. "That's big talk for a man who killed my sister and her husband!"

Nicholas's hands curled into fists, the muscles straining in his arms. "You're a lying bastard! You know that isn't so."

"Do I? I'll leave here all right, but I'm goin' straight to

the magistrate at Chestertown. We'll see what he has to say about my story."

"Magistrate Cole is a good man. He won't listen to anything from a drunken would-be rapist like you."

Bradford heaved himself to his feet, swaying. "Drunk, am I? And a rapist? We'll see about tha', too. Iss only yours and that little tart's word against mine. She was willing all the way. And I'm the twins' uncle—I should be their legal guardian. As well you know."

"I'll never let you have Celia and emily," Nicholas said through clenched teeth.

Bradford sneered again, adjusting his rumpled clothing. "You're goin' to have to, Talbot. And you'll have to give up this place to me, too, that you've worked yourself half to death to keep going. You're a fool, do you know that? Freeing all the slaves and then working twice as hard as any of them did."

Kate didn't even see Nicholas's fist move before it smashed into Bradford's gloating face. Bradford hit the floor like a felled beast, and Nicholas threw himself down upon him.

His fist smashed into the other man's face again and Bradford let out a howl. "My nose! You've broken my nose!"

"I'm going to do worse unless you stop lying and tell the truth. You're not Lydea's brother! You can't be. I heard her talk about him. He was a decent man. I can't believe he could have changed that much even in fifteen years. Who are you? Where did you get the Bible?"

The man on the floor went to pieces before Kate's eyes, all his bravado crumbling as he cowered under Nicholas's upraised fist.

"Don't hit me again!" he blubbered, holding his hand to his bleeding nose. "I'll tell you. M' name's Flynn Duncan. I met Hayes when we were serving together in the war, like I said. He died during that last battle outside Ft. Duquesne.

Right before he went, he gave me the Bible—paid me to bring it to his sister."

A look of hard satisfaction spread over Nicholas's face, but he still straddled the man on the floor, still kept his fist upraised.

"That's more like it, but he shouldn't have trusted you. Now tell me the rest of it. So you decided you'd pretend to be Hayes and see where it got you?"

Duncan cowered, shrinking from Nicholas's still-menacing fist. "No, that's not how it was. I met this man at the tavern and I asked him where Lydea's Pride was and . . ."

He hesitated, looked up at Nicholas, then went on in a rush.

"Hell, if I'm goin' down, he's goin' with me. Your neighbor Henry Aldon and me cooked up this scheme. He's been after this plantation for a long time. He started the fire that killed the girls' parents."

Kate gasped, horror sweeping over her. Henry had done that? She'd known he was a hard, cruel man, but *murder*?

Nicholas stiffened, his face turning to stone. He brought his fist down a few inches. "Is this a lie, too? Because if it is, I'll make you sorry you were ever born."

"No!" Duncan gabbled frantically. "It's all the truth, I swear before God. Aldon told me things I'd need to know; he outfitted me with clothes and the horse. I was to get you off the plantation and lay claim to it for the girls and then sell it in their best interests. Henry was going to buy it."

"At a greatly reduced price than its true worth, I'm sure," Nicholas said. "And then, I suppose, you were going to disappear, leaving the twins to fend for themselves?"

"You'd always be around," Duncan mumbled. "They'd be all right."

"Yes. With their home sold, you with the money and gone. They'd be left in wondrously good shape, wouldn't they?"

Duncan shook his head. "That was the plan, but I

changed my mind after Henry tried to kill you and shot me instead.''

Nicholas, his face still set like stone, stared down at him. "If you try to tell me you had a change of heart, I'll hit you again.''

Duncan quickly shook his head. "I decided I was going to keep on living here instead of selling it. I like it here." His voice took on a whining note. "I feel almost like I am Lydea's brother.''

"Well, you are not! I imagine Aldon was a bit unhappy with that decision.''

The other man nodded earnestly. "Oh, yes, he was. But he didn't believe I meant it. He still don't.''

"Aldon is in for a few surprises today.''

Kate shuddered at the barely contained fury in Nicholas's voice as she imagined what he'd like to do to Henry. What he might actually do.

He stood, turning to Kate. "See if you can find some rope so I can tie this animal up.''

His words were curt, but as his gaze met hers fully for the first time in days, something in his eyes told her those hard tones weren't meant for her ... that he no longer felt that bitter anger and scorn toward her.

The pain inside her eased. She nodded and hurried downstairs. In a few moments she was back with a thick coil of hemp. Nicholas soon had the other man secured.

"What are you goin' to do with me?" Duncan asked fearfully.

"Turn you over to the authorities in Chestertown, of course. What did you think I'd do? Kill you?" Nicholas asked coldly.

A look of profound relief went over Duncan's face. "I wasn't sure.''

"You almost got away with this. You're a good actor.''

Duncan's battered lips turned down sourly. "I ought to be. Thass my profession.''

Nicholas let out a humorless bark of laughter as he got

to his feet. "My God, I can't believe it. Come on, Kate. He'll be all right for a while."

While Nicholas went after Henry? she wondered fearfully. They walked out of the room side by side, Kate clutching her ripped bodice together.

Nicholas's gaze followed her movements. His face tightened further.

"I should have killed the bastard while I had the chance. I'm sorry I acted like such a jackass the other day, Kate. I'm sorry for a lot of things. When we get this muddle straightened out and I deal with Aldon, can we talk?"

Everything between them seemed to have changed. She didn't understand why, but there it was.

"I'm sorry, too. And of course I'll talk to you."

They'd reached the stairs and they had to squeeze close together to walk down them. Even through their clothes, she felt Nicholas's comforting warmth. It felt so good to be touching him.

Once downstairs, Kate found her shawl and tied it securely around her torn bodice, making herself decent again. She looked up to see Nicholas watching her, his mouth still in that hard line.

"Where are the twins?" she asked.

"At the barn with Tucker. Thank God. I'd hate for them to have witnessed this."

"Yes, so would I," Kate agreed.

A sudden noise at the door made them both turn in that direction. It opened and Devona stumbled into the room. Her hair was disheveled, and red welts on her face were turning into bruises. Behind her were Becky and Morgan.

"What has happened?" Kate hurried across the room, her arms held out in welcome.

Devona let Kate enfold her and Kate felt the other woman's slim body begin to shake. Over Devona's head, Kate looked at Morgan.

He glanced from Kate to Nicholas, his face grim. "They

need to stay here for a while. Just until I can arrange to get them completely away from the Tidewater."

"Of course," Nicholas answered.

"I must warn you," Morgan said. "Aldon will probably come looking for them here. As soon as he recovers consciousness. I hit him pretty hard."

"Let him come. He's going to have enough trouble to deal with," Nicholas said grimly. "Devona will never have to worry about him again."

Morgan gave him a startled look. "What do you mean?"

Kate heard the pain in Nicholas's clipped tones as he told them everything.

"Where are Celia and Emily?" Becky asked into the appalled silence that followed, her voice small and trembly. She stood close to her mother, her hand clutching Devona's cloak.

A look passed between Kate and Devona. This child had seen and heard far too much for one so young. And about her own father.

"They're at the barn with Tucker," Kate said. "Come, I'll take you there."

Becky looked uncertainly at her mother. "Is Papa coming after us? Will he be very angry?"

Devona smoothed her daughter's hair and smiled at her. "From now on, *everything* will be fine," she said. "I promise you."

Becky's expression changed into profound relief. She nodded to Kate. "All right."

Kate took her hand and they walked out the door and up the path to the barn. Tucker gave Kate a questioning look, but she shook her head to say she couldn't explain things now.

He nodded. "We'll be just fine, Mistress Kate. Don't you worry 'bout a thing."

Kate hurried back to the cottage. Morgan and Nicholas were deep in conversation, their voices and faces tense, and Devona was standing by the fire. Kate walked across the room to join her.

Behind her, the door was flung open so hard it crashed into the wall.

Kate whirled. Henry stood framed in the doorway, dried blood crusted on his forehead. His face was a mask of fury. His icy stare passed over Morgan and Nicholas and fixed on Devona.

"There you are," he said. "I thought you'd be here. You don't even have enough intelligence to hide from me, do you? You never have had much. But that's not why I married you."

He advanced across the room, holding his hand out imperiously.

"Come along back home with me now."

Chapter 26

Devona stared at Henry as if he were a venomous snake, his deadly eyes luring her to him. Her mouth opened as if she were going to agree with his order, and she took a step forward. Then, something happened. The frozen stare changed into fierce anger.

"No," she said firmly. "I won't go with you. I'll never take any more orders from you!"

Henry checked his rapid walk across the room. He stared at her as if she'd spoken in a foreign language that he didn't understand. "What did you say?" he asked, his voice deadly quiet.

Kate shot a terrified glance at Nicholas and Morgan. They stood, muscles tensed and ready for whatever action might be necessary.

"You murderer! I knew you were a greedy, unprincipled man, but to think you'd kill Lydea and Philip, our friends and neighbors all these years!"

Henry backed up. His face changed, the rage mingling with a look of such transparent cunning Kate shuddered. "You are obviously under a great strain, Devona.

It has affected your mind. Come, let us go back to our home.''

Devona laughed bitterly. *"Our* home? Aldon Manor has never been my home, Henry. Only yours.''

A false smile joined the emotions shifting across Henry's face. ''You are talking nonsense, my dear, but I will forgive you. Come.''

''Don't you understand? You're going to hang, Henry. Flynn Duncan revealed everything, all your evil plans.''

Henry's face and body stiffened. Slowly he looked around, for the first time seeming to become aware of the other people in the room. He cast wary glances at Nicholas and Morgan. Then his hand darted inside his coat and came out holding a pistol.

''I knew I should have taken that gun with me,'' Morgan said.

''You were a fool not to. But then, you've been one all along. And it will cost you your life.'' Henry brought the gun up, aiming it at Morgan.

Devona screamed, and Nicholas and Morgan both moved at the same time. Henry pulled the trigger and the gun went off just as Morgan reached him. The bullet went wild, missing Morgan and slamming into the wall.

''Damn you, Lockwood!'' Henry said, his voice deadly. He lifted the pistol and brought it smashing down on the side of Morgan's head. Morgan staggered and fell back into Nicholas, and both men fell to the floor.

Henry's thin lips curled as he looked at Nicholas. ''You've been such a simpleton all along. If I had time, I'd finish you where you lie.'' He turned and ran out the open door and disappeared from view.

Devona dropped to her knees beside Morgan, her face terrified. ''Are you all right?'' she asked, her new-found confidence gone, her voice trembling.

''Yes.'' His head bleeding, Morgan struggled to his feet, swaying.

"I'm going after the bastard," Nicholas said, getting to his own feet.

"No. I'm going."

Nicholas opened his mouth to argue, then closed it again after seeing the grimly determined look on Morgan's face. "We'll both go. We both have a stake in bringing him down."

Aldon was nowhere in sight. Had he headed for the docks? Undoubtedly, he'd come here in one of his boats. Nicholas and Morgan took off at a lope down the road.

A horse and rider exploded out of the stables, reaching a full gallop within seconds. Nicholas swore. He should have known Aldon would take a horse. Now he had a head start. Nicholas broke into a run, Morgan alongside.

No one was in the stables, but other mounts moved restlessly in their stalls. Both men hastily fit bridles and bits onto horses, then swung up on their backs.

Aldon had turned and headed back toward the public road. Nicholas caught a glimpse of him ahead and urged his mount on. As they passed the cottage, he saw everyone standing in the doorway with worried faces. Devona looked terrified.

Reaching the road, he saw Henry ahead, his figure dwindling.

"Goddamn it!" Nicholas swore. "Come on," he urged the gelding, bending low over the animal's neck. "Let's go!"

He pushed his booted feet into its sides again, Morgan keeping pace.

Their mounts picked up speed, and soon they'd gained on Aldon. "Good boy!" Nicholas praised. "Now go on, keep it up."

Soon, grimly pleased, Nicholas saw they were going to catch up. This time the bastard wouldn't get away!

Aldon glanced back, saw the two men closing in on him, and urged his own mount to greater speed. Then, he turned again and Nicholas caught the glimmer of metal in his hand as he raised his arm.

The shot went over their heads and Aldon's mount reared, whinnying in fear. Still half-turned, the man lost his seat and fell onto the road. His horse, crazy with fear, kept going.

Nicholas reined in his mount and Morgan tried to do the same, but his horse was too close to the fallen man.

The sickening crack of horse hooves against a human skull rang through the air. Nicholas grimaced, then rode to where Aldon lay unmoving in a crumpled heap.

Morgan, already kneeling beside the man, turned him over. Nicholas's stomach rolled as he saw the huge dent in Aldon's forehead, his lifeless face.

No longer would he abuse and terrorize Devona. Or anyone else. He'd fully paid for all his crimes. Devona was free now, Nicholas thought. She was a widow. There was no longer any obstacle between her and Morgan.

He'd set Nicholas free, too, from the awful guilt he'd felt at Philip's and Lydea's deaths. Now that he knew Aldon had set the fire, Nicholas realized he was lucky to have escaped with his own life, to have saved Celia and Emily.

Morgan still knelt beside Aldon. At last he rose, turning to Nicholas. His darkly tanned face was twisted with guilt. "I hated the man. I wanted him dead. But I didn't think I'd be the one to kill him!"

Nicholas sat with his back to Kate before the hearth fire, his book on wheat-growing open on his lap. His chestnut hair, bent over his book, gleamed in the firelight.

The twins were at Aldon Manor for a visit, Flynn Duncan awaited trial for his part in the conspiracy, and Henry had been buried two days ago.

Until now she and Nicholas hadn't had a moment alone together for their promised talk. Was Nicholas thinking about that, too?

Nervous perspiration beaded her forehead. How many times since she'd come here all those months ago had they tried to talk to each other? And never once had they come to any kind of an understanding. They'd always ended with things between them in a worse state than when they'd started.

Except for those two occasions which had ended with them in each other's arms. And even then, they'd fought afterward. How could she believe another talk had any promise of being different?

"Would you fancy a glass of wine?" she asked him.

"Yes, please," he answered without turning.

His voice sounded tight, she thought, pouring the ruby wine into two goblets . . . as if he were no more at ease than she. She moved across the room and stood before Nicholas. "Here 'tis."

He glanced up and smiled at her. "Thank you," he said, reaching for his glass.

His warm fingers touched hers during the exchange. Kate swallowed, remembering that other time, so similar to this, when a simple touch of their hands had started a fire raging between them.

Her face warmed with the memory. Was Nicholas remembering, too? Hastily, she moved her hand away, moved back a step. "I'd best see to the accounts," she said, turning away.

"Wait, Kate," Nicholas said, his voice soft, with none of those hard-edged tones she'd grown so accustomed to hearing in it. "What better time for our talk than now— while we have some privacy."

Her heart leaped. Here it was upon them. What would they make of this opportunity? Another muddle? Or could they perhaps finally speak honestly with each other? She turned back around.

He'd put his book aside. His smile lingered, but there was a questioning look in his deep brown eyes. The white of his shirt was a startling contrast to his work-bronzed face and neck. He'd undone the first two buttons, and a whorl of dark hair peeked through.

Her face warmed even more, her body heated, as memories of that other night insistently forced their way into her mind. Resolutely, she pushed them down.

"Come, sit here," Nicholas invited, patting the settee seat beside him.

He tried not to notice how the firelight made a red-gold flame of her hair, with its everlasting tendrils trailing around her delectable ears. How the bodice of her gray dress molded itself to her rounded curves.

And he wouldn't think about that other time they'd been here alone together, and how it had ended. Or that night in the barn, in the sweet-smelling hay . . .

No! He couldn't think about any of that. They must talk. He must keep his wits about him this time. He must apologize for many things and give her a proper marriage proposal.

Kate, holding her wine glass, sat down beside him, as far away as possible. Which wasn't far, considering the size of the settee. At once, he felt her body warmth. Maybe this hadn't been such a good idea. He should have let her sit across from him.

Too late for that, now. He couldn't ask her to move. He sipped his wine, then cleared his throat, wondering how and where to begin. At the beginning, he finally decided.

He cleared his throat. "Kate, you and I got off on the wrong foot. When you told me about Alyssa, I was so shocked I could hardly give credence to your words. I refused to believe she'd do such a thing to me."

"She was very young when you left her," Kate said. "And five years is a long time to wait."

"Yes. I understand that now. But as you know, I blamed you for changing Alyssa's mind. I was certain you'd offered to take her place only because you desired the prosperous life I'd told Alyssa she could have with me."

He waited, hoping Kate would say the real reason she'd

made the long journey across the Atlantic was because she cared for him.

"That was never the important reason I came here," Kate said, then paused.

Could she tell him she'd come because she'd always loved him, even if she'd not discovered that fact until recently?

No. She couldn't. He hadn't said anything about love to her.

"I wanted to see the New World," she said instead. "It sounded exciting. I was so tired of my dull life in Plymouth, running the shop, with no prospect of change."

Nicholas pushed down his disappointment at her answer and tried to ignore his rapidly increasing desire. After all, he reminded himself, he wasn't sure how he felt about Kate, either.

"I can understand that. Many women come to the Colonies to marry men they have never seen. I was much too harsh with you and I'm very sorry."

Nicholas congratulated himself. Now wasn't that a handsome apology? Those words would have to soften Kate.

"It's all right," Kate answered. "I have not always been reasonable myself."

She tried not to let her restlessness show. With every evidence of sincerity, Nicholas had just told her he regretted his past actions, something she'd never expected to happen. At last they were talking calmly and sensibly to each other, as they'd long needed to do.

And it was driving her to distraction! What was wrong with her?

She knew. She wanted to stop this exchange of lukewarm, polite apologies. She yearned to tell him she loved him! Longed for him to tell her the same.

"And I also have skills," she said instead. "I was sure that I could find employment."

"As you could. As you can." Nicholas paused, hoping his smile looked more self-assured than he felt. He searched for just the right words. "But I'm hoping, dear Kate, that you will not do that. That you will stay here with me."

Nicholas took her wineglass and placed it beside his own, then reached for her hands.

They were rough, callused from work. Work she'd done here, taking care of the twins and this cottage. A wave of tenderness swept over him, and he considered going down upon his knees, then thought better of it. Kate would not expect that from him.

"Again, I'm asking you to marry me, and I hope this time you won't scorn my offer. Someday, not too far in the future, I will rebuild the manor house. I can give you a good life. You won't have to work like this forever."

Kate looked at him, delaying her answer. His big warm hands covering hers felt so wonderful. And what he was saying should sound wonderful to her ears, too. This time she knew he'd not asked her to be his wife merely because it was the honorable thing. He truly wanted to marry her. He was offering her all she'd longed for except one thing.

Love. Not once had he mentioned that.

Nicholas had just apologized for treating her so harshly, for distrusting her. He'd agreed Alyssa had been too young to leave for so long a time.

But not once had he said that his love for Alyssa had died.

There could be only one reason for that omission—it hadn't died. And Kate couldn't marry him without knowing that he loved her as much as he'd once loved her sister, and did no longer.

But maybe, an inner voice whispered, *that will come in time. If you're only patient and wait for a while.* Kate wasn't at all sure she believed that. But she was sure of one thing.

She couldn't give him up. Maybe once she would have been able to do that, but no longer.

But neither could she marry him.

He looked back at her, his eyes deep pools of darkness.

She wanted him, all of him, heart and body and soul. And he was offering only part of himself.

"I'm honored by your offer," she said. "But I can't accept it—at this time."

Nicholas's hands tightened on Kate's. His brows drew together in a frown. What had gone wrong? This time he had done everything right and she'd still refused him.

"Why can't you? Are you still angry with me for all the foolish, hasty things that I said to you? I'm truly sorry."

Kate shook her head. "No, I'm not angry. And I'll stay here. I've grown very fond of Emily and Celia, and I like living here in this Tidewater country. But. . . ."

Her voice faltered, then she went on. "We should not marry just because we have taken our pleasure with each other. Nor, as you said, just to satisfy your respectable neighbors."

Nicholas quickly shook his head, his mouth tightening. "I can't allow you to stay here unless we marry. I want to bed you every time we're together. I could not promise it wouldn't happen again."

He saw her throat move as she swallowed. "And I am equally as desirous of you. My offer to stay did not preclude such an event occurring again."

Nicholas stared at her, shocked speechless. Finally, he cleared his throat. "Never did I think to hear such a declaration from you, Kate! Why, 'tis downright scandalous!"

Her gaze met his without faltering. "Perhaps. But that's the way it must be if I am to stay."

"This would put you in a very awkward position. There will be talk—much talk, I'm afraid."

"I know," Kate said. "I'm prepared to deal with that."

He frowned at her. "And what if I should get a child on you? Are you prepared to deal with that?"

Again, he saw her throat muscles move as she swallowed. "Let us take one step at a time and handle that problem if it arises."

Her answer pleased him no better than her proposition

had. But he saw she wouldn't be swayed. He either accepted what she offered or he gave her up entirely. And he didn't want to do that.

He couldn't bear to think of doing that.

Finally, he nodded, albeit reluctantly. "I will agree to those terms—at least for the time being. Since it seems I have no choice. But I do not like them, Kate. I do not like them at all."

Kate's gaze roamed over his strong, well-loved face, his deep-set brown eyes, his straight nose, his full, curving lips that had given her such pleasure.

She'd been so afraid he'd turn her down! Even as she thought this, she realized how ridiculous it sounded. Afraid he'd turn down her offer to be his mistress! When just a short while ago, she'd been outraged because she'd thought that's all he wanted of her.

No, they hadn't settled the muddle. They'd only made it worse. "I'm sorry," she said, smiling at him.

Nicholas watched Kate's eyes change to the sea-foam shade that did such strange things to him. Watched her full lips part in sweet invitation as she leaned toward him. A spot of red burned on her high cheekbones.

He bent his head toward hers, everything else but her nearness, her sweetness, leaving his mind. He could wait no longer to claim her lips, to pull her into his arms. When their lips met, just as had happened those other times, a fire ignited between them.

He reached for her shoulders, pulling her close against his chest, his mouth covering hers, claiming hers, in a deeper possession than ever before. He moved her down so she was half-reclining on the settee, and he slid to the floor, bending over her, kissing her as if he could never get enough of the feel of her.

The small buttons on her gown were too much for him, so Kate moved his hands aside and performed the task herself. He pushed the gown and chemise off her shoulders

and drew in his breath at the sight of her rose-tipped
breasts.

He lowered his head to one of them, suckling it gently,
hearing Kate moan and feeling her writhe with desire. Her
response inflamed him further, and he moved to the other
breast, his mouth and tongue relishing the feel of her
satin-smooth skin.

He pushed her skirts up past her smooth, white thighs.
His fingers found the nest of silky curls between and moved
among them, parting the petals of her womanhood, delv-
ing within, until Kate gasped and arched against his explor-
ing fingers.

Nicholas had grown so hard he thought he would
explode. He bent over Kate, his mouth and tongue following the path where his fingers had first gone. Kate arched
against him again.

"Stop. Please stop," she protested.

Why was she asking him to stop when he was giving her
the most acute pleasure she'd ever experienced? But it was
too intense, too strong, she couldn't stand it. . . .

Deep within her, the coiling heat began, ever stronger,
ever hotter, until waves of feeling washed over her, making
her arch against Nicholas's hands, his lips, over and over.

As the waves subsided, Nicholas moved up her body until
his lips hovered over hers again.

"Did you enjoy that?" he asked, giving her a lazy, satisfied smile.

"Yes," Kate answered honestly, "I did."

"Good."

His mouth covered hers again and she tasted herself on
his lips, his tongue. Somehow, that excited her more than
ever, made her hungrier for him.

"But I want more. I want you, all of you," she whispered
against his moving, teasing, tantalizing lips.

In answer he grasped her waist and slid her off onto the
hearth rug. She watched as he unfastened his breeches,

slid them down his legs until his manhood, huge and throbbing, was revealed. He moved over her and she reached for him, curving her hand around his hard, smooth length, marveling at the feel of him.

"If you don't stop that this instant, I cannot wait," he said.

"All right." Kate moved her hand up his flat, hard stomach, stroking and caressing, gratified when he gasped, then took her hand in his and laid it firmly beside her.

As he pushed her thighs apart, she moved, too, as eager as he for the ultimate joining. When he entered her this time, it was as if a hot, hard length of velvet came into her, his fire joining her own until both blended into an exquisite oneness.

They moved together in perfect rhythm, gradually gaining in intensity until at last they reached the spiraling center of their unity. Kate arched against him, pulling him deeper within her, deeper, deeper. He thrust, and it seemed as if he'd found the core of her that he'd sought, that she'd longed for him to find. He thrust again and she felt his liquid heat release into her as she again found her own release.

Nicholas gave a great, sighing breath and lowered his head to her breast. His forehead was damp with perspiration, his skin burning hot. Kate tenderly stroked the damp hair off his forehead, feeling the rapid beat of her heart gradually slow to its normal cadences.

He rolled over onto his side, taking her with him, his body still tight against her own. The hearth fire was warm against the bare skin of her back, and her heavy eyelids closed.

This time it was Kate who slept and Nicholas who looked down upon her with tenderness and wonder. He didn't feel for her what he had for Alyssa. This almost savage, yet tender desire was something no other woman had roused in him. He admired Kate, too, as a woman. As a substitute mother for the twins. For many things.

He didn't know what to name it. If it was love, it wasn't what he'd always thought love should be. But right now he didn't care. He was content. He buried his head in Kate's warm breasts and went to sleep himself.

Chapter 27

"Kate!" Celia came tearing into the cottage, her eyes wide, Emily behind her. "The ship from England is sailing into the wharf! Come and watch it unload."

Kate wiped the last dish from breakfast and set it on its shelf, excitement leaping within her. A ship from home! Home? No, England was no longer that. The Tidewater was. Lydea's Pride. But maybe not for much longer.

The excitement dwindled. She and Nicholas had argued fiercely only last evening.

She smiled at the girls, wiping her hands on her apron and then removing it. But she did want to see the ship. "Yes! Let's go."

The door stood open to the late spring sun, which streamed in, warming Edward's long back as he lay in a patch of it. Two months had passed since that horrible day when the fake Bradford had been unmasked and Henry had died.

Nicholas's wheat crop was planted and doing well. The hogsheads of last year's cured tobacco had been rolled to the wharf and shipped off to England. It looked to be a prosperous year, but as Nicholas often said, in planting you could never count on anything until you had the coin safely in your hand.

And maybe she wouldn't be here to see the wheat crop harvested.

Celia fell into step with Kate, slipping her hand into hers. Emily, on the other side, did likewise.

"There are presents on the ship for us. From Cousin Nicholas," Celia said.

Kate managed a smile. "What did he get for you?" she asked.

"We don't know. It's to be a surprise," Emily chimed in. She squeezed Kate's hand. "And he sent for something for you, too!"

Kate gave her a quick glance. "Really?"

Emily beamed up at her. "Yes! We are not to tell you. He wants to give it to you himself."

Perhaps he wouldn't now, Kate thought, her mind going back to last night. Nicholas had again asked her to marry him and again she'd refused.

Even though they'd lived in surface harmony since that night by the fire, tension had been steadily building between them. Not the same kind as before—not that unrequited sexual tension.

No, this was worse, at least to her. Several times they'd made love. And each time had been more wondrous than the last. The argument last night had started over that.

Nicholas had come to her bedchamber, surprising her. But she'd welcomed him into her bed. Afterward, he'd leaned up on his elbow, giving her a frowning, serious look.

"We can't go on like this," he'd said. "What if I get you with child?" he asked again, as he had when she'd proposed this arrangement.

Each month she waited anxiously for her courses. Relieved, and yet illogically a bit disappointed, too, when they arrived on schedule.

"That hasn't yet happened," she countered.

His frown deepened. "But it is a constant possibility."

Kate moved restlessly, looking away from him. "Yes," she admitted.

He cupped her chin, turning her to face him. "And what would you do then? Insist on remaining a single woman? Raise your child to be a bastard?"

She jerked away from him. "No! Of course not."

His smile was ironic, holding no amusement. "Then, it seems that I must impregnate you in order to have you for a wife."

No. What you must do is tell me that you love me as you've loved no other woman. Not even Alyssa.

Kate couldn't ask him. No doubt he would avow that he did, indeed, love her. That was no good. He had to tell her himself, with no prompting, or she could never believe he truly meant it instead of merely feeling guilty because he was taking his pleasure with her as a man would his wife.

Or his mistress.

That thought made a cold shiver slide down her spine. She'd sworn never to put herself in this position, and then she had—of her own choice. Right now she could be Nicholas's wife.

"Let us worry about that when or if we have to," she said finally.

"So, we're to go on like this indefinitely? Is that what you're telling me?" he asked roughly.

She managed a smile. "Is this life we're living so very unpleasant to you?" she countered again, trying to turn the conversation away from its grimly serious tone.

Instead, he flung himself out of the bed and jerked his nightshirt back over his head. Then, he gave her an angry, frustrated look.

"No, it is not unpleasant, as well you know. But it isn't right, and you know that, too. I want to marry, Kate. You, of all people, should be aware of that."

His words made the chill down her spine intensify. Yes, she knew that. He'd wanted to marry Alyssa. And since he couldn't have the woman he'd loved for five years, he was willing to settle for her. She'd thought that would be enough when she came here. That he'd accept her as his wife, that they would pleasure each other in the bedchamber. Eventually, have children. Make a home together.

But now she knew it wasn't. She wanted his love, too.

"I'm sorry," she told him.

He snorted inelegantly. "Sorry! Is that supposed to make me feel better? What ails you? Many women here on the Tidewater would be delighted if I made them a proposal of marriage."

"Then maybe that's what you should do," she said, the words coming out of her mouth before she knew she intended to say them. She stared at him, wanting to take them back, knowing she couldn't.

Nicholas glared back at her. "Maybe I will," he said coldly, and turned to go.

"And perhaps I should leave here," she said to his straight, angry back.

"Perhaps you should," he'd said and, without turning again, left the room.

Kate had stared after him, sick at heart. Was she a complete fool? What if she did marry him? It could be all right. She loved him, and always would. Maybe that would be enough for them to be happy together.

"Kate!" Celia's impatient voice brought her out of her reverie. "Come, let us hurry. We do not want to miss anything."

Kate let the two girls tug her along. As they came in sight of the wharf, her steps slowed. Nicholas was standing there, waiting for the ship to maneuver close enough for a crewman to throw him the lines.

He turned as they approached, his eyes going over the three of them.

Celia ran up to him. "We came to watch. Oh, Cousin Nicholas, this is so exciting!"

"Are you finding it hard to wait for your surprise?" he asked.

Out of the corner of his eye, he watched Kate. She looked rested enough. Not as if, like he, she'd spent most of the night awake. Damnation! Why was she such a stubborn wench? She mightily pleased him in bed, and in every other way.

Except in her refusal to wed him.

"Oh, yes!" Celia answered, smiling up at him.

He smiled back, remembering what a solemn, sad little girl she'd been last autumn when Kate arrived. Now, she was a cheerful, happy child. He had Kate to thank for that, as for many other things. He couldn't imagine life without her.

And now, after last night, she might leave.

He truly did not know why she refused to wed him. When that had been her express purpose in coming here to the Tidewater. Her continued unwillingness was puzzling in the extreme. And maddening. He wanted a wife. He wanted to have children of his own. And he wanted them with Kate.

But now was no time to dwell on that. He returned his attention to the incoming vessel, wishing it were the *Rosalynde*.

Morgan had given up his command of the ship and left the area. Nicholas was worried about him and his apparent guilt over Aldon's death.

Devona had not yet found another captain for the *Rosalynde*. But she'd written to several prospective candidates for the position. Nicholas was amazed at how capably she'd taken over the reins of the plantation. He'd not realized how Henry had suppressed her natural talents all these years.

Several people stood on the ship's deck, looking toward the wharf. Three or four women, bondservants he supposed, going on up the river to other plantations. He could have afforded to buy one to help in the house, but Kate had insisted he save the money for plantation expenses.

Now, after last night's argument, he would probably have to do that after all. Kate would most likely leave. Of course, he had no intention of asking any of the simpering females of his acquaintance to become his wife, in spite of what, in his anger, he'd told her.

Again, he returned his wandering thoughts to the matter at hand. One of the women on the deck was small and daintily formed, with golden hair. It reminded him of Alyssa, the first time he'd seen her in the greengrocer shop.

The woman looked directly at him. She raised her hand and waved, a wide smile on her pretty mouth.

Nicholas frowned, wondering why she was doing that, and then a jolt traveled through him, a premonition. This was like that other time, last fall, when he'd waited on the Aldons' wharf for his bride-to-be to debark.

And instead, Kate, swathed in that dull-gray cloak, had walked off the ship.

The girl on the deck wore no cloak over her sky-blue gown. It was a warm and balmy day in late May, no need for that. She waved again, her mouth forming words he couldn't understand.

Nicholas glanced over at Kate to see her mouth open, her eyes wide with shock. The premonition turned into certainty as he looked at the girl on the deck once more.

That girl was Alyssa. But what was she doing here? And where was her fiancé?

Hearing a shout from the ship, he caught the thrown lines, made them fast, and then a crewman laid the planks. Alyssa was right behind the man, a wide smile on her pretty face.

Once on the wharf, Alyssa threw her arms around her sister. "Oh, Kate! It is so good to see you again!"

Automatically, Kate hugged her back. Over Alyssa's

head, she glanced at Nicholas, and a sharp pain seized her heart. He was staring at Alyssa as he had the first time he'd seen her, that day in the shop.

As if he were bewitched by her blonde beauty. As if he could never get his fill of looking at her.

Finished with the hug, Alyssa took her arms away and turned to Nicholas.

"Brother Nicholas! It is good to see you again, too!" She put her arms around Nicholas and hugged him, too, then lifted her face and kissed his cheek.

The pain in Kate's heart intensified as she watched Nicholas's arms go around Alyssa, saw him kiss her back. Alyssa didn't know that Nicholas and Kate weren't married. The letter she'd sent on one of the first ships to make the spring voyage to England couldn't have arrived before Alyssa had left Plymouth.

"Whatever are you doing here?" Kate asked. "What has happened?"

Alyssa's arms fell away from Nicholas. She turned back to Kate, her mouth making a little pouting grimace. "It's such a long story, Kate. Can't it wait until we are at the manor house? I am very tired and I do so want a nice, hot cup of tea."

She suddenly seemed to become conscious of the two girls staring at her with wide-eyed curiosity. She gave them a smile. "And who might you two be?"

"I'm Celia and this is my sister, Emily," Celia announced, as usual, never at a loss for words.

"Oh, yes, Philip and Lydea's children. Where are your parents?"

"They are dead," Celia said matter-of-factly.

Alyssa's face took on a shocked look. She glanced from Kate to Nicholas. "Oh, my. When did this happen?"

"Right after I sent you the letter and the passage money to come here," Nicholas said, a note of accusation in his voice, blended with something else Kate couldn't identify.

Alyssa had the grace to look shamefaced. "I am so sorry

about that. But it has all worked out very well, hasn't it? Except for me, of course."

By now they were walking away from the wharf, up the lane toward the cottage, Kate and Alyssa side by side, Nicholas and the girls behind.

Kate knew she must tell her sister that she and Nicholas hadn't married, but first she wanted to know why her sister was here instead of back in Plymouth with her fiancé—or husband, by now.

"What do you mean, except for you?" she asked.

"Kate, please don't be angry with me, but I have sold the shop. That's how I was able to afford passage here."

Kate drew her breath in sharply. "Sold the shop? But that was to be yours and John's livelihood!"

"I know. But that doesn't matter anymore." Alyssa turned and gave her sister a watery smile. "John and I are no longer engaged. We had a most terrible argument and I told him I never wanted to see him again. So, you see, I had no reason to stay in Plymouth. I decided I'd come here to the New World to live with you and Nicholas."

Kate half-turned and glanced at Nicholas. The stunned look that had been on his face ever since Alyssa had stepped onto the wharf had intensified. He was staring at the back of her neck as if it fascinated him.

The pain around Kate's heart returned. Alyssa, no longer betrothed, was planning to live in the same house with the man she'd once loved.

And who, for all Kate knew, still loved her.

The time had come to tell Alyssa the true state of affairs, but instead, delaying, Kate asked another question. "Who bought the shop?"

Alyssa's smile was braver now that it appeared her sister wasn't going to scold her. "Old Mr. Oglethorpe! And he gave me a good price, too."

Kate doubted that. Cecil Oglethorpe had been her elderly suitor. He'd wanted to make her his third wife, but Kate had strongly suspected the real motive for his ardent courtship had been to acquire possession of her half of the shop.

"I have brought your share of the money, Kate. I know you don't need it now, but you can put it aside for something frivolous you might want."

Kate cleared her throat. She couldn't put it off any longer. "Nicholas and I aren't married."

Alyssa's head turned sharply and she stared at her sister in a shock as apparently great as Kate's when she saw Alyssa on the ship's deck. "Not married? Why ever not?"

The cottage loomed ahead, thank God. Instead of answering her sister's question, she said, "Let's go inside and have tea."

"Here?" Alyssa asked, her voice a high squeak. "Why aren't we going to the manor house?"

"This is where we live," Kate said. "The manor house burned to the ground."

Alyssa's eyes grew wide. "Burned? But when? Was that—"

"We'll talk about it later," Kate said, relieved when Alyssa said no more.

Kate led the way inside and hurried to make up the fire and put the kettle on. Nicholas sat down at the table. The twins, trailed by Edward, stood in the middle of the floor, still obviously fascinated by Alyssa.

As for Alyssa herself, she, too, stood and gazed around the room.

Kate tried to see it with her sister's eyes. A big, plain room, but clean and tidy. And even cheerful, with its wildflowers in the table's center and the new muslin curtains Kate had made for the two small-paned windows.

The plank floor was white from scrubbing with sand, and the rug she'd braided from rags lay before the hearth. The pewter plates and mugs on the shelf shone from polishing.

Altogether, it was a far different room from the one

she'd entered that first night she'd arrived here in this Tidewater country.

She was proud of her accomplishments even while she saw the room with Alyssa's eyes. Plain, with simple furnishings. No better than the rooms they'd occupied above the shop. Maybe not as good.

Going to the shelf for the porcelain teapot, Kate smiled at her sister even though she felt more like shaking her. Alyssa had truly and well burned her bridges behind her. There was nothing for either of them to go back to Plymouth for now.

Kate set the teapot on the table, not looking at Nicholas. "Come sit down," she told Alyssa, then glanced at the twins. "Why don't you girls go outside and play with Edward?"

Celia looked as if she were going to argue but then turned to Emily. "Come along," she said, and they left the cottage.

A few minutes later, seated around the table, Kate glanced at Nicholas. He stared at his steaming teacup as if he wished it contained something stronger. No wonder. So did she.

Alyssa sat across from Nicholas, leaving Kate at the far end, close to the hearth, her accustomed place.

Kate didn't like the way the two of them looked there, across from each other. It made her think too strongly of the many times Nicholas had been at their rooms in Plymouth, sitting like that with Alyssa.

"We need to talk," Kate said abruptly. The words reminded her of the times Nicholas had told her that. And when they'd finally had their calm, sensible talk, it had settled nothing.

They'd ended up on this very hearth rug, locked in each other's arms.

Kate felt her face warming and quickly turned the thoughts aside. She glanced at Nicholas again. He'd stopped staring into his tea and was once more gazing on Alyssa's blonde curls and blue eyes.

And Alyssa looked back at him from under her long lashes, a dimpled smile on her face.

An odd feeling swept over Kate, as if she were going back in time, to when Nicholas had been courting Alyssa.

Chapter 28

Alyssa gave Nicholas another simpering smile, her dimple showing. "I do so want to see your plantation, Nicholas."

He stared at her, still stupefied at the callow boy he'd been.

My God, what had he ever seen in this female to make him wait for her five long years? Had she always been so obvious? Why, she was no better than Georgianna Wilson! Maybe worse.

And Kate seemed as stunned at her sister's arrival as he. She was staring at Alyssa and him as if she couldn't stand the sight of either of them.

"Nicholas?" Alyssa asked again, a note of impatience in her voice.

He forced a smile. "Yes, Alyssa. I heard you."

"Are you too busy to take me around?"

Damnation! That was the last thing he wanted to do—listen to her silly prattle . . . watch her bat her eyelashes, flirting with him as she did with all males.

A sudden, disturbing thought hit him. Or did she have

something else in mind now that she was no longer engaged and she'd discovered he and Kate weren't married?

"As a matter of fact, I—"

His voice broke off. He glanced at Kate again.

She was no longer looking at him and Alyssa. Now she stared into her teacup as if totally engrossed, but her hand clenched the handle so hard her knuckles were white.

Something was bothering Kate. Something more than their quarrel last night. Something more than the fact her sister had sold the shop and come here to live.

Nicholas's dazed surprise took another direction.

Kate was showing all the signs of an acute attack of jealousy. She looked as he imagined he must have that first day Duncan had arrived and flattered her so outrageously.

Could that be possible?

He thought about it for a while, then drained his tea and stood. He looked down at Alyssa, still gazing up at him, a pout on her pretty face, and smiled.

"Today I have urgent tasks to attend to. But tomorrow I would be delighted to show you the whole of Lydea's Pride."

Alyssa clapped her hands together as one of the twins might do. "Oh! That will be such fun!"

Satisfaction mingled with frustrated annoyance inside Nicholas. He was not a devious man. He didn't enjoy intrigues and secrets.

How could he make Kate think he was once again interested in Alyssa, while at the same time not encourage the girl if, indeed, she had anything like that in mind?

But he'd do it. He and Kate couldn't go on as they had. And he'd done everything he knew to persuade her to marry him. Except this. He was going to lose Kate anyway. So he may as well risk all on this venture.

And just possibly it would work.

* * *

"This is such a tiny room!" Alyssa looked around Kate's bedchamber that evening, her blue eyes wide with surprise.

"It's adequate for me." But not for two people, Kate thought. But it wouldn't be for long.

Somehow she'd gotten through the rest of the day.

Alyssa hadn't asked Kate about what had happened between her and Nicholas and, in her turn, Kate had asked nothing further about her sister's own problems with John.

At dinner and supper, Alyssa tried to charm the twins and her former fiancé, her blue eyes sparkling, her dimples always in evidence.

She'd done a good job of it, too, Kate thought, as Alyssa threw open her trunk. The twins seemed every bit as captivated as Nicholas, who'd seemed bemused and charmed, just as he used to back in Plymouth. And yet there was something else in his demeanor, something almost guilty.

And why should that be surprising? Kate thought, clearing out two drawers of the chest. Of course there would be guilt. After all, he'd just lately proposed to her again.

"Where can I put my clothes?" Alyssa asked, looking about the austerely furnished room.

"I'll have Nicholas put up more pegs." Kate wondered where Alyssa had found the money for these expensive-looking things. She must have dipped heavily into the shop's profits these last months.

Alyssa, a frothy confection of white silk and lace thrown over her arm, glanced at Kate. "Why did you and Nicholas not marry?" she asked.

Kate drew her breath in sharply, even though she'd known this question would have to be answered eventually.

She decided to be as blunt as Alyssa. "Nicholas accused me of persuading you into breaking your troth with him. He would have nothing to do with wedding me; and by that time, he'd made me so angry I wouldn't have considered it, either."

Alyssa's eyes widened. "I am sorry, Kate. I never dreamed he'd think anything like that."

Her sister's voice sounded completely sincere, Kate thought. Maybe it was. "Neither did I. But since I owed him passage money and Nicholas needed someone to look after Celia and Emily and take care of the cottage, I decided to stay on for a while."

"Does Nicholas not even have enough coin to hire someone to do the housework—or buy a slave or two?" Alyssa asked.

Now that sounded more like the girl who was her sister. "Nicholas freed all the slaves after Philip and Lydea's deaths. He doesn't like slavery," Kate answered sharply.

"Oh." Alyssa absentmindedly smoothed the gown she still held. Then, she nodded at Kate. "I can understand that. I don't believe that I do, either."

Amazed, Kate stared at her. Had her younger sister at last begun to mature? Then another thought occurred to her. Was Alyssa trying to change for Nicholas's sake? Of course she would know that she'd have to prove she regretted breaking the engagement.

What better way than to approve of all the things that Nicholas did? Be willing to share his time of misfortune?

"Nor do I," Kate answered finally. "But it's left him terribly shorthanded. He's managed to hire a few more men to help with the crops, but he still works harder than any of them."

Alyssa nodded, then extracted nightclothes from the trunk and laid her dress back in it. "He was always like that, on his family's farm, if you recall. All the tales he used to tell about the fortune he was going to make in the New World."

"Yes." Kate decided enough had been said about this. Now, she had some questions to ask. "Don't you think that you were a bit hasty in selling the shop and coming here just because you and John quarreled?"

"No! You don't understand." Alyssa turned quickly

away. "It was such a terrible quarrel! John said I was j— just a selfish little girl. That I'd never grow up enough to be a good wife. Then, he went off to work at his uncle's shop in London. What was I to do?"

Kate expelled a breath. So that was the way of it. Alyssa had not done the jilting this time—but had been rejected herself. Considering her sister's temperament, no wonder she'd done what she had.

"I'm sorry," Kate said. "But you realize I'm not staying here much longer. I'm going to Chestertown to find work in a shop. Our situation won't be nearly as good as it was in Plymouth where we owned the shop."

Alyssa turned back to her. "Maybe you could buy a shop with your share from the sale of ours. I have a little coin left from my passage, too, I could give you."

A chill ran down Kate's back. Why was Alyssa phrasing her words like that? As if it would be entirely Kate's doing. The buying and running of the shop, all of it?

As if Alyssa had other, different plans for her own future.

"Yes, that may be a possibility," Kate told her, moving to the bed to turn back the quilt. "This isn't a very large bed, either, I'm afraid. Not nearly as large as the one we shared in Plymouth."

The words brought back memories of the years she'd cared for her sister after their mother died. Alyssa had been a sweet little girl, wanting to please.

"It is fine." Alyssa moved up beside her, slipping her arm around Kate's waist. "I've missed you. I couldn't bear to think of staying on there and running the shop by myself."

Unexpectedly, tears filled Kate's eyes. Her sister's words had been simple, genuine. "I've missed you, too." She squeezed Alyssa's hand.

They stood, linked together by memories of their shared past; then, Alyssa slid her arm away and moved back. She gave Kate a tentative smile. "So you and Nicholas have no plans to wed?"

Kate swallowed. How should she answer? With the truth, that Nicholas had asked her to marry him? That she'd refused because she couldn't endure a marriage to a man who didn't love her? That she'd given her virginity to Nicholas—and that they'd made love on several occasions since that first time? No! Her pride wouldn't let her admit that, even to her sister.

Especially to her sister, who'd once been deeply loved by the same man. Who, perhaps, still was.

She shook her head. "We have absolutely no plans to wed," she said firmly.

Something in Alyssa's eyes flickered. She cleared her throat. "Then, you would have no objections if Nicholas and I should discover that we perhaps still cared for each other?"

For a moment, Kate couldn't catch her breath. She felt as if her sister had struck her in the stomach with her fist.

"I would have no objections," she at last managed to answer.

Alyssa gazed at her, then a wry smile curved her mouth. "I'm sorry I talked you into this plan. But you seem to be happy here in the New World. You don't regret leaving Plymouth?"

"No. And you didn't talk me into it. I wouldn't have come if I hadn't wanted to."

"And *I'm* glad to hear you say that." Alyssa's smile widened. "So, you would not hate me if, perchance, Nicholas and I should settle our differences?"

That was a delicate way of phrasing what she was truly asking, Kate thought. Alyssa wanted Kate's blessing on her attempt to win Nicholas back.

"No, I would hate neither of you," she said, relieved her voice didn't reveal her pain.

Alyssa gave Kate a hug and kissed her cheek. "Thank you, sister dear. Now, shall we go on to bed? I am most fearfully tired."

"I'm sure you are. I remember how tired I was the day I arrived here."

That wasn't all she remembered about that first day. She had memories to last her a lifetime from her stay here.

And they would have to do, because that's all she might ever have from Nicholas.

Kate dished up breakfast to Nicholas and the twins. Alyssa had been sound asleep, exhausted from her journey, so Kate had left her sleeping.

As she put a steaming dish of spoonbread on the table, her glance caught Nicholas's. He had an odd, speculative look on his face, almost as if he half-wanted to say something to her but hadn't made up his mind for certain whether to do it.

"Kate!" Celia said from across the room. "Did you see the wonderful dress materials that Cousin Nicholas bought for me?"

She held up a length of peach cloth from a chair, another length of teal blue beneath it. And beneath that lay a larger length of a muted, beautiful shade of sea-foam green. Nicholas must have brought them when he came in just now.

Startled, Kate realized the cloth must be silk.

"No, I did not," she admitted.

Emily held up the second length against her plain, everyday brown dress. "See, this one is mine. Isn't it beautiful?" She pointed to the remaining bolt. "And this one is for you."

Kate swallowed. The fabric was a perfect color for her. How had Nicholas known that? Men usually didn't pay much attention to that kind of thing.

"It is, indeed, beautiful cloth." Her gaze found Nicholas's again. He still had that odd look on his face. "Thank you," she told him.

"You are very welcome," he said. "I hope this will make up for my not giving you a Christmas gift."

"I had long forgotten about that," she said.

"*I* had not."

A noise from the stairs drew Kate's attention. Alyssa came into the room. She wore a pale-yellow silk gown trimmed in lace, which enhanced her fragile blonde beauty. Her golden hair was arranged in perfect ringlets around her heart-shaped face.

"I'm sorry I overslept, but I was so *very* tired from the journey," she said, smiling prettily as she reached the table and stood at the chair across from Nicholas that she'd occupied yesterday.

"I know. That's why I didn't awaken you," Kate said, summoning a return smile. Alyssa looked exquisite, as well she must know. The twins were staring at her, wide-eyed.

Suddenly conscious of her own plain dark-green day dress, her pulled-back hair, Kate forced herself to keep her gaze off Nicholas. She didn't want to see how he looked at Alyssa; and she didn't care, she tried to convince herself.

"Can I help with anything?" Alyssa asked.

"No, it's ready," Kate answered, surprised at her sister's offer. "Go ahead and sit down."

"All right." Alyssa slipped gracefully into the chair.

After setting the last serving dish on the table, Kate sat, too.

"My goodness, do you always eat this much for breakfast?" Alyssa asked.

"Yes, always."

Remembering how surprised she'd been herself that first morning when the twins told her the breakfast Nicholas expected, and the mess she'd made of the spoonbread, Kate glanced across at Celia.

Gone was the sullen, miserable girl of those days. In her place was a lively, happy child. A pang of anticipated loss went through Kate. How could she leave these children she'd grown to love as if they were her own? Fast on the heels of that thought came another, accompanied by an even sharper stab of pain.

How could she bear to leave Nicholas?

But how could she stay?

Then, as pain knifed through her, Kate felt anger at herself.

She'd been a fool, demanding love from Nicholas when he'd offered her marriage. Love could come in time, she'd heard people say. Many people married for purely practical reasons and later grew to love each other. And even if Nicholas never loved her, she loved him.

Might that not be enough?

But Nicholas was disgusted with her. Moreover, Alyssa was in his life again; and only last night, Kate had given Alyssa her blessing to try to win Nicholas back.

She'd been a fool to do that, too. But she wasn't a person to go back on her word.

A surge of determination filled her. However, in this case she must. She wouldn't accept defeat that easily. She would go down fighting, if she went down at all. Alyssa didn't have him yet.

She looked at Nicholas, who, as she'd expected, was gazing at Alyssa, on his face the expression he'd worn yesterday. Rapt bemusement—mixed with something else.

In her turn, Alyssa was giving him one of her bewitching, dimpled smiles that could melt stone. And Nicholas was certainly not made of stone. Kate shivered at that thought, remembering the times he'd held her in his arms.

"This is Nicholas's favorite breakfast dish," Kate said. "I made a mess of it my first day here, but now I have learned to cook it to his satisfaction. Isn't that so, Nicholas?" she asked sweetly.

Nicholas turned from his apparent contemplation of Alyssa's beauty to look at her. "Why, yes, of course you have, Kate."

Kate's smile was sweet, too. "Give me your plate and I will serve you."

"Oh, yes." Returning her smile, Nicholas handed her his pewter plate.

That wasn't much, but it was a start, Kate thought, her mouth hurting from her prolonged smile.

Alyssa glanced from one to the other of them, a slight frown between her perfectly shaped brows. "I am ready to see all of your plantation, Nicholas," she said. "Will you be able to take me with you this morning?"

He took his heaping plate from Kate and set it down in its place. He gave Alyssa a dazzling smile.

"Didn't I promise you that yesterday? You'll need to put on a different gown, though. That one would be ruined in a few minutes."

Alyssa looked down at her lovely gown and her frown deepened. Then, it cleared, and she smiled. "What a ninny I am! But you know I'm not used to the country. Kate and I have always lived in Plymouth."

"The first day I came, I got lost in a wood and Nicholas had to rescue me," Kate put in quickly. She tilted her head and gave Nicholas a coquettish smile. "Didn't you?"

"Yes, I did," Nicholas answered.

Kate had a lovely smile. And she was actually flirting with him. Something she'd never done before. His plan was already bearing fruit.

He should feel triumphant, but he didn't. He felt uncomfortable and half ashamed of himself. He didn't like what he was doing. It was a deuced nuisance!

But he would keep it up as long as need be. That is, if he could manage to continue fooling both of them, he amended.

"We may be quite some time," he said. "I think it better if Emily and Celia remain here."

"Oh, Cousin Nicholas!" Celia protested at once. "Why can't we go? We do so want to!"

"Yes!" Emily chimed in. "Please."

Kate's smile faded. She fixed them both with a firm look.

"You heard your cousin. And besides, we have lessons to do."

The twins subsided and Nicholas frowned. *He'd* erased that smile from Kate's face. It had been like watching clouds cover the sun.

He *hated* this subterfuge!

But he wanted Kate.

And he'd do whatever was necessary to have her.

Chapter 29

Nicholas and Alyssa had, indeed, taken their time, Kate thought, forcing smiles for them as they came in together for dinner. He'd undoubtedly showed her every inch of Lydea's Pride.

Alyssa was flushed and prettier than ever, even if she had changed into a simple blue gown. It obviously didn't matter what her sister wore. She would always be lovely.

Kate had also changed—into her most flattering apple-green day gown. She'd arranged her hair more becomingly, too. Now, she wondered why she'd bothered. She was still elder-sister Kate, tall and red-haired, and Alyssa was still the dainty, beautiful one.

And she'd had hours alone with Nicholas today. What had they done besides walk all over the plantation? Nothing! Kate told herself quickly, horrified at her dark thoughts.

Of course she didn't think the two of them had been hidden away somewhere locked in passionate embraces.

"Oh, Kate, I didn't mean to leave all the work for you!" Alyssa said. "I will clean up after the meal."

"All right," Kate agreed, surprised at her sister's offer. Maybe she had truly changed.

But the more likely explanation was the one Kate had considered last night. She was trying to favorably impress Nicholas.

An aim which she seemed to have accomplished, Kate thought, a pain hitting her middle as she saw Nicholas's eyes on Alyssa.

"We are having the fish stew that you like so well, Nicholas," Kate said sweetly, her voice lingering on his name. She gave the pot one last stir, then got down the bowls from the shelf.

When she turned back, Nicholas was staring at her, an odd, uncomfortable look on his face. His expression swiftly turned to an even odder half-smile. "Good," he answered.

What did that look mean? Kate wondered, confused by the sudden change.

"You remember, I made it that first evening I arrived here." Turning to Alyssa, she forced herself to go on. "The cottage was in such disorder! Nicholas's servant had run away that day, and he'd expected her to have everything tidy."

For your arrival, Kate added silently. *He didn't care how I saw it.* The thought made her spirits drop even further.

"But I tidied up, and the evening turned out well after all, didn't it?" she said coyly, giving Nicholas an arch smile.

Kate felt her face warm. She was deliberately trying to make him remember he'd taken her into his arms later that evening, and they'd shared a passionate kiss.

He gazed at her, that discomfited look on his face; then, as before, his expression changed. He cocked his head to the side and gave her another half-smile, this one somehow knowing.

As if he realized exactly what she was up to and was amused, rather than intrigued, by her efforts.

"Yes," he said briefly.

Her blush deepened. She couldn't go on with this! She

was a direct, plain-spoken woman. Which Nicholas well knew. All she was doing was making a fool of herself. But neither could she let Alyssa have Nicholas without fighting for him.

With grim determination, the rest of the meal she kept up her sprightly chatter and smiles even though she felt increasingly uncomfortable.

She caught Alyssa's reflective glance on her more than once; and when the meal was over, the twins and Nicholas gone again, she expected her sister to question her. But she didn't. Alyssa, as promised, cleaned up the kitchen, then helped Kate with the work of the cottage that afternoon and also with supper.

More than ever, that evening, Kate was painfully aware they were two women vying for one man. As the evening wore on, Nicholas's face took on a hunted look.

No wonder. Kate felt more of a fool with every second that passed.

At last, Alyssa yawned hugely.

"I am very tired tonight, too. I believe I will go to bed." She turned to Kate. "Are you coming, sister?"

Kate glanced at Nicholas, absorbed in one of his books. Or pretending to be. She pressed her lips together. Alyssa was giving her a chance to be alone with him. But she couldn't bear the thought of more false smiles and eyelash-fluttering.

"Yes, I am." She might as well go upstairs, too. And she owed her sister an explanation for her behavior.

Pulling her nightdress over her head a few minutes later, Kate knew the time had come to provide it. Alyssa wore a pretty embroidered nightdress, and looked very young and innocent.

And perplexed. As well she might.

Alyssa bit her lower lip, looking up at Kate from under her long lashes. "This is a bit awkward, Kate. But last eve you said you had no plans to wed with Nicholas, that you would not be upset if . . ."

"If you and he decided you still wanted each other," Kate finished for her.

Alyssa nodded, gratefully. "Yes. Yet, today, it appears your interest in him has been revived. But you gave me to believe that you and he never . . ."

Kate felt vexed at herself. She should have told Alyssa the truth last night. No, she couldn't have! "Nicholas does not love me," she said finally. "So you need not worry about that."

There, that was the truth and was as far as she would go. She couldn't bear to tell Alyssa the whole of it.

Alyssa opened her mouth, then closed it again. She worried her bottom lip, a frown between her eyes.

Looking at her sister, seeing how her every gesture was gracefully feminine and appealing—even now, when there was no need to try for such effects—Kate realized she'd come to another decision.

She would no longer simper and flirt with Nicholas like the insufferable Georgianna Wilson. Or Alyssa. That wasn't her way, and Nicholas obviously hadn't been taken in by her foolish attempts. No, he was secretly laughing at her. If she'd not been able to win his love in all these months by being herself, she certainly couldn't do it with these strategies.

"You have my blessing to try to win Nicholas back," Kate said finally. "Just as I told you last night."

"I don't understand you, sister dear," Alyssa said, the frown smoothing out. "But I'll continue to take you at your word. I can see nothing else for me to do."

That didn't sound like a woman who still loved a man, Kate thought, chilled. But, then, why had she supposed that was the case?

Alyssa had been jilted by her fiancé, sold the shop, and come here to live with her, as she'd thought, now well-off sister and brother-in-law. Until she found a new prospective husband for herself.

Now, all that was changed. She could come along with

Kate when she left here, try to find some kind of employment. Of course, if Kate bought a shop, Alyssa could work there. But that was far from being a sure thing.

No wonder she'd decided instead to try to win Nicholas back. Whether she loved him or not. It was the best solution for Alyssa, and Alyssa had always looked out for her own interests.

On the other hand, perhaps Alyssa still loved Nicholas. Maybe it was *John* she hadn't truly loved and that was why they'd quarreled and parted.

Kate's head spun with confusion. What a tangled mess this was! How could it ever be sorted out? Maybe it couldn't. But maybe it could, if they all talked this over honestly and openly.

She glanced at Alyssa again. What would her sister do if Kate demanded to know if she loved Nicholas or merely wanted to gain security for herself?

And at the thought of marching up to Nicholas and asking him which of the two women he preferred, Kate's spirit quailed.

No, plain-spoken or not, she couldn't do either of those things.

"Good night," she told her sister and climbed into bed.

But it was a long time before Kate slept. Sometime during the night, she awoke, her mind still fogged with sleep, dimly aware some sound had disturbed her.

She rolled over on her back, realizing she now had enough room to fully stretch out in the bed. And that was because her sister's side was empty, the covers thrown back.

Where was Alyssa? Kate, now fully awake, sat up and looked around the small room. There were no nooks and crannies here to conceal anyone. The door gaped open. Nicholas had repaired the broken latch, but Alyssa had apparently not fully closed it behind her as she left the room.

A sound came from somewhere beyond the chamber—of distress—someone crying. Had one of the twins taken ill? Kate flung her covers back and padded across the bare floor. The door opened silently under her hand and she stepped over the sill, listening.

Nicholas's door was tightly closed. The twins' was ajar. Could it be Celia, after all this time, once again in the grip of a nightmare?

Then the sound came again, from downstairs, and now Kate realized it was her sister weeping.

"Oh, Nicholas, I am so ashamed of myself for what I did to you. Can you ever forgive me?" Alyssa's voice, muffled by tears but still understandable, floated up the stairs.

Kate stiffened, her hand tightening on the door latch.

"There, there," Nicholas answered. "Of course I forgive you. You were very young when I left. Scarcely more than a child."

"But I've been such a fool!" Alyssa wailed, then broke into sobs again. "I didn't know what I wanted, and now it's too late."

"Are you certain of that?" Nicholas asked. "Maybe it isn't."

Kate sucked in her breath at his response.

"What are you saying?" Alyssa asked.

"That perhaps you can make amends for your mistake."

"Do you really think so?" Alyssa's voice trembled with hope.

"Yes, I do. None of us is perfect. We all make mistakes. I have made many myself."

"Oh, Nicholas!"

Kate heard the sound of a chair scraping across the wood floor.

"Oh, Nicholas! I need to be held so badly."

"Then come here, Alyssa, my lamb, and I will hold you."

Kate's heart stopped for an instant; her body grew rigid. Then, she stepped back inside the room and very quietly latched the door. Like a sleepwalker she moved across the floor to her bed and lay down.

The night was pitch dark. No silver of moon or starlight

came through the small window. Kate lay on her back, staring into the blackness.

She'd just been given the answer to the question that had haunted her since she'd arrived here last fall. The answers to the questions she'd posed to herself before she went to bed tonight.

Nicholas did, indeed, still love Alyssa. And she still loved him. They were going to forget the past and make a life together.

She didn't know how much time had passed when Alyssa came back upstairs and quietly got into the bed. Kate closed her eyes, pretending sleep.

Nicholas's distinctive scent, a blend of tobacco and the fresh scent of the outdoors, drifted across to her. She pictured Nicholas and Alyssa, as they must have been only a few minutes ago, deep in each other's arms.

Kate clenched her fists until her nails bit into her palms. How could she face them tomorrow? Watch the happy looks on their faces as they told her their wonderful news?

But she would have to. There was no way out. At least neither of them knew how she felt. That was some consolation. Her pride would still be intact.

She'd take her share of the shop profits and try to find another shop to buy in Chestertown. Pain seized her, almost doubling her up. No, she had to go farther away than Chestertown because she couldn't stand the anguish of seeing Nicholas and knowing he would never be hers.

But that plan would be impossible since he'd be married to her sister. Naturally, Alyssa, knowing nothing of how Kate felt, would expect them to visit back and forth.

In time, there would be nieces and nephews, too.

Kate buried her head in her pillow to muffle the sobs she couldn't hold back. Finally, in the depths of her despair, another thought came to her.

She could go back to Plymouth. That was a bleak prospect since she'd no longer have the shop for her livelihood.

She would have to try to find a job as a clerk, which might be hard to do.

But nothing could be worse than staying here.

Alyssa was up and gone when Kate awoke. She saw by the sun's slant it must be near nine o'clock. For the second time since she'd come to Lydea's Pride, she'd overslept. Little wonder, since she'd stayed awake most of the night. She felt exhausted and drained, but her decision hadn't changed.

She would leave here as soon as possible.

Kate slowly dressed, her body as well as her heart aching, hoping Alyssa wouldn't be in the cottage when she went down.

Her wish was granted. The cottage was empty, bright morning sunlight streaming through the open doorway. She didn't hear the twins outside, laughing and playing as they usually were. Even Edward was nowhere in evidence.

But the hearth fire was lit, a kettle steaming. Alyssa must have done that before she went wherever she'd gone. Kate made a pot of tea and sat at the table to drink a heartening mug.

She heard the sound of the twins' voices from down the lane and quickly tried to pull herself together so they wouldn't suspect anything was wrong.

Celia burst into the room, followed by Emily. "Kate! You shouldn't have overslept! The *Fleda* has just come in."

"Another ship? So soon?" So that's where everyone had disappeared to.

Emily nodded. "Yes, and it stopped here because Cousin Nicholas had ordered some special seeds."

Kate managed a smile for Celia, who skipped across the room and gave her an exuberant hug, followed in a moment by Emily. Kate hugged them back. Oh, how she would miss them!

"And that's not all. Alyssa got a letter from England!" Emily added, her brown eyes alight with excitement.

A sound from the doorway made Kate turn in that direction. Her sister walked across the threshold, holding a square white envelope in her hand, a stunned expression on her pretty face.

Kate swallowed. "Good morning."

Alyssa nodded vaguely, then walked toward the stairs and disappeared.

Kate stared after her. Had Alyssa gotten bad news? But from whom? If the letter were from one of their Devon cousins, it would surely have been addressed to both of them. John? No, Kate dismissed that idea. Alyssa had broken with him. It was Nicholas she wanted now.

Resolutely, Kate pushed down the pain that surfaced again at that thought. She considered following her sister, asking if something were wrong, then thought better of it.

Kate moved her chair back and rose. "I'd better be starting breakfast," she said briskly. "You girls put the dishes around."

They did, then went back outside to play with Edward.

Moving about her accustomed tasks, Kate kept a watchful eye toward the door, dreading the moment Nicholas would arrive for his meal. She'd just added another small log to the fire when her peripheral vision caught movement at the stairway door.

Turning, she saw Alyssa standing in the doorway, a look of radiant joy on her face. She still held the letter in her hand.

Her eyes met Kate's and a wide smile lit her face. She moved forward, almost seeming to float across the floor. "Oh, Kate!" she said. "I am the happiest person in the world!"

Kate's heart jumped in her chest. The moment she'd been dreading had arrived. Whatever had been in the letter, it wasn't bad enough to destroy her happiness in her rediscovered love for Nicholas.

Although it took every bit of will she possessed, Kate forced a smile. "I'm glad for you—and for Nicholas."

A puzzled look mingled with the radiance on Alyssa's face. "Nicholas? What do you mean?"

Too late, Kate realized she'd given away her eavesdropping. "I'm sorry, last night I awoke and when I didn't find you in the bed or the room, I opened the door, and I—heard you and Nicholas."

Alyssa shrugged. "I don't mind if you heard us. Oh, but, Kate, listen! This letter is from John! He's sorry that we quarreled. He hasn't been able to forget me and he wants me to come back to England at once and marry him. Isn't that wonderful?"

Kate stared at her. "But what about Nicholas?"

"He won't mind," Alyssa said airily, her pretty face still alight.

"Won't *mind?*" Kate echoed. She'd been very wrong. Her sister hadn't grown up one iota. "But only last night, you and Nicholas—"

"Will you stop talking about Nicholas and listen to me?" Alyssa said, her face sobering. She gave Kate a pleading look. "There's only one problem. I don't have the coin for my return voyage to Plymouth. Kate, I know you need your share from the sale of the shop, but could you lend it to me? I *must* go back to John! I love him so very much. We will pay you back as soon as possible."

Kate felt like slapping her sister. "Then why did you ask me if I minded your trying to win Nicholas back?"

"Because I thought I'd lost John forever, of course."

"Then you were prepared to marry Nicholas even though your heart still belonged to John? And even after last night, you—"

"Never mind all that. It isn't important! Please, Kate, I have to know now. If you'll lend me the money, I can get on board the *Fleda* and go back with her on her return voyage."

"Yes, I will lend you the money," Kate said woodenly.

Alyssa threw her arms around Kate, hugging her. "You are the best sister anyone ever had. I'll never forget this. Now, I must go get my things together."

She turned and hurried back up the stairs.

Kate looked after her. If she'd thought things were in a hopeless muddle a few days ago, that was nothing compared to now. She'd just promised to lend her sister the money she desperately needed herself.

She was back to the same penniless state as when she'd come here. Worse. Now she was penniless and also had a broken heart that she feared would never mend.

And her selfish, cruel sister was planning to leave Nicholas, go back to John, after only last night being in Nicholas's arms, kissing him, making him new promises.

Kate wasn't the only one with a broken heart. Nicholas had lost his first love, his true love, not once, but twice. How would he be able to stand it?

A noise at the door made her lift her head in that direction.

Nicholas stood in the doorway, smiling at her as if he hadn't a care in the world.

Chapter 30

"Is breakfast ready?" Nicholas asked, coming into the room.

A wave of tenderness swept over him as he looked at Kate. As usual, locks of her red-gold hair had come loose from its coil and curled about her ears. He loved her hair. No other woman had hair like Kate's. He would be able to find her in a room full of people.

She lifted her head and stared at him. "Almost," she answered, then quickly turned back to the pots on the hearth.

He loved her sea-foam eyes! Her dark, winged brows and smooth forehead.

These last two days had been hell.

Trying to make Kate jealous of Alyssa had proved to be not only a distasteful undertaking, but a doomed one. He'd only confused Kate with his unconvincing performance.

And she wasn't a whit better at flirting with him than he was at flirting with Alyssa. Both of them were too blunt, too forthright, for such maneuverings.

Kate turned again and looked at him. He loved the proud way she held her head, too.

Her silly, coy expression of yesterday and last eve was gone, replaced with a strange mixture of pain and compassion.

Confusion hit him. What did that look mean?

He walked to the table and pulled out a chair. "The girls are back down at the wharf," he said into what suddenly seemed an uneasy, tension-filled silence. "They told me Alyssa received a letter from England."

Kate nodded, the movement wooden and jerky. "Yes. She did."

A sudden clatter on the stairs brought his head around. Alyssa stood there, a wide smile on her face.

"Nicholas," she asked, "will you please bring down my trunk?"

Kate hurried to the door and outside without another word to either of them.

Surprised, Nicholas stared at her back as she disappeared from view. He loved her proud, erect carriage, too.

He loved *her*.

His skittering thoughts came to a stop.

Yes, of course, he loved her. And had for a long time now. Maybe even since he'd taken her hand that first day and helped her onto the wharf.

Why had it taken so long for him to realize it?

Had he, far back in his mind and heart, thought that he still cared for Alyssa? That he couldn't forget his first love, ever be able to give Kate all of himself? Was that why he'd never told her he loved her?

"Nicholas! Please hasten!" Alyssa's anxious voice said again, and he turned to her.

Kate hurried up the lane, relieved to be out of the cottage, spared being involved in what could only be a terrible scene. In spite of her own pain, her heart ached for Nicholas.

Halfway to the wharf, she veered off toward the barn. She would see if Tucker were around and talk to him. She found him mending harness in the blacksmith shop attached to one end of the main building.

"Good morrow, Mistress Kate," he greeted her, a warm smile spreading over his face. "What brings you here at this hour? Thought I just saw Master Nicholas go up to the house for breakfast."

Kate let out huge sigh and seated herself on a stool. "Yes, you did." She didn't want to talk about what had just happened. She resolutely tried to push it out of her mind. "How are things going between you and Daisy?" she asked.

Tucker's smile widened. "Just fine. She 'bout has the new girl trained to take her place. We'll be gettin' married next month, and then Daisy can move here with me. Miss Devona givin' us a fine wedding."

"I know. I'm so glad." Kate found a return smile for him. How she wished Devona were here now! "Do you need anything else for your cabin?"

Tucker shook his head. "No, mistress. I've been makin' some furniture, and Miss Devona gave Daisy a heap o' things to bring along. Daisy is a good worker. She'll be a lot of help to you."

His words turned the knife deeper inside her. She glanced at Tucker, her mood changing, suddenly wanting to talk to him, unload her worries.

"What's the matter, Mistress Kate? You look sorely troubled."

"I am," Kate admitted. She glanced up at him. "Tucker, everything is in such a muddle! My sister is going back to England to marry the man she was engaged to."

"That don't seem like the kind of news to put that sorrowful look on your face."

"It isn't. I mean," Kate floundered, "that's not why I'm upset. Well, it is, but that's because she—"

"There you are," Nicholas's voice said from behind her. "We couldn't figure where you'd gotten to. You'd better come on now if you want to say farewell to your sister."

Kate stiffened at Nicholas's words, then slowly got up. His voice didn't sound as if he'd just lost the only woman he'd ever loved for the second time.

She smiled at the Negro man. "Goodbye, Tucker."

He nodded, returning the smile. "Good day, mistress. Master."

Kate turned toward Nicholas. He didn't look hurt or stunned or sorrowful, either. But of course he wouldn't show his feelings in Tucker's presence.

She followed Nicholas outside, and they hurried toward the wharf, not speaking.

Alyssa, dressed in a dark traveling gown, sat on her trunk, an anxious look on her face. Emily and Celia stood nearby.

Alyssa sprang up. "Oh, Kate! I was so afraid I wouldn't get to tell you goodbye!" She threw her arms around Kate and hugged her tightly. "I'm going to miss you so much."

Hugging her back, Kate felt tears behind her eyelids even if she were so angry with Alyssa she wanted to shake her sister until her teeth rattled. "I'll miss you, too. You must write."

How could all of this have happened so fast? Alyssa had arrived here only day before yesterday. And now she was returning to England!

"I will," Alyssa promised, her voice trembling. "I do hope that things can still work out for you and Nicholas." She turned to the twins, holding out her arms to them.

Nicholas handed her trunk to one of the deckhands, then turned back to the two women. "The ship is getting ready to cast off," he said. "Come kiss me goodbye, Alyssa."

"Of course I will! I'll never forget how wonderful you've been, Nicholas." She hurried to him and hugged him, too, then lifted her face to his.

Kate watched, marveling that Nicholas could control his undoubtedly distraught emotions so well, hug Alyssa like a sister, and not lash out in well-deserved anger.

It wasn't like him. But then, he must already have done that at the cottage when Alyssa told him, and now he didn't want Kate to know what had happened between them last night. Pride was holding him together.

Nicholas kissed Alyssa lightly, then moved back. "Go on. They are waiting the ship for you."

Kate remembered something. "I didn't give you the money for your passage."

"I found it in a drawer of the chest," Alyssa said, smiling distractedly. "John and I will save every shilling we can and pay you back as soon as possible. I will miss all of you—and this place. Perhaps I can persuade John to take his chances here in this Tidewater country. Goodbye!"

She waved and hurried onto the ship, then stood at the deck rail, waving as the vessel cast its lines and moved slowly out into the creek that would take it to the Chester River.

Nicholas turned to Kate. "I guess as they say, *all's well that ends well.* Shall we go back to the cottage for breakfast?"

At a loss for words, Kate stared at him. How could he act so unconcerned? As if Alyssa's leaving meant nothing to him? And why was he staring at her like that? What did that odd look mean?

"I suppose," she answered finally. She turned and walked off the wharf, the others coming, too.

"I wish Miss Alyssa could have stayed," Celia said, sighing.

"So do I," Emily said, echoing her sister's sigh. "She's so pretty. Are you going to miss her, Kate?"

"Of course I am," Kate answered, realizing that was true despite all that had happened. She and her sister had grown closer together in these few days than they'd ever been. And she'd believed Alyssa was finally maturing into a caring, unselfish woman.

Until a few minutes ago. When she'd proved she hadn't changed a bit.

Kate took an indignant breath. Alyssa had even suggested coming back here—with John! She'd told Kate she hoped things could work out between her and Nicholas! Had her sister truly no feelings for anyone save herself?

Kate's confusion grew. Something was out of kilter here.

At the cottage, she hurried to the food still cooking on the hearth. Everything seemed to be edible. She served it in silence, then sat and picked at the food on her plate.

Nicholas didn't seem to have much appetite, either, she noticed. At least *that* seemed like a normal reaction to what had happened.

Finally, the meal was over. Emily and Celia obtained permission to go to the barn and left.

To Kate's dismay, Nicholas didn't follow them.

She wanted to be alone for a while. She couldn't continue pretending she hadn't overheard that conversation between Nicholas and Alyssa last night. That she didn't know of Alyssa's second defection.

She stacked the dirty dishes into the tub, then turned to find Nicholas so close she gasped and almost dropped it.

Nicholas grabbed for the tub, setting it on the floor.

"Kate, what is the matter with you? Do you hate so much to see your sister go back to Plymouth?"

"What is the matter with *you*?" she shot back before she could stop herself. "How can you act as if Alyssa has done nothing wrong, that you truly wish her every happiness!"

Nicholas gave Kate a surprised look. Had his pretense of being interested in Alyssa been convincing after all? "But I do wish her every happiness."

"You don't have to pretend any longer. I—I heard you and Alyssa talking last night. I know the two of you—settled your differences. That you told her you still love her."

Her voice broke on the last words.

Nicholas's heart contracted with love. How he wanted

to reassure her, tell her that she need have no worries on that score. He took an impulsive step forward, then forced himself to stop.

No. He couldn't do that. He knew he loved Kate, but he didn't yet have that avowal from her.

And have it he must before he took her in his arms again and they forgot everything else but their physical passion.

"Yes, that is true, Kate. We did, indeed—settle our differences."

"How could she do that to you again! How could she be so selfish? So cruel?"

"I don't believe that Alyssa thinks she has been cruel," Nicholas said after a moment, feeling his way. "She is only following her heart."

Kate stared at him in amazement.

"I don't understand you any more than I understand my sister! Are you saying you don't blame Alyssa for what she did to you? And for the *second* time?"

Kate turned away before he could see the tears on her lashes, now rolling down her cheeks. Bitterness filled her. Her sister hadn't changed—and neither had Nicholas. He still could not bring himself to blame Alyssa for her capriciousness.

But why had she expected him to? He hadn't faulted Alyssa the first time. And he still loved her, despite her complete selfishness. He would always love her.

Kate had to face up to that, once and for all.

And never see Nicholas again.

That thought sent a pain straight to her heart. She gasped as she felt Nicholas's warm hands on either shoulder. He turned her to face him.

"What is that I see on your cheeks, Kate?" he asked softly. "Could it be tears?"

"No!" she denied, even as she felt a drop roll into her mouth and tasted its salt.

"I believe that it is," he said, his voice still soft. "Why

are you crying, Kate? Surely, those tears can't be meant for me."

She stuck her chin in the air, trying to ignore the way the sweet warmth of his hands was stealing down her arms, across her breast, into every part of her.

"No," she denied again, her voice wobbling. "Of course not."

"Then it must be that you are sorrowing for your sister, who is on her way to her love. You should be joyous for her, Kate. True love is something that is hard to find. Few people ever do."

Oh, God, how she wanted him to pull her into his arms, kiss her, hold her. As he'd held Alyssa only last night and repledged his love.

That thought made fresh tears form behind Kate's lids.

She tried to pull herself away from him. "Let me go. Why are you holding me? Why aren't you railing against the fates? Or blaming me for this latest trick Alyssa has played on you!"

"I don't think Alyssa has played any kind of trick on me," he said. "And I'm holding you because that is what I want to do."

"Why? Why are you torturing me like this? Let me go upstairs and pack my things! I will be out of here before nightfall."

"And is that really what you want to do? Do you want to leave this plantation? Celia and Emily? Me?"

Bleakness joined the pain throbbing through her. She could fight it no longer. Even though she knew he'd never love her, she had to tell him how she felt.

"No, it will be like tearing out my heart to leave the girls. To leave *you*. But I must."

"Why must you go? None of us wants you to. Why can't you stay?"

"Because I love you, you simpleton!" she burst out, anger joining the other emotions coursing through her. "I've always loved you!"

His smile widened, sweetened. "And because you love me, you must leave? I fail to follow your reasoning."

She squirmed against his restraining hands, but his grip was still firm and secure.

"Do you think I could stay here, knowing that you didn't love me, could never love me? What do you think I'm made of?"

One hand left her shoulder, and his fingers gently brushed away a tear on her cheek.

"I believe that you are made of all the most wonderful things that I could ever want in a wife, my darling Kate. And why do you think that I could never love you?"

Her eyes widened as she stared at him, not quite daring to believe his words.

"Because," she faltered, "last night Alyssa asked if you and she could start over with each other. And you said yes—and then you kissed her."

"Ah, I see. Don't you know that eavesdroppers are always punished for their sin?" he asked. "You, my sweet, obviously didn't hear the entire conversation, and misinterpreted what you heard. Otherwise, you would not be saying these things, would not be angry with your sister."

"What do you mean?"

"I mean that last eve, I was down in the kitchen, unable to sleep, and Alyssa came to me. She said she was sorry if she'd made me think her interest in me was renewed. She'd thought that might be, but now realized that John would always have her love, even if he no longer loved her. She asked me to hold her while she wept and berated herself for losing him."

"So Alyssa and you never—"

"We never so much as kissed each other. I held her as I would hold my future wife's younger sister who was in dire need of comforting."

His future wife.

"So we are back to that?" she asked him, the pain

returning, taking her breath. "You can't have your first love, your true love, so you are willing to settle for me."

The smile left his face. His hands tightened on her shoulders and he gave her a little shake.

"Kate, why are you so stubbornly determined to deny that I want you for yourself?"

"Because it's true!" she shot back. "If it were not, then why did you never tell me that you love me?"

"Because I wasn't sure myself. Even though I didn't realize that until Alyssa arrived here. Thank you, Kate, for saving me from wedding her."

Kate's eyes widened. "Then you never—you didn't—"

Nicholas shook his head. "Forgive me for all that play-acting. I wasn't any good at pretending I still cared for your sister."

She gave him a half-mocking glare. "You were good enough to fool me."

"But not for long. And you were no better at flirting with me."

"That's true." Her glare faded, replaced with a surprised smile. "I have been a fool. But then, so have you."

"Yes," he agreed, smiling back. "Don't you think it is time, past time, that we stopped being fools?"

Kate nodded. "I do, indeed. And now, if you'll let go of my shoulders, which are growing numb, I want to kiss you."

"That is a request I'll be only too happy to grant." The smile left his face and he gave her a look of such intensity Kate drew in her breath. Then, before her startled gaze, he bent to one knee.

"I want only you, Kate. I *love* only you. Can you at last believe that? Will you marry me?"

For a moment she couldn't breathe. Or talk. Finally, she looked down at him, her face radiant. "Yes. Oh, yes, Nicholas. Now, get up from there and kiss me. I don't want you at my feet. I want you in my arms."

He gazed up at her. "We will not have a placid marriage. But that would be boring, don't you agree?

"Entirely."

He got to his feet again, his hands curving around her back, drawing her close against him. Kate's arms went around his neck, and her hands buried themselves in the thick club of chestnut hair at his nape. She lifted her head and Nicholas lowered his own.

Her lips opened beneath his touch, inviting him. They stood in the middle of the floor, the kiss deepening and deepening.

Dimly, Kate was aware of a noise at the door, but she didn't look up. Her whole concentration was on Nicholas, as his was on her.

"Cousin Nicholas is kissing Kate," Celia said, her voice surprised but pleased.

"And that means Kate will truly stay here forever and ever," Emily answered.

"Forever and ever," Nicholas whispered, holding Kate tighter.

Edward wrapped himself around their ankles, purring.

"Yes," Kate agreed.

Dear Reader,

I hope you enjoyed MY DARLING KATE.

Shannon must pose as a boy until her memory returns—and she knows the identity of the man with a knife who wants her dead.

She hasn't counted on falling in love with Gareth Colby—who found her unconscious along the road and took her back to his Shenandoah Valley farm. Gareth is equally dismayed to find himself attracted to the boy he rescued!

Look for my next book in August, '98.

I love to hear from readers. Write me at: P.O. Box 63021, Pensacola, FL, 32526. For a newsletter and bookmarks, please enclose a self-addressed, stamped envelope.

Elizabeth Graham